# GOTLOST

## TALES FROM THE BEHINDBEYOND BOOK 3

### MICHAEL DARLING

Got Lost

Future House Publishing
Cover image copyright: Shutterstock.com and neostock.com. Used under
license.

Text © 2019 Lucky Darling LLC

Excerpts used from *The Rival Ladies* by John Dryden, Act III, Scene i

ISBN: 978-1-944452-95-7

Cover image adaptation by Mackenzie Seidel
Developmental editing by Emma Snow
Substantive editing by Abbie Robinson
Copy editing by Stephanie Cullen
Interior design by McKinli Wall

# Praise for *Got Luck*

"*Got Luck* is the private detective Harry Dresden would hire to solve a murder. HIGHLY RECOMMENDED."
—Paul Genesse, Bestselling author of the *Iron Dragon Series*

"*Got Luck* checks off all my 'must haves' for a gritty detective story. If I ever ran into a problem the local cops couldn't solve, I'd be lucky to have Got on my side—and so would you."
—Ali Cross, author of the *Desolation Series*

"Witty and charming, *Got Luck* is an enchanting nod to a detective noir."
—Candace Thomas, author of the *Vivatera Series*

# Praise for *Got Hope*

"Michael Darling is quickly securing a place among the rising stars of urban fantasy. *Got Hope* is an unequivocally gripping sequel."
—Kevin L. Nielsen, author of the *Sharani Series*

"Every page sparkles with lighthearted energy. Unique, thrilling, and absolutely surprising, Darling's prose sweeps you into a world of fantastic characters and unexpected twists. This novel has it all: magic, humor, and a delicious mystery that will keep you turning the pages. Don't miss *Got Hope*."
—Josi Russell, author of the bestselling *Caretaker Chronicles*

"Darling's surprising and inventive prose, powerful characters, and exemplary attention to Celtic details makes this book as intriguing as it is action packed."
—Mikki Kells, author of *The Ace of Hearts* series

# Other titles by Michael Darling
Hollowfall
"Spera Angelorum"

## Tales from the Behindbeyond
Got Luck
Got Lost
"Lucky Day"

To my children who are legion and fully understand
"Nothing Gold Can Stay"

# Pronunciation Guide

Characters and Creatures
Aighneas – EYE-ness
Aoife – EE-fah
Ardsagart – ord-SAH-gert
Báicéirfile – bo-CARE-FILL-eh
Béil – bale
Bromach – BROH-mock
Caer Ibormeith – kayr ih-BOR-may
Deamhan – day-VAWN
Dubhcridhe – dohv-CREE-ha
Dullahan – dool-ah-HAN
Fáidh Bean – FAY-ah ban
Gadharchéile – GUY-ar-KHEH-lay
Ghearradh – GHEE-ar-ah
Goethe – GUR-teh
Gabhálai – GWOL-ee
Laoch – LAY-ock
Lúbaire – LOO-beh-reh
Madrasceartán – MAW-drah-skar-TAWN
Máithrín – mah-HREEN
Miongabhálaí – meeohn-GWOL-ee
Ógbhean – OHG-veh
Petit-Palais – peh-TEE puh-LAY
Púca – POOH-kah
Seabhacmór – SHA-woke-moor
Seachmall – SHOCK-mall
Siorradh Fionnuar – sheer-AH fyown-AR
Spreasán – spress-ON
Urlabhraí – OOR-lav-REE

Places and Things

Áit Choinne – otch QUINN-ah

An Taobh Thiar Agus Níos Faide – on TAY-iv here OG-us niece FAY-dah

Barántúil – bah-rahn-TOOL

Beom Seogi – bomb SOH-ghee

Döner Kebab – DUEH-ner kah-bob

Fuilaseum – FOOL-a-soom

Liagán – leah-GAWN

Maighdinegúna – MY-dan-GOO-na

Ríocht na Bráithre – REE-ockt na brah-HEER

Scian – SHKEE-ahn

Sómasach – SOH-muh-sahk

Tír Dúchais – teer DOO-kush

Tír na nÓg – teer na NOHG

Phrases and Commands

Básaigh – BAW-sig

Buail – BOO-ehl

Codail – CAW-dle

Deus ex Machina – DAY-oos eks MAH-kee-nuh

Leigheas – lice

Prionsa Mí-ádh – PREE-ohn-sa mee-OH

Sionnach na Ádh – shih-NOHK na OH

Tine – CHIN-na

Tír Dúchais

Áit Choinne

The Fuilaseum

Borderlands

The Palisade

Ríocht na Bráithre

Alder King's Castle

An Chéad
Turas den
Greithe Laoch
Prionsa ar
Ríocht na
Bráithre

# CHAPTER 1
## A Girl and an Altar

The girl with the sapphire eyes stood like a statue against the stones of the wall. She was alone on the far side of the room but didn't seem to be lonely, staring straight ahead. Her feet were bare and filthy. Her dress was torn and frayed like she'd been chased by dogs and almost caught.

I tapped Fáidh on the shoulder. Side-by-side we stood patiently in front of an altar. The hall around us had been decorated for a wedding. The wedding was scheduled for the following day. Realistically, it was only fun because I was here with the woman I loved.

Fáidh turned in response to my touch. The hall was warm and her hair was pulled up off her neck. She was breathtaking enough to be the bride, although she wasn't. I pointed behind us.

"See that girl over there?" I whispered.

Fáidh looked, then nodded. "She has beautiful eyes. A little young to be out with no escort."

"She's been standing there for a while, and she hasn't moved a muscle."

Fáidh kept looking. Then, "Are you sure?"

"I'm not even sure she's breathing." I replied. "She's not watching anything going on. Or anybody. Just staring."

Fáidh looked some more. "Her clothes are a mess."

"Someone here should know her, right?" The group in our rehearsal party wasn't very large. Only ten or so people, and I was acquainted with most of them. As far as I knew, none of them had a teenage daughter. The girl was shivering now. She was a hundred yards away, give or take, but my eyes were better than most and I could tell. "There's something wrong."

"The groom's place will be closer to the end of the altar, sire." A hand on my elbow demanded my attention, forcing me to look away from the girl.

Bromach, my valet, had the difficult and ever-thankless job of keeping me from embarrassing myself in princely situations. I moved to stand in the spot where he wanted me. The view from the altar was spectacular, looking out over the cliff to a forest far below and gray-blue clouds in the morning sky.

"Lady Fáidh, thy place is here." Bromach pointed again.

Fáidh nodded and stepped to the corner of the altar opposite me. She caught my eye and winked. I tried to wink back but I'd never successfully disconnected whatever link existed between my eyelids and only managed an awkward blink that also twisted my mouth oddly.

The ladies-in-waiting behind Fáidh smiled shyly at me as Bromach guided them to their places. I nodded with a smile. Over the past hour, I'm afraid I'd given them rude nicknames. The lady nearest Fáidh had decided to resurrect the bustle, but it didn't quite fit her frame and she was constantly hitching it up and adjusting it, which seemed to give her derriere a rebellious independence. The second lady, to whom I was apparently related closely, had a pallor fairytale writers would call "milky," and was so pale that the morning sun reflecting off her face was like a searchlight. Or a bat signal. The third had taken a nearly fatal blow from puberty landing on her all at once, instead of spread over the course of a few normal, socially-awkward years. Her acne was closer to road rash.

Thusly, I had dubbed them Creeping Booty, So White, and Ziterella.

Biting my lips for the purpose of smirk control, I chided myself at the same time. They were very nice girls. Polite and graceful. I was only here out of duty and it was wrong of me to make my own fun while I was stuck here.

Yet, their nicknames remained locked in my dark thoughts.

My gaze strayed back to statue girl. The color of her eyes was that deep blue shade of an ocean sky at dusk. Each eye appeared to have a small star twinkling with its own light. She stared at an empty space six feet above the floor. Her hands clenched at her sides as if she were carrying invisible buckets of water. She was shivering harder now. Quivering. Pent-up energy, perhaps, from standing stock still for so long.

Bromach continued to direct the rehearsal, ordering people around, sighing when he wasn't happy and nodding to himself when he was. He looked to be in his element, running the show in the delicately-appointed wedding hall filled with fresh flowers and lace.

Torn between duty and curiosity, I turned back to Fáidh for distraction. "Do you wish our wedding had been like this? With all the pretty decorations and food and people? And a church only slightly less modest than Westminster Abbey?"

Fáidh looked around, taking in the carved pillars and the crystalline ceiling, made entirely of faceted glass. She shook her head. "We got married under a cherry tree that never ceases to bloom. What could be prettier than that?"

"I'm glad our wedding was quick. It didn't take a whole week like this one," I replied.

"Our wedding was so quick, it ended before we knew it had begun." Fáidh laughed.

Curiosity won out. Before I'd taken three steps in the girl's direction, Bromach called after me. "Sire! Sire? Where goest thou?" He sounded borderline horrified that I was abandoning my post. "Prince Luck! Please!"

Make that full-on horrified.

Halfway to the girl, I paused to look back. "Hang on, Bromach. I'll just be a minute."

He sighed. "Thy cousin and thy father will be most displeased."

"One minute," I repeated.

Bromach watched me with impatience and pickleface in equal measure. When he saw where I was going he marched in the girl's direction, determined to get to her before I did. Maybe he was thinking he could get me back to my post if he got rid of her. It was hard for me to be critical. Bromach took his work seriously and his attention to detail meant I owed him my life.

With Bromach ahead of me, I said, "There's something going on with her. She's been standing like a statue for half an hour. Maybe longer."

Bromach slowed at my words and I caught up to him.

We stared at the girl. She stared past us. Standing at arm's length, I could see she was maybe thirteen years old. No older.

A long moment passed. "She's mortal," Bromach said.

She was also Stained.

At some point, the girl had been touched by magic, and the magic had marked her. A shudder shoveled electricity down my spine. Mortals with Stains didn't often live long. I checked the pattern. It had squarish sections with little points like tridents coming out of them. I'd never seen this particular Stain before. It was subtle, subdued, and almost hypnotic to watch as the wide band of translucent light turned slowly around the girl's torso.

Bromach's words were clipped as if by a knife. "What is thy name, child?" he snapped.

"Are you . . . Prince Goethe?" The girl continued to stare blindly at a point in the middle distance, somewhere in the vicinity of the little cupola draped with cream-colored roses. Her lips were pale and dry, struggling to push out the words.

"No, miss, I'm—"

The girl's fist didn't touch Bromach, but it snapped out like a python, flaring blue with power. Bromach shot away from her, his heels skidding across the stone floor as if giant hands had clapped on his shoulders and yanked him backwards. His eyes sprang wide in surprise and he grimaced from the acceleration. With a thump, he ran into the cupola. The force that held him must have let him go because he slid to the floor next, landing hard on his butt. A cascade of rose petals descended around him like floral snowflakes.

Fáidh abandoned her post too, along with the ladies in waiting. The girl blinked, and her fist drifted down, falling slower than rose-petal snowflakes.

If she's mortal, where does her magic come from?

She'd remained in place and continued to stare past me. Past everything.

"Are you Prince Goethe?" Her voice was raspy. "I feel someone else there."

"Me?" I swallowed. My own spit tasted sour. The power inside me stirred. Wary. Ready for me to use if I needed it. "Yes. I'm Prince Goethe."

"Finally," the girl replied. My heartrate eased. Maybe I wouldn't go flying off like Bromach. Maybe I wouldn't need to use my power.

The girl raised her other fist—the one that hadn't sent Bromach sprawling—and held it out in my direction. Fingers down, she looked to be holding something. "Take this," she said, her voice rough like sandpaper.

There was a certain amount of hesitation, I admit, but I put my open hand beneath hers, brushing her skin, which was ice cold.

Like a corpse coming out of rigor mortis, her fingers uncurled with effort. I waited for some object to hit my palm.

Nothing.

She wasn't holding anything.

What the phantom menace?

Bending down a bit to better search her open hand, I checked to see if the item she wanted to give me was stuck to her palm.

Nope.

Deciding it would be best to play along with the crazy mortal girl with the lightning-fast power, I said, "I'm honored."

"The dreamer must dream."

What did she say?

Her next words almost slipped past me while I was stuck in thought.

"Mark these steps. Do not forget."

Do not forget? What . . . ?

The first little fist came up again. I felt a sudden solidity in the middle of my chest, a firm pressure that snapped against the inside of my ribcage. I barely had time to think about the odd sensation before

I found myself taking steps.

"Three steps east," said the girl.

Three steps east is what I took. I couldn't help it.

"Turn north. Nine steps north."

The pressure inside my chest twirled and I twirled with it. I had the same approximate ability to resist as a tealeaf in a tornado. The force pulled me forward again. Nine steps.

"Turn east," the girl said. Her fist didn't move but remained out in front of her.

I turned again, nonetheless.

This was making me nauseated.

"Eleven steps east."

Uh-oh.

There were several rows of benches in front of me and I found myself stepping straight into them. One step.

Poodles.

Two steps.

With a grunt, I managed to step over the back of the bench and onto the seat.

Three steps.

The next step forced me to put my foot on the back of the next bench. Staggering, squatting, and scrambling, I make awkward passage over the next four benches.

I look like an idiot.

Panting, I came to rest. My head pounded as if the bones of my cranium had grown raw nerves. I looked around, glancing quickly.

Please turn south.

"Turn north. Seven steps north."

Like a marionette in the hands of a sadistic puppeteer, I turned.

Poodle skirts.

I had a new problem. To the south was open space in the middle of the wedding hall. To the north—

"Wall!" I yelled. "There's a wall!"

One foot was on the floor, but the other foot was on the seat. As I half duck-walked down the bench, I tried to gauge the number of steps to the wall. I might avoid having my face smashed into the stones, but it was going to be close. I shot a glance over my shoulder.

Bromach was passed out on the floor, surrounded by ladies in cream-colored gowns and more members of wedding retinue.

"Wake him up!"

At the end of the bench, steps six and seven. My face was close enough to the stone that I felt my breath curl back against my skin.

Too close.

I couldn't be certain anything bad would happen going into the wall but the only way I was going to find out was a hard way. A hard-as-a-rock way. My imagination conjured up grisly details. Blood and bone on the wall of stone. The only way to be sure I'd survive being pulled any farther would be for Bromach to be awake.

"Turn west. Four steps west."

The power in my chest turned me. Pulled me along the wall. If I went north again, irresistible force meets immovable object, with me as the consequences.

"I need Bromach!" Over my other shoulder, I saw Fáidh with her hand on his forehead, glowing blue with her power, her eyes closed.

With half of my attention on the unconscious Bromach, it was difficult to focus on where I was walking, although my body was on autopilot anyway. I lost track of the changes in direction, the near misses with solid pillars, and the number of steps.

When will this end?

"Ten steps north," the girl said.

I'm doomed.

I faced north and walked. "Fáidh! Bromach!"

I heard, more than saw, activity on the floor behind me. The wall loomed close. I gritted my teeth and—blink—found myself on the other side of the wall.

Yes!

And then—

No!

The wedding hall stood picturesquely on top of a cliff and I was on the edge. No time to formulate a cry for help. A square of light unrolled in the middle of the air. From experience, I knew it was a conduit to what I thought of as heaven.

Angels are coming to take me.

I'm not ready to die. Nausea and vertigo swept over me. A woman descended from the square overhead, holding a sword made of light.

The pressure in my chest pulled me off the edge of the cliff.

My foot stepped out into space. Stepped down on the flat blade of the sword.

Holy wow.

The woman's big soft eyes sparkled with an inner fire as she smiled up at me. I stopped, standing in what should be mid-air. I tried not to look down, although the woman who'd appeared at literally the last moment was mostly below me, holding her sword at the height of her shoulder, the tip of the blade on the edge of the cliff.

A long moment passed. Then another. The pressure in my chest evaporated. No more directions from the girl with the sapphire eyes.

Clearing my throat and then swallowing took every bit of my self-control. I managed to stammer, "What's up, Hope?"

Hope gave me a dazzling smile. "You are, Got."

Looking down brought more nausea. "Yeah. You're right. Ha ha. I'm up. In the air." I forced another swallow. "So. Were you just in the neighborhood? Flitting by on a cloud?"

Hope grinned some more. "Someone ordered a fresh helping of deus ex machina, so I thought I'd oblige."

"That's, uh, very kind of you."

"You're welcome." She left me hanging for another eternity. "Do you want to scoot off the sword?" she asked.

Oh. She was waiting on me. "Yeah. Sure."

Turning around felt like a bad idea so I inched backwards, moving one foot and then the other. The fear of falling off the sword kept my pulse thrumming in my ears. Finally, when there was plenty of solid ground underfoot, I bent over, putting my hands on my knees and taking deep breaths.

"You seem tense," Hope said. She floated up from the abyss and landed lightly in front of me.

"Well, yeah. It's been a while since I was almost killed. I'm a little out of practice."

Hope laughed. She let go of her sword and it instantly evaporated, sending motes of light floating away like sparks from a campfire. She wore golden armor with a design like feathers decorating it. Behind her, bands of light extended like rippling, ghostly strips of mist ten feet across. She also had a circlet of semi-transparent gold that surrounded the crown of her head.

It was good to see her again.

"You'll have to let me borrow that sword of yours sometime."

"Can't. It's part of my essence. I can't give it away or drop it. If I let it go, it disappears."

Oh. "Guess it can't be used against you, at least."

"Exactly."

We stood for a moment, comfortably distant from the edge of the cliff. The sun felt nice. Hope asked, slyly, "Have you figured out who the girl is?"

"The little puppetmistress?" I replied. "No. But her parents are going to get a stern letter from me for allowing her to use magic out here during school hours."

The music of Hope's laugh adorned the air again.

"Do you know anything about her?" I asked.

"I know everything about her." Hope's eyes danced.

"Great. Gimme all the details while we go inside. We can make sure she doesn't bewitch anyone else."

Hope frowned. "She'll be nothing more than a teenage girl again, in a minute."

The furrows in Hope's brow worried me. "What's the matter?"

"My message is only for you," Hope said. "You cannot share what I'm about to tell you with anyone else. Not even Fáidh."

"What?"

"Promise me."

I'd been through this before. Hope's voice was urgent, so I had to

9

agree. "I promise I won't tell a soul."

Hope nodded, relieved. "The girl's name is Alyce." She spelled it for me. "A-L-Y-C-E. You're going to want to do the right thing and take her home. To her parents. You mustn't do that."

"They'll be worried." I shook my head in protest.

"You can't let her parents know where she is. You must keep her in the Behindbeyond. Don't let anyone change your mind. Not for a while."

My mind tried to formulate a reason. "That's like . . . kidnapping. Keeping her from her family."

"You have to. The survival of all the Fae depends on it. In fact, don't tell anyone that I'm here either."

"Really?"

"Yes. You'll go to investigate."

"Will I go to the Dagobah system? Go ahead and say it. 'You will go to the Dagobah system to investigate.'"

Hope blinked for a second. Even as an angel, I could still surprise her.

Heh heh.

"You haven't changed, Got. I think I'm glad. Probably." She shook her head at me nonetheless, a smirk playing at the corners of her lips. "You'll go to where she was taken to find out more. When you do, you'll want to take everything you have received from the Fae with you. Including the Heartpiece I gave you. You'll need it."

Hope was so serious about this.

Who is this girl?

The urge to ask Hope the obvious question—why—was nearly impossible to resist but her expression was a wall of stone. Lips pressed together. Jaw clenched.

When she spoke, the words sent goosebumps into a tango all the way down my back.

"The dreamer must dream."

Standing there with my mouth hanging open, goosebumps running amok, it felt like the controlling pressure from Alyce had come back and taken all the breath out of my body.

Hope put a hand on my shoulder. Different questions came to mind. "It's going to hamper my investigation if I can't tell anyone what I'm up to. Isn't it?"

"I'm just here to get you started. As quickly as possible. There are . . . situations . . . about to get out of hand. Once you're on the case, anything you find out independently you can share. Leave out the details of this conversation and how I helped and everything will turn out all right. That's all."

"Ah." I thought about Alyce and where all this might lead if I was successful. "Will she ever be able to go home? Get back to her family?"

Hope glanced up and to the side, like she was looking for an answer in the clouds. After a moment, she said, "If there ever is a time that's right, you'll know when."

That's not very helpful.

I sighed, remembering to breathe again. "Can you tell me what all that other stuff was, at least? What's up with the handful of nothing she gave me? And why did she drag me back and forth around the hall, through a wall, and over the edge of a cliff?"

"I can't comment on that." The gleam of mischief returned to Hope's eyes. "But it was fun to watch."

Someone inside the wedding hall screamed.

"That's for you," Hope said.

# CHAPTER 2
## Lost Thoughts

I am not a fan of secrets. My profession requires me to keep them when I have to but in this case secret keeping felt underhanded and unnecessary. I'd just have to trust that Hope knew what she was doing.

A golden square of light unrolled in the air and Hope vanished into it. Setting off at a run, I headed for the door of the hall. Kudos to the genius who had invented doors, built for the express purpose of letting people go in and out of buildings instead of blinking through walls.

You must keep her in the Behindbeyond.

Hope's words followed me into the hall.

The entire wedding rehearsal had come to a standstill. People had gathered in a circle. The ladies-in-waiting were clinging to each other but So White and Ziterella stepped to the side when they saw me, letting me through.

Bromach was vertical again, probing the back of his head with his fingers.

The girl lay on the floor. Fáidh held the girl's head in her own lap, her hand on the girl's forehead now, glowing blue. After a moment, Fáidh shook her head and her power trickled away.

"How is she?" I asked.

Fáidh moved a lock of hair from the girl's cheek. "I can't find her thoughts."

"What does that mean? Her mind's erased?"

"Not exactly." Fáidh stared at me. Her eyes were the emerald shade that meant she was upset. "More like her mind is hidden. Her thoughts are there but I can't get any details. Like they're behind a wall. I can feel the presence of her mind, but I can't reach it. I don't think anyone can."

Alyce. Down the rabbit hole.

Kneeling next to the ladies, I moved the girl's eyelids back. She had standard-issue pupils and irises now instead of sapphires. Gray eyes with tiny scattered flecks of green and blue and brown like the last bits of confetti after the party was over. Her pupils were equal and not dilated so she was probably okay, but I would have been happier to have a doctor check her. She was definitely sleeping. Deeply.

"Can we do anything for her?"

Fáidh shrugged. "Keep her comfortable. She might come out of it on her own."

"All right. Let's take her to our chambers in the castle and make sure someone can keep an eye on her." Fáidh and I had rooms in the castle of the Alder King, my father. "Maybe we can find out more about her."

"We should find her parents," Fáidh suggested.

Uh-oh.

Keep her in the Behindbeyond.

"Were you able to get any of her history when you touched her?" The Three Dread Princesses looked at me quizzically. To the nearest—Creeping Booty—I explained, "Fáidh is a Water Mage with the ability to see the history of an object. Who's touched it, where it's been. In the mortal realm, it's called psychometry."

"Very good," Fáidh said.

So White stared at Fáidh and backed off. The color would have drained from her face if she'd had any color to drain. I stood and put a reassuring hand on her arm. She flinched.

"No need to worry, milady," I said. "Fáidh has to touch the object to see its history."

"Oh." The girl's hand fluttered against her chest like she was trying to keep a bird from flying out. It was all she could do to manage three-word sentences that didn't make sense, taking a deep breath between each one. "I'm not really. It's just that. Or nothing to."

The private investigator side of me wondered what she was hiding.

Guess we know who's going to have the most fun at the bachelorette party.

Fáidh paid no attention to the flighty lady-in-waiting. Instead, she fingered the ragged hem of Alyce's dress. "The only item she has is this dress and it's not substantial enough to hold on to much of where it's been."

"How's that work?"

Fáidh considered a moment. "It would be similar to how certain objects hold fingerprints better than others. A bullet is very dense, since it's brass, and there isn't a lot of surface area, so I can easily get a magical reading on who touched it and where and when. This is a lightly-woven material that would never show a fingerprint, even if I knew where someone touched it. So it's not going to have much substance for psychometry either."

That's good.

I think.

Fáidh shook her head and looked at me. Her eyes were losing their green, fading back to toffee brown. "Maybe we should take her to Miami, Got. You can check missing persons."

Half nodding, half shaking my head, I replied, "It would be safer to keep her here."

And why is that? I thought.

"Why is that?" Fáidh asked.

C'mon brain. We can't say it's because Hope told us to keep her here.

"People here are better equipped to handle her."

Fáidh remained skeptical, eyebrows at full mast.

I'm going to need something more, brain.

"If we take her to a hospital, she might wake up and use magic again."

Almost there, brain.

"And if she tells a doctor to walk into a wall, it'll raise questions we can't answer."

14

Fáidh sighed. "You're right. Better keep her here."

Yes! Good job, brain!

We sent for a litter to carry the girl back to the castle. It seemed like the safest way to take her since we weren't sure what would happen if we used magic. Fáidh seemed content to remain on the floor with her. She ran her fingers through the girl's hair, gently pulling through a million tangles a few at a time. The expression on her face was mostly one of concern, but something else colored the edges of her frown. I couldn't read her further. It was as impossible for me to know her thoughts as it was, it seemed, for Fáidh to know Alyce's.

Bromach stood near the altar, surveying the wreckage of his wedding rehearsal.

"It's a pity things didn't go the way you planned." I felt sorry.

"It's all right, sire," Bromach replied. "They never do."

"My cousin will be very pleased with everything you've done."

"One hopes. The wedding is tomorrow, and we were unable to complete the rehearsal. What if someone is out of place? Or forgets their assignment?"

"It will be all right. We'll just go with the flow."

"Sire, that approach may work for thee. Respectfully, we are not all secure in 'going with the flow.'"

The sour twist that appeared on Bromach's lip made his views on flow-going quite clear.

A phalanx of guards appeared, bearing a litter. There were twenty men with six of them in armor. Seemed like a lot of men for one unconscious mortal. At the forefront stood the captain of the king's guard, Sir Siorradh Fionnuar. I pointed at him in greeting as he approached.

"Dude," I said.

"Dude," he replied. He caught Bromach shaking his head, not violently, but enough to be noticed. Siorradh amended his greeting. "Or, as I should have said, Prince Dude."

I liked Siorradh's style.

We ignored Bromach's eye rolling, which was nearly audible.

"The girl in Fáidh's lap is a mortal," I explained. "She stood by the wall for a while but when we tried to talk to her, she did some crazy magic stuff and then she passed out." I kept the details to a minimum. Helping Alyce was the priority, not giving a play-by-play.

"Fáidh hasn't been able to reach her thoughts. Could you take the girl to our chambers and make sure she's comfortable?"

There was no sound behind Siorradh's helm, which was perpetually closed. For a heartbeat or two, he might as well have been an empty suit of armor, he was so still. After a long moment, he asked, "Do you think your father will agree? We could take her to a healer in town."

"I'll talk to my father." Dad was epically prickly about mortals visiting the realm of the Fae. The girl came here looking for me personally and poor Bromach got attacked. "I'd like to keep an eye on her. Stay close to her until she wakes up."

Siorradh bowed. "As thou wishest."

With the grace and ease of the world's most gentle metal-clad nurse, Siorradh lifted Alyce out of Fáidh's lap. He laid her in the litter, which was a small bed with a four-post canopy and long poles extending from the front and back. Siorradh closed the curtains to protect her. Four guards took up positions at the corners of the litter. They lifted together, carrying Alyce out of the wedding hall to the road.

I helped Fáidh to her feet. She gave my hands an extra squeeze and I squeezed back.

Thank you, the squeezes said. And I love you.

The warmth from her toffee-colored eyes threatened to spill out. Her glance still held the wistfulness she'd had looking down at Alyce.

"Are you all right?" I asked.

Fáidh nodded.

The Dread Princesses accosted Bromach. Their duties as ladies-in-waiting required them to be elsewhere, attending to the needs of the actual bride and groom. The best man had other duties as well, but he hung back and let the gaggle of girls fight the battle with Bromach.

Bromach surrendered. Hands raised, he dismissed the party with a series of strident reminders: everyone was expected to arrive in their places in the wedding hall at least an hour before the ceremony in the morning and to not celebrate too far into the night or too fully as to make themselves late. Or incapacitated.

The best man gave a wave over his shoulder as he departed. The princesses were gone before Bromach had finished. Exasperated, Bromach gazed at me. I shrugged. Bromach sighed and turned to the cupola with the messed-up flowers. He busied himself with rearranging the vines that had come loose.

Fáidh took my hand as we walked out of the wedding hall. A carriage waited to take us back to the castle.

"Do we feel like walking?" I asked.

"Sounds great," Fáidh replied. She had on heels, but they were sensible. She never seemed uncomfortable in her shoes, even walking up and down the occasional mountain. In her highest heels, Fáidh stood over six feet tall, which intimidated a lot of people. Not me.

I loved tall.

From the top of the cliff, we could see the castle, sitting like a polished stone gift box in the middle of a velvet green forest. Behind the castle, the ribbon of a river sparkled with flickering jewels of sunlight on its way to the falls that fed the last stretch of river before flowing into the Bay of Knives.

There would be postcards with photographs of this view in the castle gift shop. If the castle had a gift shop. And if photography worked in the Behindbeyond.

In the castle hung a tapestry with a similar view. The scene included frolicking animals that would be familiar to humans from the mortal realm and other frolickers that resembled animals but were actually people. Looking at tapestries in the mortal realm wasn't the same after meeting centaurs and seeing a real unicorn. And the unicorn had been a horse's behind. Heh heh.

Fáidh remained quiet as we walked. It wasn't hard to guess what thoughts occupied her mind. Our footsteps made drumbeat riffs on the path with our strides in sync, but the sounds of our breathing made contrasting syncopations. I broke the rhythm.

"Will she come out of it?"

"It's hard to say." Fáidh looked sideways at the trees, her hand warm in mine.

"This situation is really troubling you, isn't it." I wasn't asking a question.

Fáidh nodded. Walked some more. Then, "What if it was our daughter who was missing?"

Oh boy.

That went straight to the gut.

"It would be the worst thing ever," I said.

Fáidh and I were a married couple, at least in the Behindbeyond. The Fae had a notoriously difficult time reproducing. They could live for centuries and yet only succeed in having one or two children. Three if they were lucky. My Father, the Alder King, had sired six children over his lifetime, including me. His productivity was due, in part, to rampant promiscuity. He wasn't too picky about the women he bedded and most of his women were mortal, my late mother among them. As Halflings, Fáidh and I were more likely to have Halfling children than full Fae, thanks to the mortal portion of our genetic makeup.

We weren't in any hurry to have kids. But we weren't not trying either.

Sometime between now and the end of the century would be fine, and we'd been told to expect many years of childlessness. I was relatively new to the Behindbeyond, so these kinds of things were a challenge to reconcile.

"I'm not sure I could function," Fáidh said. "If our daughter were lost. If we didn't know where she was. Or even if she were alive or dead."

Despite the brightness of the day, there was a somber feeling in the air now, as if the sun were trying too hard to be cheerful, the river trying too hard to be sparkling. There was more to Fáidh's concerns than personal worrywarting.

She was empathizing with Alyce's parents.

Without even knowing them, she'd put herself in their place and I knew what she really wanted to hear. "I'll get back to the mortal realm and see what I can find," I said. "As soon as possible."

That earned my hand another squeeze. She didn't say the words aloud because you just don't in this realm. But I got the message.

Thank you. And I love you.

For my own part, I had a different problem.

If I found Alyce's parents too soon, I'd have to lie.

# CHAPTER 3
## Middle-Aged Teen

Alyce had been washed and her hair combed, and she had been dressed in a crisp white nightgown. She rested in the middle of the bed with covers pulled up to her chest and a small pillow under her head. Lying still, it was apparent how thin she was, with dark shading under her eyes like bruises. She had high cheekbones and a small, permanent dimple on one side of her mouth. She'd grow up to be a beautiful woman, if given half the chance. For now, she was practically lost in an ocean of linens like a toddler's doll fallen into a snowbank.

Sir Siorradh stood guard at the door, moving only his helm to scan the room and follow the people caring for the girl.

I sent for a page.

The boy arrived, cheeks red with excitement, and gave a deep bow. I told him to let my father know that a mortal girl had been brought down from the wedding rehearsal. She had been used as a conduit for some powerful magic and I was concerned she would be used that way again. For now, she needed to be kept here for observation and her own protection. I needed to go the mortal realm and try to find out if she had any family there and do it all secretly, per Hope's mandate. I might not know why Hope had warned me, but I was certain she'd done so for a reason. I would return in time for the wedding breakfast in the morning.

There wouldn't be any use in trying to hide the girl. My father had probably known there was a mortal in his domain as soon as she had been brought through the gate, if not sooner. At least he would get word from me and would know why I wanted to keep her here. He'd also be more accepting of her here if he thought I had a plan to get her out of his realm.

I asked the page to recite what I'd told him and he did so perfectly, so I dismissed him to deliver his message. He vanished through the door at a run. I had no doubt that the Alder King would be informed shortly. The realm of the Fae would just have to make room for one little mortal until I could figure things out.

It would only be fair.

After all, the mortal realm had long been a place where the Fae dumped their unwanted offspring. That was one dichotomy that I'd probably never reconcile. For a race that had such trouble bearing children, they didn't value who they got unless they were full-blooded. I was something of an exception, perhaps. I'd been taken to the mortal realm to be hidden from our family's enemies but I'd grown up with a houseful of foster kids and we had all been Halflings, though we didn't know it.

Musings ended, I went to find Fáidh. She sat on a chair inside our bedroom, not too close to Alyce's door, but close enough. There was a gentle, stricken look in her eyes. This woman—the scientific analyst who could disassemble a dead body with cold candor—was practically overwhelmed by the plight of a living little girl. She was a very caring person when she opened up. That was something she'd demonstrated again and again with her first husband. But I'd never seen her warm so quickly to a person she'd never met.

"The girl's in good hands." I was careful not to say Alyce's name since I wasn't supposed to know it yet. "Shall we go back to Miami?"

Fáidh's arms were half-crossed around her abdomen, as if her stomach ached. She stared at the floor, blinking her eyes in fits and starts as if she were blinking out letters in Morse code.

Or blinking back tears.

She nodded and extended a hand so I could help her to her feet.

"Miami," she said.

Somehow, Max had known when we'd be back. He maintained the house, the grounds, and all the invisible walls that kept Very Bad

Things from coming in. He was also an excellent chef. We tilted through the portal from the Fae realm into the house and instantly smelled food.

"Omigosh," Fáidh said. Or Erin, in the mortal realm. "What is that incredible aroma?"

Women of certain breeding could use words like "aroma" and make them sound unpretentious.

"Stinks good," I agreed.

We went to the kitchen, drawn by the siren's song of smells. Erin kicked off her heels along the way, stepping silently as a Siamese cat.

Here Erin and I were, returning at 2:36 in the morning (when the hours are wee) but Max had two pizzas coming out of the oven at precisely the right moment. At my house, good help ain't hard to find.

Chicken-Bacon-Ranch.

"Dang, those look perfect," I said.

"I'm suddenly starving." Erin grabbed a plate.

The cheese was bubbly, so we ate with care, washing down the meal with what looked like wine on ice but was white grape juice. We didn't speak as we scarfed. Someone made little piglet noises. Probably Erin. The pizzas had been the same size. I finished mine, feeling a tad bit hungry still. Erin had a slice left on her plate, which she slid in my direction as if reading covetousness in my heart.

Men of certain breeding could use words like "covetousness" and make them sound ridiculous even in their own thoughts.

It was all right though. I had the last slice of pizza.

Why eat fast food when you can eat Max food?

Erin stood and stretched, as long-limbed and flexible as the aforementioned Siamese cat. "I'm sleepy. Are you coming to bed?"

"Soon," I replied. "I promised I'd check missing persons as soon as we got back."

Erin glanced at the ceiling. "Mortal realm. So, thank you." Then she kissed me.

Nice.

Although Erin kept her little bungalow in Miami, she only

stayed there once or twice a week. It was closer to her office and it saved her a drive to Coral Gables when she needed to crash for a few hours before going back to the Medical Examiner's office. Watching her slip down the hall reminded me how much I liked it when she stayed here.

With a sigh, I grabbed my laptop computer and sat in the great room. Promises being promises and all. I sat back on the couch while the computer booted up. In a browser window, I started with NamUs, the National Missing and Unidentified Persons System, which technically should be called NMUPS but NamUs was easier for bureaucrats to say. It also was less likely to cause giggles. Fergie sang about her NMUPS once. I was pretty sure.

The site was operated under the direction of the U.S. Department of Justice, but it could be used by the general public. That meant I could start a search for information about Alyce without any credentials.

Or anyone in an official capacity noticing.

The site informed me that there were almost 26,000 cases entered into the database. Some of the cases related details about bodies that had been found, with forensic details that might help identify the person who had died. The rest of the cases were people who had been reported missing. Too many of them were children.

I didn't have a lot of information to go on, but I started a new search. The advanced search would let me enter Alyce's height, weight, hair color, eye color, and any distinguishing features and had fields for the circumstances of her disappearance and lists of other options to help narrow down the details.

There was one piece of information I could use for starters. It was specific and unique and likely to get me going in the right direction.

First name: A-l-y-c-e.

Clicking "Search," I waited. Milliseconds passed.

One result.

Just like that.

I understood why Hope had given me Alyce's name and nothing more.

Her name was all I needed.

Several screens popped up. The images page had almost a dozen photos. The color in the photos was washed out and most of them were grainy, but the sunny, smiling girl with the gray eyes in each one was clearly Alyce. Some of the photos showed Alyce alone. On a beach. In a kitchen. In a car. Others had bits and pieces of other people in them, like a hand on her shoulder or the knee of someone standing next to her. The photos had been cropped so only Alyce could be identified.

The case information screen was even more telling.

Status: Missing

First name: Alyce

Middle name: N/A

Last name: Octavian

Nickname/Alias: Ally

The line that followed had to be wrong. I read it again. Then I continued reading the case section to find out if the mistake was repeated and therefore not a mistake.

The "Age last seen" made sense, noting that Alyce had been twelve years old when she'd disappeared. It was easy to believe that. But the "Date last seen" was way off, and the "Age now" was plain crazy as well.

But they weren't.

Not if we were dealing with the Fae.

Jumpin' Jehosophat and all his dancin' baby phats.

Alyce had been missing for more than twenty-five years, but she was still twelve years old.

According to the "Date last seen," she'd gone missing in the early 1990s and her current age should be 37. She'd been born in the year 1980.

Can't fight the math.

Paging through the other screens confirmed the dates, giving other information as well, including the investigating agency and the contact information of the case manager who had submitted the report.

24

Lastly, I read through the summary on the circumstances screen. The summary included shorthand references for the people involved, which was common police practice. "RP" stood for "Reporting Person," "MP" stood for "Missing Person," and "OIC" was "Officer-in-Charge."

The summary read, "On 10/17/92 RP called the Ascension Parish Sheriff's Office in Gonzales, LA, to report her daughter MP-Octavian as a missing person. RP stated that MP-Octavian had gone to a movie with friends in Donaldsonville the night before and had not come home. Deputy W. Cox responded as OIC. OIC took RP statement at the home, located at 2428 Barraclough Ave., Donaldsonville, and canvased the Epicenter Movie Theater. MP-Octavian was seen getting into a late model white van at approximately 10:05 p.m. and has not been heard from since."

In the space of ten minutes, I found out a lot about Alyce and her tragic disappearance. I found out she'd lived in Ascension Parish, Louisiana. My foster home, where I'd grown up, was in the neighboring Assumption Parish. I found out who I could talk to about her case, if they hadn't retired and moved away. Or died. I also found out why Hope had warned me off bringing her here or telling her family she was okay.

You can't explain to mortals that their missing daughter hadn't aged. Closing the laptop and tossing it on the couch, I found myself in a bigger mess than before. It had been one thing when Alyce had been used for magic, steering me around like a puppet. It was clear then that she had gotten tangled with the Fae. But this? The Fae had tangled her up for so long, she'd spent twice as long under their influence as she'd ever spent in her native realm. Mortals often reacted badly to magic. What effect would such long exposure have on a person? Especially a little girl?

Probably put them in a coma.

Like Alyce now.

My face felt itchy. I scrubbed my hands over my cheeks and chin, then went to the kitchen. There was some freshly-squeezed orange juice in the refrigerator. I poured a glass and let the cool bite of it wash down my throat.

From personal experience, I knew that time was different in the Behindbeyond. I could spend hours there and come back with a passage of only minutes here. Even more dramatically, I was 28 years old in mortal measure but I'd actually been born in the 1700s, by human reckoning. Before being brought to the mortal realm, I'd been in a sort of suspended animation for a couple of centuries. I'd been able to come out of it because I was a Halfling. On the other hand, Erin's husband Blake, a mortal, had gone missing for five years but had experienced 20 years there.

He'd come back broken.

When Alyce woke up—if she woke up—she could be dangerous. Psychotic. If even half of what happened to Blake happened to Alyce, she'd be unstable at best. That thought had me worried not only for Alyce but also for Erin. Somehow, Erin had grown attached to Alyce.

I needed Alyce to turn out okay.

Stepping through the bedroom Erin and I shared, and into the softly-lit bathroom, I brushed my teeth in twilight, muscling past the conflicting flavors of orange juice and peppermint. One of the lesser conflicts of the day, when I thought about it.

Erin mumbled, eyes closed, as I slipped into bed. "Find out anything?"

"Not enough," I replied.

"Mmm. Thanks for trying."

"I'll keep at it. Promise."

"'Kay."

Erin curled into me. Siamese cat.

Later, an hour or ten, Erin kicked and thrashed enough to wake me. "Blake. No." The pleading tones in her voice could break a heart of stone. "She's just a little girl."

"Erin. Honey." I put my arms around her, pulling her into my warmth. "It's just a bad dream. Okay?"

"Don't let him take her."

"I won't. No one will take her. I promise."

# CHAPTER 4
## Feeble Eyes

"Someone's at the door," Erin said.

"Mmrpsfl," I replied. Morning eloquence.

"Max says they look important."

Blinking made it easier to put words together. "Then let Max answer the door."

"He did." Erin poked me in the ribs. "There's a man and woman in suits."

"Sounds more like your type of people. You answer it."

"It's your house," Erin protested.

"Actually, it's my father's house. Let him answer it."

Erin shoved and rolled me to the edge of the mattress. "Go on," she said. "I have to use the toilet."

"Gross," I replied. "Besides, girls only use the bathroom to get pretty."

"It won't be pretty if you don't get out of here."

"Fine. But not dandy."

My eyes were heavy, as if the sandman had used most of South Beach to put me to sleep.

Jerk.

There had been times when Max would have knocked once and then opened the bedroom door to let me know someone was at the door. With Erin here, Max was more circumspect.

Shuffling down the hall and through the great room to the door, I struggled to identify the two dark blurs standing inside the large white blur. Sleeping well hadn't been an option. Erin kept having the same nightmare, over and over. Blake threatening to steal Alyce. Each time, I promised he wouldn't get her and Erin had gone back to sleep.

I hadn't fared as well.

One of the blurs asked, "Mr. Luck?" Even his voice was blurry.

"Sorry, whoever you are. You'll have to come back when you're in focus."

"Excuse me?"

"Nope. There's no excuse for being so fuzzy." I gestured in a circle. "When you aren't such a huge hunk of fuzzy, you can come back."

I moved to close the door but a hand stopped it.

"Sir," said a voice of warning that, if my detecting skills weren't blurry, belonged to Max.

"Didn't realize you were standing there, Max." To the big fuzzy, I said, "Who are you exactly?"

"We're the FBI."

"The Feeble Eye?"

"No." He enunciated the letters for me. "Eff. Bee. Eye."

"Like a pirate? Nice. Eff be you, then. Got be I. Pleasure to meet you, Eff. Arr."

The smaller fuzzy spoke up. "You can drop the attitude, sir. We're Federal Bureau of Investigations."

"Wow. You're the whole bureau? I somehow thought there would be more of you."

"We're not the bureau. We're from the bureau."

"My mom called her chest of drawers a bureau. I don't think you'd fit in there, so . . ."

"May we come in? Sir?"

"Well, if you're going to interrupt me before I get to the punchline, I'm not so sure."

"Know anything about abducted children?"

Dam it all to beavers.

Rubbing my eyes some more, I took a deep breath that was adjacent to a sigh and gestured for their identification. If this was about Alyce, it was serious. I squinted to read their cards. The smaller fuzzy turned out to be a female with dark hair pulled back into a ponytail. She was five-and-a-half feet tall and wide in the shoulders like an Olympic swimmer.

"Agent Madeline Scarsdale? You're from Miami?"

She nodded as I handed her ID back. "Not originally. Moved here," she said. There was an accent of some kind at the edges of her words, but I couldn't place it.

Big fuzzy was a tall man with close-cropped nondescript hair and bony features, as if a layer of face were missing. "Agent Charles Petit-Palais? Baton Rouge, huh?"

"S'right. Goin' on twenty year." I recognized the Creole in his speech, now that he'd captured my attention. My guess was he'd started in South Louisiana and never wanted to go anywhere else.

Neither of them were Stained, so it was count the blessings time.

"Your kind can't cross the threshold without an invitation, so. Come in. Have a seat." I turned to retreat to the bedroom. "I'm going to get some pants on. Max will get you something to drink."

Erin lay quiescent in the bed, her hair fanned out across the pillow. Her breathing was deep and quiet. She was finally resting well after all the nightmares. I found some khakis and a pullover and left her in the bedroom, closing the door behind me and dressing in the hall.

Agent Petit-Palais had taken a seat on the couch with a cup of spearmint tea. He'd tucked his tie into his shirt, putting the end between the buttons in case he spilled. The top part, with little gold-and-red fleurs-de-lis, still showed. Agent Scarsdale had stayed on her feet and accepted a large mug of coffee. Wisely, she wore no tie. Max also had a glass of juice for me. I took a sip and nodded. Cranberry-cherry.

I settled on a chair near the couch, the glass of juice in both hands, and asked, "What can I do for you?"

"I think you can prob'ly guess," said Petit-Palais.

"Not buying it." I took another sip of juice while I thought about what to say. It's never a good idea to volunteer information. Petit-Palais was trying to get me to cough up a few cookie crumbs without working for it, but he was on the clock, not me. Finally, I said, "When I was a beat cop, I did ride-alongs with a police detective here in Miami. Wily old dog named Jenkins. We were looking for a drug dealer and we heard from a strung-out pusher he had a friend in a certain neighborhood that could help us. He didn't have a house number, but he knew what the house looked like. We went there and knocked on the door. A lady answered and Jenkins said, 'I expect you know why we're here.' Guess what she said."

Neither Petit-Palais nor Scarsdale answered, waiting me out.

"She said, 'Did my ex-husband rat on me?' Then she spilled many beans about gambling and money laundering. We ended up arresting five people within the week. Not one of them was connected to the drug dealer we'd been looking for originally. We had no idea that this lady was anything but a soccer mom busy baking muffins but she confessed to a string of crimes because Jenkins had said, 'I expect you know why we're here' and her guilt and paranoia got the best of her."

Petit-Palais ignored Scarsdale when she chuckled. She stirred her coffee and walked around the room.

"So," I continued. "I have no reason to feel guilt or paranoia. You came to my door and said 'abducted children.' I just want to help."

It was my turn to wait out Petit-Palais. It wasn't hard. I had sixteen whole ounces of juice in my glass and no desire to chug.

After a long moment, the agent put his tea on the coffee table, which was a conflict. It wasn't a tea table, but such is life. At least he used a coaster.

He pulled a stack of photos out of his pocket. He flipped the top one toward me. It slid and turned across the coffee table, coming to rest facing the wrong way. I turned the photo around to better see it.

A cute girl with blond hair, about twelve or thirteen years old, smiled at me. I didn't recognize her. The photo looked like it had been cropped out of a family portrait because I saw part of someone else's hand on one side and an elbow on the other.

"Who is she?"

Petit-Palais looked at me, trying to see if I was pretending not to know her. I honestly didn't. He picked up his tea off the coffee table, doing little to ease the tension. "Someone tried to abduct her about a year ago."

Tried? "But she's all right?"

"She was found in the back of a van. She'd been sedated and her ankles and wrists bound. The van had been stolen."

"I'm glad she was found."

"We also caught the would-be kidnappers. They were asleep in the back of the van along with the girl."

Interesting.

"Sounds like a happy ending. I'm not sure why you're telling me this."

"The van had collided with another vehicle in the parking lot of your office building."

"Okay."

"And it occurred on the same day you reported a sniper shooting at you."

Whoa.

Now that was news.

A year ago, I'd been shot at by a man who'd mistakenly thought I'd abused his daughter. It turned out to be an attempt by some very nasty Fae to get rid of me before I could receive my powers and discover my true heritage.

"And it occurred at the same time another child was reported in the area. A child we haven't been able to identify. Or find." Petit-Palais showed the next photo. It was a sketch of a young boy with dark eyes wearing a Renaissance-style shirt.

Laoch.

There was a whole lot of story with Laoch. He'd been there that day and retrieved the bullet casing from the sniper who'd shot at me. Then he'd left the casing on my desk and disappeared. I looked at the sketch and wondered where they'd gotten it.

The most honest answer I could give was, "Sorry. I wish I could help."

Petit-Palais pressed. "You don't know this boy?"

I'd have to sidestep. "He could be the kid of any person who thinks taking a family vacation means going to Comic Con." There.

That was reasonable obfuscation. It wouldn't pass a lie detector machine, but I hoped it would fool the pair of Feeble Eyes currently staring me down.

I sipped my juice and stared back.

After a long silence, Petit-Palais dealt the rest of his cards. The next photo was a little Hispanic girl. Then a boy with a haircut almost as cropped as Petit-Palais's. And another girl of African-American descent. "These are kids we haven't found, abducted in the last six months. One from a park not far from here. Another from the parking lot of a dog track in Hollywood where you have been seen. And the third abducted one block away from The Iron Foundry, owned by your business partner."

I leaned back. "Look. I understand you're trying to play common denominator here. I admit I know a lot of people and I go all over South Florida. I don't have anything to do with any abducted children."

While I was talking, Agent Scarsdale passed behind Petit-Palais, locking onto my eyes. One of my abilities was enhanced vision. Talking had given me plenty of opportunity to look the agents over. I hadn't gotten much off Agent Scarsdale. I'd gotten bunches off Petit-Palais.

"My point is, you could probably find some connection linking me anywhere but I'm no more capable of kidnapping a kid than if I'd been born into one of the South's wealthiest families, attended a swanky prep school, and had a father who could buy my way out of any trouble I could get myself into."

Petit-Palais stood up, not spilling a drop of tea. "What are you trying to pull?" His jaws re-clenched. "You don't know me."

"You got Sherlocked, Petit-Palais." Agent Scarsdale wasn't laughing, but her eyes sparkled. "He noticed the pattern in your tie, which is your school's logo, the symbol on your cufflinks, and he knows your name. He inferred everything."

I smiled with as much cheese as I could muster.

Petit-Palais sat back down, remaining perched on the edge of his chair, disgruntled. Yep. Any gruntle he might have had was now gone. Scarsdale sipped her coffee, moving away. Some kind of shared thought passed between them.

I liked that Scarsdale understood my figuring her partner out. Maybe she was human after all. More so, at least, than the usual Feeble Eyes.

Petit-Palais put his tea back on the coffee table.

Angst.

He moved toward the door while Scarsdale stayed by the piano. It was a beautiful Steinway, glossy and black, except for the set of long gouges on the top of the lid. The Steinway reminded me of me. We'd both been wounded by things from the Behindbeyond. Scarsdale traced her fingers down the gouges. If she spread her fingers wide, she could almost touch all four gouges at once.

"What happened here?" she asked. Some people just yearn for a yarn.

"That?" I replied. "I don't know. I turned my back for a second and someone dropped a piano there. I could've been killed."

Scarsdale suppressed a sigh. "The marks on top?"

"Oh those." As if I hadn't known. "Yeah. We had a potato peeling party and things got out of hand. Thanks for coming guys."

Being seasoned experts in the art of deduction, the agents took my clue and let themselves out.

# CHAPTER 5
## Wedding in D Minor

The agents had asked a lot of questions, but they hadn't asked about Alyce. If they'd come in and asked me why I'd been on my computer in the middle of the night, researching a missing girl, I wouldn't have been surprised. The fact that they hadn't was one of a jumble of facts that didn't fit together.

Alyce had been in the Behindbeyond for twenty-five years but hadn't aged, similar to Laoch, only Laoch had been in the Behindbeyond for centuries.

Alyce was a mortal but Laoch was a Halfling.

Alyce had used magic she couldn't have generated while Laoch had his own magic.

They both had special mental abilities. Telepathy. Telekinesis. Abilities that often benefitted from touching things—or people— but that wasn't always necessary. Laoch was impressive but Alyce might be even more powerful. A gifted mortal.

If Alyce had some connection to Laoch, I couldn't think of one. Maybe Béil would know since she had been Laoch's surrogate mother for his whole existence. That was another avenue, perhaps, but I had cooked up a lead in Baton Rouge on my laptop and that would have to come first.

Ten minutes later, after hitting the computer and researching flights, I called Nat. Nat was my best friend and business partner and the Feeble Eyes knew that. He did own a health club called The Iron Foundry and they knew that too. He was also as tough as he was laconic. We'd been through a lot together, but if anybody wanted any stories about him, they'd need to ask me. Unless monosyllabic details were preferred.

He answered on the second ring.

"Iron Foundry."

"Nat?"

"Got."

"Yeah. I didn't think you'd be the one answering. Could you do me a favor?"

"Sure."

"I'm going to hang up and then call again so one of your employees can answer. I have a whole new way to mess with them, so you'll get a cryptic message to call me back."

Silence.

"Come on, Nat. You know how much I like to mess with your people."

Nothing.

"Messing with them includes monkeys."

Nada.

"'Kay. Fine. You want to fly up to Louisiana?"

"Not really."

"Me neither." I sighed. "Pick me up at one o'clock?"

"'Kay." Nat hung up.

Scarsdale had left her coffee cup on the Steinway. Without a coaster. What kind of monster does that? I wiped off the piano with my sleeve and collected the beverages, taking them into the kitchen. Behind the house, flat-bottomed clouds had gathered and the sunshine that had launched the day had been blotted out. There was no place for fickle weather like Florida. The mood of her skies could change faster than a bride could blush.

Holy matrimonies. The wedding.

It was probably time to get ready for that.

Up the hall, I heard Erin in the shower. It never took her very her long to get ready. Another of her impressive abilities.

The Steinway beckoned.

My fingers, resting on the keys, chose what to play.

Mozart's Piano Concerto Number 23. The second movement flowed out of me, haunting and heart-breaking. For some reason, the

Bureau was trying to connect me to a spate of kidnappings.

A few minutes rolled by. My fingers finished the Mozart and chose Chopin Etude, Opus 10, Number 6. The music swelled, filling the air with somber notes. Even the lighter passage felt heavy. My thoughts collected dark edges, mirroring the clouds outside.

At least the girl outside my office had been okay. But the other kids . . .

My fingers selected another piece of their own accord. Beethoven's Sonata Number 32, Opus 111. The music overflowed with oppressive energy.

"Why so sad?" Erin said. She wore her exceptionally fluffy, pure-white bathrobe and had a towel around her head, holding her wet hair. A few glistening strands descended in swooping curls, teasing her collarbones with black.

The sky, covered in angry shades, sported a single separate and distinct cloud in the middle, sitting like an obsidian baby sheep underneath the canopy of gray. "That small, dark cloud with the wispy edges is making me melancholy."

Her hand rested on my shoulder. My fingers fell still in mid-measure. The music didn't want to fade but had no choice. Sounds have a short half-life.

"Some kids are missing. They might be linked to the girl sleeping at the castle somehow." I went on and told Erin about the Feeble Eyes and their insinuations. After the first minute, Erin sat on the edge of the piano bench with me and I scooted over to give her a more spacious perch. Her hand slid across my shoulders and she slipped her fluff-enhanced head into the curve of my neck.

After reciting the last details, I said, "I found out a little about her. Her name is Alyce. With a 'y.'" It was okay to say her name, now that I'd seen her information in my own research. "She was abducted from Baton Rouge. Nat and I are flying up this afternoon, as soon as you and I get back from the wedding."

"I think you should," Erin said. "I hate seeing you upset like this." Then, "Play something happy. Maybe it will make you feel better."

"Maybe it won't."

"Maybe it will make me feel better."

"Worth it then."

My fingers chose Chopin's Etude, Opus 10, Number 5. It was the study immediately preceding the Chopin piece I'd played before. When I laughed, it was out of irony. Erin tilted her head.

"This music is called the 'Black Keys' piece," I explained. The notes ran in happy arpeggios up and down the keyboard. "The black keys are flats and sharps. When you play notes with flats, it creates music that's in a minor key. But if you play all the flats, the key becomes a major key again. So the song is happy even though the melody is all dark keys."

"It's possible to find happiness no matter how dark things get," Erin said. "There's a lesson there."

"Stupid lesson." I sighed. "I guess that's what you should expect from a piece that's French for 'study.'"

Erin laughed and stood up.

Then she kissed me.

The kiss was also French.

"There's some happiness," I said.

Erin smiled and went up the hall to get dressed.

My fingers returned to the keyboard and played the black keys.

The groom had stolen my spot at the altar. I found it hard to feel bad about that. His best man stood beside him well, a half-brother as I'd learned the day before.

The wedding was about to start and Bromach looked the most apprehensive, by far. He stood at the side of the wedding hall, at the spot where he'd blinked me through the wall yesterday. He was trying to keep his hands from wringing the outer layer of skin off.

The Dread Princesses were in their places. So White was holding down the liquid elements of a hangover with sheer willpower. Zitarella was faring better but there was a tightness behind her eyes. And Creeping Booty was as perky as a chipmunk after a morning coffee. She either hadn't partied at all or she was really good at it.

Spreasán, the groom, and his best man both looked grim. The half-brother was fully dressed but the groom stood barefoot, gripping a small coin in his hand as if it were the ticket to his last meal. The silver piece was the Fae equivalent of a penny in the mortal realm, but silver instead of copper-plated zinc. He looked like he hadn't slept for a couple of days and the tunic he wore was unbuttoned, showing a bare chest.

"Granted, I will always love that our wedding was such a surprise even we didn't know it was happening," I whispered to Fáidh. "But I'm going to need context. What's that silver thing?"

"One of the three admissions of Barántúil marriage," Fáidh whispered back. "A silver lock fastened through the muscle of his chest."

"I cannot cringe fast enough."

Fáidh laughed. "The admissions are, first, the groom wears no shoes for a week. This signifies he will sacrifice his possessions and his own comfort for the well-being of his wife. Second, he holds the coin for a week, which signifies his poverty compared to the wealth of love he will receive from her for a lifetime. And third, the lock in his chest signifies he will protect his heart and hold it sacred and only allow it to be opened by his wife."

"And it's locked into his chest?" I was stuck on that detail.

"For a week."

"Wow. And he can't unlock it or take it out?"

"Only the bride can take it out. She has the key."

"That's barbaric."

"That's tradition."

"In what painful place does the bride keep the key?"

Fáidh laughed. "On a silver chain around her neck."

"I see. So it's barbaric and unfair."

"Oh, sweetie. Women get all the barbaric stuff after the wedding."

"Ha. So funny!"

Fáidh gave me a comforting pat on the arm. "Remember, the idea of equality is almost a foreign concept in this realm. But chivalry is a way for society to connect a man's actions to his honor. Many of these girls marry and get taken far away from their families. Maybe never see them again. If we had a daughter, Got, how would we feel if a man wanted to marry her and we weren't sure he'd treat her well? If he's willing to submit to the three admissions, at least we'd know he's capable of setting his comfort aside for her for a while."

"So that's what this baboontool stuff is about then?"

"Barántúil," Fáidh corrected me. She said it with mock exasperation, figuring I'd mispronounced the word on purpose. Why would I do that? "It's been the tradition for thousands of years here, especially between royal houses."

A chorus of drums erupted in a brisk march. Everyone stood as ranks of trumpeters sounded a fanfare.

It wasn't the bride coming down the aisle. It was Dad.

Two-by-two, an honor guard of a dozen knights stormed forward. Their silver armor was etched with intricate forest scenes featuring elk among statuesque pines and wolves arrayed in proud ranks as if they were soldiers themselves. Their helms had dark slits and their emerald eyes glowed from the depths. They held pikes vertically at their sides. Behind them, four of the king's personal guard followed, armed with swords in sheaths. In the lead was Sir Siorradh, whose helm was always just black inside. Like the other elite knights in the king's guard, Siorradh was bigger than everyone in the room and his armor even more ornamented.

My father walked behind the guard.

Row by row, the company bowed as he passed, putting their own heads lower than the king's. For a few, a simple bow was sufficient to get short enough. Most had to take a knee and then bow, including Fáidh and I since we were so tall. Obviously, my stature came from my mother's side.

Dad's stature came from his strength, not his size, but the people respected him. He nodded and waved with engaging grace and the people waved back. He lived a simple life and dressed like a commoner, which endeared him to his subjects. His tunic, waistcoat, and breeches were plain shades of earthy brown and his leather boots were black. The only indication of kingliness was a silver crown that floated above his head, never touching him but moving with him. With every step, clover popped up in bunches, leaving green circlets on the stone that gradually withered and turned brown after the king left them behind.

The king arrived at the front row as the honor guard fanned out on either side of the altar. The king's personal retinue took positions in front, behind, and to either side of him. With a final nod, the king sat down. Murmurs of excitement and anticipation rose in the air as everyone sat down except the knights, the groom, and the best man.

On cue, Ardsagart, the high priest of Ríocht na Bráithre, our kingdom, entered the hall from behind the altar. His vestments were as beautifully crafted as the armor worn by the knights, only in cloth. While silver was the color of the Fae, gold was the color of Paradise, and the vestments had threads of both running through patterns that symbolized a sun and moon and stars all shedding rays of light. Bromach had introduced us to Ardsagart but he hadn't been required to attend the rehearsal. He struck me as a proud man who delighted in the benefits of his station but also took his duties seriously.

Fae theology was more complicated than I'd cared to learn, but they believed in loving Nature as much as their fellow Behindbeyonders and that sounded all right to me. They believed marriage was a sacred commitment worth formalizing in a ceremony, and that was nice too. I wasn't sure if they believed they went to the same Paradise where mortals went after they died, which I'd have to ask Hope about when I saw her again.

Ardsagart raised his hands. Silence fell over the gathering.

With a thunder-crash of sound, the drums and trumpets took up a new song.

The bride entered the hall.

Everyone remained seated but turned to behold her as she moved with quiet dignity.

Ógbhean was a distant cousin on Dad's side, and I'd found her gracious and beautiful. Today she exuded radiance in her gown, her eyes bright, her cheeks flushed. The gown incorporated the same little roses that Bromach had rearranged to cascade from the cupola in the middle of the wedding hall. The flowers were fresh and the extra long stems had been woven together to create the gown's sheath. The only parts showing any green were around the bride's ankles.

"Hopefully they got all the thorns off those roses," I whispered to Erin.

"They're Velvet Roses." The people around us ignored our whispers. "The stems are smooth and soft. They are cultivated for weddings. Her gown wasn't sewn, it was grown. Remember the Palisade?"

I nodded. The Palisade was a fort near the borderlands of our kingdom. The walls of the Palisade had been created by oak trees growing unnaturally close together, using magic.

"Each dress takes two weeks to grow, especially to fit the bride. It's called a Maighdinegúna and a girl only wears it on her wedding day." A couple of people near us glanced our way. Erin leaned closer, speaking even softer, "And by Barántúil tradition, that's all she wears."

That would make for a blushing bride.

I replied, "Remember the girl at our wedding, covered only by her hair?"

"Oh yes. She's always a scandal."

I asked, "Have you ever been scandalous at a wedding, milady?" My motto: Never let an opportunity to tease the wife go un-taken-advantage-of. Even if we were getting a glare or two.

Fáidh kept her eyes forward, tucking her lips between her teeth.

"What?" I gasped. "Details will be given at a later date."

"Shush," she whispered.

"Was it our wedding?"

Fáidh bit her lips again and slowly shook her head. I couldn't tell if she was saying she hadn't been scandalous at our wedding or she was simply refusing to answer. She strategically distracted me, pointing at the bride.

Ógbhean looked over her shoulder from the altar, enjoying her moment, smiling at her mother and her grandmother who sat next to the Alder King. I spotted the silver chain around her neck. A delicate silver key swung from the chain. Not for the first time, I realized how literal things were in the Behindbeyond. Or maybe the things that we considered symbolic in the mortal realm had come about from centuries of literal symbolism of the Fae.

Spreasán was bathed in sweat. He'd hardly acknowledged the arrival of his intended. Personally, I'd be following the bride, not only to see how lovely she was but also to make sure she had the key to unlock the hunk of silver stuck in my chest.

He cleared his throat. "Dear guests, before we begin, I have an announcement." He continued looking past his bride, over the heads of the gathering.

If he leaves this girl at the altar now, the bride won't have a chance to kill him. Bromach will beat her to it. "What happens to the lock in his chest if he dumps her?" I whispered, at great personal risk from the nearest starey-glarey types.

The groom saw what he'd been looking for behind us. He gave a "come here" gesture.

From the rear of the wedding hall, dozens of children began walking forward, singing.

This had not been part of the wedding plan. The children hadn't been to the rehearsal yesterday. I chanced a look at Bromach. He stood with his arms folded and a dark expression on his face.

The song was beautiful, though.

With bright voices, the children sang in the Old Tongue. I couldn't understand the words, but the music spoke to my heart and I understood that. Powerful music, reminiscent of Mussorgsky.

If it was odd for the groom to arrange for a musical number, the bride didn't seem to care. She clapped her hands, all smiles, as the children streamed down the aisle. In front, they divided left and right, then walked behind the altar and the high priest. There, they formed up in several rows across the front of the hall. Fáidh was captivated too. The children finished their entrance song and went right into a second one. Again, in the Old Tongue.

After the first few measures, the bride stopped clapping. Her smile went away. Fáidh frowned.

42

"What is it?" I asked. The people nearest us glared at me. I glared back.

Hesitating for a moment, listening, Fáidh didn't reply right away. Then, "I'm trying to remember where I've heard this before." She shook her head. "I can't place it, but it feels wrong."

When the children finished the first verse and started singing the chorus, the groom raised his hand high in the air. His middle and ring fingers bent down to touch the side of his thumb. He used his fingers to make a biting motion, while he raised his forefinger and little finger like the ears of a bunny. The gesture sent an icy river of understanding through my veins.

Without thinking, I stood and bolted for the altar.

The groom was Dubhcridhe.

# CHAPTER 6
## Don't Blink

Time struggled to move as I ran at the groom, shouting, "Everybody get down!" and calling my power from the center of my being. Figures dressed in black blinked into existence at the edges of the children's choir, the displacement of air making puh-whoosh sounds. The groom's half-brother saw me coming. His hands flared blue and he came at me, preparing a spell. I didn't know what his plan was, but I knew it wouldn't be good.

Pumping my arms, head down, I accelerated. My hands traced bright blue arcs in the air. The brother swung his hands toward me, trying to adjust his cast, and some kind of sparkling white spell erupted in my direction. I ducked. Brought my arm up under his. Shifted to the side of him. My arm deflected his, redirecting his sparkles at the ceiling as my hand clamped down on his neck. With momentum carrying me forward, he came off his feet and I lifted him higher, pulling him along. He had no chance to catch his balance as I drove him down, slamming his back against the ground at the groom's feet. His breath went out of him in a rush.

Spreasán's eyes flared wide. "Tine!" I yelled. By the time he had power coloring his hands, I had grabbed him by the back of his hair and my fire was in his face. I spat, "Hands down, unless you want to feel your brain fry from the inside." The groom hesitated for half a heartbeat before dropping his hands to his sides. His power flickered out. I let go of his hair and popped him on the chin. His eyes rolled up and he crumpled to the floor.

The children.

Turning my head, I saw tragedy in progress. Half of the kids had already been kidnapped. The bad guys were so fast. Screams pervaded the air like a shimmering curtain of sound.

A black-clad kidnapper appeared, phoosh, and slapped his hands on a boy who looked to be no older than ten. The stones at the man's feet suddenly thrust themselves up, clamping around his legs all the way up to his knees. In the next moment, the bad guy tried to blink away and take the boy, but the stone interfered with his magic. Instead of teleporting and taking the boy, the bad guy blinked forward a few inches. Wet cracking sounds were followed by a shriek loud enough to break glass. The boy landed safely, looking shocked, while the bad guy fell. Blood sprayed over the stones.

Jiminy and a million crickets.

The stone had held the man's legs while the rest of him had tried to blink. He'd snapped his legs off below the knees.

The spectacle was almost irresistible to watch. The man rolled in agony on the floor, inches away from the two columns of stone holding his bleeding stumps. I pulled the boy into my body with my unlit hand, shielding the kid's eyes, but we were both probably in for some therapy.

I blinked. Hard. And looked away.

The Alder King—my father—knelt on the floor, the most powerful Earth Mage in existence. His fists were jammed into the stones. His eyes were dark as they locked on mine. He'd been the one to snare the bad guy's legs. His grin was more than victorious. It was vicious.

He enjoyed this.

The thought made me shiver.

Everything was happening so fast, but it all needed to stop. Right now. We'd just keep losing children to the bad guys.

Or the bad guys would keep losing limbs to my father.

Dad's personal guard had done their jobs well. They'd stayed in place and turned outward to protect the king. The honor guard was simply too slow to be of help. The bad guys were blinking in and out faster than the knights could get at them.

I shoved a huge gout of flame from my hand, pushing it in an arc over the honor guard and what was left of the children. It splashed on the stones in a flood of flame. I chanted "Tine," and made the fire curve around and come back. In moments, a wall of orange heat encircled me and the kids. Experience had taught me that blinkers couldn't blink to a place they couldn't see. The wall of fire was thick enough to hide everyone and everything inside the ring.

"Children!" I yelled. "Stand with me!"

Wide-eyed, the children came forward. Some on shaky legs. Others with tears streaming. A couple of the kids put their arms around the bride and she knelt to hug them back. In the chaos, I'd forgotten Ógbhean. She'd stood bravely in the midst of all the ruckus in her spotless gown of roses.

Her day was ruined. Along with everyone else's.

The Alder King came into the circle. Just walked through my wall of fire like it wasn't there.

Either his skin was made of stone or he was immune to fire.

Interesting.

"Good idea," he said. He dropped to one knee again. His fists popped through the stone floor like hammers hitting a mud puddle. Stones to the side of the altar climbed upward, forming walls and little towers and finally a roof with another tower on top.

It took ten seconds for him to build a miniature castle. With a grin, the Alder King made the drawbridge tilt open.

"In with ye," he said. "Where ye shall be safe."

Dutifully, the children filed into the castle. A couple of them managed a laugh, choosing to find a moment of fun in the disaster. Good for them. When they had all gone inside, my father pulled his hands out of the floor and stationed himself on the open drawbridge, arms crossed over his barrel chest, smiling savagely.

Awestruck a bit, I stared at him. Dad was a mean little man, but he had style.

He caught me looking. "Douse the fire, son," he said. "Lest the building burn down."

Right.

The flames dwindled as I let my power fade. When the roar of the flames died out, there was only silence. Scanning the hall for bad guys, I stood in place for a heartbeat. Then two. The attack had ended.

Each magical blink included a millisecond of a blur, so I had an inkling where the kidnappers had been coming from. They had accessed the hall through the large doors at the back, which had been opened to let in the air. I ran back to check. Sniffles and sobs floated up to me as I dashed past the company. Most had ducked for cover under the benches like I'd told them. A few peeked out to see what was going on.

Trees. A road. Short cliffs. Meadows. Wildflowers. More trees.

I had excellent vision but saw no bad guys.

Even if they stood in view, I couldn't have caught them, but I wanted to get a look at their faces. Bromach would be able to chase them down, perhaps, but wouldn't have the stomach for it.

To be thorough, I walked outside and took a turn around the hall. A few of the honor guard joined me and we checked the grounds and stared at the trees and found nobody.

The bad guys were gone and they'd taken dozens of children with them.

Inhaling deeply, then exhaling a sigh, I tried to clear my mind.

Whoever was behind this would be hunted down and made to pay.

Thoughts of punching the face of a bad guy until it turned bloody entered my mind, colored my thoughts. I shook my head, shoving the image down. It wasn't anger that made me want to mete out retribution in pain, but justice. Still, I'd let my feelings get away from me before and I couldn't let it happen again, even if my motivations were noble.

I'd do this by the book.

That's the way it had to work.

That's what Hope had asked for.

That's what Alyce needed.

That's how I'd been trained.

Vignettes of disaster played out inside the hall.

Fáidh knelt in a pool of red far larger than it should be. A lot of blood could come out of one person, and she attended a very pale bad guy. After losing his legs to my father's Earth spell, he was staying conscious, barely, and groaning. The pain was either too much or not enough for him to pass out. With hands equally blue and crimson, Fáidh healed the skin around the stumps, but it was taking time. No answers would be forthcoming from him. Not for a while. If he survived.

Sir Siorradh and the king stood beside the little castle, dispensing children to anxious parents. The ten-year-old who'd almost been kidnapped by the recently-shortened bad guy came down the drawbridge and was caught up in a smothering of tears and hugs. There were a lot more parents waiting than children. Some of the parents had lost track of their kids but hoped they hadn't been taken. Some of the kids' parents weren't even here. Their children had come to be in the choir. A lot of parents would be going away distraught today. A lot of other parents would have distraught land on them later.

Unless they were like the Fae who left their kids in the care of strangers. For them, distraught might not be a factor.

Ógbhean stood rigid and straight, not crumbling into a soggy mess on her mother's shoulder. Her resolve was impressive. She'd put her arms around her family but remained stoically upright, facing the company, tears streaming down her face but not wilting. Her mother whispered words of comfort to her and she nodded periodically.

Spreasán was still laid out on the floor along with his half-brother. I wanted to ask them both some questions.

"Sire. There are others missing from the wedding party besides the children."

My father nodded. "List the names of the missing."

The bits of my brain that felt like magnets rolled together, thoughts attracting thoughts. "Find out if they were Halflings," I told him.

Bromach bowed to me.

I hated that.

"Goethe. What thinkest thou?" Dad could tell I had suspicions.

48

"Spreasán gave the sign of the Dubhcridhe before the attack," I replied. "The Dubhcridhe are interested in Halflings."

Dad nodded, his expression somber.

Sir Siorradh and the king's guard shifted to block an approaching knot of subjects. They were led by a man with a maroon doublet. The color matched the complexion of his face.

"We would speak to the king." The man's fists were white at the knuckles, his fingertips buried in the meat of his palms. The edges of his eyes were tight and hard. I'd seen that expression on men before. His intention had nothing to do with speaking to the king. His intention was written on his face and it was murder.

The king's schedule was kept by his Chancellor, but the wedding was a private event and the Chancellor wasn't on duty. In his absence, the duty apparently fell to the king's guard.

Siorradh remained implacable. "Ye may petition the king, as always, on market day."

"We demand justice." The man who spoke jabbed a finger toward the groom, who was still on the floor. Unconscious.

"The king is ever a friend of justice."

"We want Spreasán. He will pay for what he's done."

A second collection of figures gathered, their apparel highlighted by bright blue collars and insignia from a neighboring realm called Sómasach. They'd seen the mob come forward and moved closer in their own cluster, looking haughty.

Siorradh turned to the side a fraction. "Spreasán is in no condition to pay for anything."

The man in the maroon doublet looked like he was about to chew up his own teeth and spit them out. The cluster of blue collars from the other side of the aisle looked at each other and Siorradh but waited to speak.

The Hatcoys and McFields.

The king stood nearby. His hand rested on the shoulder of a father whose arms were around his wife. He would certainly be able to hear the heated words of the mob but didn't spare so much as a glance in their direction. With quiet words, he consoled the young parents. Their child must have been taken.

"Thou shouldst yield, sir knight." Maroon doublet took a step toward Siorradh. But only a step. Siorradh was a foot taller. And clad in armor.

Spreasán chose that moment to stir. He moaned. His hand went to his chin where I'd popped him. His eyes worked independently for a moment then snapped into focus as he realized where he was and who was staring at him. With a dark scowl he got to a knee and managed to stand. He gave his half-brother a kick to rouse him. Misery wanting company. The other man stirred with a curse.

"Him too." Maroon pointed at the half-brother. "We want them both."

"Stand down, sir." The head of the blue collar cluster finally broke his silence. "As kin, it falls to us to discipline the two of them."

"If we cannot have them, ye shall not either." Maroon gave a gesture of dismissal. "They'll vanish into one of your mud huts, in one of your filthy backwater villages, never to be seen again. That's not justice."

The groom's father sniffed. "Sadly, your wealth cannot buy your daughter's way out of being a Halfling."

Wow. Somebody got burned and it wasn't my fault.

Maroon Doublet had a knife in his hand, appearing as if by magic.

Of course, it could have been magic.

A moment later, there were a lot of daggers and a few swords and the two sides were squaring up again on opposite sides of the aisle.

If not the Hatcoys and McFields, the Montelets and Capagues.

My father stepped between them, clover springing up beneath his feet. When he raised his hands between the groups it was both a calming and a warning. "These men are under arrest."

Maroon opened his mouth.

"Brother." Ógbhean's voice sounded more penetrating because she spoke so quietly. In that one word there was a full definition of heartache. In that one moment, a year's worth of pain. "Stop."

Maroon Doublet's gaze shifted sideways to meet his sister's eyes.

The dagger remained in his hand, pointing idiotically now at the king. He paused, then took a deep breath and half a step back. His flushed cheeks became mottled as his blood pressure went down.

There was a collective return to breathing in the room.

Everyone watched the bride. She held her head high, tears streaming down her cheeks without shame. She looked again at her mother and tried not to tremble. Her lips quavered as if whole sentences full of words were all crowding together at the tip of her tongue, fighting for pronouncement. Yet she remained silent. Her head refused to hold still any longer after that, slipping free of stillness, bobbing, trembling as she turned. She'd been wholly incapable of smiling or talking or putting words together but her hands knew what to do.

Ógbhean, in her brilliant gown of roses, reached up and took the silver chain from around her neck. The sparkling strand carried the key to the lock buried in Spreasán's chest. She let the key dangle at arm's length, holding the chain in her tiny fist. Spreasán reached for the key. Ógbhean let go.

The silver key caught the light, flashing as it dropped to the stones. He sighed and bent down to pick up the key and chain, missing the manic glimmer that came into Ógbhean's eyes.

He straightened. Ógbhean's hand flicked out, lightning fast. She grabbed the lock on Spreasán's chest, screaming a Valkyrie's scream.

And pulled.

Spreasán's scream was louder, but my cousin's scream held more pain.

Blood streamed in a sudden fall down Spreasán's pale skin as his eyes rolled wide. Ógbhean took a step back, then threw the lock. It struck Spreasán across the bridge of his nose.

The lock was off.

So was the wedding.

# CHAPTER 7
## The Price of Truth

"He's asking for a healer," said Sir Siorradh.

"I thought he might." My father gave a nod to Fáidh and me.

He'd invited us both to accompany him to the castle. Fáidh had done her best to help the kidnapper who'd lost his legs, but she hadn't been able to save him. The man had died silent and trembling on the wedding hall floor.

The argument could be made he'd essentially done it to himself. Witnesses confirmed he'd taken other children before coming back, so stopping him was justified. The timing was critical. If the king had cast his spell a moment earlier, the kidnapper might have realized his legs were bound and might not have tried to blink away. To end the way it did, the spell had to be timed precisely to bind his legs with stone at the very moment the man tried to teleport.

As unforgettable as my father's feral expression was, I wasn't about to ask him how he'd mastered the skill.

Water had been brought. Fáidh had cleaned the blood off her hands. After that, we'd been escorted straight to the dungeon, which was as cold and dank and miserable as a dungeon could ever be. I'd been down here before and I wasn't thrilled to be down here again.

My father gave my elbow an iron-hard squeeze. "Time for thee to go to work."

He wanted me to interrogate Spreasán.

"Great," I replied. "I'll send you an invoice."

Dad ignored me. Instead, he gestured down the blackened stone hallway. "As they say in the mortal realm, I've got your back."

Something large moved, filling the hallway. The light and air at the end of the passage were cut off while deep and sonorous breathing rumbled along the stones, felt as much as heard.

A heavy tread, also felt and heard, announced the approach of a large creature.

Toto!

The beastiest of beasts paused, looking down at us with predatory eyes. Her name was Madrasceartán, the giant, sometimes-invisible liondog that was my father's pet assassin. She shook her massive head and shoulders, settling the mane of hair around her neck. What would she be doing here? Probably keeping Spreasán from getting away.

"Kill any tasty squirrels lately?" Madrasceartán's gaze settled on me like a bucket of cold water. She'd tackled me to the floor once and used her claw to etch a spell into my forehead. The look in her eyes let me know she'd be happy to do so again. The beast inhaled a sigh and it felt like all the air in the passage went away for a moment. When she exhaled, there was only the aroma of a sunny day in springtime after a rain.

Instead of meat, maybe she'd eaten the month of April.

"Let's get this over with." The door to the cell was heavy but hadn't been locked. It swung inward on silent silver hinges.

Spreasán looked miserable.

The lock Ógbhean had yanked out of his chest and thrown at him had struck forcefully enough to break the skin of his nose. Inwardly, I both grimaced and giggled. Twin trails of blood decorated either side of his nose like war paint, except he'd lost the war. He had a white handkerchief pressed against the wound on his chest where two more trails of blood ran down to his breeches. One of the things I needed to know was how deep in the Dubhcridhe organization he had gotten himself. I suspected he'd been influenced by a man named Urlabhraí. I'd seen the Stain of people affected by Urlabhraí before. A quick glance at Spreasán's Stain told me he hadn't been touched by Urlabhraí's magic.

Crap.

It would have made some things easier to understand if he had.

He looked up when he saw me and started, "Finally, a heal—"

His mouth clamped shut, making his teeth click together. He stared at me and shook his head like he was thinking, "Just when I thought this day couldn't get any worse."

He might not be wrong.

"Do you know who I am?"

He rubbed his jaw unconsciously where I'd popped him. "Prince Luck."

"That's right."

"I want a healer."

"Okay." There had been plenty of times when I'd been the tough guy. I was big enough to be intimidating and I knew how to hit without breaking anything if I wanted. Or hit and break anything. If I wanted. That approach wasn't always the most effective. Sometimes the thing that had to be broken had to be broken gently.

I had a healing medallion in my pocket. "Hold still." He looked confused for a moment, then saw what I was doing. With the medallion barely in contact with his nose, I called up my power and said, "Leigheas." Blue light leaked through the coin, washing over his wound in flickering little tongues. When the left side of his nose was healed, I turned the coin carefully across the bridge and over the right side as I repeated the word of power again.

It only took a few moments. He tapped his nose with his fingers and gave me a nod. "I knew not thou hadst a healer's touch. What of this?" He'd left the handkerchief on the wounds in his chest for too long. The blood had partially dried and when he tried to peel the cloth away, it pulled. He hissed as he detached the handkerchief bit by bit. Patiently, I waited and watched as the wound oozed fresh red.

"That looks painful." I nodded sagely.

"Canst thou heal it?"

"I canst." Placing the medallion on the table front of him, I said, "The first one is free. The second one costs."

Spreasán leaned back. The shaky wooden chair he sat on creaked. I guessed Spreasán had no healing powers. Even if he did, it didn't work well at all to try and heal yourself. "I see."

"Hey. You had to know we'd be asking questions. The Alder

King is outside the door. His reputation is no secret either."

The man's grim expression told me he knew about my father's lack of patience.

"I figured it would be worth it to try a different way. If we help each other then it's a lot easier."

Toto moved up the hall outside the cell, brushing along the door. If it felt like a thousand pounds of large animal stalking by, there was a reason for that. Spreasán looked at the door out of instinct and back at me.

Pretending I hadn't seen his nervous glance-o-matic, I said, "I heal you, you tell me what I need to know. I heal you some more, you tell me some more. Pretty quick, we're all good."

Madrasceartán gave a little dungeon-basement rumble, somewhere between a growl and a groan. It was easy to hear, even through a foot-thick wall of stone.

"Not yet," I hollered at her. "He's being nice."

"What did the creature say?" Spreasán looked at me and back to the door and then back to me.

How should I know?

I breathed a sigh, as if I didn't want to tell him, which gave me a moment to make something up. I cleared my throat. "First, the creature is a 'she.' And it was all I could do to keep my father and his assassin beast out of here."

Spreasán's face got tight.

"Assassin beast isn't the best—" I paused. "Look, I'm not trying to scare you. It's what she does. One of the things she does. But I'm in here and she isn't, okay?" I leaned across the table as if I didn't want the beast to hear. The key to good-cop-bad-cop was a believable good cop. The bad cop wasn't the hard part. A lot of grown men can play threatening. The hard part was being a convincing good cop. Unless the suspect honestly feels the good cop is trying to help, they will feel they have no way out and just shut down.

Pointing to the coin, I whispered, "I want to heal you. All I need is information we can use, okay?"

All I got was a stare. Spreasán wasn't buying my good cop yet. I needed more time.

"You gave the sign of the Dubhcridhe, but you're an Eternal. Why help the Halflings?"

I got a longer stare.

"We need to understand why you did what you did." He hadn't turned me down. That was a crack in his resolve. A crack was the start of an opening and an opening was all I needed. "You must have had a reason. Your family will want to know what it was. We might as well all get on the same page."

His resolve stiffened again.

Maybe a different approach.

"Thirty-nine." I said. He looked at me. Curious. I waited him out. I knew he'd heard me. I needed to keep him talking. Even if it was just to ask me a question.

He finally asked, "What's that?"

"That's how many children the Dubhcridhe took. Fourteen."

"What's that? The number of adults?"

"Yes. One hundred six."

"What?"

"One hundred six," I repeated.

He looked confused again. Finally, "What's that?"

"The approximate number of parents whose lives took a tragic turn today. It may be fewer. They might not all be living. What's that total though? One hundred fifty or more? How many people were brothers or sisters or cousins? Double that? Three hundred? What about the relatives who couldn't be here? Double that again? Six hundred? Six hundred people who were affected by this." I did the Carnivorous Bunny. "You did it to them. "

"So what?" The words were loud. He swallowed, his eyes turning hot as he blinked repeatedly.

"Six hundred people who expected today to be a celebration of love. Now, instead of crying joyful tears, they're mourning the loss of their children and friends."

"I care not."

"Spreasán. The guilt is pouring off you."

Spreasán shook his head but the denial was not for my benefit. He stopped looking at me, focusing the heat of his eyes on the table and my healing medallion.

"I'm telling you this to help you. Those who were abducted weren't all on Ógbhean's side. A third of those taken were from your family."

At that moment, Spreasán clenched his fists. There was anger in that gesture that told me events had not gone the way he'd expected.

"You clearly didn't want to marry into Ógbhean's family. It's one thing to make enemies of them. But you've made enemies of your own kin, Spreasán."

The man wasn't stupid. He knew where I was going with this line of thought. "My father shall protect me."

"He'll try. I know my father would prefer it if I were a full Fae. Your father must feel very protective of you. Especially if you are his only heir. So what kind of magic is there in your family? Is it enough to protect you from an assassin that can blink to you from a dozen miles away? Instantly?"

No answer.

Pointing at the walls, I kept my voice even. "The best bet to keep you alive is to put you in a dungeon with no windows. But think on this." I tapped the table. "Is the trouble you've caused more than you're worth? I don't mean to be disrespectful. You know the politics of the Behindbeyond better than I do, but you may have more value as a bargaining chip at this point. What concessions could be gained if your father—I'm not sure how to say this politely—surrenders you to those who wish you dead now?"

Madrasceartán's breathing was the most noticeable sound in the moments that followed.

"I can think of one advantage in working with us. Nobody will know where you are."

Spreasán glanced up at me.

Remembering his clenched fist, I probed, "You didn't get everything they promised you. Did you." I didn't say it like a question. It wasn't a question.

He frowned. "How dost thou know it?"

Pressing the advantage. "If they didn't give you what they promised, why protect them?"

Leaning back away from me, he looked at the ceiling. The blood on his chest had stopped painting lines, but the gash looked swollen and tender.

Feeling like I should hold my breath, I waited him out.

"Aighneas and Ghearradh."

The words made me blink.

Yeah. That explains a lot. Of course. I mean, a little Aighneas is one thing but you add some Ghearradh to it and then. Like. Whoa. Right?

He was talking at least. The crack growing wider.

"The Dubhcridhe promised to abduct them both."

Aha. It was people he was talking about. In the hallway, Madrasceartán growled. She knew the politics of the Behindbeyond better than I did too.

"Why would you want Aighneas and Ghearradh abducted, more than other Halflings?"

Spreasán sighed and scrubbed his eyes with his knuckles.

"They aren't Halflings. They precede me in line to the throne."

Figuring Spreasán's motives from there was easy. Madrasceartán growled again. Louder.

"With them gone, you'd be next behind your father?"

He answered with his eyes staying on the door. "Not exactly. I have two more sisters and a brother who are older than I. However, women do not rule if there's a male heir and my brother is the progeny of a concubine, giving me precedence."

With a sage nod, I replied, "As I said, I don't understand politics in this realm very well."

"Have ye no royals in the mortal realm?"

"Oh sure. I don't understand that either." I shrugged. This wasn't the time to explain a democratic republic. I needed to keep him focused on the reasons he was betrayed. "The Dubhcridhe are taking Halflings to recruit them. They are looking to rebel against full-blooded Fae. Maybe they figured out Aighneas and Ghearradh are full-blooded and don't really have a use for them. Maybe they weren't taken as you wanted precisely because they weren't Halflings."

Spreasán shook his head. His hands were clenched so tightly, they trembled. "He promised me it would be done regardless. As if they'd made a mistake."

This was it. What I needed. I picked up the medallion, showing it to the wounded man.

"He broke his promise to you. But I won't."

In his face, I saw the longing for help. He believed me now. Believed I was on his side.

Give me information I can use and I will heal you.

I saw a shadow pass over his eyes and then it was gone. I knew that was the moment when he decided to tell me everything.

"I know not his name." Spreasán's hand went to his chest. To the wound. Not touching it, but close.

"What does he look like? Where can I find him?"

"I never saw him. He always spoke through an intermediary. That's how he taught me the sign. How he taught me about the Dubhcridhe and what they hope to accomplish."

"Messengers taught you? What did they look like? Where did they meet you?"

"No, no. I mean, yes, they were messengers, but they were always different. A few of them weren't even human. And they always came to me. So I never knew who would be talking to me. Or where."

"Wait a second. A few of them weren't even human? How did they talk to you?"

"That's what I mean. He always spoke through an intermediary. Through."

Something cold and slimy reached down my throat and settled around the base of my spine.

I cleared my throat. "Did the voice sound like it was coming through a pipe? Like a voice coming up from the sewer?"

Spreasán snapped his fingers. "Indeed! Since he wouldn't tell me his name, I thought of him as Sir Garderobe for that very reason!"

Garderobe was a quaint medieval name for toilet.

The chill that started in the pit of my core crawled up to my heart. "Was there a dark cloud nearby? Like a nasty black mist that felt wrong when you looked at it?"

Spreasán nodded, so helpful now. "Yes. Sometimes I was approached at night but in the daytime, there was a dark cloud like that. I felt nauseated when I looked at it. So I stopped looking."

It had to be Urlabhraí. He must not have used any magic on Spreasán so his Stain had never been changed. But it must have been Urlabhraí who had approached him. Had put the thought into his mind to bring the children to the wedding. Had tricked his way into setting up the abductions here.

I thought he might be dead. Hoped.

"I may know who tempted you. And betrayed you. Have you heard the name Urlabhraí?"

"Wait." Spreasán looked up. "I know that name. Is he not of The Máithrín's court?"

"Yes. Or he was. Could it have been him?"

"I don't know what Lord Urlabhraí sounds like. But the voice had a certain—" There was a snapping sound in the middle of Spreasán's chest. His eyes grew wide. He tried to swallow but there was a click instead of a gulp. Madrasceartán growled louder, shaking the door on its hinges.

He seemed to be mildly surprised at first. But then his mouth dropped open far wider than his eyes. He froze that way. When he started shaking, the liondog snarled and snapped behind the door and then roared so loudly that I flinched.

In full shiver, I stood. Spreasán's skin erupted in purple-and-black curlicues. Lines and whorls traced dark patterns under his skin. The blackness seeped up as if his bones had started oozing ink into the tissues of his body. He tried to speak. The only sounds he made were gagging sounds as if the ink were burbling into his lungs. For a split-second, he was beautiful, like a figure in a stained-glass window backlit by a sunset.

Until the sunset melted the glass.

The door flew open. A hairy mountain shouldered through the door. Teeth clamped on my shirt. Breath like a dew-filled meadow drifted over me as Madrasceartán dragged me out. The last I saw of Spreasán was the black filigree on his skin splitting open and molten orange lava crisping the air.

Mads dropped me to the stones of the hallway like I was an errant cub brought back to the den. The Alder King already had his fists buried in the floor. As soon as the doorway was clear, he raised a thick column of rock to seal the room. The stones crushed the heavy timbered door like paper, and shards of wood flew into the corridor.

Behind the newly-built bulwark, a massive thud rumbled through the rock, shaking the floor and the walls and the ceiling.

Spreasán had detonated.

A shockwave moved through the castle, expanding away from the epicenter, rolling up and down and sideways. I struggled to my feet. Madrasceartán stared, her fuzzy face unreadable, while my father looked concerned and Fáidh looked afraid.

"I didn't know," I said.

# CHAPTER 8
## Girl Attorney

Keeper was a keeper of all things arcane and strange. Concern knit together the overstuffed white hair of his eyebrows. "Ya couldna known about the curse."

The words did not help me feel better. I knew well how spells need a word to be triggered. Or several. The spellcaster might not have been Urlabhraí, but talking down a sewer pipe through another person was a trick he favored. He might have taught it to someone else. Someone who also cast the curse that had killed Spreasán. It would prevent anyone from asking more questions if they started to get close to the truth about the abductions.

There are more of them.

I shuddered.

More nasty mages like Urlabhraí.

I felt lousy. Responsible for the man's death. My questions had triggered the curse. Or made him say the words. The curse could have been triggered by anyone. I knew that. But I was certain Urlabhraí and whoever else was involved would be perversely delighted that I'd been the one involved.

I hate you too, Ur.

"This isn't good, Keeper."

"No, lad."

"In the mortal realm, a suspect dying while in custody means somebody will lose their job. Or resign, at best."

"Kings and princes cannae resign."

"His family will have to be notified."

Keeper tilted his head a notch. "In time."

"We have to tell them."

"Spreasán was a criminal, sire. There were witnesses, including the lad's own kin. The king may hold traitors and such indefinitely."

I didn't like it. The longer we waited to tell them, the worse it would look.

"'Tis nae good how he died. Spreasán burned to death and, if ye'll forgive me, ya are famously able to set anythin' on fire."

Keeper had a point.

This was bad.

Really, really bad.

"I'll have to find out who cursed him. If I can do that, we can lay the blame where it belongs."

Keeper gave a short nod. "There's good thinkin', lad."

It was my turn to nod. Exhaustion settled in my bones, stress taking its toll.

"We'll nae be able to open that room." Keeper shook his head. "Not for some time. Take a look."

Keeper handed me what looked like a silver spoon, except it was completely flat instead of curved in the bowl or in the handle. He had used silver mirrors and silver implements for scrying before. I looked at the circle of silver.

All I saw were blobs of black.

Moving the silver scryer was like moving a camera inside the room. By shifting and turning it, I got a good idea of what it looked like inside. The walls of the cell were spattered with black splotches. Bits and pieces of Spreasán were strewn everywhere. More strange and terrible were the droplets of black, like tar, hanging in the air. The room looked like it must be full of water and filled with a dense school of dark, deformed fish, all dead and frozen in time.

"There's all kinds of befoulment in that cell. Magical and elsewise," Keeper said solemnly. "We dinnae know what it will take to cleanse it."

What a disaster.

Today my luck was bad.

There was one place where my luck could improve.

Back in my chambers, I found Fáidh tending to Alyce. She'd

come up to check on her while I was talking to Keeper.

"How is she?"

"Stable."

"Has she said anything? Woke up at all?"

"The nurse said she's slept. That's it."

The chair complained when I sat in it. The complaint sounded a lot like me.

"Are you all right?" My wife's cool fingers traced lines on my forehead while my eyes closed.

"I will be."

"Sleep for a bit before we go back to the mortal realm. There's time before you need to go with Nat."

"I would argue, but I'm on your side." It had been a long day already and it was far from over. "Come with me. You can tuck me in and then I'll tuck you in and we'll take a nap."

"Will that work, really?"

"We'll make it work. Together, we can do anything."

Fáidh kissed me on the cheek as she helped me up. "Of that, I have no doubt."

We held hands as we left Alyce's room and went to our own. I stretched out diagonally across as much of the bed as I could and closed my eyes. "Shoot. I've fallen and I can't get up."

"That's fine," Fáidh laughed. "I'm going to the little princess's room. When I get back, I'll bring a pry bar. Or Sir Siorradh."

Mostly to the mattress, I mumbled, "That's my girl."

Soft footfalls carried her away.

My breathing deepened. The yarn of the old-fashioned quilt fluttered against my face as air went in and out.

Soft footfalls returned. High heels.

"Are you all right, honey?" I asked. "You seem to be making a lot of quick trips to the bathroom lately."

"I'm fine." There was something a little off about the voice, but I was too sleepy for it to register.

"I could probably move over. You should start with bribery. You have all kinds of things I want."

"Sire. We don't have much time."

Sire?

I heard the difference in the voice more clearly, but it wasn't enough for me to open my eyes.

"That's a terrible bribe. In fact, it's not even a bribe. Do you know what a bribe is?"

"Your Highness?"

Churro-chucking chihuahuas.

The voice was not my wife's. My eyes popped open.

The heels she wore were as red as rubies. Skinny legs, but cute. A dark pencil skirt with a hint of a pinstripe starting at the strange girl's knees, held by a narrow leather belt. Above that, a white satin blouse with a smart jacket that matched the skirt. A ruby brooch sparkled at the edge of my vision, pinned to the blouse at her neck. Her manicured hands were folded together in front of her and the color of her fingernails matched her brooch. She rotated almost imperceptibly back and forth. Impatient? Needing the little princess's room? I couldn't tell.

My nap would have to wait.

I pulled myself toward the edge of the bed and sat up. She was already moving to leave the bedroom, heels clicking on stone, but she checked over her shoulder to make sure I was following. I caught a glimpse of warm, brown eyes. Horn-rimmed glasses sat perched on the end of her nose. She had a lot of makeup on; lashes long and dark, cheeks one shade too peachy, and lips dramatically crimson. Her hair was pulled back away from her face in an elegant chignon.

The obvious question finally came to me. "How did you get in here? There are twenty guards outside the door."

"Please follow me, sire."

Maybe she was an attorney for Spreasán's family. If so, she looked really young, despite the makeup. In the Behindbeyond, an attorney looking young wasn't odd. An attorney in the Behindbeyond at all was odd.

As I got off the bed and followed her, a few mental magnets aligned.

In the adjoining room, a liagán stone presumptuously occupied the center of the floor. The girl waited beside it. The stone was open. Darkness waited on the other side.

Never mind how it got here.

"Where does the portal go?"

"No time for chit-chat, sire."

"Sure there is. This is an enchantment of some kind. Or a dream. And anyone who can put a portal stone in my living room can give us all the time we need."

The girl sighed. "It goes . . . someplace you've visited before."

That didn't help. I'd been to a lot of places and a lot of them were places I didn't want to visit again.

"Hold on a minute." There was one person who had controlled my dreams before.

Béil.

I strode across the room. "Hey!"

She spun around to face me. Her eyes grew wide and she was suddenly not wearing glasses anymore. I half-expected to see Béil's face but it wasn't her. The girl had Béil's determination but her features weren't familiar. "Who sent you?"

"Sire, I—"

Her hair undid itself and fell to her shoulders.

For a long moment, she studied my eyes. I wanted answers but I must not have appeared threatening. "There are things you need to know." She spoke with authority again. Her hair went back up behind her neck. Thwip. She moved her hand to adjust her glasses, which reappeared on her face as if they'd never vanished. "Follow me."

The girl stepped into the portal.

I followed.

A lightless nowhere.

No up or down or left or right. I saw my own body when I looked, but reaching out with my hands offered nothing tangible. Without a point of reference, an instant dizziness hit me. I couldn't tell which direction I was facing or if there was such a thing as direction.

Yet there was a sense of place, feathering out at the edges of my awareness. Like the shelf of books in your peripheral vision or the table behind the couch, parts of the room that you would usually not recognize as being there because you were noticing other things, but you didn't question their existence. When I did consider their existence, I felt them. Saw them. Like they didn't exist until they came into my thoughts.

For example, the floor underfoot. Once I quelled the queasy wave of nausea from being lost in empty space, I directed my thoughts to logic. There wasn't anything there but I had no sensation of falling, therefore I had to be standing on something and so it was there. A black-and-white checkerboard pattern of tiles beneath me fading off into a darkened distance.

This place was familiar, resembling the place where I'd received my powers. I'd been alone with my own magic self in that place and someone had tried to murder me.

More logic. Portals and gates invariably kept your destination in front of you. As far as I could tell, I was facing the same direction here as when I'd arrived. So the exit should be straight ahead. All I needed was a destination.

And there it was.

An old door presented itself a few yards away.

If you think it, it will come.

This was not the usual way for a portal to work, but this was someone else's realm and rules weren't made to be broken for the Fae. Rules were made to be ignored, revised, or eliminated.

Speaking of which.

Next to the door was an umbrella stand, because what else would there be next to a door? In the umbrella stand was a child's plastic parasol. The handle was pink and the shaft was silver. The parts of the canopy sticking up out of the stand were transparent and there were little ducks wearing raincoats on it. The ducks weren't the only birds in attendance. Perched on the handle was a big, black raven.

My raven. Midnight Dreary.

I said, "Hey."

The bird croaked in reply.

"What a nice surprise. I'm afraid don't have any snacks. I wasn't expecting to see you."

She turned her head to the side and ruffled her wings in a convincing shrug.

I pointed at the door. "Are you coming?"

The raven flew up to my shoulder as I grasped the doorknob. She croaked, "The dreamer must dream."

The doorknob wouldn't turn. Very possibly because my hand had ceased to move.

There was no need for me to ask what the raven had said. She'd spoken clearly and there was nothing wrong with my hearing. I turned my head enough to catch the raven's eye. She tapped my head with her beak. Not hard. Soft dit-dit-dits on my temple. I interpreted the taps as her saying, "Think about it."

Time to go.

The doorknob rattled and turned.

The door swung open.

We crossed into a dusty foyer. Simple furniture covered in a thin layer of gray huddled under a ceiling pregnant with shadows. On one wall hung a painting, abstract gunmetal shapes with a slash of red, ten feet tall. On the facing wall, a tapestry with a thousand faerie creatures gamboling over a landscape stolen from the easel of William Turner.

I had been here.

Ail Bán Dearg. Béil's home.

My visits here were always a mix of bliss-and-miss. Laoch was cool. Béil was usually cold.

Girl Attorney stood with her arms folded across her abdomen. She held her mouth in a twist. Her glasses had slipped to the end of her nose and her eyes were suddenly blue. "You had to come, huh?" I caught the line of her stare. She wasn't asking me, she was asking the bird. "We don't have time for these delays. You know what will happen if we're here too long."

Midnight Dreary squawked by way of explanation.

It was hard to tell if Girl Attorney accepted the squawk as she reset her glasses and her eyes went back to brown. She spun around and stalked off into the shadows. Her hair had transformed from a chignon to a more practical ponytail and the ponytail swung and bounced as she walked away.

I followed, my raven perched on my shoulder like a feathered bodyguard.

We climbed a set of stairs and proceeded down a short hallway. The artwork on the walls held to a theme, but the theme had twisted sideways. Modern settings with Renaissance figures jammed in and the thousands of imps and satyrs and dryads had stopped gamboling. Now they were murdering each other.

With claws and teeth and little angry knives, the creatures swept across the scenery in mobs of slaughter. The tapestry was drowning in red.

A shiver ratcheted up the vertebrae of my spine.

Girl Attorney turned a corner and ascended more stairs.

I followed. At the top of the castle was four thousand square feet of floor space, but it was all one room.

Béil's bedroom.

I tried to remember if I'd ever been here in the real world, but I couldn't recall. It felt odd that an entire floor would be devoted to a sleeping chamber. No columns supported the tons of rock that would be the ceiling and even in the Behindbeyond, that would be a miraculous feat of engineering.

This wasn't exactly the Behindbeyond.

The room was a vast, hollow cavern of gray stone and grayer mood. The emptiness served to emphasize the only piece of furniture in the space: a bed. Scaled huge as well, bigger than king size. More like emperor size or, in this case, empress.

The bed had four pillars, holding up a gauzy gray canopy over the bed.

Midnight Dreary launched herself from my shoulder and flew up to the corner of the pillar where she could perch and watch.

Underneath the canopy, Béil's sleeping shape was like a child's doll. She wasn't a tall woman by any means. Here, under the voluminous gray satin sheets, she was so very small.

I knew her power had little to do with her actual size.

"I was. Worried. Thou wouldst. Not come."

A shapely apparition whispered to us, standing in a pool of moonlight like a starlet in a film noir. Béil wore a modest satin nightgown with only her shoulders exposed, perhaps in deference to the younger girl in the lawyerly business attire. Béil enjoyed the attention of men and the envy of women, and she was well equipped for both.

Béil regarded Girl Attorney. "Well done. Thou didst. Deliver. As promised. If only. A bit late."

Girl Attorney curtsied. "We were delayed in the portal. The guide wanted to come."

Béil smiled and it wasn't entirely cold. "She is. Doing her duty. As you. Have done. Mortal."

Girl Attorney curtsied again.

Mortal?

I let my head tilt to the side. The motion helped the mental magnets of my intuition line up and click together somehow.

Facing Girl Attorney, I imagined her without glasses. The glasses vanished.

I imagined her with gray eyes and they were gray.

I imagined her hair down again. It fell in a tumble over her shoulders.

Béil laughed.

I imagined her with her makeup gone and her features were instantly without adornment.

Béil's grin was wicked.

The girl was no stranger.

Alyce.

# CHAPTER 9
## Key to Escape

Jabbing a finger in Alyce's face, I said, "I have some questions for you."

Alyce clamped her teeth down on her lower lip. After a moment, she nodded. "As soon as we're finished."

Béil gave me a smirk before extending a graceful hand in the direction of her own sleeping form. "I am. In need. Of rescue."

The Béil in the bed looked okay to me. She reposed with her hair in a perfect fan on the pillow. Her hands were clasped at her chest holding a single white rose.

Classic Sleeping Beauty.

Of course.

I looked back at the talking version. "How?"

"That's not. Really me." She looked up at the ceiling for a moment and took a deep breath, then sighed. "Explain. Alyce. Lest I wake."

Alyce nodded and started machine-gunning sentences. Unlike Béil, she could talk a mile a minute.

"What you are seeing is a vessel, projected here by Her Ladyship's subconscious. Her Ladyship's physical body is being kept prisoner. In sleep, she is able to project a facsimile to this realm. The facsimile is, however, not able to speak undetected, but Her Ladyship also embedded a manifestation of her consciousness in the vessel to speak for her. To her captors, this will be difficult to detect but not impossible. She must remain circumspect even now."

Alyce took a deep breath and smiled.

Wow. Vocabulary.

This made Béil a riddle, wrapped in a mystery, inside an enigma.

More so than usual. Or a ghost of a spirit in a specter.

"Two. Of us. Are held. Myself and. Laoch."

Laoch too?

"I need. To know. He. Is all right."

"Where?"

Béil put her hands on her hips. "Tír na nÓg."

Midnight Dreary croaked and waggled her head as if hearing the words was unpleasant. "Who's holding you captive?"

Béil shook her head as she stood up and pointed at Alyce. Alyce whispered, "Caer Ibormeith." Then she said, "May all dreams be to her glory."

Monkey chunks. That sounded like another Fae name spelled with the letters left over at the end of a badly-played Scrabble match. "Anything else?"

"In my. Pocket." Béil said it to Alyce, who nodded and crawled onto the bed. "Take it. To open. A barrow."

"A barrow? Isn't that a mound where dead people are buried?"

Béil nodded.

Super. I'd grown up not far from one of those, if local legend were to be believed.

Alyce was having trouble crossing the stadium-sized bed, scampering over the satin sheets in her heels.

"Can I get it?" I asked.

Not that I wanted to be in a bed with Béil.

"It has to be me," Alyce said. "Her body is warded against contact by an Eternal or a Halfling. Only I can touch her. Or the key."

"All right."

"Oh no," Béil said.

The room tilted. The ceiling groaned as if it finally realized there was nothing holding it up, and now that the whole place was moving it would be a good time to fall. The air swirled, catching Alyce's hair.

"Hurry!" Béil shrieked. "They are. Waking me."

Alyce screamed. The bed tilted more steeply and she slipped on the satin sheets. The room went past off-kilter all the way to precarious, and my shoes lost traction in the dust on the floor. I

72

caught myself by grabbing the pillar of the bed. Alyce had monkeyed her way up to the headboard where there were carved leaves and vines.

The version of Béil that was sleeping hadn't moved at all. She was still in her same relative position in the bed, her hair still fanned out perfectly over the pillow. Her vessel was obeying the gravity of the place where her body was lying, not the place of her dream.

Alyce and I weren't so lucky.

The Girl Attorney Ninja screamed again as the room shifted again, turning in another direction.

"My pocket!" Béil cried.

Alyce let go with one hand and reached for the pocket at sleeping Béil's waist. The room was way closer to vertical than it had any right to be. With a crunch, the corner of the room vanished, bitten off like a saltine cracker nibbled by a giant. The swirling air accelerated to a rushing wind, fleeing through the hole in the corner of the room to fill the void behind.

"They wake me!" Béil cried.

"What if we die here?"

"You die. In. Reality."

Of course.

I pulled myself up onto the pillar, wanting to help with no clue how.

Alyce's hand scrambled inside the pocket.

"It's empty!"

"Other! Pocket!" Talking Béil was becoming more ghostly by the moment.

Another bite of the room disappeared.

The roar of the wind cranked up to hurricane.

"We have to get out of here!" My voice barely carried.

"Not without the key!" Alyce gamely stretched for Béil's other pocket but she was still just a twelve year-old girl. She screamed before she dropped, knew her grip was failing.

Her hand slipped from the headboard. She flailed, grabbing at anything and everything; my instincts kicked in.

I jumped.

Alyce rocketed past Béil's vessel. I met her in midair. She grunted as my shoulder slammed into her and my arm wrapped around her waist. My mass was far greater than hers, so my momentum carried us across about a mile of bed to the other side. I turned as we hit in an attempt to avoid squashing Alyce between the stone of the pillar and my chest and got my arm over the opposite pillar.

Above us, another chunk of room got bitten to oblivion, taking the headboard with it. The wind rushed faster.

"The key!" Alyce cried.

Even if I stood on the pillar and boosted Alyce on my shoulders, she'd never be able to fish Béil's pocket.

"We can't reach."

Alyce looked up. "I can climb the sheets."

I admired her pluck but there was zero chance she'd' make it.

The room lurched again.

We were almost completely vertical.

I let us drop a little. Alyce screamed again. I caught the edge of the pillar with my hand. If we slid down the floor before it tilted further and if the wind added some drag, we could make it to the wall opposite the bed and work our way to the door without dying.

I hoped.

Now or never.

I let go.

With Alyce in one arm and the other arm against the floor, I kicked the soles of my feet against the stone. The dust worked against me, defrictioning our descent, but the wall of moving air was grabbing at us, slowing us a little.

We slid for about a week.

The castle lurched again. Another chunk of the dream world disappeared. Where we had been heading toward the wall, we were suddenly heading for the archway of the room now.

Not helpful.

Beyond the arch there was an open stairway. If we hit it at this angle we'd be falling forty feet into a whole set of hard, angular edges, likely to our deaths. The wind moaned and whined so loudly around the corners and through the passages now that I couldn't hear Alyce screaming.

Good.

She couldn't hear me screaming either.

Time felt stuck in honey. The edges of the world turned golden, and it felt like the world's most unfair joke prolonging the set up to the punchline. My brain was high on the chemicals of fear, which made me want to run, but I couldn't see a safe place to run for.

This is a dream world, Luck.

Think.

If I made Alyce's glasses go away with a thought—

Then—

In a split second, I considered a cargo net, a trampoline, a jungle vine.

Keep it simple.

Dad could move stone.

Try. I imagined a ramp emerging from the floor, curving up to the ceiling.

The stone curled.

We hit the ramp. The g-force pressed me down. I couldn't hear myself grunt but I felt it. Despite the screwy angle, I kept my legs in front of me. We hit the top of the ramp, not as hard as we could have. My legs took our weight. With my arms around Alyce and her arms around my neck, she didn't even slip out of my grasp. We slid back, coming to rest at the bottom of the curve.

Score one for the visitor's team.

Alyce said something to me. I saw her mouth move but the wind stole the sound.

Behind us, Béil was gone along with half the room.

We had a long way to the portal.

Pointing right, I nudged Alyce off the ramp. She scooted down the floor about six feet to the wall and scrambled to the archway with me hot on her heels.

Negotiating the stairs was an exercise in vertigo. Too many angles and all of them wrong. Half the staircase, which had been steep before, was now upside-down, making the other half practically flat.

Screw this.

I made my own stairs, forcing up hunks of stone with my thoughts.

We scampered to the hallway like squirrels on beachside boulders, but we were losing ground to the fading of Béil's dream.

"Run!" I yelled, even though Alyce was already running and she couldn't hear me anyway.

The hallway tilted oddly. One wall served as our sprinting track while the other made a makeshift ceiling. The tapestries above hung down like old laundry while the others lay like rugs. The imps in the tapestries laughed at us. I stepped on their faces as we ran along the wall.

The wall/ceiling vanished as we made the next set of useless stairs.

I improvised more stairs.

Alyce stepped off and the wind took her. She flew off the stone and hit the wall above her. Her face twisted in a grimace with the impact. I had to force up a stone so I could climb on it and grab her.

"I'll hold you." She didn't hear. Couldn't.

Arm-in-arm, I jumped down stone to stone. The wind snarled and grabbed at us like an angry animal, buffeting us so hard that every drop to the next stone was a breathtaking leap of faith.

Alyce squirmed out of my arms when we made it to the next floor so she could run. I felt more than saw the hallway above us collapse and disappear. We streaked along the last wall like our tails were on fire, maneuvering over the tapestries.

At the edge of the wall, Alyce abruptly stopped. I almost ran her over.

She'd stopped for good reason.

The portal was ahead of us but too far. With the floor tilted the way it was, we'd have to jump and slide into the portal to escape. I might be able to make it but Alyce wouldn't.

Duh.

I'll make a slide.

It took only a thought and boom. Instant slide.

Yes.

The slide disappeared.

No!

A huge swath of the room had been chewed to oblivion.

The dream was at an end.

And so were we.

I wanted to conjure another slide, but Béil's waking up was eliminating options. I had the bit of hallway behind us but it wasn't enough. The wind had reached its peak. A beastly mass of unforgiving, unrelenting air.

Alyce turned to me, pressed her little body against me, and looked up. Tears streamed from her eyes only to be stolen by the wind. I couldn't hear her question. It wasn't hard to read it from her lips.

Are we dead?

I wanted to give her an answer. I didn't have one.

Midnight Dreary streaked past, a glossy black bullet.

I'd entirely forgotten about her.

Happens when you're fighting for your life.

The raven flew past us, heading toward the portal. She gave a miniscule flap of her wings and the wind tossed her up in a blur. She tucked her wings in and sliced down, cutting through the wind like an arrow.

At least one of us will get away.

She didn't go.

She flapped again. Shot up and away from safety.

She's waiting for us.

I had an idea.

A tapestry, covered with the giggling, profane little demons of a nightmare. I pulled, tearing it off its brackets. It tried to fly off but there would be no escaping my iron grasp.

Precious seconds ticked by. I looked at Alyce and saw a spark of hope. I prayed it wouldn't be misplaced.

The tapestry fought to get away. I jammed two of the corners into Alyce's fists. She held on like a little tiger.

We were out of time, but the details nagged at my mind. We'd need to run and jump and then sail over the empty void, but I was so much heavier than Alyce. If our bodies weren't linked together somehow, she'd fly up and we'd fall into oblivion.

Stupid physics.

While holding my corners of the tapestry, I bent down and picked Alyce off the floor. When I pulled her legs around my waist and patted her knees, she nodded and locked her ankles behind me, then squeezed.

I should be first off the ledge. I backed up as fast as I could move and shoved as hard as I could. We rose in the air, describing a graceful windblown arc.

The sum of a million desperations.

With a sickening realization that gravity still existed, we fell.

The wall we'd just jumped from crumbled and shattered into empty, heartless nothingness. Alyce and I spread our arms. The wind blew and the constant roar sounded like rushing death.

Death caught the tapestry at last.

With inhuman strength, we kept our corners. The fabric ruffled for a moment before snapping into a lopsided canopy. We floated under the world's ugliest improvised parachute.

Blessed stars.

It wasn't working great.

But it was working.

Momentum and aerodynamics and sheer, stupid luck carried us toward the portal. The air bucked and swirled, but all we really needed for it to do was keep blowing.

My pulse thundered in my head. We sailed for just another second. Then two. With nothing else to give a point of reference, I prayed we'd be over the portal.

Almost.

Now.

I let go of the tapestry. The wind cried havoc, released from captivity.

I put my arms around Alyce.

We dropped as one. So fast.

The tapestry ripped itself from her hands. She threw her arms around my neck. A flash of sparkling black drew a streak of light as Midnight Dreary plunged into the portal. My butt landed on the last solid piece of castle right before it vanished.

We bounced through the ring.

Bank shot.

# CHAPTER 10
## Alyce in Dreamerland

We skidded across stone, me underneath her, skin scraping and burning, then we stopped with a bump against some furniture. The first thing I noticed was the pain.

Pain was good. Pain meant we were alive.

And yet.

Ow.

The next thing I noticed was the quiet. There had been a wind monster in Béil's dream house. No such monster here. Maybe I'd gone deaf.

But no.

I heard our breathing. I just had to listen harder because it was muffled as if there were cotton in my ears.

It took some effort to get to my feet. Alyce was wrung out and limp and could hardly stand.

She cried against my shirt. She needed to let it out so I stood in place, savoring the relative calm. Compared to the maelstrom we'd left behind, Tropical Storm Alyce was a springtime refresher.

Finally, I felt her backing away and I let her go. She sniffed and cleared her throat. Her glasses popped back out of nowhere and I hadn't realized her hair had fallen down again until it rearranged itself into a lawyerly bun.

She noticed my shirt and reached out like she wanted to brush it off but didn't touch it.

"Ew. Snotsville," she half-laughed. "What a mess."

She didn't apologize, but she didn't need to. Even though we weren't in a place we could label "reality," this was still the Behindbeyond and she knew the rules.

"All right?" I asked.

Alyce stared at the floor. "We failed. We went through all that and didn't get the key Her Ladyship wanted me to give you."

"How did you arrange all of this the first time? Using your dreamland to access Her Ladyship's dreamland? Maybe it can be done again."

I didn't want to do any of this again.

Alyce sighed. "Laoch."

Laoch? "But Béil said he's captive along with her."

"They were separated. The children were taken to a different place."

"He only looks like a child."

"I know." Alyce nodded. "He and I are a lot alike. Living in bodies that never age, only I'm mortal." Alyce swallowed hard but more tears stood in her eyes. "Or I used to be. I'm not sure what I am anymore. And I don't know if we will be able to arrange things again. If the others woke Her Ladyship, they may have sensed something and figured out what's going on."

I felt the need to change the subject. Maybe something cheerier. "You'll have to show me how you do that thing where your glasses appear out of nowhere."

"That? Oh. That's just how I see myself. I wanted to be an attorney when I grew up. Ever since I was little. My appearance in my dreams is always like this."

"Huh."

"Your appearance changes too. Did you know?"

"That's crazy." I looked down. "How long have I been like this?"

Alyce giggled. It improved the look of her face immeasurably. "Since I brought you into my dream."

"Are you sure?"

I looked down again. I was covered in armor. Not the decorative armor of the king's guard. My armor was the dented, pitted silver of a knight errant. One who had traveled far and fought hard, seeking adventure and rescuing maidens. I'd never seen the armor before.

"We don't always see ourselves clearly." Wise beyond her years, she looked at me and pressed her lips together.

"Do I look like this because you see me that way? Since this is your dreamland? Or is this how I see myself?"

Alyce thought about it. "Does it matter?"

Swell.

She's profound and enigmatic.

"Um." She looked at me with a sudden shyness. "If it helps, I do see you as a knight."

Midnight Dreary chose that moment to land on my shoulder.

She leaned out over the space between Alyce and me and dropped something. Something small and hard that clattered on the floor. She croaked as if saying, "Here."

Alyce cried out in surprise. She bent down and snatched the item off the floor and held it in her hands, looking in wonder from there, to the raven, and back again.

"Did you get this from Her Ladyship's pocket?"

Midnight Dreary ruffled her wings and croaked as if to say, "Of course. What else?"

"You amazing, marvelous, wonderful bird!"

The raven ruffled her wings and croaked again.

Of course. What else?

Alyce smiled at me. "The key. This is what Her Ladyship wanted you to have. Now that a raven and a mortal have touched it, the others will have a very hard time finding out where it went." She held her hand out in front of her, fingers down.

Flashback.

"Huh. We've done this before." It felt strange going through these actions again.

"We have?" Alyce squinted at me, perplexed.

"Yes." I almost put my hand beneath hers and then I remembered what happened afterward. "Wait. When you did this gesture before, you weren't holding anything. Then you controlled me with magic and made me walk up and down inside a building. I went through a wall and over the edge of a cliff."

"I did that?" She pressed her hand against her chest.

She didn't seem to grasp the severity of the situation. "It was very traumatizing. If it hadn't been for, um, a few friends who were there, I'd be dead. Probably."

Furrows took command of Alyce's brow. She opened her hand and looked at the key for a moment. "I wish I could remember. It must have been Laoch. Everything I've done has been what he commanded me."

"That makes sense. As much as any of this."

"Tell me exactly what happened."

I started with my noticing her at the wedding rehearsal. I skipped the part about her force-fielding Bromach and explained how she'd held her hand out to me but hadn't had anything to give me. Then she'd magically pushed and pulled me around the wedding hall, over benches and nearly into solid objects. Bromach had been able to blink me through a wall and I'd almost fallen off the cliff. I didn't mention Hope.

Alyce scrunched up her face some more, which was pretty cute. Her hand rubbed against the middle of her chest like it had a mind of its own. She said, "I don't think there will be significant consequences after I give you this. Based on my substantial experience, it's extremely difficult to connect one spell with a different spell directly. So the spells are probably intended to accomplish different results. Just to be safe, though, please close your eyes."

She'd given me no cause to mistrust her so far. I only hesitated for a moment before doing as she'd asked. The world went dark and she said, "Open your eyes."

We weren't in my chambers anymore. Instead, we were in a grassy meadow. The light was flat, as if someone had forgotten to put a decent source of illumination in the world. The wispy green blades of grass stretched out in every direction as far as the eye could see. Which was, apparently, forever.

"Now if another spell goes off, you can walk safely as far as you need to." Alyce smiled.

I looked around some more. "Cool. Why did you want me to close my eyes?"

"Changing the dreamland is kinda nauseating to watch." She stuck out her tongue. "The first time I did it, I threw up. So I close my eyes too."

Now that she wasn't being analytical and in charge, Attorney Girl's speech had a little less vocabulary and a little more chill. Our location was a little more chill too. It was probably the empty space where there is no direction. The place where I'd picked up Midnight Dreary earlier.

"You're quite thoughtful."

Alyce beamed. "Ready to take this?" She stuck out her hand.

"Guess so." I put my hand under hers.

She opened her fingers.

The key dropped to my palm. It was cool to the touch.

Last time, she'd said, "The dreamer must dream." This time she didn't say anything.

I hunched my shoulders. If she was going to make a puppet out of me, it would be now. I made a face, pre-flinch. Her eyebrows went up a fraction.

That was it.

We looked at each other. Looked around.

"If you like your climactics anti, this is perfect," I said.

Alyce smiled. "Whatever happened is going to be linked to something later. Something tangible, like the key."

"Are you sure?"

"Pretty sure."

"Guess it makes sense."

I held the key in my hand—the hand that was wearing a battered gauntlet—and checked it out. It was a carving a little larger than a game piece from a set of dominoes, made of bone. The carving was a Celtic knot. One of those circular shapes with the interlocking rings or the line that runs over and under itself and ends up going back to the same place if you trace it with your finger.

This is a key?

I looked at it. Turned it and twisted it. It was just a carving.

"Do you know anything else about this?"

Alyce shook her head.

"Okay. I'm, uh . . ." Unsure now what to say. Then I nodded and smiled. "You did great, by the way. Attorney Girl."

Alyce giggled. Her glasses winked out for a minute and her hair fell to her shoulders. She was just a girl for a moment.

Looking down, I saw my armor in its full, beat-up glory.

Of course.

"I should probably—"

"Don't go yet." Alyce blurted out the words.

"Oh. I—"

"Like you said, this is my dreamland. We have all the time we need. To, um . . ." She struggled with her thoughts. "I just haven't had anybody to talk to for . . ." Her eyes got misty again and she looked up at the non-existent sky. ". . . a really long time."

"Hey. It's great. I was about to say I should probably ask you some questions."

Alyce bounced her head up and down. "Oh! Good. Okay. About the night I was kidnapped?"

"And about Laoch and Béil. First, I did look up your family. I might know where your mom and dad are."

Alyce suddenly found her ruby shoes to be fascinating. "My dad was a piece of garbage. Mom was a little bit better, although she let my dad be a piece of garbage."

Some things take time to heal. Some things never heal at all.

"Whatever happened, it shouldn't have happened. It was a long time ago. I can at least see what they're up to, if you like."

"How old am I?" Alyce shrugged off the other topic.

She was a smart girl. Who knew what she'd been through? Or how the days had passed?

"Based on your age when you disappeared, if you were the mortal realm, you'd be thirty-seven years old now."

She took it pretty well. Looked up from her ruby shoes. Turned her gaze to the side, absorbing the data. I didn't know if thirty-seven was older than she expected. Or younger. Either way it was probably a shock.

"That was the age of my mother when I was abducted."

"Sixty-four then. She'd be jealous over your anti-aging secret."

Alyce laughed. "She hated her wrinkles." She bit her lip. "I wouldn't mind a few."

Whew.

"I grew up thinking I was a mortal, but Laoch and I are both a couple of centuries old. He looks better than I do. But it's very close."

Alyce smiled. "He and I are a lot alike. I said that before, I guess. That might be why he asked me to help. Even the Fae underestimate those who appear to be children. They forget I'm staring down middle age."

My turn to laugh. "You can get away with a lot."

"I'm easy to ignore."

I had a feeling she meant that in more ways than one. Even now, it was hard to reconcile how mature her thinking was because she looked so young. Luckily, I'd had practice with Laoch.

"I'm glad Laoch found you."

"There's a story. It wasn't easy to work out a plan. We only saw each other every few days. Our duties are in very different places."

"Well. He chose the perfect conspirator."

"I am a girl. Girls are good at conspiring."

"True. Just don't go overboard like Lady Béil."

"Okay." She laughed.

"Good. And now it falls to me. I'll take this key and figure out how to use it. Then I'll rescue everybody. Simple, right?"

"No. Not simple. Be careful. The goddess will not relinquish her servants lightly. In fact, I think she might have let me leave to be here, but I can't begin to guess why."

"Okay. Careful it is. And we will take the best care of you as well. We have the best healers and priests in the Alder King's court watching over you. If there's a way to wake you up—"

"It's okay." Alyce squirmed, standing on the grass. She wasn't accustomed to people making a fuss over her, I expected. "Get the others out first. I served in the places bordering the mortal realm and Tír na nÓg. Lady Béil would have been kept in the tower with the

Eternals, but Laoch is in the castle, separate from everyone else. Just know the realm of dreams is vast and dangerous."

"Okay. One thing at a time. How about your magic? Did Laoch give it to you?"

"No. Maybe. I don't know." She put her hand to her chest again. It was the third time she had done that.

"All right." I had more unpleasant questions. Questions that could prevent more tragedies. "What can you—"

"What's it like to kiss?"

Oh.

Oh boy.

"I'm not sure how to answer that."

"It's okay. I'm thirty-seven years old. Is it fun?"

The full weight of the subject and its implications landed on my shoulders.

Ow.

She persisted. "I mean, I've been kissed on the cheek but that's not like getting a big ol' wet one on the lips. Right?"

"Alyce, I don't know—" Her question had me flustered.

She shrugged. "I might not get the chance to ask again." Then she stared at me.

She really wants to know.

"Let me ask you a question. Have you ever had a boyfriend?"

"No. There was a boy I liked though. He was ahead of me in school. Eighth grade."

"Ah. An older man."

Alyce laughed. "Yeah. He and his friends were supposed to meet me and a bunch of my friends at a movie. They never showed."

"Their loss. What did you go see?"

"A River Runs Through It. Since my future boyfriend didn't show up, I decided I'd marry Brad Pitt instead. Have you heard of him?"

"Maybe. Gray hair? Three hundred seventy-five pounds? Played left tackle for the New Orleans Saints?"

"Huh?"

"Weird because he never touched a football in college. He was badminton champion."

Alyce semi-smiled. "You're making that up."

"Sadly, Brad took a helmet to the face. He was so disfigured, he had to start acting to make a living."

"Uh-huh." Her eyes sparkled.

"Not being able to eat for a couple of months took off the weight though. Things turned out okay for him. I liked that movie a lot."

Alyce shook her head. "Is he still acting?"

"He is indeed. Now that I think about it, you remind me of his first wife. Her name is Jennifer. You have the same girl-next-door look as her."

"So if I ever grow up, I have a chance?"

It was my turn to laugh. "His tastes may have changed. He was into dark-haired women with hardcore maternal instincts for a while."

Alyce blinked at me. "I don't even know what that means."

"Don't worry about it."

"Okay. So. Kissing. Fun or what?"

She really, really wanted to know.

Sheesh.

I had to be honest. "Yeah. It's great."

She nodded, her mouth twisting sideways a little. "Thought so."

I felt bad for her. "Maybe, someday—"

"No big deal. Anything else you want to know?" Alyce asked the question with a chill eye, almost a challenge. If there was anything else she wanted to know, she no longer wanted to ask.

I shifted gears, back to detective mode. "Okay." I cleared my throat. "The night you were taken. Do you remember anything about the kidnappers?"

"A little." Alyce looked across the endless grass, her mind changing gears too. "My friends had had giant sodas, so they were in the restroom after the movie. I went outside. I couldn't wait to smell the fresh air after watching Brad Pitt fly fishing for two hours."

"I love the outdoors too."

"I remember standing outside in the dark, all by myself, staring at the moonlight on the clouds, which was stupid. Because the next thing I know, there's a huge hand on my face so I can't scream and more hands grabbing me and throwing me into the back of a van. Then I felt something like a bee sting in my neck and I passed out."

"They drugged you." Keeping to cold facts would help her get through the story.

Alyce nodded. "I woke up and everything was dark. I tried to move and for a minute I thought I was paralyzed. I finally realized my arms and hands had gone numb from being tied behind me and laying on them. I rolled over a little. There was a blindfold over my eyes. That's why it was dark. I tried to move the blindfold by rubbing my face on the floor, but people noticed I was awake. Someone sat me up. The blindfold had shifted a tiny bit. If I looked straight down, I could see a sliver of daylight."

"What did you see?"

"It was hard to even think. My arms and hands were tingling and I was scared. And mad. When the guy touched me again, I started thrashing." Alyce started acting out what happened, taking the role of her abductor. "He grabbed my shoulders and said 'they don't want to hurt you' in a quiet voice. And the way he said 'they' was like he wasn't one of the kidnappers. You know?"

"Those kinds of people are manipulative."

"Then he said that me and some other kids were already out of the country and I would be given a new home. The kids that were cooperative always got the best places while the kids who made trouble were sent to a workhouse. I didn't know if any of it was true, but I cooperated."

"Just in case, right?"

"Yeah. Anyway, when he grabbed my shoulders I could see his wrist through the bottom of the blindfold. I was hoping he'd have a tattoo or something. Or a scar."

My heart rate ramped up somewhere near the underside of my cranium.

"But there wasn't anything."

"It's okay. In movies, there's always that telltale clue. In reality, there's often nothing."

Tell that to my pounding detective's heart.

Alyce returned to her narrative, speaking in a low voice.

"The whole thing made me more mad because he lied. The older kids went somewhere else but us younger kids were taken to a workhouse. For months, we worked every day, all day, making electronic things in a hot room that always smelled sweaty and stinky. People with shotguns, including women, were always watching." Alyce paused. The memories opened old wounds, brought up old emotions. She started to cry and I let her have a moment.

"To make sure we didn't have friends, we sat by different kids every day. We bunked with different kids too. If we were good workers, we got extra food and clean sheets. And we got ten minutes to have a hot shower every other day by ourselves." Her voice hitched. "There weren't any doors, but there were heavy shower curtains. A woman with a shotgun was always in the hall but if you could forget about that, you could almost pretend you were in a fancy hotel somewhere. Or home with your family."

There was no stopping the sniffles. Her sniffles were noisier than mine. Lots noisier.

"It's unbelievable you went through that."

Alyce took a cleansing breath. "After six months, they pulled me aside. I couldn't imagine what I'd done wrong. They didn't always need a reason. Two strangers told me I was being promoted, which really meant I was being sold. That's how I ended up at the castle of the goddess."

"No more people with shotguns or kids throwing up on the floor?"

Her eyes were clear and dry and full of meaning. "I've seen worse since, but that's a story for another time."

Listening to Alyce speak, I'd almost forgotten where we were. Forgotten that the grass underfoot wasn't real and the perfectly even light had no discernible source and wasn't just an overcast day of gray.

"Will we meet again?"

"In my dreams." Alyce shot me a wry grin. Looked at her feet again. The mixed-up girl lost in her own Wonderland but wearing Dorothy's ruby slippers that would never take her to no-place-like-home.

"Would you do something for me? I thought I wouldn't care about my parents, but I do. Could you check on them for me? Make sure they're all right?"

# CHAPTER 11
## A World Beyond

Blinking my eyes, I rolled on my side with no idea how long I'd been asleep. It hadn't been long enough to be restful. Or restful enough to be restful, which happens when you spend 83.7% of your dream trying not to die.

I needed a nap after my nap.

"You decided to share the bed after all, huh?" Fáidh's bare feet had made no sound on the floor. "That is suspiciously thoughtful. A girl might wonder if you have ulterior motives." She slid into bed behind me, sliding her arm around my chest.

"Not just ulterior, super-mega-ultra-terior. And that goes for interior and exterior."

Fáidh giggled. Her hand was warm through my shirt.

"What day is it?" I yawned.

"Huh?"

"How long have I been asleep?"

"You fell asleep? I went to the bathroom two minutes ago."

Two minutes?

A cold thread of fear ran down my center. Where was the key? I wasn't holding it.

Lost it already?

After all Alyce and Béil and Laoch had done?

I jammed a hand in my pocket.

What a relief.

The key looked different in the real world. A piece of bone, more gray than brown, the Celtic knot worn down.

Maybe the real surprise was the key coming back as a physical object from Alyce's dreamland.

"What is that?" Fáidh asked.

"Apparently, dreams come true."

Fáidh kissed me. "Yes, they do."

I kissed her back before launching a rundown of my trip to dreamland. Telling her how the girl now sleeping in the room nearby had been kidnapped twenty-five years ago and had been serving a goddess named Caer Ibormeith in a place called Tír na nÓg. Béil and Laoch had arranged for her to control me this morning and deliver the key.

I left out a few of the details. Like Alyce asking me about kissing. Or me using a tapestry as a parachute. I'd save that one for when I needed something to brag about in case Fáidh forgot what a knight in beat-up armor I was. It still took five times longer to explain than it had taken Fáidh to tinkle.

"We should check something." I moved off the bed. "Come with me."

"Aren't we taking a nap?"

"Too much on my mind. Come on."

Fáidh followed me to Alyce's room. The attending nurse sat vigilantly and stood when we entered the room.

With a nod, I asked, "Would you help with something?"

"Of course, Highness."

"This girl's name is Alyce. I met her in a dream just now."

The nurse regarded me with no change of expression and no eyelashes batted.

Because Behindbeyond.

"As a mortal, she shouldn't have any magic, but she does. I think Alyce has something in her body. I don't know what. But she touched the center of her chest when she talked about magic. She did so without thinking. I'd like you to check. Both of you, if you would."

Alyce was so vulnerable. Defenseless. Part of me felt like a jerk for asking strangers to examine her body in such an undignified way. Intruding on her privacy even though she'd never know. That thought made it worse.

Fáidh and the nurse turned the covers down and I looked away.

Maybe we'll find out something we can use, I told myself. Maybe we'll find a way to bring her home.

Sheets rustled. People moved. I waited.

"I found something," Fáidh said.

"What is it?"

"You were right, Got. She has silver in her chest."

"Seriously? In her chest?"

"An emblem, the size of a thumbnail. Underneath the skin. Attached to the sternum."

"So she might not even know it's there?"

"It's enchanted. She wouldn't notice it consciously."

Poor kid. She's been a puppet too. That made me mad all over again. "What is it with the Fae controlling people? It's insane."

Fáidh didn't answer. I stayed turned toward the wall. It was easy to imagine Fáidh lost in thought with that cute look of concentration she got when she was focused on a problem. Brows converging. Eyes going toward squint. Lips slightly ducky. She'd heard what I'd said though. "Mortals control people too. They just have different ways of doing it. Alyce was kidnapped by mortals. Isn't that what you said?"

"Good point." I sighed. Fáidh conversed with the nurse in soft tones.

After a minute, she said, "The emblem seems to work as a permanent battery. Magic energy can be stored in it but the spell that uses the energy comes from somewhere else. Otherwise, the emblem would only be capable of doing one thing."

"Alyce did different spells at the rehearsal."

More whispering. Then the sheets were drawn back over Alyce. "Keep a close eye on her." I turned and nodded at the nurse.

Bromach met us in the hallway.

"Sire." His dead-flat expression and fidgety hands portrayed panic.

"What's happened?"

"Spreasán's father is asking after thee. He wishes to speak with Spreasán and he is . . . not satisfied . . . with the information given him."

94

"What has he been told?"

Bromach wouldn't meet my eyes. He held a hand out toward me and Fáidh both. "His Majesty, the Alder King, requests that I escort the two of you back to the mortal realm. For your safety and theirs."

"Theirs? What does that mean?"

"Sire. They have vowed to throw themselves upon the weapons of the guard if they are not heard. His Majesty feels it will be best for you to go."

This was nuts.

They couldn't just come into my chambers, could they?

In my own father's castle?

"Sire. It is not a request." Bromach frowned as he put his hands on our shoulders.

Blink.

"Hey!"

Blink.

"Knock it off—"

Blink.

"—for a second."

I shrugged Bromach's hand off my shoulder. Bromach had blinked Fáidh and me from our chambers to the shore of the lake in back of the castle, then to a treeless hilltop, then to the clearing in front of a circle of liagán stones. There was no line of sight from our chambers to the circle, but Bromach had bounced us from one point to another to get here in moments.

"By the king's command, sire." Bromach's chagrin gave his face a conflicted twist.

"I understand." He was just doing his job. How could I be angry about that? "Do all rulers have an Air Mage in their employ?"

Bromach tried to smile and halfway succeeded. "Those who wish to see another day certainly do."

Holding Erin.

Hugs and kisses.

These top the list of the best things in life.

I kept Erin in my arms. "Something on your mind?"

She squeezed me tight. "It can wait."

"Are you sure? You don't need anything?"

"As long as I got you Got, I got all I need."

"Gotcha. Glad I got you too."

Fáidh smiled. "You gotta go."

I thought for a long moment. Long. "I got nothin'. You win."

Nat honked outside. I said, "The time at the horn is one p.m. o'clock. In the afternoon." I didn't want to leave. Erin and I gave each other another hug and kiss. Nope. Still didn't want to leave.

"Hurry back," Erin tried to pull away. She failed but didn't seem to mind. She hadn't really tried that hard. More hugging and kissing. "Mmf mu doonf gm, ym cmf cm bkf," she said.

I took my mouth off hers. "What was that? I don't speak smooch-ese."

"Oh, you are fully fluent in smooch-ese." Erin's laugh was throaty and soulful. I loved that laugh. "I said 'if you don't go, you can't come back.'"

"Oh." I nodded slowly. "So you think I should go."

"And hurry back."

"Okay. I'll go." I took a step away, then reversed. "And I'm back."

Erin laughed again. I wanted to somehow put the sound of it in a bottle so I could take it with me.

"You did say I should hurry back."

Nat honked again. For a big truck, the horn was super whiny.

Erin gave me a final peck on the cheek. "I hope you find them."

Right.

I did have a purpose.

Time to take care of it.

"Love you."

"Love you too."

I left, striding out the door like I wasn't going to look back. Then, at the end of the driveway, I looked back. Erin gave me a wave.

Nat nodded as I clambered into the shotgun spot of his Navigator and tossed my overnight bag on the floor. He had dark shades on and his hair trimmed down almost to invisibility. Instead of his usual black-on-black, he wore denim jeans and a baby-blue button-down shirt with a white collar. The sleeves were rolled up to let his muscular python forearms breathe.

"You got a date in Baton Rouge?"

Nat gave with the minimal turn-and-tilt of his head so he could let me know he was throwing me a stink eye behind the shades.

I shrugged. "Just saying you look nice."

Nat pulled away.

"Me, I'm running out of red sticks. Don't want to let my supply get too low. Yup. Never know when a stick—a red stick specifically—is going to come in handy. That's why I'm going to Baton Rouge."

Nat headed north on state road 953, which was also SW 42nd Avenue, named after 42nd Street in New York City. Someone had wisely changed "Street" to "Avenue" to avoid copyright infringement. We passed Valencia Street, named after a city in California, and then Aragon Avenue, named after the Spanish Queen who got really lost and ended up ruling England co-dependently with Henry VIII. We drove past dry cleaners and dentist offices and beauty supply shops and lots of people going about their business. None of the shops had a surplus of letter "Rs" so I could change all the street signs to Aragorn, named after the dude in Lord of the Rings.

"You carrying?" Nat's stink eye rested on my overnight bag.

"My gun's locked up, unloaded, in a hard-sided box just the way Great Aunt TSA likes it."

Nat rewarded me with a patented micro-smile. "What's the plan?"

"Little girl was abducted from Donaldsonville, Louisiana twenty-five years ago. I want to check into it. Solving her disappearance could help other kids."

Nat nodded, checking off a mental box.

"From there, I plan on going back to my old stomping grounds."

"Visit The Mama?"

Nat, of course, knew about The Mama.

"Maybe. Might take a few days. If you need to come back home, it's cool. I probably just need backup tonight."

There was an exhale and an inhale while Nat thought. "We'll see."

I told Nat how the FBI was trying to connect me to recent abductions and my research into Alyce's past. I left out the fact she still looked like a twelve-year-old.

"I don't know if these incidents are related. They're twenty-five years apart."

Silence prevailed after that. I ran through a mental inventory of things I'd brought. Besides my sidearm, I had clothes and toiletries along with my Silverpoint and the Heartpiece from Hope. If I needed to find people who had eaten a hunk of deamhanlord heart, that item would be handy. Dumb Dubhcridhe. I also had my healing medallion and a fully-charged shield coin.

Ready for anything.

I had the key from Béil's pocket on me. It looked so unimposing in the afternoon light. Like a boy scout had carved it at summer camp. There wouldn't be any reason I could think of to keep Nat from seeing it. It didn't do anything as far as I could tell.

We'd turned down an unfamiliar road near the airport.

"We aren't going to parking?"

Nat offered no explanation.

The road led to private aviation where small planes and millionaire's jets were kept. Nat passed a Cessna and a Beechcraft and a beautiful De Havilland before stopping behind a silver and blue Piaggio Avanti twin turboprop.

Two ladies waited for us, a blonde and a redhead, wearing snazzy uniforms and big smiles.

They were both Stained.

The Stain was mine.

White filigrees of magic circled around their bodies at a lazy pace, and I jumped from the SUV before it rolled to a stop.

"Brandy! Carlene! Holy mostaccioli!"

Brandy was Nat's girlfriend. She laughed as she put her arms around my neck. I hugged her hard. Carlene was Brandy's roommate. As soon as Brandy let me go, she jumped up and clung to me like a baby barnacle and I swung her around with her feet in the air while she squealed.

I'd saved their lives, preventing them and Erin from being eaten by a deamhanlord, which they couldn't remember and would never again know. That's how they'd come to acquire my Stain.

"What a great surprise!"

I kept my speculations vague. The uniforms weren't commercial or military so there wasn't any insignia to clue me in. The girls looked like they could be the most sophisticated flight attendants ever to board a plane, but somehow it felt like they were something more.

"He didn't tell you we were pilots?"

There we go.

"You know how Nat is, ladies. Talks non-stop about everything and never gets around to making a point."

"Yeah." Carlene nodded sagely.

"That's Nat for sure."

Nat was busy unloading bags out of the back of the SUV, pretending he wasn't listening.

Carlene led me to the door of the plane and ushered me aboard. "Welcome to 'A World Beyond Air Services,' Mr. Luck."

"A World Beyond?"

Both Carlene and Brandy said, "Yep."

That's a little on the nose.

"How did you come up with that?"

"Don't know." Carlene gave a little shrug. "It just felt like a great name."

Okay then. "I like it."

Carlene gestured toward the cabin, which was beautifully appointed. Big leather seats faced in all directions and there was a refrigerator and open shelves with all kinds of snacks. "Sit wherever you like. The food and beverages are included in the service, so help yourself."

"Wow. This is nice." I wandered down the aisle. I preferred

facing forward but I might try sidesaddle today. "Have you been a pilot long, Carlene?"

"Actually, I don't have my pilot's license yet. Brandy got hers a few months ago but I only need a few more hours. Flying to Baton Rouge and back will be all I need to finish my qualifications. So, thank you!"

"My pleasure. Although the credit goes to Nat."

Brandy boarded the plan with Nat right behind her. He dropped the bags he'd been carrying and they landed with a thud. Whatever he'd brought was heavy.

Brandy gave Nat a quick kiss. "We wouldn't have the plane without him."

"Ah. So Nat made a donation to the cause. Very noble."

"It's not exactly a donation," Carlene corrected me. "He our Chief Financial Officer."

"So it's a partnership. Smart."

Nat spared a moment to focus my way. "Less risky than other ventures."

"Oh. I see. You're referring to me now? Partner? I'll have you know, there just might be enough money in the petty cash box at the office to cover all the utilities. Including the phone bill. Possibly. Maybe even some of the rent. So. Not that risky."

Nat's face didn't twitch at all. No tilt of the eyebrow or curve of the lip. His face wanted to smile though. I could tell. Nat was just holding his face back from expressing its inner feelings.

I stared straight at Nat as I reached for snacks, taking a bag of chips with a no-look grab and, from the sound of it, knocking a few other bags off the shelf. With great deliberation, I took a second bag without looking as well. Then I held both bags up as I slid into the nearest seat.

Nat's face twitched.

Good.

"You realize, by the way, I have to spend tomorrow trying to get a refund for the airline tickets I bought."

Nat returned my stare for a solid three count and then said,

"Sucks."

   Fine.

# CHAPTER 12
## Monarch

Reasons why flying in a private plane was a great idea: One, not only was Nat helping his girlfriend and her roommate get their business off the ground—heh heh—but it was also a two-hour, non-stop flight instead of a six-hour ordeal with a stop in Atlanta. Two, Nat wouldn't be stuck with me at an airport, which would keep him from getting cranky. He invariably got pulled aside for a search and he wasn't a big fan of large public spaces full of people he didn't know. Three, guns.

Nat and I remained seated with our seat belts securely fastened about us while Brandy and Carlene taxied the plane out to the runway. We waited maybe two minutes for clearance. Then we cruised around the corner and what sounded like a couple of bumblebees the size of space shuttle boosters wound up for takeoff. The power building in the turboprops was intimidating. Like the offspring of Conan the Barbarian and a nuclear power plant had grabbed us by the throat and said, "We go bye-bye now."

Takeoff time was about half that of a commercial jet, which meant we got shoved against our seats twice as hard. One of the passengers yelled, "Woo-hoo" with hands raised like a kid riding a roller-coaster for the first time. Nat looked at me sideways. I defiantly kept my hands up until we leveled off.

At cruising altitude, we were free to move about the cabin.

I popped open a cold can of ginger ale from the fridge.

Nat popped open an arsenal.

Taking one hard-sided carrier at a time, Nat opened each one on the mahogany counter in the middle of the plane. He removed each firearm from its carrier, gave it a quick check, and put it back before moving on to the next. He checked a sniper rifle, two assault rifles, a pair of Desert Eagle pistols and a 12-gauge semi-automatic Remington 1100 shotgun.

"We're going to Baton Rouge. Not the Alamo."

Nat packed up the shotgun. "Scout's motto," he said.

Yeah. I got it.

Be prepared.

"Got yours?"

"Got my motto? Sure. Same as Teddy Roosevelt's. Speak comically and carry a big stick. I got dibs on the shotgun."

Nat held out his hand. "Your sidearm."

I pulled the carrier for my Glock out of my bag and unlocked it. Nat took it and put it on a soft cloth. Then he disassembled it and opened his kit for cleaning and oiling. He checked the gun's every component from barrel to butt, cleaned it, and oiled it.

"Lemme know if you find any polyps," I said. "I've been feeding it high-cholesterol bullets."

When he was done with all the parts, he put the gun back together. It looked like I'd just driven it off the showroom floor. Except for the polymer frame. And the aftermarket rubber grips. I used those because, you know, Halflings touching steel is ouchy.

"Guess what the boy scout said when he fixed the car horn."

Nat didn't even hesitate. "Beep repaired."

"When you tell Brandy," I said, "give me the credit."

Nat put a companionable hand on my shoulder. "Sure," he said. "Thanks for coming, man. And thanks for arranging all this."

It was good to be on assignment again with my best friend. It was also nice to have someone I could say "thanks" to.

We landed in Baton Rouge before four o'clock. The power-buzz of the engines wound down and Carlene was first out of the cockpit.

"How was my landing?"

"Whoa. We landed? It was so smooth. Are you sure we aren't still in the air?"

Carlene laughed and put her hands together. "Two more hours! That's it! Then I'll be a full pilot."

"So happy for you."

Nat and I got the luggage out of the plane and loaded everything into the back of a rented Honda Pilot. We drove south for about ten seconds and stopped at the Hilton Hotel where Nat had arranged for three rooms. One for him and Brandy, one for Carlene, and one for me. Stretching out on a bed for a few hours sounded like a great idea, considering the last stretch had not been restful in the slightest. Unfortunately, I had work to do.

Once the ladies were settled, Nat and I got on Interstate 110, southbound. Nat pinned our speed to the posted limit, obeying all traffic laws.

"Head south to Interstate 10. We could head west across the mighty Mississippi river towards a town called Grosse Tete but we'd just have to turn around at Grosse Tete because Grosse Tete is not Donaldsonville, which is the other direction from Grosse Tete."

Nat let that sit for a full ten seconds. "'Kay."

"Instead, Donaldsonville is 45 miles south, where someone abducted Alyce Octavian. I anticipate raising an average-sized ruckus. After that, we'll head mostly west for about 20 miles, which won't really get us any closer to Grosse Tete, until we arrive at the town of Pierre Part, where I won't have a chance to say Grosse Tete for the rest of the day."

Nat nodded. "Love that."

"I will instead repeatedly refer to Pierre's parts, partially, in Pierre Part."

Nat drove on without a twitch.

Thinking about Alyce and other kidnapped kids—those in the Behindbeyond as well as in the mortal realm—put a damper on the day. Someone was up to something bad. And they'd been getting away with it for a long time.

Out of habit, I scanned the road ahead of us and checked the rear view from time to time as well. A few miles passed. A dark gray sedan stayed behind us. Not too far, not too close. The driver kept the same distance as other cars came between, then pulled out after a while. Mere mortals would not have been able to see the faces of the driver and his passenger.

Mere mortal I was not.

"Bet you a shiny nickel that Cadillac follows us all the way to Donaldsonville."

Nat said, "No bet."

"Where did they pick us up?"

"Airport."

If I believed in magic, I'd wonder if Nat was psychic.

"Still want dibs?" Nat asked.

"Don't think I'll need the shotgun." I gave Nat more details about the FBI agents who had visited me a year ago. Or this morning. Whichever it was. They'd asked some nosy questions I'd been less-than-willing to answer. And they must have flagged me and noticed my purchase of two airline tickets to Baton Rouge, which would have given them plenty of time to come up this way and sit around. When I didn't use my tickets, they must have tracked my known associates and found out we'd chartered a plane with A World Beyond Air Services to here.

"They're thorough," I said. "Or maybe they've decided I'm innocent and think I'll lead them to different suspects."

Maybe they're right. Things just got more complicated. Stupid Feeble Eyes. On the other hand, their game was one I knew how to play.

My mobile phone was sitting in my pocket, handy as hecknation. I pulled up my list of contacts and sent a text message to a private detective I referred to as Penny Andy. Four minutes and eleven seconds later, he'd accepted my offer of three hundred dollars and texted he'd get back to me.

As predicted, the gray sedan followed us all the way to Donaldsonville. The town sat on the other side of the Mississippi River and was mostly notable, according to my extensive research, for having been originally named Donaldduckville. I directed Nat to Alyce's house at 2428 Barraclough Avenue. The sedan stopped and parked a half-block away. The agents didn't know about Alyce, so it would be a test of their patience, wondering why we were here.

The house squatted as the homeliest of homes on a solid acre of grass in need of a good barbering. A place once owned by Alyce's dad and mom. According to her, the garbage and the garbage-enabler. The neighbors to the west had a home with a little more art in the architecture—there was a portico over the porch—along with an aboveground pool. The neighbors to the east were likely quiet, except on Sunday, because it was a church.

Here was where Alyce grew up.

Until she didn't grow up any more.

Stepping out of the passenger side, leaving the more intimidating Nat in the truck, I strolled up the hardpack and gravel driveway toward the front of the house. An ancient Chevelle was parked at the end, by the side door, and it was hard to tell if it was a recipient of spare parts or a donor.

I had my private investigator's license in hand as I rapped on the door. There was a squeal from inside. Tiny feet ran over a wood floor.

"Junie! No!" A heavier tread—not much heavier—sounded on the boards as well. Two little smacks smacked against the thin front door and started to bang.

"I said no!"

Another squeal. Then a cry as the banging stopped.

"Git yerself away."

The screen door rattled as the door behind swung open. The screen part of the door was only on the upper half, so I couldn't see the munchkin below who renewed the banging on the metal panel.

"Stop it."

A girl bent over to pull the child away. She stuck herself between the wood door and the jamb so the child couldn't bang anymore. The crying wound up again, louder. I stood at the edge of the top step and gave a wave and a smile to the girl when she looked up. A second child, lots of curly blond hair, straddled one hip.

"What's this?" The girl's voice had a Southern lilt. She looked at me guardedly with eyes that would be pretty if they weren't so tired. She was either an older sister or a very young mother.

"Hi." I held up my license but didn't make a deal out of it. "I'm looking for the Octavians. Do they still live here?"

"Who's this?"

"Octavians. Lorna and Robert."

"Naw."

I persisted. "They'd be about sixty years old. They lived here about twenty-five years ago?"

"Naw."

"Did you maybe buy the house from them?"

"Naw. We're rentin'."

"I see. May I ask who you're renting from?"

The girl pressed her lips together. "What's this 'bout?" She was tired but she wasn't stupid. Good fer her. The crying child behind the door downshifted into sniffles as the conversation continued. Easy up, easy down.

I moved closer to the door, putting my license within reading distance. The girl stepped up to the screen to look. The smell of ammonia coming off the infant was potent enough to stun-startle a grizzly out of hibernation. The girl had the baby in a cloth diaper with plastic pants that had given up trying to be a barrier to anything gaseous. It was all I could to keep from coughing. As it was, my blink rate ratcheted up to "Hummingbird."

Flashback. The choice of cloth diapers was likely economic for this family. The Mama, on the rare occasion when she accepted an infant, would use cloth diapers because they were cheaper than disposables. And more odiferous than a treatment plant.

"I . . . uh . . ." Wow. The other kid must be contributing to the ambiance. I could almost see the vapors. "I'm a private investigator. My client is looking to reconnect with family, and the Octavians were close to her mom and dad." It was a half-truth, but maybe close enough to do the trick.

The girl looked up from my license. "What's yer name? Goaty?"

I pulled my license back away from the door. Before the plastic melted. I looked at it as if I hadn't reviewed my name for a while.

The girl would be more cooperative if I didn't correct her. "Uh, yes. Goethe is German for Goaty. That's surprising you knew that.

Do you speak German?"

She looked me up and down liked I'd asked her if we could make a baby together right on the porch. So we had forged some kind of connection at least. "Naw."

Super. And also duper.

"So. Do your landlords know the Octavians? Or how I could reach them?"

"Doubt it. House was bought by my parents. They got it a year ago from some couple like us. Younger folks. Then my dad got work up in Shreveport so me and my husband are rentin' from them."

"I see." Through the space under the young mom's elbow, I caught a glimpse of the elder stinker waddling toward the back of the house. The kid had long blond curls like the infant and was cowboying across the room with about two liters of damp between the knees.

Clearly no useful help here. "Well. Thank you for your time."

"Yup. An' I hope yer client finds their family."

"Thank you. That's kind of you." I gave a nod as I turned back toward the SUV and a great big beautiful world of breathable air.

The little mommy's footsteps retreated into the house. Through the screen I heard, "No! Junie, no!" followed by an exasperated gasp. "Spit that goldfish out right now!"

Somehow, I knew the little mommy wasn't hollering about a goldfish cracker.

Nat read my expression as I got back in the SUV and darn near laughed. "Any information?"

"Naw. Just an education."

We drove north again, back across the river, and found the Parish Sheriff's office in nearby Gonzales, arriving two minutes before five o'clock. The Cadillac had followed us and I couldn't decide if they were really bad at tailing suspects or just didn't care if we knew.

Nat and I both went inside. The deputy at the front desk had cut her hair short at the sides but had a little ponytail in back. She looked like she was getting ready to leave for the day, shouldering her bag.

"Help you?" She smiled like she was just starting her workday instead of finishing it.

I showed her my license and introduced myself. "There was a kidnapping about twenty-five years ago. Alyce Octavian."

The deputy put her hand up. "Hold it." She dropped her shoulder bag on her chair and stepped back to a door with the words "Sheriff Monarch Holden" painted on the glass in gold and outlined in black. She tapped politely on the door and stuck her head through.

"Sir, some gentlemen are here. Wanna talk to you 'bout Alyce."

"Show 'em on back, deputy." The springs of a heavy chair groaned and two big shoes landed on the floor. I pictured the sheriff with his feet resting on the desk while leaning back to relax, then sitting up again with visitors about to come in.

The deputy turned to Nat and me and waved us back. "C'mon y'all."

Sheriff Monarch Holden waited for us with his thick fingers interlaced on top of his blotter. He possessed a glorious mane of silver hair that octogenarian Elvis would be proud to own, and a deeply-tanned face with creases earned by many hours out among his townsfolk. Or, considering the ten fishing rods on the wall, many hours on a sunlit lake. I got the impression the sheriff could have retired by now but liked the office.

The deputy checked with her boss. "Need anythin'?" she asked.

"You go on home, Macy. Have a nice evenin'."

The deputy scooted out of the office. Nat and I sat in the chairs offered by the sheriff.

"She's good with the public." I stuck a thumb in the departing deputy's direction.

"Macy? Yeah." The sheriff nodded. "She don't never put more than two words together at a time but she's likable as a baby tiger, so I don't mind if she looks like a boy from the front."

I smiled and nodded. There was a touch of Old South prejudice in his comment, but I didn't think he was being malicious.

The sheriff sized me and Nat up with a glance. His clear eyes had seen a million officers and a million more perpetrators, and he'd know the difference in a heartbeat. He took time to read my private investigator's license thoroughly and handed it back with a certain economy of motion that spoke of efficiency and power restrained.

"You're here about Alyce Octavian? I knew her family. We were all devastated when she was taken."

The man was soft-spoken but his authority came through every word. He'd undoubtedly be able to keep being sheriff as long as he kept his health.

"Yes, sir."

The sheriff waved a big hand at me. "Ain't no 'sir' after five o'clock 'round here," he said. "Please call me Mon. All the Jamaicans do." The sheriff laughed at his own joke, a slow boomer, and I grinned as well.

"Thank you, Mon. My friends call me Got. I hope you'll do the same."

"I will. What about the Octavian girl brings you here, Got?"

My story for the sheriff was a little different than for the baby mama from earlier. "My client is interested in finding out what happened to Alyce."

"What would make someone interested in a kidnapping that happened twenty-five years ago?"

"A girl. Twelve years old. She may be related."

"You don't say."

"She looks like Alyce."

The sheriff stared at me for a moment, assessing. "You got a photo?"

I'd thought of this possibility. "No, Mon. I don't. Her current guardians are . . . how to put this . . ."

"Guarded?" Mon offered.

"Ha. Uh-huh. That's a good word for it."

Mon stared at me again. Every word I'd spoken so far had been the truth. Her age, her relationship, her protected situation, her uncanny resemblance to Alyce.

"All right." He believed me. "What'll help?"

"They don't want to involve the girl until we know for sure. I'm hoping I can find enough information to convince them it's worth pursuing further. They have a name, Alyce Octavian, and not much else. I can have the girl's DNA tested but you know that takes weeks."

"That's sure."

"But I've seen her, and I've seen the report on the National Missing and Unidentified Persons System."

"You think they're related? This girl is Alyce's daughter?"

I shrugged. "Unless Alyce's parents had another child."

"Well," the sheriff continued as he eased out of his chair, "that's not possible. Like many families, the loss of their child killed their relationship. Robert blamed Lorna for not keepin' a better eye on Alyce, although he was hardly home and, by most accounts, his parenting skills left more than a lot to be desired." Mon took a seat on the corner of his desk. To its credit, the desk didn't complain.

Solid desk.

"Robert took the loss of Alyce as further reason to drown in hooch. He died five years after Alyce disappeared, which would be five years before the girl you're tryin' to help was conceived."

"Sounds about right."

"As for Alyce's mother, depression took hold on her. After the divorce and after Robert's death, she made her way to the brink of death once or twice. Found her way back with professional help, but she was never truly right. Lost her house. Stayed in a women's shelter for a while but disappeared. Up and walked out and nobody seen her since. Like daughter, like mom."

The sheriff leaned forward to get momentum off the desk and walked back toward the door. I turned around in my seat as Mon said, "Gentlemen. Let me introduce you to the missing persons of Ascension Parish."

I hadn't noticed what was on the wall when we came in. Much of it had been behind the door and I'd been focused on the sheriff as we'd come through from the lobby.

The wall was covered in photos.

# CHAPTER 13
## Mallard

So many children.

"They're weren't all abducted." Mon scanned the wall like a grandfather looking at grandchildren who had moved away, leaving him all but forgotten. "We have our share of runaways. A few who came of age and just moved on without tellin' anyone where they were goin'."

A piece of string stretched from floor to ceiling, separating roughly a fourth of the photos from the others. Mon pointed to the smaller group. "The remaining few are likely dead. Killed by their husbands or lost to the bayou. Their bodies will likely never be found."

Mon took a step to his left. The larger group was all kids. Their photos were not only a record of tragedy, like layers of sediment accumulated over eons, but a history of photography too. The upper rows were mostly Polaroids and school photos with phony canvas textures. Boys with wide collars and girls with bangs sprayed high using a gallon of Aquanet. After that, the school photos got glossy and the photos printed from film had lost the white borders and turned less square. Better hairstyles. Straighter teeth. Near the bottom of the wall, the photos were more uniform, school photos and candids spat out by a laserjet on eight-and-a-half-by-eleven bond paper. The kids with their hipster glasses and smiles as white as the paper.

"My first year as sheriff, two kids went missing." Mon looked with resignation at top left corner. "It seems like more and more kids disappear every year."

He pointed a thick forefinger at a photo well above the middle of the wall, second from the right. I'd already picked out Alyce's face.

"From what you tol' me, that there's the mama of the girl you came to ask me about."

Bending closer, I said, "It must be her. This photo is much clearer than the ones on the database report. May I have a copy?"

"I can sure do that, Got."

Mon pulled the thumbtack out of Alyce's photo and took it down. The whole wall turned out to be one big corkboard, but it had been blanketed with photos so densely, the cork had been all but buried.

Nat and I stared at the faces. So many kids. The sheriff came back a minute later and handed me the copy of Alyce's photo.

"Thanks, Mon. I'll take this with me and see if the girl's guardians will give me permission to follow up."

"Welcome. Anythin' else?"

"Come to think of it, is there a chance Alyce's mom has resurfaced? Maybe she quietly returned to the area or something?"

The sheriff smiled a half-smile. "I can sure check around. Give me somethin' to do that'd help you, an' that'd be my pleasure."

"Much appreciated."

Mon crossed his arms over his barrel chest. "This all raises some big questions. Is Alyce still captive anywhar'? If so, how is her child free? Or did Alyce get away, settle down somewhar', and have herself a baby? If so, what happened to her?"

"There are a lot of possibilities," I agreed. "They've been troubling me as well."

"I'd sure like to find out what happened."

I held up the photo Mon had given me. "So would I."

"You'll let me know, won't you, Got?"

"I will, Mon. That's a promise."

Nat and I shook Mon's hand in turn and he gave us a nod before we took our leave.

Outside, I spared a glance in the direction of the gray Cadillac. I took a moment to check Alyce's photo in the sunlight, mostly so the FBI would see the paper. The agents wouldn't know what was on it, but they'd see me coming out of the sheriff's office with something they could rightfully assume I hadn't had going in.

Across the street, I spotted a grocery store, which gave me an idea.

"Hey, Nat. Do you mind standing out here for a couple minutes?"

Nat planted his feet in the middle of the sidewalk and took out his phone.

"Be right back." I stepped across the street, in no particular hurry, with the paper in my hand. I bet myself a shiny nickel Nat would be snapchatting Brandy. He'd probably use the filter that made it look like he had puppy ears.

After I had engaged in covert activities inside the store, spending ten minutes and two hundred dollars, I watched a tall man in his early thirties walk across the parking lot pushing a cart full of groceries. In my hand, I had a paper bag with a few items I'd purchased and a piece of white paper.

Timing was everything. The tall man stopped at the back of his car and popped the trunk. He began transferring his purchases into the trunk. After the first bag went in, I walked out of the store with my paper bag in hand. As the tall man put the last of his groceries into the trunk, I arrived beside him and offered him the piece of paper. He didn't take it but started reading. When he finished, he looked at me and said, "Okay." I slipped my paper bag into his trunk and closed it for him as he took the paper. I walked away.

Listening, I heard his car door open. As he settled into the driver's seat, the springs made soft adjustments. The door slammed shut. Moments passed. I was almost to the sidewalk when the car's ignition cranked momentarily and the engine turned over. There was only a little traffic and I hustled across the street. Nat saw me coming. Behind me, I heard the tall man's car pull out of the parking lot and drive away, heading back along the road in the direction where we'd come into town. I'd made a point of not looking at the gray Caddy but I caught it passing up the road in my peripheral vision.

Nat and I swung into the SUV and Nat pulled smoothly out of the parking space.

"One stayed." Nat checked the rearview mirror as we took a

sedate drive out of town. "Male. Six-two. Fair hair trimmed short."

"That would be agent Petit-Palais," I said. "If the other agent is the same one who dropped in on me this morning, it would be a woman, five-six, fluffy hair in a ponytail."

"That was her."

"Well. Since it looks like we're going to be friends, she'll be Mully and the tall guy will be Skullder."

Nat smirked.

"His face fits the part."

We drove for a block.

"Mallard?" Nat asked.

"Yup."

Mallard was our name for a dodge we'd pulled before. It referred to using an unwitting civilian to act as a decoy to pull attention away from yourself while you ducked out of a situation.

Heh heh. Ducked out.

The tall man was acting as my mallard. He wasn't entirely unwitting. I'd approached him in the store and he'd been more than happy to help. The hundred-dollar bill I'd given him had done most of the talking. The scene in the parking lot had been for the benefit of our onlookers. I had neglected to mention that doing me a favor would likely result in him being followed and questioned by one or more Federal agents. On the other hand, unless he was already committing felonies, Mully would figure out what was going on and let him go.

For now, she'd follow him to see where he was going, which was the goal.

Skullder, on the other hand, would be trying to find out what we'd asked good ol' Sheriff Holden about.

Sorry 'bout that, Mon.

They'd catch up with us sooner or later. I simply wanted a little lead time. All I'd needed to do was sow seeds of intrigue and let FBI procedure take over.

For the moment, it was working.

We tooled south and west on LA-70 for half an hour and found ourselves in Pierre Part, a small village at the north end of Lake Verret. The town had changed a bit since I'd left. The trees a little taller. The bushes a littler bushier. There was an inn, a couple of hotels, a cozy cafe or few, a gas station, and a couple of fast food places. One of my favorite hangouts had been the steel bridge that could be raised to let the shrimp boats motor up the tributary to the Avoca Island Cutoff. We didn't get that far south. Shortly after getting inside the city limits, we turned off I-70 onto Bayou Drive.

I was going home.

My pulse started ramping up. I hadn't seen The Mama's place for almost ten years. Would it resemble the ramshackle hovel I had kept in my memory?

I told Nat to slow down. The road to The Mama's barely qualified as a road. When it was used, it was used by kids in bare feet, and any vehicular traffic was the kind with two wheels. Finally, I saw the path between a couple of houses, wide enough to drive down but grass-covered and lined with trees hung with moss, sentinels of a former age.

We made little sound as we rolled up a short incline. The moss hanging from the trees whispered over the roof of the cab as if giving us their blessing as we passed. The Mama's house had always been on the verge of being swallowed up by the bayou and, for a moment, I wondered if perhaps the trees had finally consumed it. When I saw the clapboard front of the house emerging from the gloom, my heart jumped in recognition.

The air was heavy as we stepped out of the SUV. Nat had pulled up almost to the steps. A thin cloud of gnats flew around us, inspecting the new arrivals while in the deep, a chorus of frogs croaked. A dank aroma prowled the air as if someone had bottled the atmosphere of a Mesozoic swamp and released it as a greeting.

"You grew up here?" Nat seemed impressed.

"Aw." I grinned. "It's so nice you think I grew up."

The corner of Nat's mouth twitched.

The treads of the old wooden stairs popped and protested as we walked up to the front door. For the most part, the treads were

116

traveled by kids. The only time they had been burdened with a heavier step was on shopping day and on Sunday. Those were the only times The Mama ever left the house.

Felt more than heard, I knew there were people inside. Running and yelling in the house wasn't tolerated and offenders would find themselves bruised and going without meals if they misbehaved, so it was quiet. I banged on the screen door with my knuckles. The whole house seemed to stop whatever it had been doing and held its breath.

Silence prevailed. I knew there was a possibility The Mama wouldn't care to see me. She'd executed her responsibilities in my regard and I'd been discharged. The Mama wasn't the sentimental type, unless you were bold or beautiful. Maybe young or restless. Or potentially spending a day of your life at the general hospital.

After ten seconds, I banged again.

Footsteps stepped, locks unlocked, and latches unlatched. The heavy door pivoted open and a mop-headed boy with round, solemn eyes peered at me through the gap. He was Stained with an intense red band circling his torso. The pattern reminded me of a duke who led the Alder King's infantry, which meant he was likely his offspring.

"Hey," I began. "Is The Mama home?"

The boy turned the handle on the screen door and opened it wide enough to shove a slip of paper through. The paper had been torn off a pad and still had a bit of the gummed edge across the top. I accepted the paper and opened it. At the top was printed the name of a nearby grocer along with a cartoon drawing of a bloodhound and the phrase "Hunting down the best prices for you!" A note had been scrawled across the middle in a looping hand. "The dreamer must dream." It was signed "La Mere."

A troop of goosebumps began an expedition climbing my spine.

By the time I'd looked up from the note, the doors were closed.

"Mean something?" Nat asked, looking at the note.

I tried to think of a rational response while fighting a goosebump assault. "Means we're done here, I guess."

We went back to the SUV. Putting the house behind me felt disconcerting. On the one hand, it appeared all was well. The

Mama and her charges were safe and sheltered from any would-be abductors, which was the whole idea behind a half-hidden foster home for Halflings in the mortal realm. On the other hand, The Mama's handwritten message caused me to wonder if everyone knew more about my mission to help Alyce than I did.

I chewed on sinewy thoughts as we backed down the road. The headlights of the SUV shone on the porch in twin pools that got bigger but dimmer as we reversed. At the edge of town, I directed Nat to head south. My phone blinked at me. I had a message from Penny Andy. The message was brief but I had to read it twice. Then a third time.

Agent Petit-Palais is on probation. Looking for a score. Agent Scarsdale is in Arizona on bereavement. Mother died. Funeral was last week but she's off for two.

Puddles and doodles.

I didn't know how Penny Andy got his information, but he was scary accurate, based on past experience. That meant I had two problems on my hands and they both carried a badge. Petit-Palais was looking to make a major case out of this to get back in good with his superiors. There was nothing more rabid than a Federal agent wanting to make an example out of someone. As for Scarsdale, I didn't know if her deal was better or worse. If she was off-duty and in mourning, what had she been doing in my house?

Stuff was wrong.

At State Road 997, we turned north, straight into the heart of the bayou. The light was seeping out of the day and the trees were as dark as my thoughts. Civilization soon became a distant memory as we moved deeper into people-don't-belong-here land.

Ten miles up the road, I pointed to a row of shacks with a neon sign from the 1950s.

The sign blinked "Gatorbait Excursions" and below that, a hand-painted sign proclaiming "Your Guide to Louisiana's World of Wonder."

"We going fishing?" Nat asked.

"Exactly." I got out of the SUV. "And I have a friend named Eustace who's just the fisherman we need."

A gray Cadillac pulled into the parking lot behind us.

# CHAPTER 14
## Blinkies on the Bayou

The agents must have picked us up near The Mama's house. The location would have been on my background file and, despite my attempts to delay them, they had caught up to us. Scarsdale got out of the Cadillac on the passenger side and stood with her arms folded. Petit-Palais got out and put his hands on his hips, but not before shifting his jacket so we could see he had a gun in a shoulder holster.

A narrow thread of electricity sang in my veins. He wasn't coming at me with his weapon drawn, but he wanted me to know it was close.

"Mr. Luck." Petit-Palais called as if we'd accidentally bumped into each other at the bowling alley.

"What's up?" I replied.

"On a scale of one to ten, how much do you enjoy wasting taxpayer money on wild goose chases?"

"Not sure what you're talking about. Agent Skullder."

My freshly-announced nickname derailed his train of thought. "What did you call me?"

Happily, I got to repeat myself. "Agent Skullder. And your partner Agent Mully. Hey, Mully. How's your mom?"

Agent "Mully" Scarsdale didn't react, which was impressive. No change even when I asked about the health and well-being of her mother, recently dead and laid to rest.

"The truth is out there, Skullder. Go get it, boy!"

Agent "Skullder" Petit-Palais winced like he was sad.

"I guess this is a game to you," he drawled. "Some kind of joke. Kids have been abducted and you decide to pester an innocent mom and a hard-working sheriff about some girl that disappeared twenty-five years ago? And send us after some fella who had no idea why we were showing our badges and inspecting his trunk? Is that funny to you?"

There was a sarcastic expression of concern on my face when I said, "It sounds like you were following us, Agent Skullder. I dare say we did talk to a young woman and a sheriff today. Is it against the law to work on a case that has nothing to do with you?"

"If you really have a case."

"And if you spoke with Sheriff Holden, he told you enough to know I do."

"The daughter of a girl who vanished decades ago? Sounds phony to me."

"It's not." Not entirely. "Agent, I hope you didn't scare the good Samaritan I pressed into service at the grocery store."

"Mr. Hinks was very cooperative. He seemed more confused than scared."

"Okay. Good work."

"Do you want to tell us why Mr. Hinks had a trunk full of diapers?"

"And Desitin," I added.

"Desitin?"

"For diaper rash."

Petit-Palais scratched his chin, giving me the exaggerated look of a man pretending to care. "According to Mr. Hinks, he has no children. You understand why I have questions about your actions."

I nodded with mucho sagacity. "Let me clear everything up for you. If you visited the mom in Donaldduckville, were you wearing biohazard gear? Because you should be able to figure this out."

"What?" Petit-Palais's fuse burned short. It hadn't been a long fuse to begin with.

"The woman I visited lives in the house where Alyce Octavian once lived. She's the girl who disappeared. The lead didn't pan out."

"Yet you sent her diapers?"

"Sure. She was super nice and helpful, but you should have smelled the little sewer-on-a-stick she was holding."

Petit-Palais was reduced to repeating me. "Sewer-on-a-stick?"

"What's the matter, Skullder? They don't teach creative writing at Quantico? I'll say this slow for you. Her baby was stinky. And the other one was a walking cesspool. I thought I'd do her a favor and get her some supplies. Make her life a little easier for being kind enough to answer my questions. I asked Mr. Hinks to help because I have a case to solve and I'm very, very, very efficient."

For my trouble, I got a livid Skullder in my face. He walked up close enough to me I could see the capillaries in the skin of his nose and smell the peppermint on his breath.

"No. What you did is set up a stooge for yourself because you knew we'd follow him instead of you."

I kept my eyes locked on Skullder's while I said, "Hear that Nat? They were the ones following us after all."

Petit-Palais fumed, blowing peppermint-scented air out his nostrils. I let him fume.

Finally, he backed away. I hadn't done anything illegal. Not even mildly unethical. He buttoned his jacket and smoothed out the wrinkles that didn't exist. He turned to Nat. "Why do you hang out with this guy? Huh? He save your life or something?"

"Yes." Nat shot back. "But that's not it."

"Then what? Why do waste a single minute with this bozo?"

Nat deadpanned, "He makes me laugh."

Skullder looked at Nat, then looked at me, then looked at Nat again. Not even a blink. Then he shook his head and went back to perch his butt on the hood of the Cadillac. After a day of Louisiana driving, there were probably six hundred species of bug squished on the hood, but hey, it was his polyester.

Mully decided to take a turn. She sauntered forward. I couldn't get over her eyes, which made her seem older and wiser than the usual agent. They were the eyes of someone who had seen a lot and a lot of it had been bad.

"Did you find anything at your foster mother's house?" She sincerely wanted to know.

"Nothing to find." The words felt sour in my mouth. I wasn't about to mention we hadn't gone in. Or the handwritten note.

"Any more thoughts on the other kids who were taken?"

"My guess? Whoever took those kids is a professional. And they've been doing this for a very long time."

"Same people who took Alyce Octavian twenty-five years ago?"

I raised a pointed pointer finger and wagged it in Mully's face. "That's what I like about you, Agent Scarsdale. You don't say a whole lot, but you know how to put two and two together."

Skullder shook his head some more. He'd caught that I'd called Mully by her real name and complimented her.

That's the way life goes, Skullder. Some people earn respect while other people are you.

"What's your next move?" Mully asked.

"Here's the thing." I smiled but it was artificial. "I'm trying to help a little girl who just wants to know if her mama is Alyce Octavian and which, even better, doesn't concern you."

"Who's the little girl? Maybe we can help."

"Yeah. As much as I'd love to complicate my case with Federal intervention, I think I'll pass. On the other hand, if you want to dredge up the file on Alyce Octavian, maybe we can swap information. How 'bout you look into that and get back to me?"

Agent Scarsdale pursed her lips, considering. It was clear I wasn't going to give up any information for free and they couldn't force me to tell them anything unless they wanted to see if there was a file for Alyce they could pull out of a dustbin somewhere. If there wasn't a case already, there'd be zero chance of opening one. Too much time had passed and there were higher priorities. They knew it and I knew it.

She had no response, so I stared at Skullder, which got boring real fast. I whistled the first six notes from the X-Files theme. "Woo wee woo woo wee wooooo."

Our business concluded, according to our panel of experts— namely me—I turned to the Gatorbait building. Nat followed me, and Mully followed him. I wasn't sure what Skullder did because I stopped paying attention. And I also didn't care.

The teenage girl behind the counter gave a bright smile as we entered. "We're fixin' to close up shop," she said. She had a push broom in hand that she was using to shoo a small pile of dirt into a corner. The girl wore a t-shirt depicting cypress trees and a cluster of azalea blossoms and the words "I Got Swamped in Louisiana." She had a nametag with "Anna-Louise" on it that was a close anagram of "Louisiana," and I wondered if it was her real name. There was an unfinished bottle of soda with a straw in it next to the cash register and a Calculus textbook open to a chapter titled "Implicit Differentiation and Related Rates," which indicated that the girl was fixin' to go to college, if she wasn't already. She tapped her broom on the floor to knock loose any clingy bits and then leaned the handle against the wall. "What kin ah do fer you?" She ended the question with another dazzling smile.

"Well, Anna-Louise, my friend and I would like to rent a boat." I returned her smile, suspecting mine was substantially lower on the dazzle scale.

"Ah kin do that, but y'all shoulda come afore dark. Ah'll hafta charge extra."

"Okay." I pulled out my wallet. "Are you afraid we won't bring it back or something?"

The girl gave me an eyes-wide nod that I found ominous. "'Xactly. We lose more boats'n y'all kin believe after dark."

Golly-bob-howdy. She's serious.

"All right. And what boats do you have available?"

"Ah suggest sit-on-top kayaks. They're easy to paddle and you won't hafta git a secon' mortgage fer the security deposit."

Louise was very personable. I liked her. The rather large man lurking in the back of the shack had probably figured out the girl was good for business and he was correct. Between Deputy Macy and Louise the kayak girl, women were taking over commerce in Louisiana.

"Sit-on-top kayaks then." I handed my credit card to the girl. I liked the idea of kayaks. Nat and I could out-paddle Mully and Skullder if they decided to follow us. And if they decided to waste a boatload of taxpayer money on a boat, I knew where we were going and they'd be hard-pressed to catch us.

Louise made me sign a three-page contract after that. With all the indemnities and waivers, it would have been faster to donate a kidney. At least we'd have a head start on the agents. Finally, Nat and I headed out to the dock to get kayaks and paddles. About ninety seconds later, Mully and Skullder sauntered out, Skullder brandishing a receipt and smugness in equal measure.

"You commandeered kayaks?" I asked. It was the only way they could have gotten through the red tape so fast.

"It's good to be the Feeble Eyes." Skullder removed his jacket and loosened his tie as he lobbed my words back at me.

Touché.

Touché-au-lait even.

"You wanna tell us why we're going for boat rides, Mr. Luck?" Petit-Palais sounded like he was hoping to avoid the water.

Good.

"You're from Louisiana and you've never been on the bayou? You should know there are only a few game trails, let alone a drivable road in here. Disney wasn't fooling around when he built 'Pirates of the Caribbean.'"

I shook my head and Nat jutted his chin at the water.

It was on.

We dropped our kayaks into the swamp and jumped aboard. Within seconds, we were paddling away from the dock, leaving the agents scrambling to get on the water and follow.

With strong, measured strokes, Nat and I glided into the bayou. The cypress trees were pillars of shadow. We paddled between the guardians and followed the curve of water to remove ourselves from view of the dock. The swamp seemed eager to hide us as the dark trunks of the trees slipped past and the depths of the bayou opened like a black mouth. A few water lilies glowed softly under the light of the moon, but everything else remained charcoal and midnight.

We paddled without speaking, murmuring wakes trailing after us.

A shout and a splash sounded in the distance, followed by cursing. The bayou played with the noise, making it hard to tell where it had come from. Skullder's voice was unmistakable though, and I almost wished I could watch him pull himself back onto the dock, soaking wet and swearing.

I permitted myself a chuckle as Nat and I moved deeper, choruses of frog-calls cheering us on.

While I'd never rented a kayak from Gatorbait Excursions, I'd been through this bayou a zillion times. It wasn't hard for a kid surrounded by old logs and scavenged twine to come up with a raft and a pole to push it with. Especially after Miss Letourneau had us read Huckleberry Finn in fourth grade. Some of the kids hated reading, but that book captured my imagination from the moment Tom Sawyer helps Huck escape from the Widow Douglas and her sister. By the time Huck runs into Jim, the runaway slave, and they find a raft, my only goal in life had been to build a raft of my own.

The bayou was no Mississippi River, but that was probably for the best because the current in the swamp was gentle. For a while, I'd rafted into the bayou every chance I got, pretending to be Huck Finn looking for Jim.

Then I'd found him. Except his name was Eustace.

He'd been okay becoming my surrogate Jim: a black man who was big and good-natured like Jim from the book. And I'd never known he worked for the Fae until many years later after I'd gained my power and recalled our conversations about barrows and monsters in the swamp.

I pointed at three trunks sticking up out of the water to make sure Nat spotted them and then gave him a "thumbs up" to indicate we were on the right track. The trunks were broken cypress and collectively they resembled a mandible of teeth as if a giant's jaw had been snapped off and dropped into the drink. It was easy to imagine the flesh being stripped away over time and the teeth rotting and chipping down to bony points.

Like a forest, a bayou doesn't change radically from year to year. The landmarks I remembered from a decade ago were still there, although the living things had grown and the dead things decayed. Still, Nat and I followed along the river roads, zigging and zagging through tall gray ladies with their hair brushing the water. After a mile or so, we might as well have been on another continent, in a bygone age before humankind was a glimmer in the plans of the universe.

We slowed. Somewhere should be a thick tree slumped onto its neighbor, like an old man on a cross-country bus asleep on a stranger's shoulder. When it seemed like we'd gone too far, we worked our way back. Finally, I spotted the tree and grinned. The stranger had been overcome by the old man. Now, two trees leaned over instead of one, gradually burdening a third cypress. The world's slowest row of dominoes, falling one by one.

The trees pointed the way. Nat and I sailed on.

With the shadowed deep before us, and our paddles barely needed, the water bore us farther away from our pursuers in close-cool quiet. I listened for sounds. The little frogs that plied the lilies greeted us, and the katydids pronounced their accusations from the trees.

I waited for the blinkies.

Lightning bugs refused to fly over open water. Close to land was their domain, and Eustace's cabin was their Shangri-La. The first blinkies were few and far between, like floating faerie lanterns that had drifted away to explore the unknown. Gradually, as we moved up-bayou, the blinkies gathered to welcome us home. By the time we saw the lanterns on Eustace's dock, the air was peppered with flickering, flocking dots of golden light.

We slid past a short spit of land, the sky full of bouncing yellow stars like a Van Gogh painting re-imagined by Guillermo del Toro.

From the shore, the sound of a shotgun racking a shell ripped into the quiet.

# CHAPTER 15
## Skulls

Certain sounds make your guts clench and your heart stop, instantly encased in ice. The chick-chack of a pump-action shotgun chambering a shell was one of those sounds.

"Who dat?" The voice was hard and rough like barbed wire scraping over gravel.

"Eustace," I spoke as clearly as I could. "It's me. Goethe. From The Mama's."

"You ain't Goethe. Too big an' too old."

My hands stayed where he could see them. "It's been ten years, Eustace. Of course I'm too big and too old." Eustace preferred buckshot shells, I knew. The last thing me and my unperforated skin wanted was to provoke was a hasty pull of a trigger. Solemnly, I said, "Human beings can be awful cruel to one another."

There was a long quiet moment. I thought I saw the glint of moonlight on metal in the brush, but it could have been my imagination.

"Why you said dat?" Eustace's voice carried softer. The barbs on the barbed wire eroded smooth.

"C'mon, Eustace. It's what Huck said to Tom Sawyer at the end of our favorite book."

More time. More darkness. More listening to my heart pounding in my ears.

Then, "Y'might be Goethe after all. Get on to the dock. Meet y'all there."

Nat and I paddled deeper into the bayou while I tried to convince my heart to remain confined to its cage. Eustace was part panther. He made no noise moving over the soft ground even though he had to be less than twenty yards away.

The lightning bugs swooped and flitted around us, so many they should be flying into us or each other. Yet the murmuring buzz of their wings swept past without contact. Tiny biplanes in the night.

We found the center of glowbutt city, which was where Eustace had his home. Eustace kept a generator in back, which was cranking up as we docked. A line of 40-watt bulbs gradually came to life, running on a wire from a woodshed. The lights illuminated the front of the house and then came out to the end of the dock for our benefit. Strangers from a place where people had forgotten how to live in harmony with the cycles of the sun and the moon.

The satellite dish was new.

Eustace waited for us on the porch, standing next to the spindly rocking chair where he'd sat when he and I used to watch the sun drop low over the swamp. His wary eyes gathered us in. He'd seemed both timeless and ancient when I'd been a kid, and nothing had changed over the past decade. Eustace had the demeanor of an old man, but at the same time he seemed to be pretending.

Nat followed behind me and I saw Eustace measuring his stock over my shoulder. When he looked at me, he nodded. "Been a spell, L'il Huck."

"Sure has."

"Bring y'selves on in."

We followed Eustace through the screen door, which was decorated with a handful of lightning bugs looking to roost. The interior of the cabin was just as rustic as one would expect from the outside, with gaps between the floorboards and a dusty old couch that looked like a sharecropper's hand-me-down sulking under the front window.

"I be right which'oo." Eustace shuffled to the kitchen, leaving Nat and I to bake in the semi-stagnant air, heavy with leftover heat from the day. Neither of us wanted to sit on the grungy couch. At one time, the wallpaper had been brightly colored with vertical stripes and a pattern of miniature frogs. The walls were faded now, and it was only after I squinted at the frogs that I remembered what they were.

Eustace reappeared, carrying a tray with several large mason jars and a plate of shortbread cookies. There was ice in the jars and a clear liquid and condensation already running down the sides. He put the tray on the little table in the middle of the room. There were five jars and I wondered if Eustace had brought extras in case we were really thirsty.

"Dis da comp'ny 'shine," he said, handing the first jar off the tray to me. "Better'n my home 'shine."

I took a sip and realized Eustace was having a little fun. Instead of moonshine, the glass held Perrier water, which was quite the continental beverage in the bayou.

Once Nat and I had both received a glass and cookie, Eustace nodded. He didn't seem to be offended we were still on our feet. "Whatch'oo needin' then?"

Shoving the cookie in my mouth, I freed my hand to dig in my pocket. I retrieved the carved bone key I'd brought back from Alyce's dreamland and handed it to Eustace. He and I were both well versed in keeping Fae secrets, and I was sure he would know what I wanted without my saying so in front of Nat.

Eustace looked at the carving. "Dat's a Faerie key," he said, handing it back.

For a moment, my thoughts derailed. Was Eustace losing his mind?

I looked at Nat to gauge his reaction, but he was as good as carved from stone.

"Faerie key, huh?" I turned the piece of bone over and over in my hands.

Had Eustace forgotten our past conversations? Granted, we'd never mentioned The Behindbeyond by name because I hadn't known about that, but we'd talked about the magical strangers who often visited The Mama and he'd specifically talked about the barrow of the dead where ghosts of the Fae tormented those who got lost in the bayou.

Maybe I remembered wrong.

130

Eustace made it worse. "A key like dat opens Faerie mounds, which're gateways to their lands." Eustace looked at me and then at Nat. "If'n y'all believe in that sorta thing."

Saved by mythology.

"Where dat come from?"

"It was given to a girl by her mother. I'm trying to find out if she has family near and I knew you were familiar with these old superstitions."

Ha. I incorporated his story into mine.

The old man moved toward the front door. "Y'all's friends finally found us." The porch creaked as Eustace opened the door. I realized why he'd brought out the extra jars.

He's got hearing like a panther too.

Agents Mully and Skullder.

Eustace presented them with mason jars and cookies. "Here y'all are."

Mully followed Nat's example and sipped, smiling at the taste. Skullder looked lost, like he'd never taken a drink from a canning jar before and didn't know the procedure.

I didn't introduce the late arrivals. Satellite dish notwithstanding, Eustace wouldn't get the X-Files reference and they weren't my friends in any case. In fact, I was moderately ticked they'd found us at all. Our dash through the bayou hadn't kept them from finding us. I sipped more Perrier and took the opportunity to grin at Skullder's damp clothing.

"Nice night for a swim, Agent," I said. "My friend Eustace was just sharing his best moonshine with us."

Skullder took a sniff, then a sip. "Mineral water."

With a straight face, Nat said, "Earned that FBI badge."

Skullder fumed, his face reddening, but he had the good sense to keep his mouth shut. Still, Eustace checked our expressions, reading the situation.

"L'il Huck." He extended a narrow thumb over his shoulder. "C'mon. Somethin' back here."

I followed Eustace to the kitchen and then to a side room. He turned on the lights and memories flooded back to me from a decade ago.

Skulls.

"Wow. I'd forgotten about these."

Eustace made his own display cases with glass and wood and he'd filled them with the cleaned, bleached skulls of animals from the swamp. Some smaller skulls huddled in rows in a case by themselves. Other cases held skulls from related species or larger skulls. I found I could still identify a lot of them. Eustace had taught them to me. All assortments of mammals and reptiles and birds.

"Squirrel. Muskrat. Mink. Otter. Opossum. Skunk. Rabbit. Raccoon."

Next case.

"King snake. Cottonmouth. Snapping Turtle."

Next case.

"Quail. Wood Duck. Turkey. Heron."

And the larger creatures that called the bayou home.

"Beaver. Bobcat. Coyote. Deer. Panther. Bear. Alligator. Crocodile."

The gator and croc were the famous big boys of the bayou. Florida was known for alligators too, but the crocodile was the largest. With its narrower head and snout, which allows it to move between trees and hide better, the croc was also more dangerous.

Eustace addressed me in a voice that was as deep and quiet as Lake Pontchartrain. "Son. I never tol' you, but Faerie mounds all have they own watchers."

I still had the key in my hand. With thin, dark hands, Eustace held mine and gently pulled my fingers open. He tapped the carving. "An' fo' this'n, it's me."

A watcher?

Eustace does serve the Fae.

"What's going on?" Skullder burst into the room like he'd heard Al Capone was selling nuclear missiles to John Dillinger in here. He narrowed his eyes as he found the object we were discussing and snatched it out of my hand. "What is this?"

"Congratulations, Agent. You've confiscated a tchotchke."

"A what?"

"C'mon Agent. With a name like Petit-Palais, you must have run into your share of Yiddish."

"Petit-Palais is French," Skullder sneered.

"Well, there you go. And in the tradition of the French, you're trying to claim something beautiful that doesn't really belong to you. Like Canada."

If Skullder followed what I was saying, it didn't register on his face. Maybe he was just getting better at ignoring me. "What's a tchotchke?"

Eustace answered. "Dat's jus' a kid's carvin'."

Picking up the thread, I said. "My client had it. I'm trying to find out where it came from. One of the few leads I've got. Like I keep telling you, Agent Skullder, I'm working my case."

Petit-Palais stared at me.

"If you just go home, it wouldn't be the worst decision. If I find out anything on your missing kids, I'll let you know."

Skullder took a step toward me to give the key back. "I don't like you, Luck. I know you're not telling me the truth. My gut tells me not to trust you. The fact that you're so convincing right now tells me I really shouldn't trust you."

No sale.

"All right, Skullder. Tag along, if you can." I gave him my hard stare back. Puppies have been known to whither beneath that gaze. Kittens even. "Just consider which of us is wasting the taxpayer's money."

Skullder nodded like he was seeing a piece of my plan. "Really, really, shouldn't trust you."

With a final point of the finger in my face, Skullder left.

"He don' listen," Eustace said.

"No he don't," I agreed.

"He should." The tone of Eustace's voice hinted at a very good reason. Without another word, Eustace gestured for me to follow him again.

"Keeping secrets. I had no idea you guarded a burial mound."

"Jus' part of the job. I need to show you 'nother part."

Eustace led me into the yard behind his house, which consisted of a path bordered by lilies, leading into the bayou. A milky way's worth of lightning bugs illuminated our way. After a hundred yards, I could barely see the cabin over my shoulder. After another hundred yards, we might as well have been on a different planet.

"You know 'bout ley lines?" Eustace asked.

"Sure."

"Mm-hm. An' you know 'bout portals to dat Behin'beyon'?"

"I do."

"Mm-hm. So there's more ways to get to the Fae realms. Like burial mounds."

"Aren't barrows the same thing as burial mounds?"

"That's them."

"You used to tell me about the ghosts of the dead buried in them."

"Dead Fae, to be precise."

I had remembered right.

"Why would the Fae bury their dead in the mortal realm?"

"Centuries ago, it were safer here than the Behin'beyon'."

"Safer? Safer from what?"

Eustace nudged me with an elbow. "C'mon, son. Can't think of a reason for hidin' the dead?"

It took a moment. "Necromancy."

Eustace nodded. "Yup. Nothin' more evil. When da Fae were strong, dis country was pristine. A few native tribes an' dey were superstitious."

"Which gave the Fae a lot of secret real estate for hiding their dead and no one to bother them."

"Mm-hm. Hid away from all de worl'."

It made perfect sense.

I asked, "Do the ley lines give power to the barrows then?"

Eustace nodded. "'Xactly. Ley lines give magical power to de barrows. And de keys let anyone come here from de Behin'beyon' or

134

go back to it."

The Fae usually needed to be summoned to come to the mortal realm.

"So the barrow keys gave them a shortcut?"

"Mm-hm. An' de keys were guarded by armies of de Fae."

We arrived at another shed, tucked away in wild wood of the bayou. The door was held closed with a heavy chain. The iron in the steel hummed at me, shunning the blood in my veins, warning me away. Eustace handed the silver lantern to me and I stood at a respectful distance, waiting for Eustace to fiddle the padlock. He politely dragged the chain around the side of the shed, then came back and pulled the door open.

"One more thing 'bout de ley lines," Eustace said. "Power goes to barrows so de Fae can come an' go. But power also goes to de protections keepin' de barrows hidden and safe. Some of de protections are magic . . . an' some ain't."

Eustace took the silver lantern. He held it up over a tarp, which looked like it was covering a small car, about eight feet long and five feet wide.

Showing a flair for the dramatic, Eustace pulled the tarp away in one smooth motion.

The skull was an ivory-white color, more matte than glossy. Instead of a radiator at the nose, there were nostrils. What sent a chill all the way to my knees, however, were the sockets where the eyes had been and the rows of six-inch teeth.

This wasn't a small car, suitable for weekend picnics with the kids.

This was the skull of a grand-daddy crocodile.

# CHAPTER 16
## Eustace the Third

"That thing can't be real."

I found myself backing away.

"He's real," Eustace said proudly. "I thought f'sure he was goin' to outlive me."

Looking at the monstrous skull triggered something primal in my head. An instinct that didn't want to allow me to accept the truth. The instinct that told me that the sort of thing I'm looking at eats things like me for lunch. I bumped into the corner of the door.

"You sure you aren't kidding?" I asked.

"He lived for sixty year, thereabouts. Named him Eustace, Jr."

"With my condolences to you and the missus, I'm glad he's dead."

"Mm-hm. He were kilt by his son. Eustace the Third."

"What did Eustace the Third do? Push dear old dad down the stairs?"

Eustace shook his head at me.

"What then? Run him over with a tank? Throw him under a freight train? Accidentally drop an ocean liner on him?"

Eustace half-smiled. "Eustace the Third got bigger'n his daddy and bit him in half."

When blood stops running through the veins and goes chill, it hits hard.

Can't be real.

Big lizards like crocodiles have heads disproportionately large for their bodies. Even so, Eustace Junior had to have been forty or fifty feet long. Twice the size of the biggest alligator in Florida.

Can't be real.

If Eustace Junior was the size of a semi-truck, how big was Eustace the Third?

"Fae magic super-sized them?"

"Mm-hm. Livin' on ley lines makes 'em big quick."

Staring at the skull did nothing to make me accept it better. Eustace, the human, moved toward me and the shadows cast by the lantern in the eye sockets moved with him.

"Make him stop looking at me, Eustace."

"Don' gotta worry 'bout him. His boy you gotta watch out fo'. Gotta get past'm to get to de mound."

Yeah, sure.

"Okay. So how do I do that?"

"Beats me." Eustace shrugged.

"Aren't you the guardian?"

"Mm-hm. I guard the gate by guardin' de beast."

"C'mon. Can't I put him to sleep somehow? With music or something?"

Eustace gave me a sideways glance. "Kin you sing?"

"I can try. Will it help?"

"No. I'd pay good money to watch tho'."

"Thanks."

"Mm-hm."

The two of us stared at the skull. Put some wheels under that thing and Fred could drive Wilma to the drive-in and still have room for Barney and Betty in the back.

The barrow key was still in my hand. It was small but suddenly felt heavy.

They needed me. The kids.

Laoch.

And Béil.

I have to find them.

Eustace faced me. "You know you gotta be goin' to de mound alone."

Pushing breath through my nose in a sigh, I nodded. Then, "I know. I can't take my partner. And I'll have to lose the FBI agents."

"Good luck. Seem like dey can track."

I nodded. "I think Agent Scarsdale is part Sacajawea."

"Mm-hm. An' th'other part's hound."

Drat.

One problem at a time. First, I'd need to get Nat to return to Baton Rouge without me. I could tell him it would be best to let Brandy and Carlene know we'd be here overnight, at least. That was reasonable.

Losing the agents would be a different problem.

Then there would be the minor issue of Eustace the Third. The lizard that could take down a ton or two of daddy for giggles.

As if reading my thoughts, Eustace said, "Watch out if you're usin' magic." His voice was leaden with meaning. "De same ley lines dat make these crocs grow also make them resistant to bein' spell't. Understan'?"

"Yeah. Using fire for baking croc-cakes is probably not an option."

We trudged back through the bayou to the cabin. The little fuzzies on the back of my neck kept watch in case the bones of Eustace Junior forgot to stay dead, promising to throw their little follicles in the air and scream like first graders at any sign of danger.

Nat waited for us on the back porch.

"Did Mully and Skullder take their ball and go home?" I hoped.

Nat shrugged. A shrug leaden with meaning.

The lightning bugs had slowed in their paths of flight as if they had gotten distracted by the people and forgotten they were busy writing cursive in the deep-night air. We sauntered down to the dock. At least, it felt like a saunter. It was somewhere between an amble and a mosey, and where else on this beautiful Earth would those words even occur to a person? Only in the bayou.

At the dock, four kayaks.

"They're still here somewhere." Me. Detectivating.

I listened. The cool air over the water made inroads, pushing back the warm air around us. Sound carries better over water, and I tried to ignore the sounds of frogs and insects making their little concertos in the dark.

The scream seemed miles away. The sound battled through the stands of somber cypress and over bush and weed and flower and grass, diminishing with each moment. It sounded like Petit-Palais's bad day was getting worse. I moved toward the yell, which had been full of pain. Two gunshots rang out, stabbing the silence; I stopped and drew my pistol. While I wasn't making contact with the metal parts of the weapon, the steel buzzed in the background like electricity waiting for an excuse to do damage.

Eustace handed the lantern to me and disappeared, probably to get his shotgun. Nat fell in behind me. His presence was reassuring, like a mountain backing up a meadow.

We pushed through the brush, sidearms out, senses heightened. Quiet. Then the cursing drifted in. We found Skullder on his back, a crush of honeysuckle beneath him. Mully was there. She'd torn the sleeve off Skullder's white cotton shirt and she'd started tying it around Skullder's leg. I held the lantern to the side, so she could see better while he cursed some more and grimaced. His left leg was dark and shiny. The tang of his blood was unmistakable in my nose.

"Who shot?" I asked. I needed to make sure we weren't under fire.

"I did," Mully said.

"Okay." Parallel slashes adorned Skullder's outer thigh. He was lucky. If those cuts had been on the inner thigh, he'd be dead in another thirty seconds. "What happened?"

Mully shook her head. "I heard something." She cleared her throat and swallowed, perhaps choking down fear and guilt. "Moving around in the brush. Came over to check it out."

"Looks like you found it. Or it found you." I knelt on the other side of Petit-Palais. "Did you see it, Agent?"

Through gritted teeth, Petit-Palais nodded. "Just a glimpse. It came out of the dark. Tan fur. Big panther. Snarled once and took a swipe at me. Claws cut right across my leg like I was paper. Then it bolted back into the trees."

I looked at Agent Scarsdale. "You hit it?"

She shook her head. "Never even saw it. I fired off two rounds to scare it off. That's it."

Holding the lantern higher, I scoured the ground nearby and found something of a paw print in the soft earth. There wasn't a lot of detail but there was enough to see that the animal had been large. I'd seen a big cougar on a hike in the Rocky Mountains. In Louisiana, the same cat was called a puma or panther and they were about the size of an adult human male. This one was bigger.

Maybe the ley lines make the cats supersize here too.

I'd have to remember to come out again in the daylight to get a better look. This was Eustace's home, so it might be worthwhile to bring him out too. He might know what had been here.

"Probably surprised it as much as it surprised you," I told Petit-Palais. He glared in reply.

Scarsdale finished binding the wound as I heard an engine approaching. Eustace pulled up about a hundred yards away. The lights from his truck cut holes between the trees.

"That's all I can do," Scarsdale pointed at her bandage job. "You guys help him up?"

Nat and I each hooked an arm under Petit-Palais and got him to his feet. He cursed some more and tried hopping on his good leg.

"We could carry you," I offered.

"Get lost."

He didn't really mean it. Probably. Either way, he kept his arm around my shoulder and leaned in, dividing his weight between Nat and me. We made it as easy on him as we could, our mode of movement anything but a saunter. At Eustace's Jeep, we pushed him up into the passenger's seat as he tried to hold on to his dignity.

"I can take you to the dock," Eustace said. "You'll have to get him in a kayak and tow him back."

"You can't drive me to the hospital?" Skullder's frown devolved into a snarl.

"Road washed out in 2005. I ain't drove to town since."

Skullder blinked his disbelief. "How do you fill up the gas tank?"

"Shrimp boat carries back more'n shrimp."

Without a word, Nat climbed in the back of the Jeep, making the vehicle tip and sway. He'd help get Skullder into the kayak.

Eustace pulled away with Skullder muttering curses and I found myself alone with Agent Scarsdale. I retrieved the lantern as the taillights painted red on the trees. The bayou got quiet. My ears searched for sounds of an oversize cat. The lantern was probably enough to keep it away, but I kept my pistol drawn just in case. Maybe I could get the panther to follow me to the croc pond and they could have tea while I found my way to the barrow.

Just because a plan is stupid doesn't mean it won't work.

Scarsdale's footfalls brushed over the grass behind me.

"You didn't want to help your partner?" I asked.

Scarsdale didn't laugh but there was a tinge of humor in her voice. "Little me isn't strong enough to help a big guy like Petit-Palais."

Looking over my shoulder, Scarsdale appeared as a ghostly presence just outside the glow of the lantern.

"Maybe not," I replied. "I have a feeling you're stronger than you look."

Scarsdale waited to respond as we drifted through the flickering cloud of lightning bugs. Then, "Maybe I just wanted to observe you in your natural element, Detective."

"Mm-hm."

"Or maybe I saw it as a chance to get away from an insufferably pompous partner for a few minutes. Not that such a thing would ever occur to me."

I looked over my shoulder again. "I believe you."

Not entirely. It could be an almighty coincidence that circumstances were falling into place, so I could find the barrow alone. Or maybe it wasn't my good luck but Petit-Palais' bad luck working to my advantage.

It was pretty dang convenient.

I didn't trust convenient.

Scarsdale could be with her family, grieving the loss of her mother, but she was here instead. She could be getting a ride to the dock, but she was walking with me. Maybe she was letting circumstances work to her advantage too. What would that advantage be?

We walked on in silence and I felt Scarsdale's eyes on me the whole way.

Getting Petit-Palais from the Jeep to the kayak had undoubtedly been awkward and embarrassing. I was sorry I'd missed it. Anyway, Nat had the agent situated by the time Scarsdale and I strolled up, which was nice for him. He sat in the little boat with his arms folded like a kid who'd been told he couldn't ride It's a Small World anymore. While Nat tied a towrope to Scarsdale's kayak, lightning bugs hovered at the edge of the dock as if to wish Skullder farewell.

Scarsdale stepped to the end of the dock and stopped. She put her hands on her hips and hummed as if trying to decide something. Nat and I looked at each other. I didn't mind calling her out.

"Hey, Mully. You might want to let your passive know your aggressive is showing."

"Hmm?" She looked at me like she didn't know what I was talking about.

"My friend Nat here might be willing to lend a hand. Just ask nicely."

She looked at Nat as if she'd forgotten he was there. "Hmm?"

From the dark water, Skullder yelled, "Can we please get going?"

Scarsdale took a step, so she could put her hand on Nat's shoulder. "That would be great." She shot me a quick look and went to Nat's kayak, leaving hers open for Nat.

That's a saunter.

Definitely a saunter.

As Mully settled in, Nat boarded Scarsdale's kayak with a smooth action. He cast off and started stroking downriver. The tow rope went taut and Skullder's kayak jumped forward, making Skullder grunt.

"Tell Brandy and Carlene hello," I called. "I'll see you in the morning."

Nat waved farewell. In moments, the three were swallowed up into the dark bayou, trailing lightning bugs like tiny comets.

"Mm-hm," Eustace said. "Now you got all the time you need to get to the mound."

"Yeah," I replied.

Convenient.

# CHAPTER 17
## Gateway to the Barrow

Eustace offered to let me bed down in his cabin until daybreak. He offered again when I yawned. I was tempted but decided to take a reconnaissance trip instead. He said I could take any supplies I wanted and refused my offer to pay. We chatted while he sat on his decrepit couch with a plate of cookies.

"Isn't there a way of getting past Eustace safely?"

"The Faerie key itself used to hold guardians of the burial mounds at bay. That was when the Fae wanted their lovers to find them. Those days are long gone. The key still opens the mound, but it won't hold the guardian."

"Okay. And opening the mound?"

"Mm-hm. Jus' walk 'round the barrow seven times."

"Okay."

"Make sure you go in the direction you want. Counter-clockwise if you want to come back. Clockwise if you want to stay forever an' not be found. Once you pick a direction, you can't change your mind."

There's a wrinkle. I guessed some people would prefer to visit. Others would want to escape and never return. "Anything else?"

"Mm-hm." Eustace took a bite of cookie and showed me the cookie with the missing piece. "Don' get et."

Thanks.

Through the screen door as I departed, the voice of Pat Sajak announced a word puzzle. At least Eustace was putting his satellite dish to good use. And what was I doing? Heading out on a sleep-deprived quest to find a fifty-foot, magically-enhanced crocodile named Eustace. The third.

I'm the nutcase.

The back shed was right where we'd left it, complete with skulls. I found a rucksack and loaded up with an extra lantern and some rope and a hammer and other odds and ends. They went into my bag with the other things I'd brought from Miami. Stuff useful in this realm and the Behindbeyond.

Good to go.

I did not stop at the shed with the head of Eustace, Jr. Just walked right past. Didn't need to see it again. Knowing it was there was creeps enough.

A clear path led into the bayou, comprised of parallel tracks left by Eustace's Jeep. I hadn't thought to ask where to find the burial mound, but it had to be north. So, north I went, with a lantern in one hand and my gun in the other.

There's a spiritual communion that takes place when a man is alone with his thoughts in the wilderness. At least for me. After a few minutes, I felt the stillness of the untamed swamp as it slumbered. The moon was descending in the sky, but I turned the lantern off and let my eyes adjust and found there was light enough to see. The tire tracks on the ground turned silver under the moon's shared illumination. Silver. The metal of magic.

All around me, the cypress cathedral besought heaven with upraised limbs while the cherub bugs flickered in holy reverie and choirs of insects sang their oratorios. High above, the exalted stars bowed in reply and the reverent stillness of Nature penetrated my soul with a balm of peace.

This is where I'm meant to be.

My path lay ahead. And my fate.

Glory, hallelujah.

I hiked for an hour. Often, I came across sturdy wooden bridges connecting pieces of land. Crossing each bridge felt like passing a marker from which I couldn't turn back. After the last one, I realized something was changing—had been changing gradually but had only become noticeable after a time.

The lightning bugs had diminished, and here—as the land started to bend to a higher elevation—there were none. I put my things on the ground and took a drink of water. The hill in front of me was two hundred feet higher than the bayou. For a moment, I wondered if it could be the barrow, but the tire tracks went straight up the incline, and I decided the hill was just a hill. Only a fool would drive over a burial mound. Especially one where the bones of the Fae were at rest.

Stepping on the hill ground felt like walking on concrete, and I didn't really like it. Moving from the softer land of the bayou was like leaving a comforting friend. I was still in the bayou, but the hill ground was an intruder here. Cold, unnatural, and out of place. It was almost painful to step up the rise. My feet jarred as if striking anvils with every fall of my boots. The climb was enough to raise my heart rate and I reached the top of the hill slightly out of breath.

The pyramid of human skulls at the top of the hill put me out of breath even more.

The skulls were set in an alcove to protect them from the elements. Large stone slabs had been stacked and held together with mud and sticks to create a shrine of sorts at the side of the path. Most of the skulls looked ancient—but a few on the top of the stack were free from discoloration and significant age. I had no way of knowing more. I hoped the skulls were those of Native Americans who had chosen to honor this path with their dead. I didn't know if that was even a thing, but it was a better thought than the alternative.

These were the victims of the barrow guardians.

Another striking surprise met me beyond the skulls. The trees were different here. The narrow cypress had given way to oaks with heavy trunks. These were not oaks that grew in Louisiana naturally.

These oaks were the kind that grew in the Behindbeyond, and they shouldn't be here. The bayou was too warm and wet for these oaks to be healthy, yet here they were.

And they felt like a barrier. Or a boundary, at minimum.

The ley lines help the trees grow.

That meant the croc was close.

The twin paths led straight between the two largest oaks. They reached skyward like a pair of massive gateposts, except the gate was

146

gone. All it needed now was a welcome mat. Stepping between the trees generated a wave of goosebumps that ran up my back and along my arms.

It's cooler here.

The drop in temperature was at least thirty degrees.

Perfect for the oaks.

The barrow waited.

Almost as if lit from within, the burial mound stood under a faint emerald glow on the other side of a long, narrow valley. It looked to be a hundred feet tall. No trees grew on it, but it was surrounded by oaks, and their branches were lightly intertwined as if the trees were holding hands all around the hill.

The barrow was a quarter of a mile away. The twin trails ended ten feet in front of me. There was a swath of grass for a short distance, and there the ground dropped off. Beyond was only blackness.

A pit hunkered down between the trees, separating the road from the barrow.

Tentatively, I took a step toward the empty space. Then two.

The roots of the oaks went deep. A few stuck out from the sides of the pit as if tasting the air. The sides of the pit were sheer and stony. Someone had taken house-sized slabs of granite and used them to line the sides. The stone had long scratches in it. And many of the roots had been chewed.

It's a wonderful life, Mr. Stewart.

If only I could shift like Bromach. I'd be on the other side in a heartbeat.

Unless the ley lines monkeyed up the magic, as Eustace warned.

If that happened, I'd either end up in the pit playing crocodile rock or I'd end up blinking myself all the way to Ontario.

For a moment, I thought about taking advantage of the darkness. Maybe I could sneak across the bottom of the pit and ninja my way over before li'l ol' Eustace the Third caught on. If he didn't know I was here already, I could be out of here with nothing more life-changing than a song in my heart.

I sighed. The only sane plan would presume the croc knew I was here already. Crocodiles are ambush predators. Much like panthers. They may run for a short distance if necessary, but they mostly lie in wait for something meaty and stupid to get close. And the claustrophobic configuration of the valley made sure I'd be close.

Better take a look at what's waiting.

The lantern made me flinch when I switched it back on. The light was so bright and brilliant it nearly blinded me, and I wasn't looking directly at it.

Maybe it would blind the croc as well.

I let my eyes adjust for a minute—no sense in being the deer in the headlights—then I inched forward toward the edge of the pit, holding the lantern in front of me like a talisman.

In my imagination, I pictured the croc waiting below the rim and as soon as I got close enough, he'd launch himself to take a bite, snapping through my arm and leaving a bloody stump. Not to mention eating my lantern.

Nothing happened.

The water at the bottom of the pit was still and dark, like ink. There was no way to tell how deep it went. The shapes breaking the surface were dark and round and bumpy. It would have been easy to mistake the shapes for a crocodile's nose or brow, but under the light they were revealed to be nothing more than logs and branches.

Hm.

The makers of this place had crafted a brilliant design. There was no obvious way to safely cross the pit.

Maybe there was a way to go around.

I backed away from the pit and went back the way I'd come in. The sudden rise in temperature and humidity as I re-entered the bayou was like being smacked with a wet wool blanket.

At some point, there'd be a space between the hand-holding oaks for me to sneak through. All I had to do was find it. I sauntered around the gatekeeper tree and moved north, tramping along a course that would be parallel to the edge of the pit. After passing a dozen oaks, I turned again, treading carefully between the trunks. The last thing I wanted to do was fall into Eustace the Third's kitchen.

I hedged between the trees, checking to the side for a sign of the glowing emerald barrow.

All I could see were more oaks.

Maybe I'd gotten the angle wrong, but I had a well-honed sense of direction and distance. Still, I tried stepping at a cautious pace between two more trees. On the other side of them, I found more.

The pit was gone. The barrow was gone. As far as my eyes could see—which was pretty dang far—there were only trees.

Curse the Fae and their enchantments.

Retracing my steps, I picked my way back to the gatekeepers. Between them, the barrow glimmered insolently in the distance with the deep, dark pit in the middle.

I got it. The space between the trees was the only way in. Like a portal.

Because I'm stubborn, I tried going around in the other direction, but I knew what the result would be. All I accomplished was a discouraging stroll into a forest that shouldn't exist.

Twenty stupid minutes later, I was back to the gatekeepers.

"Wow," said a voice. "That looks interesting."

My head, not prone to sudden snapping, snapped around nonetheless. A short figure stood on the grass, a step off the trail, wearing her jacket around her waist.

"Agent Scarsdale?" The lack of credulity in my voice was obvious.

"Detective Luck," she replied, without an ounce of sarcasm. She seemed happy to see me. Or happy to see me confused.

"What . . . ?"

When no more words came forth, she finished the question for me. ". . . am I doing here?"

"Yeah. That."

She shrugged. "We got Petit-Palais to the hospital. Nothing more I could do. So, I went back to your friend's place and followed you here."

It sounded so simple and reasonable when she put it that way.

"And Nat?"

"I came without him." Scarsdale nodded. "It didn't seem like you wanted him with you."

She stared at me with confidence in her eyes. If she was expecting a response from me, she'd be waiting for a long time. I wasn't about to share any details. A long moment passed with our eyes locked together. I couldn't read her at all.

In my head, I calculated the time it would take for Scarsdale to have paddled back to Gatorbait Excursions, get Skullder in the car, take him to the hospital and have all the paperwork started, then come all the way back to Eustace's place to track me down.

I decided it was possible. I'd chatted with Eustace for a while and collected supplies. Then, coming here, I hadn't been in too great a hurry. And I'd lost a little more time trying to find a way around.

So, it was possible Scarsdale had done what she'd said.

Possible.

It would have been more convincing if she'd been out of breath. At least a little.

Inhaling, slow and deep, I reasoned that I couldn't keep this person from following me despite my best intentions. But Eustace had told me I needed to be here alone. Exhaling, long and low, I decided I couldn't be responsible for her persistence.

One more chance. Up front.

"You can't follow me." I let my eyes bore into hers.

Please listen. Take my advice.

I went on, "This is a dangerous place. I have something I need to do here. I can't do that and worry about you. I tried losing you more than once. If you're smart, you'll go back to the cabin and let Eustace make you breakfast. Even though he may very well give you cookies, you'll be a lot better off than if you don't leave me alone."

Scarsdale tilted her head at me and took a fraction of a step back. "Does this have anything to do with the disappearance of those kids?"

If I answered her directly, I'd have to lie. I didn't mind lying to Petit-Palais. I had a somewhat higher regard for Scarsdale. I dug the Faerie key out of my pocket instead. "This came to me from the girl I told you about. I thought the girl's parents might know what it means, but couldn't locate them. I knew Eustace was familiar with these sorts of keys and he mentioned an ancient site up here in the bayou. So I've come here. This is the reason I have to go forward alone. My case. You have to let me."

Scarsdale folded her arms across her stomach. She looked at the key and then at me. She stepped close and picked up the key, turning it in her hands. I let her look as the silver moonlight caught its edges. The wind rattled the leaves while she looked. Her gaze drifted from the key to the gateway trees and the scene beyond.

She held out the key then and dropped it into my palm. Her expression landed somewhere between amused and mollified.

She might leave.

She might.

"Fight me," she said.

"What?"

"Fight me. If you win, I'll leave."

I sputtered, trying to come up with a response. She untied the jacket from around her waist and dropped it on the grass. She filled the empty space created by my confused delay with a taunt. "C'mon Detective. Are you afraid to hit a woman?"

Afraid? "No. Just unwilling."

Scarsdale unbuttoned her sleeves and rolled them up. "Good." She grinned. "It'll be a short fight."

I raised my hands in surrender. We both unfastened our shoulder holsters and dropped them to the ground. I took my turn rolling up my sleeves while Scarsdale kicked off her shoes.

"What constitutes a win?" I unbuttoned my shirt and took it off. She might use it to grab and throw me. Or try. "I wouldn't want to leave you out here unconscious. What if the panther comes back?"

"Good point." Scarsdale had a t-shirt under her button-down. She removed the button-down, which was fair. Thankfully, she stopped there. I had no plan to grab her by the shirt. It would just rip and the goal was to fight, not embarrass each other. Scarsdale added, "First to land three clean hits is the winner."

"Okay."

I swung my arms a little and shrugged a couple of times to loosen my shoulders. A small thrum of adrenaline set my heart pumping. "Whenever you're ready."

She launched herself at me, covering the distance between us in a heartbeat. Her flurry of punches came fast and surprisingly hard. I kept my hands up with my arms vertically in front of me and moved efficiently to block her fists.

She backed off. I sidled to my left and lost her for a moment in the dark. A light flared up in my peripheral vision. Scarsdale had snatched up the lantern and switched it on. I tracked the lantern as it fell to the ground again. A split second later, my leg flared in pain.

She'd kicked me.

Ow.

I backed off. Her feet made soft sounds on the grass. I heard my own breathing rise, but she appeared to be as calm as milk in a bucket.

"That's one," she said.

"Yeah."

"I did say three hits. Not three punches."

"You did."

"So that's one."

"Yeah. But it'll be the last one."

She laughed. "Ready?"

Why not?

I brought my hands up in front of my chin and nodded.

She came at me again. I focused on hem of her white t-shirt. Soccer players are taught to watch the belt line of their opponents and fighters are taught the same. Players can move their feet to deceive you or try to fake you out with a nod of the head. But the direction their body commits to follow will always be at the center of their mass.

She moved around me, fists poised. I stayed in place, pivoting to keep her in front of me. She tested my defenses with quick attacks that I fended off with my arms and a dodge or two. Patiently, I let her come at me again. Then again, looking for a pattern I could exploit.

Any predictable motion. She tried another kick and I just stepped away, out of her range. I was taller, so I had reach. She favored jabs with her left hand, followed by a compact cross with her right. She mixed in the occasional hook, but I—there! Quick jabs with her left fist again. I took them on my forearms and unleashed a cross of my own, aimed at her shoulder.

Cripes.

She ducked my punch and came under with a quick shot into my ribs.

Ow-ow.

I should have gone for her gut, then I might have caught her. But she was short and I was reluctant to hit her in the face.

"That's two." Her grin wasn't mocking me. She thought this was fun.

I stepped away and lowered my hands, shaking off the tension. I rubbed the spot on my side where she'd landed her fist. That bony, hard-hitting fist.

"They update their training at Quantico?" I really wanted to know.

"Actually," Scarsdale replied, "I followed Hilary Swank's movies, like when she did The Next Karate Kid and then I got into boxing when she did Million Dollar Baby."

"She dies in that one. You should try following her example and be sweet like in P.S. I Love You." As I spoke, I sauntered in her direction and finished with a lunge of my own, followed by a quick left and right.

They all missed.

She ducked under my first punch and rolled to the side. It was like fighting smoke. How was she so quick? She laughed again. Now it was annoying.

Bouncing up and down on her bare feet, she grinned and said, "Next one is on your face. Right here." She pointed at a spot between her eyebrows.

Seriously? She's calling her punch? And why am I the only one breathing hard?

Scarsdale's face turned serious. She shifted her stance, putting most of her weight on her left foot with her right foot in front of her, the balls of her feet on the ground, and her fists at her sides. In Taekwondo, it was called Beom Seogi. The tiger stance.

She's changing fighting styles?

Oh, nifty.

I turned sideways to give her a narrower target. Her stance was an attack stance, but it was easy enough to dodge from as well. I closed on her and stepped into a roundhouse kick, hoping to power my way past her block before she could escape and then hit her in the side. She caught my shin on her forearm with a solid block that never broke her defense. It was, however, the leg she'd kicked before and her block was hard.

Ow-again-some-more.

We sparred. I was down 0-2 and wanted to land a solid hit. She dodged and blocked but didn't attack, waiting for me to make a mistake. I launched a few shots that would have been bell ringers on most people, but she slipped away every time.

I focused and threw a straight shot from the shoulder. She ducked under and caught my arm, spinning inward. My arm ended pinned beneath hers and as she spun, she raised a backhanded shot aimed for my face. I caught her fist, expecting the shot, since she'd so thoughtfully told me where she was going to strike. With her shoulder against my chest and our arms momentarily useless, she grinned.

And kicked me between the eyes.

Ow. Ow. Ow.

"Who is even that flexible?" I rubbed my forehead.

"That's three."

At least she had the grace to not point out I hadn't scored.

"And zero for you."

Never mind.

Scarsdale sighed with obvious satisfaction. I'd count that as panting. She put her shirt back on and good-naturedly tossed mine to me. "So." She grinned. "What do we do next?"

# CHAPTER 18
## Crocodile Rock

The monster was down there, in the dark water. Standing near the edge of the pit, a cold knot wound itself around my stomach.

"What are you looking at?" Scarsdale stood beside me, shoes in hand, looking for the next fun thing.

I wasn't going to tell her the whole story, but there was no sense in lying outright.

"There's a crocodile down there."

"We have guns," she said brightly.

I eyed her sideways. "We aren't going to kill it."

"Why not? Shoot it between the eyes. Same place where I kicked you."

Ha. Ha ha. Ha ha ha.

"Yeah, Mully, your skill is impressive. And your enthusiasm for your work is equally impressive but also disturbing. You need to be more careful. There are things in this world that are different from what you know. For the last time, don't follow me. The crocodile down there is more dangerous than you could ever imagine possible. A few bullets aren't going to be enough." If guns will even work here. "Trust me. Go home."

Scarsdale listened. Listened and looked at me with clear eyes.

"Thank you for your concern, Detective. I'll be okay."

Maybe she's not that smart after all. I looked at the trees bordering the pit. Their bark was smooth, their branches high.

"How are we getting down there?" Mully peered into the pit.

Her sudden perkiness grated on my nerves and gave me uncharitable thoughts. "Jump. If you find a safe way across, come back up and let me know."

Mully looked into the hole some more. "What aren't you telling me?"

"Sure. When I get sarcastic, you listen." There was a thin, broken ledge along the pit. I stepped carefully so I could touch the first tree. The bark of the oak was warm and textured like glass. I had the hammer in my back pocket along with some nails. They both had iron in them, so I had gloves too. With the gloves on, the metal didn't burn. Over my shoulder, Mully watched. I set the tip of the nail against the tree and shifted my grip on the handle of the hammer. If I could string rope from one tree to the next, I could create a safety line to traverse the side of the pit.

The head of the hammer rang out as I struck. The tip of the nail sparked and flew out of my hand, spinning off into the pit.

Piglets.

The nail hadn't even scratched the bark.

I tried once more, knowing it was hopeless, but trying anyway. Holding the nail securely, I struck again. Then again, harder. The thick nail bent against the impenetrable bark.

Curse the Fae and their enchantments.

Logically, the nail should have disrupted any magic. Magic cannot abide the touch of iron. There was something special about the trees to protect them, perhaps, or the magic was exceedingly powerful. In any case, there was no time to figure it out.

I went back to my bag and stowed the hammer and nails, feeling Mully's eyes on me. I had several coils of rope, each about forty feet long, and the trees had plenty of branches. If I couldn't traverse the rim, I'd have to go over it instead.

A solid branch, about fifteen feet up, looked like a good candidate. I took a few loops in my hand, which would be enough to send several feet over the branch. From there, I'd be able to climb up with more rope.

With a swing and a fling, I tossed the rope. It sailed up smoothly, the loops unwinding.

A brief flash of green flared over the surface of the tree.

The rope bounced away, rejected by the magic in the tree.

Crap. Crap. Crap.

The Fae thought of that too.

Curse them.

Something massive moved in the pit. A huge body shifting in the water. The rope I was holding went taut, pulling me off my feet. I let go of the rope, but I was already heading over the edge. My hands hit the ground, skidding, then grasped open air. My abdomen slammed halfway off the edge. I felt like I was going to break in two.

Below me, more movement, shiny on glossy. Bony, plated skin. Emerald eyes. A maw filled with ivory daggers. The mouth opening. Rising.

Hands grabbed my belt and hauled.

With a roar, lengthy jaws slammed shut, crushing the world an inch from my face. A rush of air swept over my nose, rich with the aromas of decay and death. The momentum of the monster's leap carried upward. A glowing green eye with a black slit at the center focused on me. The jaw opened again, preparing to snap once more. I rolled to the side. The head cracked the stone when it struck. The epicenter was next to my skull. Thunderous shockwaves kicked up the dirt around me.

The ground trembled as the beast slipped back into the deep. On my hands and knees, I crawled in reverse, scraping the skin through my pants, the pain a sharp burn.

I shifted to sit. My heart threatened to pound out of my chest. The bloodrush was deafening in my ears.

Mully stared at me, eyes wide, panting for real.

"Better idea," I said. "You go on. I'll head back."

Mully looked at the pit. "What was that thing?"

"Eustace. The Third." I started to get up. My knees begged to differ. I sat back down. "Go on over and introduce yourself."

"Don't be a jerk. I just saved your butt."

"Sure. After you kicked it."

"No. I kicked your face, not your butt."

I ignored her. I laid back on the ground and waited to see if my heart rate would slow or if tachycardia was my new reality.

Mully stayed close, standing so she could keep an eye on me and the pit at the same time. "I don't think that crocodile is natural."

"Nope."

Mully paused. "You going to tell me what's going on here?"

"Nope."

"You're very annoying."

"Yep."

She paused again and sighed. "Takes one to know one. I admit."

"Yes."

She nodded. "Is this job personal for you?"

Didn't expect that.

"Why do you ask?"

Scarsdale looked away, thinking. She started to take a step toward the pit and thought better of it. "Private investigators run the gamut. On the one end, you have those who don't care about anything but the paycheck. On the other end, those who would do anything to help a client. Most fall in the middle."

"What's your point?"

She extended her open hand toward the pit. "This is something more. Nobody would do what you're doing for a paycheck. And I suspect on a normal day, this would be more than what you'd do for a client. Somehow, you're doing this for you."

I thought about the work I'd done. How far I'd gone to help someone who didn't have anyone else to help them. I'd gone pretty far to rescue Erin once. Before I really loved her. In the last day or two, for Alyce, I'd gone pretty far. A whole lot of people were hurting and all their pain had brought me here. If I were honest with myself, helping Alyce was important. Helping Béil was important too. Helping Laoch was, admittedly, an act of self-preservation, but important too.

Scarsdale's question had made me realize something though. About myself. About why I was here trying so hard.

If I looked past everyone else and everything else, I'd find myself. Me.

And Urlabhraí.

He'd done terrible things to people I cared about. And he'd done terrible things to me. He hadn't stopped. And he wouldn't.

Not until I stopped him.

If I were being honest, I was doing this for me.

I was here, risking my life, because Urlabhraí had gotten away and because following this case to the end could mean putting an end to him.

And if I were being completely honest, I wanted to end him in the worst way.

My legs had strength again and I stood up. If Scarsdale wanted to stay, she could stay. And if she was going to stay, I might as well put her to good use.

Scarsdale had her hands on her hips. "Are you going to answer my question?"

I locked eyes with her. "We need to get something to eat."

Scarsdale looked confused. "You hiding a Burger King in that knapsack?"

"Not for us."

I laid out a plan including what I knew about crocodiles. She was skeptical at first. "You're obviously an excellent tracker," I said. "Search to the east and see what you can find. I'll search to the west. We'll meet back here in an hour."

Scarsdale nodded but I saw questions in her eyes. "You aren't trying to get rid of me, are you? Go ahead without me?"

"Nope. Don't think it's possible. I tried." I gave her a half smile. "Now you can help."

"Okay." She galloped into the trees. The fun back in action. "See you in an hour."

Not a standard agent.

All the skulls on Eustace's wall were animals found within range of his cabin. With my lantern and gun and the beckoning west, I looked for tracks in the dirt and places where game might seek shelter. Life in the bayou was abundant, and while I found an opossum in a tree and ticked off a number of nesting birds, the largest tracks I found were raccoon.

I needed something larger.

After an hour, the deep purple sky had bled to pink. Dawn approached.

I made it back to the gatekeeper trees to find Scarsdale waiting, arms crossed, grin smug.

"I see why your last name is 'Luck,'" she said as soon as I go within earshot.

"Yeah? If my first name is 'Bad,' you're on to something," I replied. "You look like you've been waiting for a while."

She shrugged. "Forty-five minutes."

"Really?"

"Let me show you." She headed eastward. Sauntering.

Five hundred yards into the forest, we came across a small clearing with a conspicuous pile of leaves and branches. Scarsdale walked over to the pile and pulled the branches away.

There was a deer underneath.

"He's wounded," Scarsdale said. "I don't know how long ago. He tried to run when I found him, and it opened up his wounds again. There's fresh blood down his side and along his hindquarters." She pointed to the wounds. Multiple gashes. Similar to the ones inflicted on Petit-Palais. Scarsdale went on, "Maybe he was attacked by the same panther that got my partner. Somehow the deer got away and came up here. Passed out. He's lost a lot of blood. The panther, still hungry, ends up near your friend's cabin."

I looked at the deer. His eyes were barely open, and he had lost the will to fight or flee. The wounds were serious. Mortal. He wouldn't survive another day. Not out here.

"There's that word again," I muttered.

Scarsdale heard. "What word?"

"Convenient."

Scarsdale acted miffed. "Look a gift horse in the mouth, Detective, you'll get your nose bit off. Can you stop being paranoid for a minute? Things happen."

I nodded.

Without another word, I checked my bag of supplies. The

circumstances Scarsdale had offered were plausible enough. I might have reasoned out a similar story; however, I'd had things go a little too well before and it had ended in disaster. It's a challenge trusting good fortune when bad fortune keeps wearing it like a second skin, tearing it away at the worst moment and laughing in your face.

In any case, I was having a much better day than the deer.

"Sorry, buddy." I knelt by the deer with a length of rope. "I wish I could tell you this wouldn't be painful. But I need to do this. I'll never forget you and your sacrifice."

It took some shoving and rolling but I finally got the rope under the deer and tied it around his back and behind his front legs. I tied a second rope around his neck.

Handing the end of the second rope to Scarsdale, I warned, "If he tries to bolt, he'll be stronger than you think. It will take both of us to hold him, and even then he might get away. If you can't hold on, let him go and we'll track him until he drops. Okay?"

Scarsdale glared at me. "If you can hold him, I can hold him."

Swell.

"You want, you can carry him then. You hauled me away from the edge of the pit and I weigh more than the deer."

She rolled her eyes at me.

The ol' Luck charm kicking in.

I didn't want to carry the deer to the pit either. If I got blood on me, I'd smell like dinner to the croc. And the panther. And, for all I knew, to Special Agent Scarsdale. Still, it bothered me to drag him over the ground and I hoped he was past feeling it. For most of the way, the ground was grassy, so it wasn't as rough as it could have been.

Everything was quiet at the pit. For a creature whose job it was to lie in wait, the crocodile was employee of the year. In a minute, we'd give him a reason to end the wait, which would buy time, I hoped, for us to get to the other side of the pit.

"Remember, if this works, his tail will still be a threat. He could swing it. Break our backs or necks with it." I sounded like I was delivering a lecture. "And although his legs are stubby, they're powerful and he has claws."

"I know, Detective."

"All right. Class dismissed."

The dawn provided a cool blue ambiance. The water was still black, but the granite walls were lighter gray and distributed the weak morning rays through the pit. I couldn't see the croc among the black, bobbing bits of flotsam in the pool. Perhaps his eyes were closed. Or he was submerged. Or he was waiting us out under a rock at the edge of the water. Aside from the beast, I needed to make sure there was a way out. If we managed to subdue the animal, it would be pointless to cross to the other side with no escape.

"There." I pointed to a narrow set of stairs across the pit.

The stairs had been built into the granite slabs. They were narrow. Too narrow to be of use to a massive reptile, but adequate for a couple of human beings who hopefully would not be running for their lives.

At the bottom of the stairs, a landing of stone crossed the back of the pit and gave access to a series of stone slabs along the side of the pit. The slabs served as a walkway and at the near end, the walkway faded out of view under shadows. Logically, there had to be a stairway on this end as well. If it was built like the one on the other side, the top of the stairs would be near the left edge of the rim. It had been overgrown with tufts of grass, but I found it right where expected.

"Good." I pointed to the start. "When we're ready, we'll go down the stairs here, run up the side, and get out the back."

"Detective. You talk too much."

The blood drained out of my face as Scarsdale shoved the deer over the edge of the pit. It thudded on the granite and rolled into the water with a modest splash.

A number of quality words came to mind but there wasn't time to spew them.

I ran to my scattered collection of equipment and threw it all into my bag. I slung the bag over my shoulder, sparing only a moment for a baleful glare at Scarsdale, who stood, unrepentant, at the rim.

Pistol drawn, I headed for the top of the stairs. I moved cautiously. One step down. Then another. I had to wait for my eyes to readjust to the gloom, and while my heart pounded, I listened. There were drips and small swishes of little things in the water. Possibly dirt knocked loose by the falling deer, crumbling into the tiny sea. Only these small sounds, with no sign of Eustace the Third.

Part of the plan included holding onto the rope we'd tied around the deer. Giving the croc a snack was only half of my intention. Using the croc's instincts against him was the second part. Either Scarsdale had forgotten that or she'd just gotten impatient.

One of the ropes lay on the stairs below me. The other had fallen into the pool. As quietly as I could, I shifted down one more step. Three more to go, and I'd be able to grasp the frayed end. I slid down another step. The pool beneath me erupted in a fountain of dark water.

The sound of the crocodile's roar was deep and powerful, making the ground thrum and resonate in the bones of my chest. Sharp yellowed teeth flashed up to slash and rend. I backed away, retreating up the stairs. The bite missed my boot and I kicked out, shoving the snout down. The ebony skin of the croc was as hard as Siorradh's armor.

The deer's plaintive cry of fear echoed from the bottom of the stairs. That small sound made my heart quaver, but I prayed it would also get the croc's attention.

There's food. Alive and kicking. Just the way you like it.

Refreshed, perhaps, by the water, the deer tried standing up. I could see a patch of tan shifting in the shadowy murk and muck. He had three legs that worked, although he had to be hurting.

Come on, reptile. Obey your instincts.

The strike was businesslike and fierce. Maybe Eustace the Third was ticked at missing me twice, or maybe he just decided a little appetizer would be nice. With an angry growl, the teeth were suddenly there, in an instant, clamping down faster than a bear trap on the deer. The deer made no noise. Eustace withdrew, a pair of legs sticking out of its maw, the croc's eyes emerald slits.

Sorry, little one.

The thought returned, unbidden.

Now, reptile, do your thing.

Crocodiles prefer live prey. Once caught, unless the catch is very small, they almost invariably do something else.

They roll.

And I was counting on it.

Come on, Eustace.

Roll.

You can't choke that deer down in one piece.

Roll.

Make sure the deer isn't going to get away.

Roll.

The wait felt interminable. I hunched down at the top of the granite steps. My pulse thrummed in my throat. I consoled myself with the thought that if he didn't roll, at least I'd be able to get mad at Scarsdale.

Finally, there was a thrashing sound in the water.

Eustace was halfway around, his belly up.

Praising the gods of instinct, I ran.

I ran down the stairs, searching for a rope all the way. Just one. I spotted the frayed tail of an end as Eustace continued to roll. Pounding to the bottom of the stairs, I yelled in frustration as the rope vanished beneath the black surface. Launching myself from the step, I dove into the water. The sudden immersion in the chill of the deep shocked my system. I almost inhaled ink.

Flailing under the surface, I prayed to catch a rope. One hand brushed against something soft. A plant. The other caught a twisted length of rope.

Hallelujah.

I held it tightly. Took a single stroke upward. Emerged into the air.

Eustace. Right in front of me.

The rectangular scales of his ebony skin glistened in the blue-gray light as if an armored tank had been forged into flexible plate mail and oiled.

It was beautiful.

Easier to appreciate if there hadn't been bloody chunks of deer in those long teeth, and if the monster's emerald eye wasn't tracking my every move. So close.

I could touch him.

I backed away, the end of the rope in my hand.

The deer twitched and the croc made a rumbling sound.

The croc rolled again. His immense body created waves that pounded the sides of the pit. I was drenched already, but here in the water, I was hit with a fresh tsunami every few seconds.

"Get ready, Scarsdale!" I yelled as I swam backwards, drawing the slack in the rope. If left to drag, the rope might have wrapped itself around the jaws of the croc, but those loops would have been loose, and Eustace would have been able to shake them off in moments. The loops had to be tight. At last, the slack went and the croc kept rolling. Like a winch drawing steel cable, the rolling action of the croc bound the rope around his jaws. After eight or nine loops, I was running out of rope, getting pulled toward the monster.

A few strong strokes got me to the granite steps. Scarsdale had made the descent and helped me out of the water, carrying my bag. She stared at Eustace. The water in my mouth tasted like the bottom of an aquarium. I spat and sputtered, yelling to explain. "He won't be able to bite until the rope unwinds. The muscles for biting down have a force that could crush a pickup truck, but the muscles to open the mouth are weak."

Scarsdale yelled back, "Thanks, professor."

"Shut up and run. Watch out for his tail."

As if he'd heard me, Eustace stopped and turned to watch us run. His tail thudded against the other wall of the pit. I felt the impact. If he lashed out at us, at least we'd see it coming. He didn't attack. He stopped rolling and held still. He gave a chirping, croaking sound instead. We'd almost made it to the stairway on the other end of the pit. The chirping, croaking sound resembled a call. Like . . . oh, no.

I scanned the ground and the stairs and found a round, black rock. It had broken open and was hollow inside.

"Oh no," I repeated. Loudly.

Ahead of me, Scarsdale skidded to a stop.

"What?"

"This croc has the wrong name. He's not a Eustace. He's a Eunice."

# CHAPTER 19
## Storming the Barrow

I pointed at the broken black rock and spotted even more. A dozen at least. "Those are eggs. And that sound she's making? She's calling her babies."

"Are you kidding?"

As if to prove my point, an angry hiss drifted from above. A croc skittered over the stairs, heading straight for us. It hissed again, narrow enough in the body to navigate the stairs.

"Up there!"

Holy roly-poly guacamole.

Scarsdale had her pistol out and shot three times. The sound was muffled, and while the bullets found their marks they didn't slow the reptile down. She retreated to the wall, eyes wide.

I leapt onto the stairway and caught the baby by the tail.

The "baby" was still ten feet long.

Twisting sideways, the croc tried to turn and bite. I kept yanking backward. There was a drop-off of two feet into the pool, and I swung sideways. The croc's claws scrabbled on the stone, but I flung it over. It hit the water with a splash.

Another croc came over the edge. Scarsdale shot again. "What's wrong?" she yelled. "It's like the powder is wet."

Or there's magic here.

"Stay behind me." I shoved my gun into my bag and shoved the bag into her hands. Pulling my knife out of my belt, I faced the next beast. The thing wasn't built for going down stairs, mostly sliding, but it hissed at me, gaining speed. It went for my leg. I jumped up, turning in the air. As I came down, I plunged the knife into its eye, and with a snap, the blade penetrated the center of its head and it went still.

"Up the stairs."

We needed to get out before more crocs spilled over. And the one I'd tossed into the pool might come up behind us any second.

I was more than halfway up when I heard another hiss, and a snout appeared above my head. As it came over, I caught it under the neck and belly and used its momentum to throw it over the side of the stairs. It chirped a cry that almost sounded like "Mommy" before it slammed into the stone below.

"Sorry, Eunice."

I surged up from the stairs, knife in hand. Two more crocs came plodding forward over the grass. They'd been slow to answer their mother's call and would likely be spending the morning in timeout. Scarsdale was still climbing.

I called up my power. "Tine!" The sizable fireball I'd planned to unleash fizzled out with a lukewarm pop.

Yup. Magic here. The kind that stops mine. Eustace had warned me.

The nearest croc hissed at me, twenty yards away.

"I want to kill them." Scarsdale came up beside me. She was almost breathing hard.

"Take out your frustrations later. Right now, run up that hill."

I took off at a sprint. Crocs could move fast when they wanted, but only for short distances over flat ground. The runts gave chase but gave up when we climbed the knoll.

At the top, the burial mound waited a hundred yards away.

A choir of angels was singing. Probably. Somewhere.

I collapsed onto a patch of grass, keeping an eye downhill.

It felt good to be on this side of the pit. It felt good that I hadn't killed Eunice to get here. Eustace the First would be surprised to find out his guardian crocodile was a girl, but he'd learn to be okay with it.

Having caught my breath, time for the next item on the agenda.

In front of the burial mound was a circle of standing stones, similar to a liagán circle, except there were only four stones.

"Well, Mully, here's another place you should stay away from."

She stole a glance back toward the pit. "Not sure going back is an option."

"You can make it. Dodge the little ones and hurry past Eunice. She'll be tied up for a little while longer."

"Ha. Funny," she retorted with half-closed eyes, somewhere between cynicism and sarcasm. Then, "Your trick was more effective than I thought it would be, actually."

"In the immortal words of Joan Jett and the Blackhearts, 'I love croc 'n' roll.'" I smiled. Full cheese.

She put her hands on her hips. "I refuse to accept an adult would say something that stupid."

"Refuse away, Mully. This is my world and you're just along for the ride."

"There may be some sad truth to that statement." She sounded like she was having second thoughts.

"Come on." I hadn't been kidding. It had been her decision to follow me, and I wasn't going to take a lot of time to explain. She was along for the ride indeed.

With the Faerie key in my hand, I stepped into the center of the standing stones. Most magic exhibited a visible effect, as if the employees of Industrial Light and Magic retired to the Behindbeyond. This time, a wind arose, enough to ruffle my hair.

If Scarsdale noticed, she didn't ask. She moved to check the left exit.

"Not that way," I said. "This way."

"Does it matter?"

Actually, it does.

"If you don't want to get lost." Forever. "My world, my rules."

"Why is that way different from this way?"

"Uh." Eloquence in a syllable. I grabbed her shoulder and shoved her to the exit.

We left the circle and the wind stopped.

Scarsdale didn't seem to notice.

The burial mound dominated the landscape to the left as we

walked. I wondered what would happen if I tried to go back. Would some power prevent me? Having been under control of an irresistible force previously, I wasn't eager to feel that way again. I spun around, in part to make sure Scarsdale was following, and I saw that the stone circle had vanished.

That answers that.

Can't go back to the beginning if the beginning is no longer there.

The corner of the barrow was roughly a right angle, although it was rounded and smooth like a curve on a suburban street. The air shimmered as though there were a mirage, but the air was far too cool to generate rippling heat like a desert. The next corner was rounded the same, and unless the compass points were altered, we turned around the northeast corner. Scarsdale kept up, not speaking, content to keep pace.

Like the south side, the north side of the burial mound was several times longer than the east and west. The scenery in the distance blurred as if behind a thin waterfall. The leaves on the trees quavered, vibrating, as we moved. At the foot of a stone wall rested a pile of bones and a skull with prominent canines. Perhaps the creature had fallen from the wall. Eustace would love to have the specimen.

We continued on.

We rounded the northwest corner, then the corner at the southwest. The stone circle would have been in front of us, fifty yards away, except it had been carried off by the wind. Scarsdale stopped.

"We just walked in a circle." She looked ahead. Then she looked all around. "Didn't we?"

I didn't answer.

No sign remained of the stones. We walked over the patch of grass where they would have been with no sign that we had completed our first circuit.

Above, on top of the barrow, a line of gray figures looked down on us with solemn expressions. Some had armor. Some had robes. Some had crowns of laurel or staves of oak. I felt their eyes upon me as they bore still, silent witness to our intrusion.

Not my world. Theirs.

Onward.

Two more corners. The sun across the north side seemed higher than it should have been. The shimmering curtain of light brighter than before. Scarsdale looked at the trees and squinted. Where the bones had been previously, I saw a dark pelt and muzzle. Though distorted, I could tell it was a black bear. The wall of stone above it remained unchanged. It was hard to tell if the bear was dead or holding still.

I felt compelled to keep going. A subtle urge. A craving to just take the next step, then the next. Maybe Scarsdale felt the same as she kept pace.

Go with the flow.

I chuckled a little. I'd been told I go with the flow habitually, especially when things get weird. Around the south side, Scarsdale tilted her head when the circle of stones was still missing, but she kept walking.

Twice around.

More specters on top of the barrow. We kept walking.

The trees looked different, once we made the turn. It could have been another variation of the light or a shift in the shimmering curtain. The wall of stone was the same as before.

Third time around.

The wind returned along the south side, swirling around like a square dance of zephyrs. Along the north side, the scene on the other side of the glimmering curtain was dark, as if the sun had just set on a brewing storm about to break.

Fourth time around.

The wind increased, yet the scenery was quiet, as if holding its breath for us. The burial mound bore a crown of ghosts. Hundreds now.

Fifth time around.

We weren't impeded in our walk, but the wind was hard to ignore. The curtain seemed to have slowed its rippling motion, and the trees were lit as if by a spotlight behind, casting fingers of shadow over the top of the stone wall.

Sixth time around.

The wind objected to our forward progress, pushing against us, snatching at our clothing, and pulling our hair. On the north side, there were few details not swallowed by a bright glow. In this direction, however, the wind encouraged us on. A thousand phantoms were standing witness.

Push. Shove.

We came around the final corner.

The circle of stones had returned.

Scarsdale sauntered to a stop. Looked at me sideways. I returned the look, keeping my face neutral, and walked on. The wind calmed as we approached the circle, and died away altogether as we stepped inside. The opening to the south—which should have been to my right—was blocked by a new stone. We had first entered the circle from that direction, but now that we had found our way to this circle, we couldn't get out that way. Instead, the exit was through the north side.

Into the center of the barrow.

I left the circle and stood in front of the mound. A passageway had been carved into the side of the barrow. On the ground, there was a circle. The circumference of the circle resembled a Stain with a pattern of knots and runes glowing softly with cerulean power. The center of the circle was perfectly, brilliantly white, like a movie screen after the film had ended but before the projection lamp had been extinguished. Whatever waited for us on the other side was obscured.

"What is this?" Scarsdale whispered, finding her voice again.

"Some hole-in-the-wall place to hang out," I replied.

She shot me a look that said grow up. "Where did it come from? First the miniature Stonehenge disappears and then it comes back. And then the side of the hill has a tunnel in it."

"Yep."

Above us, the spirits had vanished too. I'd tried to prepare mortals for the Behindbeyond before. Explained what the place was. How things worked. The human mind isn't always able to deal with what they might encounter. I'd tried to be a good host in the past. Today, I was too tired. Scarsdale had followed despite my best efforts. She'd have to figure things out on her own. I had no patience and no time.

I shifted my bag on my shoulder to secure it and offered a simple "It's magic, Mully," then I stepped up to the circle and fell in.

Turning the corner into the Behindbeyond had become routine for me. I was accustomed to falling forward and walking into the Fae realm.

The snowstorm was a shock.

A frigid wall of cold air blasted me with tiny flakes of ice that felt like needles. The sudden drop in temperature took my breath away, and I had to force myself to inhale. Instinctively, my eyes squinted shut to block out the blizzard, but I had the presence of mind to step to the side. A few long moments passed. My skin was going numb already. Mully must have jumped into the middle of the portal instead of following my example and tilting around. She shot out of the circle and landed on her butt with an oof and a curse.

Against the howling wind, I shouted, "Welcome, Mully."

She got to her feet, wiping snow off her backside and giving me a dark, withering glare. She hunched into the cold, untying her jacket and putting it on. "Where are we?" she yelled. The wind threatened to steal her words away.

I yelled back, "Never been here before."

Behind us, the portal blinked and disappeared.

Mully yelled again. The words were meant for me, all right, but their meaning didn't require a response.

Spruces and pines surrounded us, nodding in the wintry wind. Ahead, there was a gap in the trees, which had to be a road, although the way was buried in snow. I trudged off, wishing I had taller boots. The snow was up to my knees and my feet were instantly turned into blocks of ice. Mully followed grimly behind, bent over against the storm.

With the wind chill, the temperature stood well below zero. We had very little time before hypothermia set in. Already shivering, I could no longer feel the biting snow on my skin.

"This way." It was the only way that made sense.

Circumstances may have changed over time, but if the Fae gave keys to mortals to access their realm on their own, they would have accommodated the mortals in other ways. Like providing shelter. Or a welcoming committee with blankets and hot cocoa.

Or maybe making sure there wasn't a stupid blizzard in the first place.

On the other hand, the fact remained that mortals weren't welcome in this realm anymore.

I held on to my opinion, hoping for the best in any case.

Ahead, the landscape widened. The storm eased up enough for me to look into the valley. In nice weather, it would be a stunning view. In this weather, the view took the heart out of me. I stood at the crest, panting, numb, and trembling. With the exception of a few burly spruce trees, there was only an endless blanket of white as far as I could see.

# CHAPTER 20
## Tracks in the Snow

Scarsdale shivered so badly, it looked like her bones were trying to escape her skin.

We couldn't stand here. If we don't keep moving, we die.

And if there was one thing I could do well in this place, it was fire.

I led Scarsdale into a stand of fir trees that screened us somewhat from the full brunt of the storm. Her steps were slow and determined. Fighting the cold was making her tired.

One benefit of an untended forest was the abundance of dead material on the ground. There were plenty of small branches under the boughs and even a pair of heavier logs. Those I carried and piled together ten feet away from the screen of firs. The sticks that didn't snap off I cut from the trunks with my knife. Scarsdale saw what I was doing and carried wood to the pile. The work helped keep us from freezing.

"You'll never get that wood to burn." Scarsdale stared at the pile, her arms wrapped around her middle. "Everything's wet."

I nodded sagely. "Care to make a friendly wager?"

Scarsdale snorted. "We're freezing to death and you want to make a bet?"

"If I can't get a fire started within one minute, I owe you a steak dinner. If I do, you owe me one."

"Deal. I'll take my steak rare."

"Loser." I fed power into both hands. "Tine!"

Gouts of red-orange fire erupted in twin streams from my fists. My fire could melt rocks, so it wasn't much of a problem to set the damp wood aflame. The pile sizzled and popped as the moisture boiled away. Once I'd achieved a merry crackle, I ended the spell and the bonfire was bon by itself. Scarsdale glanced at me guardedly before she stepped into the warmth and stuck out her hands, rubbing them together.

"Just when I thought this day couldn't get weirder." She looked at me with mixed emotions. Curiosity. Fear. Regret for having kicked my butt by way of my forehead, perhaps. And guilt, as if she'd seen something too personal about me, like she'd caught me walking around in my underwear and it was her fault.

"Medium." I tried to lighten the mood.

"What? Medium? What's that?"

"Medium, Agent Scarsdale, is how I like my steak."

She snorted. When she shook her head it was from appreciation instead of scorn.

We stood in front of the fire. My hands tingled as they thawed. The warmth was welcome, but a whole lot of smoke was rising into the air. On a clear day, the smoke would be visible for miles. If anyone saw the smoke, they'd come to investigate. I didn't know where we were, which meant I didn't know if the beings here were friendly or dangerous, and I didn't like not having that answer. The wintry day had the one benefit of obscuring the black column from distant eyes. The light was waning as well, and it would be getting dark soon.

Small favors.

Minuscule miracles.

Bite-sized blessings.

With all the bluster, I hoped to find a large drift where I could dig out a snow cave. Unfortunately, it seemed the snow was only a foot or two deep. We'd have to make do with piled up branches, donated by the fir trees, to make a lodge of sorts where we could stay warm.

The fire would last for about 30 minutes. I told Scarsdale I was going to scout ahead and see if I could find a better place. She nodded and I slogged down the hill while she turned in place, warming herself on all sides like the meat for döner kebab roasting on its vertical spit.

After a quarter of a mile, about to give up, I found what I'd suspected would be here—or what remained of it. The dome was broken. Pieces of stone had crumbled and crushed the stove or whatever had been at the center of the little way station set off the side of the road. There were runes carved in a partial ring of silver, the script ornate and ancient. I recognized some of the characters engraved in the ring, but it was the Old Tongue and I couldn't read it.

The prospects for the evening were growing less desirable by the minute. With the dying of the light came a drop in temperature, and the thin gray light turned the world flat and bitter. I dragged myself back up the hill. My previous tracks had been nearly swallowed up and I found myself straying off the center of the road to follow the border of trees where it was more protected.

Scarsdale and I were in for a long night.

The snow shifted. I caught the movement out of the corner of my eye and stopped.

A footprint.

Where there hadn't been a footprint before.

I traced the line of my tracks to the broken down waystation and my tracks heading back. There were other tracks. A long moment passed. I felt less tired. Fear substituted for rest.

I bent over, inhaling deeply, as if I'd only stopped for a breath. Facing back up the hill, I took another step. In the side of my vision, after the slightest hesitation, another track pressed itself into the snow.

Thirty yards away, something invisible was moving alongside me. It stepped when I stepped to better hide the sound, but my eyes were sharper than a normal human's, and it couldn't hide the marks it made in the snow.

As though unaware, I trudged on, senses on high alert.

Whatever it was, it was large. Like all living things, it had to breathe. I heard it exhale and the breath was deep. Two narrow streams of vapor appeared in the air, teasing lines in my peripheral vision. The breath emerged eight feet above the snow.

This thing was large. Very large. And invisible.

A liondog. Like Madrasceartán. It couldn't be her. She wouldn't be hiding from me. We were friends. And, setting that all aside, there was another problem.

I heard two of them.

The first one was following a path parallel to mine. The second one was coming up behind me. I heard it breathing too. They hadn't revealed themselves. I had no idea what that meant. I hadn't known there were others of Madrasceartán's kind, although, upon reflection, there would have to be.

A dozen unanswerable worries coursed through my thoughts. These liondogs could be feral. Untamed. Predatory. They had claws and teeth for hunting prey, after all. And they were stalking me in stealth. Maybe they were curious. Nothing more. I couldn't risk it.

The least I could do would be to warn Scarsdale.

With little hope of making it back to the fire, I broke into a run.

The liondogs ran too.

Chunks of snow flew into the air as eight paws chewed up the ground.

Yelling, "Tine!" I sent a lance of flame at the beast to my right. It was built for maneuverability, even in snow, and it pulled up short, changing course. I spun around and took a shot at the one behind me. The fire bathed the snow in a pool of rippling orange light. The flame vaporized a cloud of snow kicked up by the creature as it dodged.

They were too fast.

Reflexes too good.

"Scarsdale!"

What would I tell her?

Run? Hide? She was defenseless.

Please let her be okay.

Guns were all but useless here. I'd hold them off with fire, then. At least until I ran out of power. Or I'd use the Silverpoint, sitting in my bag. I'd used it once before. It allowed me to touch the power of the Earth and doing so had nearly destroyed me. That had been in the mortal realm. Here, in the realm of magic, with ley lines strong, I'd most likely kill us all.

Running, staggering, I kept yelling Scarsdale's name. Kept flinging fire at the unseen beasts. The invisible tracks in the snow sent daggers of fear through me. My fire never hit. The only results were new tracks showing how the liondogs dodged. Worse than anything, they made me feel like the beasts weren't really there. As if it were all some sort of trick to make me waste my power.

More puffs of steam, hanging in the air.

The liondogs are there all right.

They didn't seem to be in a great hurry. They were far better equipped than I to traverse the snow, but they hung back instead of running me down. Grr. I threw more fire at the liondog on my flank and another gout at the one over my shoulder. It never occurred to me that they were herding me along.

Not until I ran straight into the third one. A heavy paw slapped me down and everything went black.

Warm.

The sense of walls nearby.

No shivering.

Worry?

Hypothermia victims feel warm.

Then they die.

Something more.

Fur.

Warm fur.

A coat.

Scarsdale found a coat.

That's nice.

Maybe from the fir tree.

Heh heh.

Fur tree.

Erin would laugh.

She's sweet.
Sleepy.
Not shivering.
Not dying.
Warm.

The second time I realized I wasn't dead was better than the first. I didn't fall back to sleep the second time.

My head was pounding, but it was okay.

Dead guys don't get to feel head pounding. I did.

My eyelids wanted to stick together as well. Eventually, I won the battle and looked through slits at a room. A fire. A ceiling. Honest-to-poodle walls holding things up. Not to mention keeping the winter out.

Wait.

Where am I?

It took far longer than was graceful to get up. My legs wanted to wobble and, even worse, they wanted different rhythms. Left Leg wanted to tango but Right Leg wanted to cha-cha.

Cha.

Why wasn't it called "Cha-cha-cha" anyway? Calling the dance "Cha-cha" left out a "Cha." Some lazy Spaniard . . . never mind. Not important.

Ow. My head.

The room was big. Scaled for people ten feet tall. The bed not a bed so much as a . . . nest?

A fur-lined nest.

My feet told me they were bare when they hit cold stone. They hurt too.

Where . . . ? Architecture? Okay. The structure resembled the waystation I'd run into before. My brain just needed a little time to reboot and make connections. Columns. Dome. A silver circle with script in the Old Tongue etched around the circumference. In the circle, a warming fire.

Someone had rescued me.

Hold on. Scarsdale had been . . . Where was Scarsdale?

My nesting room was empty, except for me. My boots and socks sat next to the wall. I put them on—they were dry—and wondered what could have happened to Scarsdale. Hopefully, she'd be in a room near mine. We could grab our stuff, make nice with whatever Faerie creatures had pulled us from the jaws of death, and find out where to go to get away from the giant carnivores.

The door to my room had no lock or handle, but opened silently at a touch, swinging inward.

My round room turned out to be part of a larger round edifice. A circular chamber lay before me with a number of doors identical to mine. Across the chamber, a hall led to what I hoped would be freedom.

A sparkling confetti outline shimmered around the form of a liondog. The creature had been sitting guard, blocking the hallway. It turned solid as sparks drifted up to the ceiling.

I wasn't getting out that way. Not with a ten-foot tall wall of fur-plus-teeth between me and the exit.

Nagdabbit.

Where was Scarsdale?

Keeping an eye on the guard dog, I moved to the door of the room next to mine. If it didn't have an occupant, maybe it had another door. I'd even settle for a window. I touched the door and it swung away and I stole a glance.

Empty. No door. No window.

The liondog let me check another room. I kept an eye on him anyway as I passed the room where I'd been sleeping and tried the next one.

Empty.

As I turned back toward the middle chamber, the guard dog started panting. Bits of those rainbow scintillas flickered in his eyes. Panting started looking a whole lot like laughing.

Pointing at the next room, I asked, "Is that one empty too?"

Guard dog tilted his head a bit but kept huffing with his tongue out.

"You want the shirt that goes with those pants?" I asked.

Guard dog closed his mouth and regarded me with a curious expression.

"I can guess what kind of breed you are. Jerkshire terrier."

With a sigh, the liondog settled on his belly, letting his paws stick out in front of him. He resembled a canine sphinx, only without the headgear, and started panting again. Or laughing.

Guess he's letting me off the hook.

I checked the last two rooms in my little cul-de-sac and found I had the whole place to myself. No Scarsdale. No way out.

Well, puppy nuggets.

Regrettably, I was stuck. On the other hand, I still had one trick. I called up my power and said, "Tine." Fire bloomed in my hand. In these close quarters, and me able to see the liondog, I was pretty sure I'd be able to even the odds if it came to it.

Guard dog pricked up his ears and pulled his tongue back in his mouth. He didn't growl and he didn't move from his spot blocking the exit. My fire made red-orange swirls in his eyes.

He did the darnedest thing.

He lowered his head and sniffed, shifting his nose around. Then he raised one paw and reached out as if he wanted to touch the fire. With me standing ten feet away, he rolled onto his side and reached out with the other paw, scooting a few inches closer.

Neither afraid nor aggressive, it was like he wanted to play.

What kind of guard dog is this?

He inched closer, switching from one paw to another as he swatted gingerly toward the fire. I stood where I was, watching the creature scoot toward me while at the same time opening the way out.

"You like the pretty fire?" I ignited my other hand, waving twin flames. He paused for a moment, his head moving back, suddenly serious. Then he resumed his panting and pawing. Grinning at the pair of dancing lures he moved toward me a foot or two at a time.

"Do you want to play?" I wheedled. "Come on. It's a nice fire."

Finally, drawing close, the liondog sniffed again. His muzzle inched forward, then backed off with the heat, then cautiously moved closer to sniff again.

He sneezed and my flames went out.

The chuff of air surprised me. "Hey!" I said.

The liondog rolled over on his back. The floor shook as his weight dropped to the stones and he resumed panting. His tongue lolled out the side of his mouth like a thick wet blanket, the noise he made sounding more like a laugh than before.

On his back, with his paws in the air, he seemed to be begging.

"I'm not rubbing your belly." I called my power to reignite my flames and said, "Tine." The hall was open now and—what in blazes or the lack thereof? My power wasn't working. I couldn't call it up. I tried again, looking for a droplet of blue power to materialize in the palm of my hand.

Nothing.

Oodles of poodle doodles.

The liondog turned his head and rolled his eyes in my direction. He half-laughed, half-barked and I had the feeling his sneeze hadn't been entirely accidental.

He was either the most idiotic puppy ever, or he was the most adorably diabolical saboteur.

His sneeze had left me powerless.

# CHAPTER 21
## Misunderstandings and Baggy Pants

Being disconnected from my power left me shaken. I'd only been using magic for a year, but I'd grown accustomed to feeling the quiet thrum of energy ever present in my core. With it unavailable, it felt like suddenly going deaf or losing my sense of touch.

Was it simply deactivated? Or completely gone?

The liondog stopped panting, or laughing, long enough to listen to my question. "Was that on purpose?"

In response, the beast made a sound between a chuckle and a bark.

"That's not helpful," I retorted. "A guy can't trust anybody around here. Can you hear the rue in my voice? I speak ruefully. My voice is full of rue. You can hear rue, right?"

The liondog laugh-barked again.

"This is your fault."

The dog rolled, getting his feet under him. I shuffled to the side to get out of his way.

"At least you aren't trying to eat me."

The dog stared at me. He licked his chops, but it wasn't clear if he was thinking that sounded tasty or disgusting.

"You haven't eaten my friend, have you?"

He responded only by stepping behind me and crowding my space. To stay out of his way, I moved toward the hall.

I'm being herded again.

As if hearing my thoughts, he nudged me with his nose, propelling me down the hall. Like an errant, weakling pup, I stumbled along the passageway, sore at being tricked or letting my guard down.

Granted, I wasn't the most well-versed mage in the Behindbeyond, but I'd never heard of anyone losing their power. The only time I'd ever been without mine since my ten-thousandth dawn was when I'd used it all up. Eventually—quickly, usually—it recharged on its own.

Meanwhile, I was a liondog's push toy.

"I'm going, I'm going." Perhaps he felt the need to keep bumping me, although it wasn't mean or malicious.

Maybe they're just nice to their food, up until the dinner bell.

The bump-and-stroll was doing nothing to alleviate the throbbing in my head.

"Hey, Clifford, you aren't the one that smacked me in the head, are you? Because if that was you, I want to register a complaint with the A.S.P.C.H. They have offices everywhere. You've heard of them, right? Animal Society for the Prevention of Cruelty to Halflings?"

Bump.

Swell.

The passageway was curved. A fact I finally noticed after colliding with the wall due to not watching where I was going. That earned me a laugh-bark.

The room where I'd been herded was a huge rotunda of sorts. There were broad terraces made of stone, climbing to an elevated platform with a wide throne. The throne turned out to be one big doggie bed, but no dog sat in the throne.

Scarsdale did.

She chatted with another human figure dressed in earth-tone robes. His pants were the parachute variety. Baggy and loose. And the shirt looked more like a vest than a shirt. Gold buttons decorated the front, but the man was muscular enough the buttons could never have been introduced to their companion buttonholes, let alone fastened. Scarsdale was short enough that her legs didn't reach the floor from her perch, and she swung them as she smiled at her companion. If I didn't know better, I'd say Scarsdale and the man were long-time friends, but that made no sense at all. The man had a tablet or a slate of some kind, which he showed to Scarsdale. She read it and laughed and put her hand on his arm. Shoot. With that level of intimacy, they could be dating.

How long have I been unconscious?

"Mully."

Scarsdale turned away from the prince of muscles. "Good morning, Detective." She eyed me with a clear stare. "Sleep well?" She gestured over my shoulder to someone at the border of the rotunda. In moments, a rolling cart laden with food was at my elbow. The aromas of a roadside diner wafted up to my nose and my stomach decided to give me a poke. I hadn't eaten for hours.

"We weren't sure what you'd like." Scarsdale smiled. "There are pancakes, waffles, eggs, bacon, ham, toast, hash browns. There's also coffee, tea, juice. Do any of those work for you?"

"Sure." Somehow, during naptime, Scarsdale had inexplicably been elected queen of the dog pound. "Might as well have some of everything. After, we can go outside and make sure this place landed properly on the Wicked Witch of the East. Then I'll collect my ruby slippers and head on home."

Scarsdale exchanged a look with M.C. Hambone in the baggy pants while Clifford came around the side of me, shaking his big, fur-bearin' noggin. He gave me the laugh-bark again.

"I can give you an explanation. You're in my world now."

Scarsdale's body erupted in a shower of multi-colored sparks like a Skittles factory had detonated from inside her, except the Skittles all glowed with an inner light. Each glowing Skittle rose to the ceiling and winked out one by one like a miniature galaxy fading with the dawn.

I stared at the creature who stood before me.

"Madrasceartán?"

The liondog nodded her head then shook herself all over. She dropped to a sit and used a hind leg to scratch behind her ear.

"Okay," I began. "First, points to me for saying your name correctly even though I am freaked to the core. Second, what is going on?"

Madrasceartán blinked at me.

"I like surprises, but I hate a liar, Mads. How long have you been impersonating a Federal agent? Which, by the way, is a felony in the mortal realm."

Mads shrugged.

"That long, huh? Is Scarsdale aware you're pretending to be her?"

Saying I was freaked to the core was only half of it. This felt like a setup. I hated setups more than secrets. All the events of the last day landed on me like Dorothy's Kansas home, which really set me off. "And back to personal matters, why did you hide from me? I thought we were friends. What about that fight back in the swamp? I'm still sore where you kicked me in the face. And I just about killed myself getting past the crocodile pit while you were playing at being a human? Why?"

Mental magnets clicked together. "Poodles. You slashed Skullder's leg. And you wounded that deer in the woods. I knew that was too convenient." Accusations. "You harmed a mortal. You could have helped me but instead you hurt me. You've been lying and hiding things from me, and the only reason I can think of for doing that is because you find it amusing. And you're the one who knocked me out. In the snow. Smacked me to the ground like a pancake."

Mads got back on all fours and stretched herself, loosening her big stupid muscles after they'd been cramped into Scarsdale's form. She bowed to Baggy-Pants-and-Biceps and they pressed their foreheads together. He stroked the side of her dumb fuzzy face and then she turned back to me. There was pain in her eyes. I didn't care.

"People are depending on me," I snarled, betrayed. "You've made everything worse."

Mads turned tail and sauntered out of the room.

I watched her go. The sound of my breathing hung heavy in the air.

The guy in the so-small vest had a wounded look on his face too. The liondog that had bumped me in here walked around the back of him and sat, looking at me accusingly.

Baggy Pants had an eraser and chalk. He swiped at the slate with a brisk stroke of the eraser and then hammered down some words with the chalk. He turned the slate so I could read what he had written.

That's my wife you're shouting at.

I looked up from the slate. "Who are you?"

He pressed a hand against his chest. His features were dark and his expression of concern made them darker. He erased the slate and wrote a word and showed it to me.

Gadharchéile.

"Great, Gad . . . Guy . . . Or—whatever. Leave me alone."

Gadharchéile pressed his lips together in a hard line.

There was breakfast that needed eating. I grabbed the handle of the cart and rolled it over to a stone bench. A chair sat waiting, but I wanted to be away from anyone annoying, which meant anyone else. I sat and ate. The food wasn't the only thing I chewed on.

Scarsdale had arrived with Petit-Palais on what I thought of as yesterday. She'd stood in my home. I'd provided her with refreshment and witty congeniality. She'd asked about the scratches on my piano, which she had caused herself. Madrasceartán, the liondog, had defiled my Steinway. The gouges in the wood were her fault and I'd left them there as a reminder that there were things I didn't understand but should be wary of. She'd given me cause to be wary again today. Even though I couldn't have known it was her at the time, I had welcomed her into my home. In return, she'd bludgeoned me into hers.

I sighed.

I was being a jerk.

And the waffles were really good.

Furthermore, there was the small matter of Mads saving my life. She'd prevented me from being obliterated by Spreasán, the exploding groom. My father's castle had a room full of floaty gunk bits. My bits could have been in there as well, if Mads hadn't pulled me out.

Still, she could have helped get across the croc pit. She could have told me we were heading into the territory of the liondogs. Territory she seemed to know like the back of her hand. Erm. Paw.

She could have trusted me as I'd trusted her.

With a final bite of bacon, I stood up from my breakfast. My stomach was full and the time for me to whine at an end.

I gave Guy-or . . . Baggy Pants a nod. "The food was exquisite." I hoped he would accept the compliment as a gesture of conciliation. I didn't feel so cranky after eating. Sleeping hadn't done any damage either.

It worried me a little that Nat would be looking for me this morning. He wouldn't know what to tell Erin.

"Is there a way to get a message to someone in the mortal realm?"

Baggy Pants fixed me with a stare so medium-average I couldn't tell at all what he was thinking. Maybe he didn't know the answer. Maybe he was peeved at me and didn't want to answer.

Maybe I couldn't blame him.

Finally, he gave the shortest possible bow and extended a hand to an archway leading out of the rotunda. I went where he indicated. He followed close behind, giving me the feeling again of being herded. The hallway curved one way and then the other. We passed more doors and more hallways.

As we walked, I explained. "My friend will be looking for me. If I don't get a message to him, he'll have a search party combing through the swamp."

Baggy Pants tilted his head and nodded to let me know he was listening.

"And my wife will worry. Is there a way to tell them I'm all right?"

No answers. All I got from Baggy Pants was the palm of his hand, held up in a way that begged my patience.

I wasn't exactly overflowing with that.

We descended some steps. The air in the rotunda had been warm. Here, it started to cool. The swirling music of a small creek drifted up from somewhere ahead.

"Look, I need to contact my people. If I can't, I need to leave and come back, but I really can't spare the time." I felt my voice get louder to the point of being strident.

Baggy Pants shook his head and his finger at me with equal vigor.

"Are you saying I can't go back to the mortal realm? I walked around the barrow counter-clockwise so I could. That's the rule, isn't it?"

189

With a nod, Baggy Pants finally used the slate. He wrote three words:

Five minutes. Follow.

Begging patience again with his hand, he gave a gentle smile. I saw some formidable dental work behind his lips, including canine teeth that were very canine. Long. Sharp. Did I mention long?

I sighed.

Baggy Pants led the way to another set of stairs. We emerged from the building into a familiar wintry landscape. Here, at least, the bite of the wind was cut by the round castle and the trees. We followed a path that ran parallel to the creek that burbled and sang through a grove of little maple trees. The points of their leaves were so sharp and so red they seemed to have cut open some creature's veins and taken the blood into themselves.

Baggy Pants stopped along a quiet stretch of water. We stood on a broad boulder flat and round enough for King Arthur and all his knights to sit upon.

My host picked a red leaf from a low branch and let it fall in a slow arc to the water. Because he seemed so intent on watching the leaf, I watched too. The leaf drifted on the current and got caught in an eddy that pulled it back upstream. It swirled around in a full circle. When it reached the place where it had first touched the water, the little red leaf vanished with an audible fwosht and became seven large, green leaves.

Baggy Pants grinned at me.

"Nice work, Mr. Copperfield," I said dryly. "If you can do that with Vegas showgirls, you'll have something."

I got a sidelong glare.

"If you haven't noticed, he can't explain in words."

The woman's voice was loud, skimming over the fallen crust of snow with perfect clarity. I turned to find a familiar face.

Béil.

# CHAPTER 22
## Púcaland

Words weren't often elusive for me. For a brief moment—or many—they were.

Behind Béil was another guy in baggy pants and a tight vest. He had large canine ears with tufts of fur on the ends and he gave me a grin that was happier than not. He all but let his tongue loll out of his mouth and, if I had to guess, he was the big puppy who had sat watching the hallway outside the room where I'd awakened. He stood behind Béil protectively like a bodyguard.

Béil was dressed in a fur-lined cloak, the leather red like the leaves, with a silvery gown beneath it. Her expression was coy and smug, like she knew how shocked I'd be to see her. I found myself shifting to a conciliatory stance, forcing nonchalance.

"All right," I finally said. "Consider yourself rescued. Let's go get Laoch."

"Similar to Gadharchéile, yet different, I can't explain," Béil said. "Not directly. You have to figure it out."

The words had to sink in for a moment. Then I caught on. Sort of. "Wait a second. The way you speak. You're speaking smoothly."

"Yes, I most certainly am speaking smoothly."

Béil spoke haltingly as a rule, as she had with Alyce and me in her cavern of a bedroom. It was a side effect of a deal she'd made with a deamhanlord, and it made her speech staggered and strained. She could only say two or three words at a time before pausing.

With one exception.

"The only time Béil has spoken smoothly was in my dream," I said. "But we aren't in any dream. I know what that feels like and this isn't it."

"Correct."

"It seems unlikely that the deamhanlord's curse has been lifted. Deamhan curses tend to be binding until death."

"Also correct."

"So you are not Béil, although you look like her."

"Very good."

"Is Oz around?"

Oz was one of only a handful of Seachmall mages who were able to make people look like other people. He'd made me look like a woman once, for an awkward three minutes.

Béil—or the person who looked like Béil—shook her head. "There are neither illusions here nor glamours."

"Okay." Heat began rising along my neck. This had been fun for a minute. No longer. "Then you are a person who likes to become other people and be devious and generally unhelpful all day, every day, so I can only make the assumption that you're Madrasceartán wearing yet another phony body and torturing me again. Thanks for nothing. Please show me the exit. I have things to do."

Béil sighed. The downturn of her eyes and tilt of her head were evidence I'd wounded her. Wounded Mads. I only felt a little bit sorry.

"May I ask you a question, Prince Luck? Several questions, actually."

"Sure."

"You have come to understand that words of thanks are an acknowledgment of debt—a contract that can bind one's soul to servitude—have you not?"

"Yup."

"And you no longer give thanks in the realm of the Fae?"

"Nope."

"That is good."

"Dandy. Can I go now?"

She ignored me. "This place, the home of my people, lies on the borders of Tír na nÓg. Is that not your destination?"

I crossed my arms. "Yeah."

Mads went on, showing more patience to me than I would to her. "You are in the realm of the Goddess of Dreams. A place where the name Caer Ibormeith must be spoken with reverence." Suiting deed to word, she curtsied. "Her name be ever blessed."

Clearly, Mads-Béil had a point to make. I'd let her make it.

"The customs of the Fae were strange to you at first, but there are reasons for them. In Tír na nÓg, the reasons are far more strange, and therefore the customs more important in their following."

"So I'm never going to get a straight answer here and I have to be content with that." I shifted my weight to the other foot and tried to ignore the cold seeping into my shoes. "Got it."

Mads-Béil gave me a narrow-eyed glance. "It's true we can only hint at things you might want to know. Unlike any other realm, the goddess here has never had to share her kingdom or its secrets. This makes her more jealous and more careful than any other. We remain here on her borders at her pleasure. Our fealty has been forsworn for millennia. Our duties as protectors of those who visit are secondary only to our duties as protectors of her home."

"M'kay."

Mads-Béil stepped closer, placing a hand on my arm.

"When we dream, the experience is passive. We have little control over what happens and we have little explanation. Occasionally, we may find the power to make choices and guide the experience. Some may be able to interpret the meaning of their dreams, but the gift is rare. The things of Tír na nÓg are no different." She lowered her voice. Almost a whisper. "And the deeper you go into her realm, the harder it is to know what's real. We can't answer questions for you, but we will mind a clever one if one is clever in the mind."

Two can play at the rhyme game. "So. I'm in the middle of a riddle?" Mads-Béil almost smiled. "I'm so excited I could piddle."

The almost-smile went away.

"Look, Mads. I'm listening. I know you're helping in some way and I'll pay attention and try to get what you're hinting at. Okay?"

Mads-Béil offered a sour expression.

"The leaf in the whirlpool thing. Amazing. I'll figure it out, I promise. Meanwhile, is there a way to contact Fáidh? Or Nat?"

"There is no need. Figure out the meaning of the leaf and you'll understand."

"You're just going to keep telling me to figure out the leaf?"

Mads-Béil nodded, doing nothing to soothe my concerns.

Fine.

I'll do what I came here to do, quickly, and get home.

"Okay. If you can't tell me anything immediately useful, can you help me find the real Béil or Laoch? And how come you look like Béil anyway?"

With another nod, Mads-Béil turned around and led the way back into the round castle.

Maybe she'd give me something useful after all.

We returned to the hall leading back to the rotunda. The guy with the puppy ears bounded ahead, but the rest of us walked. Puppy Guy waited for us at the top of the stairs. As soon as we arrived, he loped away again. Mads-Béil detoured to another set of stairs going up, and I followed.

Puppy Guy met us on the landing of the next floor, bouncing on the balls of his feet like he couldn't contain himself. When Mads-Béil stepped onto the top step he dashed off once more.

Somebody give the kid a jerky treat already.

We trooped down a short, curving hallway that ended at a large, heavy door. Silver inlays depicted liondogs and humans speaking with one another and drinking together from chalices. Exquisitely crafted. Epically ancient. It appeared that liondogs and the Fae had been acquainted for centuries. I had only a few moments to appreciate the artistry of the door before Puppy Guy opened it for us. He gave a bow that straddled the line between servitude and sarcasm.

Beyond the door lay another rotunda. The domed ceiling had more scenes of liondogs in full frolic, but the human figures seemed more stern. Around the perimeter of the room stood door-sized slabs of agate. There were at least thirty pieces of the thick stone, polished to a mirror-like gloss. The banded patterns in the rock were a riot of different hues. The edges were natural, for the most part, leaving

194

few straight lines. Whoever had worked with the rock had left them irregularly shaped, and no two stones were the same. Natural history museums would go to war to have such pieces in their collections.

Puppy Guy waited, unable to stand still. His grin was barely disguised. If he got any more excited, he'd blow a blood vessel.

We stopped in front of a slab that had white and pink bands of chalcedony and quartz. The pattern curved and folded through the rock as if Mother Nature had been trying to write a word on a billboard in some foreign script and gotten lost. Each of the slabs had a pedestal of stone in front of it holding different objects. Coins, locks of hair, and assorted other items. On the pedestal in front of us was a silver necklace.

Mads-Béil nodded at the slab of agate, bigger than a king-size bed. "Watch." She put her hand on the necklace. There was a hum in the rock that turned into a note like a bell. A soft light rose within the stone, making it appear much deeper than the four inches of its actual depth.

Inside the stone, as if standing in a display window at the mall, a woman's image faded into view.

Béil.

She appeared to be asleep. No different from last time I saw her.

Mads-Béil explained, "Her image is here for as long as we need it."

"It looks perfect. Why do you have it?"

"We were commanded to hold her essence. As she is an Eternal, we are not allowed to take more."

I let her words sink in. A growing sense of dread started to burn in my core as I figured out what was wrong with that statement.

"You're not allowed to take more of an Eternal? More than what? Are you saying you can take actual people if they aren't Eternals?"

"Let me show him!" Puppy Guy spoke at last, his voice gravelly and rough. Heh heh. Ruff.

Mads-Béil nodded.

My fists were balled up at my sides as I followed Puppy Guy. Whatever he was about to show me, I felt certain I wasn't going to like it. He led me out of the rotunda of agate into the adjacent room.

Here, there were tombs.

Constructed of the same beautiful stone as the slabs, the tombs were exquisite, but a coffin is a coffin as sure as jeebies come from heebies. The room was lit dimly and, I couldn't be certain how many coffins there were. A lot. Near the door, Puppy Guy walked around the back of a coffin and rested his hands on the edge, leaning in to look at the body occupying the tomb. Part of me didn't want to look, but the badge sitting on the pedestal by the coffin was an adequate clue. I looked.

Special Agent Scarsdale lay in the coffin, but she wasn't posed like a dead person. Instead of lying face up in the usual way, she rested on her side. Her hands were curled together under her cheek and her legs drawn partway up in a natural curve. And there was no cover on the coffin. It was open to the air and the only odor was one of shampoo and soap.

She sighed and stretched. I found myself taking a step back as the jeebies took over, because this was still creepy. Mads-Béil appeared at my elbow.

"Again, Mads, kidnapping is a criminal offense." The words tasted sour. "You have to wake her up and send her home."

"I have my orders," Mads-Béil replied. "If you want to understand, figure out the leaf." She left the room.

Puppy Guy grinned. Either he'd gotten the reaction he wanted out of me or he just enjoyed the general weirdness. I glanced again at Scarsdale's sleeping form. She seemed comfortable. Blissful even.

I found Mads-Béil beside the essence stone, hand on Béil's necklace. The light within the stone was diffused, a blue chiaroscuro that illuminated her in romantic shades.

"I don't understand this." I didn't look at Mads-Béil as I spoke. Rather, I looked at her shadowed reflection in the essence stone. "But I can guess. This is my father's doing. He asked you to take on the appearance of the mortal. Am I right?"

Mads-Béil nodded.

"He asked you to follow me and not tell me what was going

on. But he didn't ask you to keep me from following my case. That means he doesn't care about me doing my job, which tells me this is about something else."

"Good." Mads-Béil smiled thinly. She looked down at the necklace. "You're right. I can tell you that Spreasán's family demands your arrest over his death. They want to interrogate you to find a reason to execute you. As a Halfling, you are adept at lying. They have concerns."

"What? I'm too good at lying?"

"In part. Eternals can always tell when a mortal is lying. Not so with Halflings. There are other issues."

"Like what?"

"You might be in league with Urlabhraí and the Dubhcridhe."

Heat flared in my collar again. "Seriously?"

"That is the rumor. You are a Halfling. Therefore, you could be sympathetic to their cause. You had an opportunity to kill Urlabhraí, but he escaped. Therefore, you could have let him go."

It was pointless to raise any protest. Mads wasn't judging me. She was explaining facts.

"Furthermore, you could have decided Spreasán had become a liability and therefore you could have murdered him to keep the plans of the Dubhcridhe safe."

All I could do was nod. Mads had been with me while I'd been talking with Spreasán, but she couldn't be certain I hadn't used magic. I was very good with fire. A fact that had been pointed out to me more than once.

"So, under the guise of a mortal, you followed me. You were very convincing."

"It is our most singular skill. When we take the essence of someone, we also take their way of thinking. It allows us to feel the way they would feel. Think the way they would think. Act the way they would act."

I understood. "That's why you make such good assassins." There was no need to be shy about the purpose for their skill. I knew what Mads did when she worked for my father.

"Yes."

"If I may turn the tables for a moment, why haven't you assassinated Urlabhraí yourself?"

The shadow Mads-Béil turned to look at me in the face. I turned to look back.

"If you were in league with Urlabhraí, you would have led me to him."

Ah.

"How long have you been following me?"

"Since Spreasán's death. If you were working for the Dubhcridhe, you would have contacted him by now. Or received a message of some kind. But you haven't."

"My father doesn't trust me." I was only half surprised.

"Your father isn't the suspicious one. Just because he gave me the order to follow you doesn't mean he did so from a lack of trust. The idea was suggested to him."

"Who planted that stupid idea in his head then? You?"

Mads-Béil's eyes lingered on mine but I couldn't read her. "I can offer testimony that will favor you."

"You didn't answer my question."

"Indeed not. I will happily testify, however, that you are fair in your treatment of others. I have observed your concern for other mortals, even those whom you despise. You made certain Petit-Palais would get the medical attention he needed. You provided goods to a complete stranger to better care for her children. You went out of your way to preserve the life of a rather annoying mortal when faced with the task of overcoming a rather large and vicious crocodile. For which I am grateful and impressed."

"Sure." I rolled my eyes. "I'm a peach of a guy. But you didn't need my help getting past the crocodile, right?"

"You didn't know that."

"True. But you could have dropped the pretense, right? You could have returned to your liondog form if you needed to, right?"

"We are not liondogs." Mads-Béil's eyebrows fell together and her lips twisted.

"What are you?"

"We are called Púca."

"Púca?" I nodded repeatedly, savoring the word. "That has a tasty sound. Is there, by chance, a Winnie-the-Pooh-ka?"

Puppy Guy laughed. I looked at his ears and remembered where I'd heard the word Púca before: an old movie with Jimmy Stewart. "Oh, man." I shook my head at Puppy Guy. "I am so calling you Harvey from now on." Harvey frowned and tilted his head.

Mads-Béil growled. "Mock us at your peril. To answer your question, I didn't wish to drop my cover until its purpose had been served. It is easier to retain it than resume it."

"I guess I understand." I allowed a grin to steal across my face. "Out of curiosity, in a battle between a giant crocodile and a Púca, who would win?"

"I believe, Prince Luck, it's time for you to go."

"Wait." I looked at the other members of the liondog club. "These guys are wearing essences, aren't they? But Harvey has ears like a Púca, and your husband, I noticed, has fangs."

"Yes. We all retain a part of our natural selves, even when assuming the guise of another. My nephew always has his ears. This makes it a challenge for him to pass unnoticed, but there are hats." She put her arms around her husband's waist. "As Púca, we do not have the mouth parts for speech. As a human, my beloved remains silent. He is, however, a most deadly opponent."

Baggy Pants gave Mads-Béil a squeeze and a warm, toothy smile.

"What about you, Mads?"

Mads-Béil sighed and lifted the side of her cloak. A long, tan tail emerged with a silky tuft of hair on the end. She let it twitch like the tail of a cat and, by her expression, dared me to say something rude.

Intuition told me my life depended on the next words that came out of my mouth. With all the sincerity in my soul, I said, "A tail, Mads. That's amazing. And beautiful."

# CHAPTER 23
## Hew

After surviving the initial reaction test, there had to be a line I could try to cross. In any case, teasing Mads was better than being mad at Mads.

"Does your tail wag if someone scratches you behind the ears?"

"Dear Prince, shut up."

"If you're wearing pants, does your tail run down the leg or curl up on your butt?"

"Hardly appropriate."

"If you have to tail someone, you can really tail someone. Am I right?"

Mads-Béil handed my bag back. "Don't make me slap you down again."

About that. "Why did you knock me out? My head still hurts."

"You were already on the verge of exhaustion."

"Afraid I'd singe someone's fur?"

"Yes. Or set the forest on fire."

"Point taken."

"You need to know that Púca are not the only creatures in this realm. Other creatures sense magic and you'll attract them. Be careful, my prince. This may be the realm of dreams, but dreams can kill."

For a moment, my mood had turned happy again. Now it was murdered. Again.

She is an assassin.

"Prince Luck, you said you're here to find Béil. May I ask why?"

I shrugged. "She asked." That wasn't all. "I also need to find Laoch. The Dubhcridhe have abducted a lot of other kids. I'd like to bring them home. I think she could help. And, if possible, I'd like to do something for Alyce, the girl who appeared at Spreasán's wedding rehearsal."

Mads-Béil listened with a focus that was almost palpable. "Would you like some advice?"

"All right."

"Don't do this."

Was she serious?

I took a step back. "Don't do this? Why not?"

"The goddess." Mads-Béil looked at the floor, composing her thoughts, her tail twitching. "It rarely ends well when taking a thrall from the service of Caer Ibormeith, great be her name. If you are not careful, Béil could become insane."

That ship's barely still in the harbor.

"Or you could be made to serve her yourself."

That would be bad.

"If you go after Béil in the land of dreams, go with eyes wide open. So to speak."

"Holy crap, Mads. You just made a joke." I had to grin.

Mads shrugged. "Jokes can be useful, in the right time and place."

If she'd meant to imply I didn't always know the right time and place, it was okay. She wasn't wrong. A long moment passed when neither of us spoke. "Mads, I—"

"You have nothing to feel apologetic about, Prince Luck."

She was quick to catch my intention. "No. I do. I said some things I shouldn't have said. Both to you and to your husband."

Mads-Béil dismissed me with a wave of her hand. "You have more worrisome concerns ahead of you. There is no sure path to follow if you want to help Béil and the others. Like a dream itself, the place where you're going is a different kind of reality. Unpredictable. Ever changing. At times, without meaning or direction. You'll need to get to the heart of Tír na nÓg without being noticed. Once you have awakened Béil, you will have the attention of the goddess. You will need to get away before she catches you, and her resources are many."

"Okay, Mads. So come with me."

She shook her head. Not forcefully. "That would violate the pact that we have with Caer Ibormeith, ever the regal and mighty." Mads-Béil curtsied again as she paid tribute to the name of the goddess. Then she smiled and there was a certain sparkle in her eye. "That doesn't mean I cannot provide you with another."

"Who is this guide?"

Snow flew past and the wind rushed in my ears, snatching my words away. Mads-Béil and I rode in the world's grooviest sleigh, being pulled by Baggy Pants and Harvey in Púca form. The warm maple wood of the ancient sleigh had been polished to a luminous gleam, and the silver fittings had been elegantly crafted into leaping stags and charging boars. Storming down the mountain from the Castle of the Púca, sailing past the decrepit little way stop, I felt like a prince indeed, thundering over the snow in such a handsome conveyance with two white liondogs straining the traces. Their oversized paws barely touched the snow as they charged ahead. The runners of the sleigh hissed as we coursed along.

Santa Claus would wither with jealousy.

"We call his kind grand-gabhálaí." Mads-Béil shouted the answer to my question. "They serve as intermediaries between the goddess and all who dream." The wind did its best to rip her words to tatters.

"All who dream?"

"The goddess collects dreams, from every people, from every realm."

Every people? From every realm?

It was hard to fathom what that entailed. Or the results. Billions of people dreamed every night. Did she collect all of them? Collecting implied choosing from the options available. I knew I dreamed often, although my dreams usually evaporated upon waking. Still, I had to wonder if the goddess of dreams had one or two of mine in her collection.

Many of them had been ugly.

202

The evergreens swept past in a blur. Baggy Pants was the stronger Púca, but Harvey was having more fun. He ran with his tongue flapping in the wind.

Ahead, a stone wall rose up as if growing out of the ground. We slid to a stop like the coolest high school seniors ever to be late for chemistry class in Alaska. Baggy Pants shook his body, throwing off a cloud of snowflakes. Harvey plopped down on his butt and proceeded to scratch his ear with his hind leg.

I disembarked from the sleigh, running my hand appreciatively over the beautiful wood. If I ever needed a vehicle other than my beloved Mustang, I'd have a sleigh like this one. It'd look great driving around Miami.

Mush Púca.

Baggy Pants was handsome as well, in his wild animal way, taller than me at the shoulder, with massive rippling muscles and a glossy bone-white coat that was lots easier to notice when he wasn't being invisible. I stood in front of him and waved goodbye. He closed his eyes and gently lowered his face in a bow of sorts. I caught on after a second or two, remembering the gesture shared between him and Mads. I pressed my forehead against his. His face was warm and furry, and I felt a wave of gratitude. He'd been far too gracious after my bad behavior. The Púca were trained to be excellent hosts, it was true, but I hadn't earned such a warm welcome and didn't deserve such a warm farewell.

"I hope to see you again." I meant it.

Stepping to the side, I passed in front of Harvey. He dropped his chest to the snow, forepaws splayed out, leaving his hindquarters raised and his tail thrashing the air.

I scrubbed my fingers over the top of his head, ruffling his fur. "Hope to see you again too, pup."

Turning away from my new friends, I scanned the massive stone wall in front of us.

Mads-Béil regarded the wall with me. "You are familiar with Dante's Inferno?" There were steep crags and sharp-edged crevices in its face. Even with climbing gear, getting to the top would be a challenge.

"Sure. The first poem in his Divine Comedy. He depicted Hades as a having nine concentric circles of torment for the wicked."

"Exactly." Mads-Béil's eyes continued to search the stones.

It wasn't hard to reason why she'd mentioned Dante. "You're kidding. Inferno is based on Tír na nÓg?"

"Dante visited often. He was a favorite of Caer Ibormeith's court. May the night skies praise her name. There are many layers to Tír na nÓg. Dante adapted the geography for his own agenda."

"Then Inferno should be subtitled 'based on a true story.'"

Mads gave a little smile and a nod. "In the interest of full disclosure." She unfastened the harnesses, setting Baggy Pants and Harvey free. Baggy Pants sat in the snow, where he assumed an expression of vigilant calm, surveying the trees and stones. Harvey took a sniff and bounded off into the forest, kicking up snow.

Another waystation stood near the rough wall of stone. Mads-Béil led me there. The roof was mostly intact. A modest gap let snowflakes drift in like crystalline motes of dust that turned and sparkled in the light. The silver ring in the small table was whole. Mads-Béil touched the silver with her finger and the ring glowed blue. A fire sprang up from the middle of the circle, floating above the stone table like a torch without any of the torch parts.

"The guide should be here soon," Mads-Béil said. "He's not the most predictable, however. Have a seat."

"Usually, I call Midnight Dreary to guide me. Would she know this place?"

Mads-Béil shook her head. "The Behindbeyond is vast. Although your raven might be familiar with the lands outside the kingdom of your father, it's unlikely she would hear your call. Even if she did, it would take far too long for her to get here." She wore a subtle smirk that was both cryptic and annoying.

What did that mean?

I remained on my feet. The snow outside was falling again in earnest. The wall in the distance hunched, foreboding and dark, as if using the shroud of gray to hide its details. There was silence and

204

cold, softened by the weather, which made them somehow more suspect.

I looked back at Mads-Béil. "Do you need to keep wearing Béil's essence?" It was exasperating to have her acting and speaking like someone else.

Mads-Béil remained elusive. "I have reason to keep this form."

I nodded. "Sure. Yup."

Moving on.

"If this guide of yours is unpredictable, why have a guide at all?"

Mads-Béil gave half a smile, happy to have a change in topic. "He's a bit unique in the realm of dreams. He knows the ways of the goddess. While his kin usually deal with Eternals, he has ways to commune with Halflings and mortals equally. If there's a way to get Béil and Laoch out of Tír na nÓg safely, he'll know how."

"Wait a minute. He worked for Caer Ibormeith?"

"Closely. Her name be praised always and forever."

"But he helps people from the outside?"

Mads-Béil shrugged, losing patience. "Did you not hear me well, Prince?"

"I heard you. I just need to know where his allegiances are. If he worked so closely with such a powerful being, can I trust him?"

That smirk returned. Mads-Béil raised her chin and folded her arms. She said, "Why don't you ask him yourself? He's standing behind you."

I turned. The guide wore a skull for a helmet. I didn't recognize the species, but the eye sockets were slanted and the teeth as sharp as knives. Heavy bone covered the guide's shoulders and chest. His entire ensemble, in fact, was comprised of skeletal remains, turning ivory with age. He carried a spear with another bone, sharp and serrated, on the end of a polished black shaft, inlaid with silver.

Under the armor, his tunic and pants were furry and dark. He wore the skins of beasts, if he wasn't a beast himself. Most strikingly, through the sockets of the skull, the guide's eyes were fierce blue rings set in obsidian.

He presented a savage and dangerous figure.

He was also two feet tall.

I'd missed him at first. After Mads-Béil warned me to turn around, I looked behind me and saw the waystation wall. Then I looked down.

I strenuously resisted the urge to say, "Hey, little guy!" The spear he carried was pointy and aimed, purposefully or otherwise, at the environs of my femoral artery. If he managed to stick me, I'd bleed out in minutes.

"Hail, Mother of Púcas." The guide's voice was oddly gruff even though it was pitched in the soprano range. He sounded like a schoolgirl imitating Batman.

"Hail, Slayer of Nightmares." Mads-Béil's response sounded serious and genuine. She respected this little warrior.

The guide strode around me, hefting the spear as he walked. "This is the son of the Alder King?"

"Indeed."

"He's not much to look at. His father, as I recall, is a barrel-chested, brawny man."

Yeah? You'd have to stand on his head to be taller than me.

Mads-Béil tried to vouch for me. "Prince Luck makes up for his lack of stature with cleverness and bravery."

Lack of stature? What about the shrimp with the barby over there?

"Yup." I ignored the jabs and extended a hand. "Call me 'Got.' As in I 'got' cleverness. And also 'got' bravery."

"We'll see." Instead of a shake, my hand got a stare. "Call me 'Hew.' As in I 'hew' down all those who oppose me. Or annoy me." He shook his toothpick-slash-butter-knife at me for emphasis. "You stink of Halfling magic."

I cleared my throat and took a half step back as a favor to my femoral artery. In self-defense, I said, "I make up for it with great hair."

Hew stared at me for three full seconds before he spoke. "You what?"

"I have great hair. It's a perfectly-balanced combination of wavy and curly."

Hew looked at Mads-Béil while he kept one eye on me. "Does he do that a lot?"

Mads-Béil gave a shrug. "Mostly when it's least appropriate."

Hew grumbled and glowered. "And we're trying to find a woman?"

"Yes." Mads-Béil turned in a circle to show herself off. "This is her essence."

Hew regarded her sharply. He tilted his head in quick motions that were almost birdlike, taking in Béil's face and form. "Got anything of hers?"

Mads-Béil handed Hew the barrow key. "She had this at one point."

Hew took the barrow key and examined it, then popped it into his mouth.

"Hey!" I protested. "I need that back."

Hew spit it out and held for me to take. "The more of this woman's essence I can get, the easier it will be to track her down, but suit yourself." The key glistened with saliva.

Yuck. "I'll get it back later."

Hew stuffed the barrow key into a small pack and walked all the way around Mads-Béil, sniffing at her clothes and her hands. He beckoned for her to bend forward and sniffed her hair.

"Got it," he nodded. "We'll find her." He shifted his gaze to stare at me. "Assuming we don't get eaten."

Those are the kind of comments that require more information. "Why would we get eaten? Exactly?"

Mads-Béil answered. "Like I said, some creatures sense magic."

"And some creatures eat magic, along with the mage," Hew growled. "You reek of it. Your magic is new or unbridled. Or both." He stepped toward me and turned his head so his left eye could appraise me fully. "But don't worry, with that great hair of yours, you'll make a right handsome corpse."

Nifty. "I've never felt more prepared for a mission. Show the way, Hew."

Mads-Béil clasped forearms with Hew in a way that suggested familiarity. It was like a handshake if the hands overshot their target and grabbed halfway to the elbow. I felt left out. Like they were part of a secret fraternity and I hadn't been invited to rush.

Hew didn't bother to look over his shoulder as he trudged out of the sheltering waystation. The snow had stopped completely, leaving the sky open and bracing cold. Small clouds like delicate feathers drifted in clusters of wispy white.

Mads came out just behind us. She released Béil's essence as I watched, and the change was startling. Footfall turned to pawfall from one step to the next. Béil vanished—her body, her clothing, her demeanor and carriage. In her place, a tall, shaggy creature floated across the snow, drifting over the crystalline whiteness like a wraith. She touched noses with Baggy Pants and they loped back up the hill, impromptu clouds of snow flying skyward in their wake.

I found myself alone with my little guide.

Ahead, the black wall of rock loomed. Foreboding was too gentle a word. The cliff looked like it wanted to swallow us whole and then chew us up, crushing meat and breaking bones. Hew disappeared into the maw of rock, but I stopped at the entrance.

"What's in here?"

"The liagán circle of Caer Ibormeith. All hail queen of the night places."

Onward.

The floor of the cave was uneven and slick. I squinted into the shadows for secure footing. An electric thrum beat within the walls as if there was a power plant somewhere behind the stones. My eyes adjusted to the gloom. The walls sported jagged edges and protrusions like axe blades. Overhead, the ceiling was a haphazard dome with no birds making nests and no bats hanging by their feet. Whether intentional or otherwise, the hum kept the wildlife out. As it was, the feeling and the sound set my teeth on edge.

The cave didn't penetrate far into the rock, and the liagán circle waited two hundred yards inside. Like the cave, the stones were rough and jagged.

Hew waited in the circle. Nine stones with symbols carved in them.

"Your woman is mostly likely held here." Hew pressed his hand against a stone. It flared blue and there was a change in the atmosphere, but the stone remained black and bleak.

"Is it open?"

"It's night. Follow closely and stay silent."

Hew hopped through the portal.

# CHAPTER 24
## Into the Night Places

Stagnant air hung heavily all around. The change from crisp and mountainous to dank and dead made it difficult to breathe.

"It's like being in a tomb. Anyone hear of a cool evening breeze?"

"Sometimes, people dream about them. Now shut up."

Okay.

A narrow path wound through tall rocks. Hew set off at a quick pace. He was quiet and quick, despite his armor of bone and the tools he carried. Silver implements with bone handles I hadn't noticed before were arranged across the back of his pack, and I had to wonder what they could be for.

Feeling like a three-year-old kid in a graveyard overcrowded with monolithic headstones, I followed as quietly as I could. I wasn't supernaturally quiet like Nat, but I'd hunted animals in forests and tracked terrorists in cities and could capably hold my own on different kinds of terrain. Dodging rocks twice my height was almost fun.

Hew moved with purpose. Being small, he had no trouble slipping between the pillars. It took more effort for me. A few times I had to turn sideways to pass, but I managed to get by almost grunt free.

The rocks got shorter after a bit, with more space between them. Finally, we emerged into a grassy glade surrounded by maple trees with a scattering of short stones. A sliver of silver light came from somewhere, although I was unable to find a moon overhead. Still, the grass and the twilight made me want to enjoy a jog through the scenery despite the dead, unappealing air.

Hew stopped in his tracks in the middle of the glade and I nearly ran him over.

Tempted to ask him what was happening, I refrained and watched instead.

For a few long moments, Hew froze. Then his free hand moved and it did so smoothly, reaching into a pocket and withdrawing a piece of silver and bone. I looked where Hew looked.

Movement among the trunks. Dark and misshapen.

"Prionsa mí-ádh," Hew muttered under his breath. I knew the first word meant "prince" but I wasn't familiar with the second word. From the way he said it, he'd called me a name that was far from complimentary.

Hew handed me his piece of silver, which was held by a detached bony hand.

Yikes.

"That's a dullahan in the trees. By all the sleeping stars, you stink. Pardon my saying so."

"Pardon granted. What's a dullahan?"

"A fair nasty beast. A most vile eater of magic and meat. The one thing I'd hoped to avoid most. He must have caught your scent the moment we arrived. He'll lay by for a time, but he'll come for thee. Make no mistake."

The chagrin I felt must have shown on my face. Hew patted my knee and tapped the tool in my hand. "Give this power then draw a circle on the ground with it and leave it at the joining. Understand?"

Nodding and feeling even more like a child, I knelt on the ground. The process for feeding power into the silver piece was the same as using the healing medallion. The blue light was comforting in my hand and channeled almost instantly into the shiny talisman.

The bony handle in my hand, I started a circle, using the silver part to draw an arc of glowing blue on the ground. I turned as I dragged the silver over the dirt and grass until I'd gone all the way around. As soon as the line met the beginning point, the silver piece stopped by itself as if welded to the earth, refusing to move. With a snap, a thin wall of power leapt heavenward; its light was decorated with intricate filigrees and whorls. As it rose, the light thinned out.

A couple of feet above the ground, it seemed to fade completely, although I felt its power radiating in at me from much higher.

Hew nodded, satisfied. "Whatever happens, don't leave the circle."

"Sure."

"And don't use any other magic. You'll ruin the spell." With that, Hew looked toward the trees as if I'd ceased to exist. He headed off at an angle and within moments, he was a scant shadow among the shadows.

No other magic? All I do is wait?

Movement through the distant trees caught my eye.

This is so not good.

If my guide was afraid, then I needed to be afraid as well.

My training and my instincts told me I was exposed and vulnerable here, which made everything worse. I needed to find cover. Here, with no rocks or brush or trees to screen me from whatever had Hew spooked, I was tactically naked. And naked was as good as dead.

Okay.

Not quite naked.

I had a thin wall of magical power surrounding me. My guide thought it would be enough.

He seemed to know what he was doing.

Mads trusted him.

With an angry sigh, I tried to relax. My hands felt sweaty. I wiped them on my pants. A chill set in my guts. Little I could about that. My pack sat beside me in the circle. With an eye on the distant maples, I felt inside for a knife and found the one made of sterling silver.

Something to hold on to.

The patch of dark had detached itself from the trees. It came loping toward me on four legs like a horse with a weirdly misshapen rider. The thing didn't have a well-defined Stain, but it was surrounded by a dark mist, as if it were leaking clouds of hate and badness. Its gait was ungainly but heavy, and I felt each landing of its hooves as it galloped closer.

In my mind, I planned the action I'd have to take.

If the thing breached the wall of my circle, I'd duck under it and slash at its belly. I pictured the thing flying above me as I turned and cut, slicing into the soft flesh and releasing its guts to spill over the grass.

But I'd only get once chance.

I didn't know where Hew had gone. The dullahan came at me, leading with a long protrusion resembling a horse's face on a long, sinewy neck. Two eyes bulged lightly from the sides and two holes like nostrils opened at the end of the nose. A rictus of a grin showed teeth, and they weren't broad and flat but narrow and pointed like needles. It had ears more or less in the same place as a horse. A flash of recognition struck me in a single clear moment as it thundered to my magic-fed cocoon. My eyes caught the details.

It wasn't a horse. It imitated one. A seahorse resembled a horse but was a completely different creature. I saw it in the eyes. The eyes had no life. No motion. No focus. The eyes were a sham like a circular pattern on butterfly wings. Painted eyes that were no more real than a horse on a carousel.

Then there were the feelers.

Some of the wisps that tasted the air around the dullahan were like smoke. Dark and thin at the edges, they dissipated as they drifted off. Some, however, had a defined shape. They waved like dark, jagged tongues sensing the surroundings.

Smelling the stink of my magic.

I crouched with my knife in hand.

The dullahan swept toward me. At the last moment, it swerved. Maybe it was trying to frighten me into leaving the safety of my circle like a hound to a pheasant. Maybe it just didn't notice the circle until it had nearly pounced on me. Either way, it angled past suddenly, side-swiping the shell of power surrounding me. Glowing patterns flared into view where the dullahan struck. A sound like a hundred fingernails shrieking along a hundred blackboards shot through the silence.

Small shockwaves reverberated inside the circle, vibrating against my clothing, my hair, my skin.

The dullahan wheeled around and stopped, giving me a better chance to examine it. The half-formed monstrosity sitting on its back seemed to take greater interest in me. As I looked at the thing, an image of a headless horseman came to mind, and the fit was uncanny. There was no saddle or reins or stirrups, but there was a lumpen mass on the back of the horse that could easily be mistaken for a person without a head, sitting on the horse's back. Along the side of the mass was the dullahan's true face, as if the head were being carried under the rider's arm. The off-kilter positioning dropped shivers down each of my vertebrae like ice cubes falling down stairs. The image was the creepy stuff of nightmares. The kind that shock you awake in the dark hours, trembling with cold sweat.

The dim gray eyes, its real eyes, regarded me with hunger.

The way it wandered back toward me was unnerving. It would have been better if it had charged again. Instead, it stepped closer slowly.

Sauntering.

Like it had all night to get to the soft, chewy center of a life-sized Tootsie Pop.

And I was the soft, chewy center.

"Stay back, nasty." I swallowed. My throat clicked.

The nose of the horse face nuzzled the boundary of the protective shell. The wall crackled, and spiderweb patterns flared to life. The wall held.

Lips peeled back. A tongue that was not a tongue slipped out, licking the boundary. A silver tongue, flat like a sword with a pointed tip. It rolled over the shell, tracing languid lines on the wall.

Gross.

The tongue thrust itself against the barrier. Lightning-flowers blossomed. The tip of the tongue was as pointed as an ice pick. A snapping sound shuddered in the barrier. The blue patterns of the wall turned to sickly green.

It's eating the magic.

The tip of the tongue pressed through the shell. The odors of many burning things came in with tendrils of smoke. Burning hair. Burning teeth. Burning innards.

To be consumed by such foulness would be a horrifying end.

Where are you, Hew?

The wall cracked.

A small herd of white things dashed by. Faster than I could follow, the dullahan pulled away from the barrier and struck. A quick, mist-shrouded hoof caught one of the small creatures, pinning it to the ground by the leg.

It squealed.

The dullahan used its other foreleg to turn the creature onto its back. There was a pop of muscles and tendons that turned the poor creature's squeal to a scream. Eyes wide, the little fluffball kicked, trying to get away, but to no avail. It panted and chittered words I couldn't understand.

The dullahan's tongue shot out again, cutting into the fluffball's abdomen. The poor thing continued to pant but its eyes lost their focus.

Moments passed. The fluffball stopped kicking. The dullahan waited briefly before taking a step back. It sniffed its victim, now lying inert but breathing.

A wave of shock swam over my skin.

He's not going to kill it before he eats it.

The tongue lashed out again, slicing the belly of the fluffball. I braced myself to see intestines but—thankfully—only a layer of glossy silver was visible.

For a moment, it seemed things couldn't get any more strange and disturbing.

I was wrong.

The top of the dullahan split open like an upside-down armadillo. Long, spindly legs—so many legs—quivered in the air as the "rider" part of the monster unfolded. The dullahan laid on its side and the real head curved around on a serpentine neck. Jagged, mismatched teeth—so many teeth—gnashed on nothing, but the sound was frightening.

Bile rose in my throat as the dullahan rolled over. The horse legs pointed skyward, lax and useless, and the head of the horse hung limp, an appendage forgotten.

The real dullahan sniffed at the fluffball once before the teeth crunched down.

The other fluffballs had scattered. A blur came through my peripheral vision. I was distracted enough I almost swore because it caught me by surprise.

With a swish of his weapon, Hew yelled, "Buail!"

A crescent-shaped flare of blue light tracked up the dullahan's neck to its chin. It lifted its maw from its meal with a throat-torn shriek. Its face shuddered and then split in two as the stroke of power, as thin as a scalpel, sliced meat and bone. Gray-green ichor sprayed across the grass.

Hew dodged as the dullahan fell sideways. The bulk of the thing's body slammed into the shell of my circle, making more shockwaves. Making me jump. Then the carcass slid to the ground.

I stared at the thing, half sure it would get up again. Hew stepped to its neck and prodded with his weapon. Perhaps he had the same concern. The dullahan didn't move.

Hew turned and looked up at me. "Are you well?"

"Mostly. Thanks for the front-row seat to the freak show. I may never sleep again."

Hew nodded as if I were a sage. "Might be for the best." He saw the knife in my hand and pointed at it. "What were you going to do with that?"

The dullahan's corpse was large. The horse part looked more like an insect's carapace now that it wasn't moving. I made a slashing motion at it with the knife while at the same time understanding it was a pathetic gesture.

Hew chuckled. "You might have given him a scratch to remember you by. Dullahan are nearly invulnerable unless they're eating."

I looked at the half-chewed fluffball. "Did you send these? To give that thing a meal?"

216

"Aye. There was a nest of them nearby."

I knelt by the little creature. It looked like a children's doll with all the stuffing pulled out. Its oversized eyes were bright blue, and it had a pair of curled little horns. He had hooves on his hind legs but hands on his forelegs. The hands were rough but very nearly human. They hadn't hindered him at all when running on his four legs. He looked a bit like a mix between a sheep and a bear.

"We have to keep moving." Hew shifted his pack on his shoulder.

I touched the little creature's hand. "Thanks." I said it softly. Among the living, I couldn't say it. For the dead, it was the only thing I could say.

On the other side of the glade, more tall rocks waited. Hew led me through the gaps. Many of them were narrow, and I again found myself shuffling sideways so I could make it through the maze. I didn't complain. Dullahan would never fit.

"Is there anything I can do to be less . . . odorous? To the things here?"

"Yes. Get older."

That was helpful.

"Your power is fresh and new. With use, and time, it will be less so."

Wonderful. Doomed because of my "new car smell."

"What kind of creature was that tiny guy?" The sound of my voice got lost in the tangle of stones only to echo back to me from unexpected directions.

"He was a miongabhálaí." Hew gave the name no particular reverence. It came out of his mouth like a fact, not a tribe of living things. He saw them, perhaps, as a means to an end. He had used the little herd to accomplish a task. Never mind that one had died. "They serve Caer Ibormeith, sovereign of dreams and nightmares."

"What do they do?"

Hew didn't answer. Instead, he changed direction, angling away from the course we'd been following. After a minute, he stopped and pointed.

I looked down into a hollow filled with fluffy white creatures.

They were all sleeping around and on top of each other. Some had a little hoof in the nose or a curly horn in the eye, but they didn't seem to mind.

Hew pointed again. "Miongabhálaí," he said, as if that explained everything.

"Looks like the Guinness World Record winner for a bowl of giant popcorn."

Hew and I watched the fluffballs sleep. A few of them twitched fitfully. I wondered what Hew had done to roust out a nest of these guys and chase them in front of the dullahan.

"What do they do again?"

Hew shrugged. "You saw they have no internal organs, didn't you?"

"Yes. How does that answer my question?"

Hew ignored me some more. "Legend tells of the early times when humans first began to dream. Raw and wild as a race, their dreams were powerful, filled with unexpected glories and untamed imaginings. Caer Ibormeith, her name above all others, had magic to catch dreams. She was captivated by human dreams most of all. She would do nothing but sleep for days at a time, gathering dreams. Her father thought that her obsession was unhealthy, naturally."

"Naturally."

Hew gestured for me to follow. We left the fluffball nest behind. As we walked between more tall rocks, Hew's voice meandered along strange paths. He continued the story of the goddess in whose land we trod.

"Her father finally gave her an ultimatum: give up hunting dreams or be exiled to a place where dreams could not be found."

We continued through the labyrinth of stone. I waxed poetic. Within these jagged sentinels, may the fluffballs sleep safe from harm.

We came out into an area marginally wider. Hew waited for me to extract myself from the passage, my arms scraped up and my knees aching. A mist gathered among the stones. Hew's echoing voice said, "That was when the young goddess decided her father had to die."

# CHAPTER 25
## Tower of the Dreamers

"The girl would never be able to murder her father outright. He was wary of everyone around him—especially his family. But he had a particular fondness for swans. In his gardens, he kept the largest swans in the realm on a private lake. Caer Ibormeith, may she reign forever, bargained with a witch to turn her into a swan so she could wait in the garden as a surprise for her father. She flew to the lake, her feathers spotless white. Her father took his customary walk, and she floated along the shore. When he came near to admire her, she struck, stabbing him in the heart with her beak. Unknown to her, her father's clothing was enchanted, designed to burn anyone who touched him. The fire turned the swan's neck black, and a drop of heartsblood clung to the tip of the swan's beak. If you should ever see a white swan with a beak tipped in red and a black neck, you will know she is the goddess."

Wow. I just became allergic to large white birds.

"Hold on. She's always a swan?"

"When the witch heard how the goddess's father had died, she altered the spell. The goddess has her human form in the castle she inherited. When she leaves the castle, she becomes a swan again."

"I see."

No wonder she's cranky.

Hew raised a hand to stop me. "Stay here." He didn't wait to see if I had heard him. He trotted off between the pillars, leaving me to wonder what he was up to now.

Minutes passed. I jumped a fraction of a hair when he reappeared behind me.

"The path is clear. Follow me."

I followed. Hew moved at a comfortable pace. At some point, he started singing. I missed some of the first verse but caught the chorus.

Stranglers in the night,
Exchanging pantses.
Wondering in the night,
Where are their handses?

"Is that supposed to be Frank Sinatra?" I had to ask.

Hew glared briefly over his shoulder. "Not supposed to be. It is Frank Sinatra."

"Well." I tried to be gentle. "It's strangers in the night. Not stranglers."

He cleared his throat. "I sang that."

"No. And 'where are their handses' isn't right either. Maybe if there was a Broadway musical version of Lord of the Rings and you were Gollum."

Hew rolled his shoulders in annoyance and stopped singing. I felt bad.

Wending our way between more stones, we emerged at the top of a short cliff, twenty or thirty yards off a sand-covered space—like a beach without an ocean.

Hew pointed. "That's where the woman you seek will be found."

The pit before us was roughly the size of a downtown Miami block. From my vantage point, I couldn't see the bottom. The pillar in the center was even more striking.

The structure was assembled from a mish-mash of different architectures. There was a modern glass house with neon lights at the corners that looked like a single-story Las Vegas hotel, dropped on top of a quiet craftsman from a Midwest suburb. A Polynesian grass hut sat diagonally atop a Bavarian castle while a Chinese pagoda rubbed shoulders with the columns of a French Colonial. Both were crowned with a moss-strewn wall of rock with firelight flickering at the opening.

"Is that a cave?"

Hew shrugged.

The buildings were moving.

A narrow New York townhouse with Tiffany lamps flanking the door retreated, leaving a shadowy space between a split-entry crackerbox and a California ranch with stucco walls. A Mediterranean villa slid into the space from above. One at a time, the buildings over each subsequent space moved down until a log cabin rotated sideways and stopped the cascade.

It's a giant, three-dimensional sliding puzzle.

There were castles as well. Lots of castles. Windows with keystone arches and heavy oak doors in gray stone thresholds.

"What is this place?"

"These are the elite dreamers. Seers. Oracles. Dreamers who have dreams that come true. They see the future. They see the hearts and minds of powerful people. Their dreams are potent and valuable, and the queen prizes them above all others."

It was easy to understand why Béil had been taken. I'd seen her go into a trance and deliver a prophecy. The words she had said had all come true. And a dream was similar to a trance. It was possible that Béil's dreams were predicting all sorts of future events.

I sighed. It wasn't going to be easy to steal her back.

"How do we get in?"

"Do you have the ability to shift?"

"No." I had to correct myself. "Well. I did it once. But I can't shift whenever I want."

"Pity. The hard way then."

Hew trudged off down a path so overgrown with ferns it was barely discernible. I followed. He walked for a few yards and then stopped.

"What is it?" I whispered. My heart rate was bumping up. "A dullahan?"

Hew shook his head. "Guards. Like me. Get down."

I crouched in the path. Ferns tickled my face and neck. One presumptuous tendril gave me a floral wet willy, but I didn't move.

221

Hew's senses were more attuned than mine. I couldn't see or hear anything, but he remained at attention with his weapon ready. All I got was damp seeping into my pants as we waited.

Finally, without warning, Hew ran. I launched to my feet.

Catching up to Hew wasn't a problem. The problem was not running him over. He didn't thrash his way through ferns and underbrush to make it easy to see where he was. Instead, there was a flicker of a fern here and a bounce of a leaf there. Running after him was like playing a high-speed version of connect-the-dots. There was a spot, run there. Next spot over there. Go.

After a few hundred yards of that, Hew stopped in a small open space where I could see him. He spoke before I had time to say, "Phew."

"Over that bridge," he ordered.

His weensy, gloved hand pointed at a round tube supported haphazardly with vines. The tube ran from the edge of the giant sinkhole to the pillar of domiciles.

"That's not a bridge," I pointed out. "That's barely a drain pipe. I can't fit in there."

"That's why I said go over. On top. Miongabhálaí go through. I'll see you on the other side."

I checked the pipe again. "Do I look like a Cirque du Soleil kind of guy to you? People are not meant to go over things like that."

"That's why nobody will catch you. They won't be looking for you there."

Hew trotted into the tunnel, ending any discussion.

"I'm going to strangle him," I muttered. "Then I'm going to strangle Mads for hiring him."

The pipe swayed as I stepped onto it. I'd done enough high-adventure trips to be secure on my feet in precarious places, but rope bridges at least had guide ropes to hold.

This was insane.

The vines holding the pipe were set randomly and the knots all looked suspect at best. I prayed they would hold my weight. It also helped to have a goal to watch in situations like this. A stable, visual anchor directly across the way to focus on.

My visual anchors wouldn't stop moving.

Spiffy.

The span was too far for me to just run and let momentum carry me across. I took another step. Then another. The pipe bounced and shuddered with the shifting of the pillar's parts. Halfway across, I knew I was going to fall. My footing and my balance couldn't compete with the moving houses, and the closer I went to the pillar, the more pronounced the shaking got.

I dove to the pipe before it bucked me off.

With my legs straddling the pipe and my arms wrapped tightly, I inch-wormed another foot. And another. This was going to take time. As long as I didn't slip . . . I started to slip.

Oh, dang. Oh, dang. Oh—

I managed to lock my ankles together as the slippery pipe sent me sideways. My hands weren't sliding but they wanted to; I locked my fingers together, too.

If any guards see me now, it won't be a problem. They'll die laughing.

Using my best tree sloth impression, I scooted up the pipe. Looking down in this position was practically impossible.

Small favors. I didn't want to know what waited below me if I should fall. My dignity could shrivel as long as I hung on. I proceeded. Not gruntlessly. The pipe angled up, steeper the closer I got to the pillar.

A different thought. That's what I needed.

My friend.

Nat had trained me well. His relentless training meant my shoulders and arms and legs were strong enough to hold me, bless him. While exertion pushed exhaustion into my muscles, I eventually found myself able to drop to a soft patch of grass outside the door of a very nice tiki hut on stilts. I sat and shook out my muscles, stretching.

Hew appeared behind me. "Let's go. Slowpoke."

Really?

I stood and followed the little sadist between buildings. Behind the buildings was a hub of sorts. A central space consisting primarily of a spiral staircase. Whatever apparatus enabled the buildings to rise and fall and slide and turn wasn't apparent. A short hallway led to a stone bridge. The bridge led to the other side of the pit.

"Uh. Why didn't we come in that way?"

"Too many guards." Hew said it before he stopped to look.

"Guards?" I looked too. "Where?"

Hew padded silently down the passage and stopped. Padded farther. Padded to an archway. He leaned around the edge of the wall and then padded back.

"Huh. No guards. You're right. The bridge would have been easier. Follow me."

Grumbling, not just to myself, I took long strides up the stairs. Some of the landings had handrails, but the stairs did not. I wasn't sure how far off the ground we were, if there was any ground at all. Staying away from the gaping hole in the middle of the pillar seemed like a genius idea.

"What kind of building are we looking for?" Hew wanted to know.

When Alyce had taken me into Béil's dream, she'd been in her own bedroom there.

"A marble castle," I replied. "Pink. That's where she lives in the Behindbeyond."

Major movement started. The sound of stone scraping over stone rumbled up to us from somewhere below.

"A dreamer awakes," Hew said. "Run!" He set the example, loping up the stairs on all fours like a dog. After a couple of flights, I envied his versatility.

"For a place all about sleeping," I puffed, "the exhaustion factor comes as a surprise."

Hew continued upward while I gamely lagged behind. Finally, flights later and out of breath, I caught up to Hew as he sat on a landing. It looked like he was picking his teeth with the business end of his weapon, pointed tip of the jawbone working at something under the skull mask.

"You aren't worried." I had to inhale. "About slicing your face off?"

"Doesn't cut without magic," Hew replied. "Smell anything?"

"What?"

"Smell anything?" Hew repeated. "I do." He tilted his head.

We were standing in front of a door, which was the entrance to a marble castle. Pink.

"Impressive." I bent over, just breathing.

"You aren't catching the scent?"

"Of course not."

"Poor human. Missing half of the good things in life."

"Yup. Armpits. Diapers. Vomit. All day long. Missing out."

Hew exhaled through his nostrils.

"Is it safe to go in?" I had my hand on the door.

Hew looked at me with one eye centered in the orbital socket of the skull. He hesitated. Then gave a tiny nod. The door wasn't locked.

Inside, a simple bedchamber and Béil. The head of the bed had a nest with a snoozing fluffball. This fluffball was identical to the others I had seen, except it had a glowing dot in the middle of its forehead. The dot pulsed. Béil looked small in the small room and the small bed. The covers were pulled up to her chest, her hands resting one upon the other. She'd lost weight.

Welcome to the Caer Ibormeith spa. Her name be ever parasitic.

Béil's eyes were closed. They appeared to be larger than I remembered. Perhaps because her face had thinned and her lids were dark, almost bruised. Under the lids, her eyes moved.

Hew came in behind me. "Don't they feed her?" The tone in my voice was accusing.

"They feed the dreamers well. Food is brought in abundance. The dreamers don't always choose to eat."

Béil's sallow skin was gradually turning to paper. Small blue veins threaded their way up her exposed arms, chest, and neck.

"We need to get her out of here."

225

"She has great value. The queen will not surrender her lightly."

"The queen doesn't have to know."

Hew looked at the floor. "The queen knows everything. Disturbing a dreamer will alert her and bring her guards."

I considered gathering Béil up in my arms and making a run for it. I was tired, but she wouldn't be heavy. If I could make it to the forest of stones, I could lose any pursuers. Or take them out.

"If I might suggest." Hew's voice was soft. "Find out what she dreams. See what has captivated the goddess. And talk to your friend before doing anything rash."

"Do we have time for that?"

Hew shrugged. "Time is different in Tír na nÓg and different still in dreams. A day's adventure in a dream takes only moments in time."

That was true. I'd experienced that with Alyce.

Hew promised, "If anyone approaches, I will let you know."

"All right. I'll want time to get her out of here."

"I'll do what I can."

Hew seemed sincere and if he was like the Fae, he couldn't lie. "What do I do?"

Hew pointed at the fluffball. "Hold the miongabhálaí."

The little guy was curled up and cozy. One of his horns was a little more crooked than the other. His hands moved as if he were conducting a legato symphony for an orchestra. I asked, "Won't touching him wake him up?"

"He sleeps for as long as the dreamer."

Seems legit.

I sat on the bed beside Béil and slid my hand beneath the fluffball. He was surprisingly light. Like a bird. And warm. I cradled the fluffball in my arms and closed my eyes.

# CHAPTER 26
## Béil Out

The lightning had frozen.

A soft orange glow emanated from warehouse windows, bleeding through the butcher paper plastered over the safety glass. The air was gelid with a rain like needles of ice. Visibility was less than a city block. This was a city, certainly, but it was hard to tell which one.

The jagged rain continued to fall, making circles in the street, but the lightning bolt striking the ground was an immobile shaft of blinding brilliance.

"I wouldn't touch. That if I. Were you. If you. Want to get. Burned touching. Something. Touch me. Instead."

Béil had materialized at my side. Or I had materialized at hers.

"Hello Béil."

She wore the same nightgown she'd had on in the last dream we'd shared.

"You used. The barrow key."

"Yes."

"Well done."

"Why is the lightning stuck?"

"An anchor."

"An anchor? For what?"

"In dreams. Something. Is flawed. To anchor. The dream. To reality."

I nodded as if that made perfect sense. "That makes absolutely no sense."

Béil swept her hand toward the bolt of lightning. "This dream. Feels normal. The lightning is. Clearly not."

"Okay. In other words, this whole conversation, which is

delightful, by the way, is going on in the time it takes for lightning to strike, and the lightning reminds us that this is not real?"

"Yes."

"Got it."

The electricity moved up and down, slowly and visibly, as it traveled through the lightning shaft. Fascinating.

"How have you been?" My question came out softly.

"All right." Béil looked at the warehouse with the papered windows and the lightning. "I tire. Having. The same dream. Over and over."

"What's in there?"

"I know not."

The windows beckoned. I tried not to let curiosity get the better of me.

"Someone said that dreams are a reflection of the soul. So, Béil, if this is your soul, it's probably empty."

She gave a pinched expression.

"Heh heh." I faked a laugh. "Kidding. Heh."

"I've seen. People go in."

"Anyone familiar?"

"No."

"Let's take a look."

"No. I'm trying. To get out. Not in."

"I have a friend watching over us. He'll wake us up if there's a problem. Where did you see people go in?"

"A door. Right side. But we don't. Have time."

"Sure we do. We have at least a lightning bolt."

Béil gritted her teeth. "I regret. Telling you. About the timing." She sighed dramatically but started walking toward the warehouse. "Let's. Hurry."

As we left the frozen lightning behind, the little hairs all over my body settled back down. I hadn't realized they'd reacted at all. Somehow, this was . . . familiar. I found myself relaxing as well. My shoulders unhunched and my fists unclenched. This wasn't monster chasing. This was detective work.

228

So good.

A thin orange line was painted on the ground, courtesy of a narrow gap in the door of the warehouse and the light within. I crept up to the door and, in my most professional private eye move, privately eyed the opening.

No one stirred behind the door. There was a late model Honda in the space between the door and a workbench. A couple of empty happy meal boxes sat on the top of the bench along with a short stack of magazines. I couldn't tell who was on the cover, but the title of the magazine was People.

I shifted to get different angles but didn't see anything else I could identify through the door. Around us, the buildings were generic. There were deciduous trees. No palms. No pines or spruces either. A salt tang hung in the air. If this place were real at all, I'd guess we weren't in the south but we were near an ocean, more likely east coast than west.

Not a lot to go on.

"Someone's coming." Béil pulled on my sleeve.

We retreated to the shadows. I wasn't sure if there was danger to us, since this was a dream, but my natural snoopitude wanted to snoop. If anyone saw us, the conversation would change and snoop would have no fun.

Two guys strolled around the corner. The happy meals had not been enough, judging by the soda bottles and bags of potato chips. The guys were big, with windbreakers and jeans and black shoes. They didn't speak, although one guy coughed so roughly it sounded like he was trying to hack up a twig wrapped in sandpaper from his lungs.

The two guys went up to the door and stopped. They didn't open the door. They didn't knock. They just waited. The one guy coughed.

After a minute, the door opened.

I pressed my hand against Béil's back. "Come on."

The lightning bolt around the corner flickered as we ran to the door. Béil asked, "Your friend. Will wake us?"

"If there's any hint of trouble."

We ducked through the door, skimming along the wall like rats into a dark corner. The door closed itself. The room we were in was used as a garage. There were two panel vans with the name Harborside Exquisite Coffees painted on the side.

The men we'd followed had vanished around a corner. The rain pattered on the roof as a reminder the air outside was fresher. The garage smelled of motor oil and cigarette smoke and manual labor. Sticking to the shadows, we scuttled to the other side of the room to see where they'd gone. There was a narrow hallway connecting to the next room. It was well lit, with metal walls and slits that could be used for watching whoever was passing down the hall.

Or shooting them.

My kingdom for a blink.

The next room was filled with dark blocky shapes and a low-wattage light. The shapes looked to be desks and shelves. There was a small refrigerator and a microwave oven against the bit of wall visible from our vantage point and a workbench with papers on it.

I wanted in there.

A trickle of a tickle ran down the center of my back: the thrill of being somewhere I shouldn't be. Even in Béil's dream, the trickle was real. If I had to choose a criminal career path, I'd go with cat burglar. It would be the most fun.

I leaned into Béil. "Can I take stuff from here?"

Béil shook her head. "What exists. In dreams. Can be. Remembered. Only."

"So when I got the barrow key it was because you brought it with you from the waking world." I knew the answer already.

"Yes. Planned. Ahead of time. A complex. Spell."

Crap.

Time to make some memories, then.

There was no avoiding the hall and its dark, ominous slits. With no options coming to mind, I'd have to trust to dream realities, of which I knew precious little.

Moving out of the shadows, I whispered "Stay here, Béil," and sauntered down the hallway.

Sauntered. Hardcore. Made it. No yelling or shooting. Just walked right down.

Directly to the computer. The screen was dark. The keyboard ignored my tapping. Either the computer was off, or electronics didn't work in the dream. A clipboard on the end of the desk had a stack of papers on it. The top sheet had the Harborside Exquisite Coffees logo and several columns of information assembled as an inventory sheet.

| VANILLA | BEAN | 12 | + | NON |
|---|---|---|---|---|
| SALTED | CARAMEL | 14 | + | NON |
| ISLAND | COCOA | 13 | - | NON |
| FRENCH | VANILLA | 16 | - | NON |
| TOASTED | ALMOND | 12 | - | NON |

The information was screwy, but I was at a loss to see why exactly. The flavors seemed to be normal, although I'd never heard of "Island Cocoa." Could be a coconut or pineapple flavor mixed with chocolate, which sounded disgusting. The quantities seemed odd as well. Commodities were sold by the tens or dozens. Maybe the number meant thirteen dozen Island Cocoa. Plus and minus weren't symbols I could interpret. Neither was "Non" unless it was all non-fat.

Down the page, another entry snagged my attention:

| VANILLA | BEAN | 17 | - | NON |
|---|---|---|---|---|

There had been that flavor earlier. Come to think of it, the word "Vanilla" was in the first column here but appeared in the second column elsewhere. And the quantity was different. And a minus instead of plus.

I scanned the page twice, committing it to memory, so my mental magnets could click up an answer.

It'd worked before.

There were more files to flip through. Utility bills. Phone records. Voices.

People were coming.

I went back through the hall, sauntering faster this time.

Béil looked annoyed. "Can we. Go now?"

"Just a second."

The roughed-up voice matched my expectations. From the shadows, I caught a glimpse of the guy who had been coughing at the door speaking in a matter-of-fact tone. The person he was speaking with stepped into view and my heart nearly stopped like a stone hitting sand.

I knew her.

Her hair had changed. Her intense green eyes had not. Neither had her nose, which had been broken once and never set properly.

Her name was Aoife.

Processing the shock took my focus. The warehouse might be somewhere—that thought derailed. Behind Aoife a half-open door gave me a glimpse into the room beyond. My focus shifted there. The door closed.

I'd almost missed it.

"Let's go." I took Béil by the hand, feeling sick. I had to get out of here and back to the mortal realm. Now. We hurried to the door, which was still closed. I looked for a button to open it and couldn't see one. The very real possibility that there wasn't one occurred to me. The door had opened by itself when coughing man and his snack pal had waited outside.

Ice ran through my system, chilling my nerves, seizing my guts.

Waking my brain.

Whoever controlled the door must use security cameras or another device, but I didn't see any cameras.

Nuts.

Well. I always had my version of a sonic screwdriver.

Hesitating for maybe one-sixteenth of a heartbeat, I remembered what I'd been told about magic in dreams.

"Tine!" I pulled up my power and threw a tiny fireball at the

232

cross brace holding the door.

The wall-sized explosion took out the cross brace. And the door. And tossed Béil and I back on our butts.

"What did. You do?" The sound of metal crashing made it hard to hear. I helped Béil to her feet. Our clothing was intact and, most importantly, my hair had not ignited.

"I picked the lock. Let's go."

The jagged hole looked dangerous with all kinds of pointy, sharp edges. Luckily, there was a ten-foot gap between them all. We stepped through, played a quick game of dodge-the-lightning-bolt, and hurried back to the spot where we'd entered the dream.

All the while, my body had cold chills. And my mind had cold thoughts. A plan. One Béil would not like. I held Béil by her shoulders.

"I need you to stay asleep. If you wake up, your room will move and the fuzzballs will catch us. It will only take a few minutes to make sure we can safely get you out."

Béil searched my eyes. "What aren't you. Telling me?"

I sighed. "I realize I'm the one saying there's no time to explain. Can you stay asleep?"

Something was fishy with my story and Béil knew it. As an Eternal, she was a living lie detector, even in dreams, but I was a Halfling and hard to read. She also knew I was her ticket out of here. I waited her out. It wasn't easy.

"I have to. Trust you. I guess."

"Great. So how do I wake up?"

"That. I can. Help with." There was a nasty twist in her smile as she slapped me in the way only an expert mean girl could, and I woke up.

I was still sitting on the bed. Still holding the fuzzball. Still feeling the sting on my face so sharply, I had to rub my cheek.

No time.

I placed the fluffbutt back in his nest. He continued to dream Béil's dream, the dot in his forehead pulsing. Béil was breathing softly, but she had the same nasty twist in her smile, still dreaming about the slap she'd delivered.

I promised to take you, Béil.

Forgive me.

Hew followed as I crept out of the room like the sneaky jerk I was. The stairs were clear and I made no sound as I descended to the landing below, where I stopped.

Hew regarded me eye-to-eye, standing on the steps above me. "Was not your purpose to bring her with us?"

"Not now. I have to get back to the mortal realm."

Hew swiveled his head, uncertain. "Did you see something in her dream?"

I nodded but offered no details. "Can you get me out of here?"

The rooms shifted. Someone was waking up. It might be Béil.

Hew wasted no more time. He led the way down, finding a landing with a bridge. It was higher than the one I'd seen before, but it took us out of the tower to the woods. We concerned ourselves with putting distance between us and the tower. Hew kept pace easily, galloping on both hands and feet.

The icicle that had started running up my center in Béil's dream hadn't thawed. If anything, it had grown colder.

Trees and midnight-black shapes flashed past us. I paid attention to the path in front of us and little else. Gratefully, we reached the stone forest. A few steps in, we came to a stop.

Panting, Hew asked, "Will she be angry?"

My worries obscured everything. "What?"

"Your friend. You left her behind. Will she be angry?"

"Angry will be the only polite way to say it. She's going to go nuclear."

"I'm familiar with many things from the mortal realm. I don't know 'nuclear.'"

"Oh. Angry enough to destroy a city."

"Ah. You may wish to leave her in the tower then." Hew took a moment to spit, the bit of foam zipping out from under the skull helmet. "The guards may be able to handle her better than you."

"You may be right." I had some compelling reasons to lie to Béil and leave her here. I couldn't be certain she'd see things the same way. "I'm not very bright though. I'll be back to get her."

Hew shook his head and led the way through the stones. We passed the fluffball nest and after an hour, emerged from the stones.

A shiver had begun between my heart and my shoulders. There was a chill in the air that hadn't been here before. The icicle in my gut was growing as well.

Hew stopped. He looked over his shoulder, scanning the sky. Then he knelt on the ground. He laid his weapon on the grass in front of him. Then he took a step back and knelt again.

"What are you doing?"

He shifted his shoulders under his armor of bone.

"We need to go, Hew."

"I did what I could, Prince Luck." He looked at the sky again.

I tracked the direction of his gaze. My eyes picked out three patches of movement heading our way.

"What's going on, Hew?"

"I told you the queen knows everything. The question is always what she'll pay attention to."

The patches in the ink of the sky moved fast. Two birds were black, but the bird in the center was white. As they got closer I could see the white bird was a swan. The swan had a black beak with a spot of red.

My muscles tensed.

Hew sensed my intention. "Don't run. It will be better for both of us. Her seabhacmór—those giant hawks—will tear us to pieces."

Crap-a-matic.

Circling overhead, the black birds—seabhacmór—screeched with the sharp, harsh shrieks of a thousand predatory nightmares. Their warning calls added to the chill in my heart, and I didn't dare to move after that. Their wings displaced a minor hurricane as they landed, the white bird between them.

The swan remained silent, calm, and relaxed; yet she was far more terrifying. Waves of power thrummed over the ground like aftershocks of an earthquake, advising of magical strength not unleashed but held in check, only barely. The swan regarded me with a clear eye. She ruffled her feathers as if preparing to nest. Then she preened her chest, her long neck arching gracefully.

A small figure descended from one of the black guards. A fluffball. Her eyes were large and dark, dilated as if she'd been drugged. She wore a silver circlet on her head and her pace was sedate as she moved across the grass to stand beside her mistress.

She touched the wing of the swan and closed her eyes. The silver circlet flared blue, and she spoke in a soft voice that still managed to cut the air. "Hail and well met. I am Caer Ibormeith, Goddess of Dreams and sovereign of Tír na nÓg."

"Hail, goddess." Hew bowed his head as he spoke.

Not being a complete idiot, I followed Hew's example. "Hail, goddess."

The fluffball who spoke the goddess's words mimicked her attitude and manner or, at least had a whole lot more attitude than she'd had at birth. She opened her eyes and looked at Hew with a bemused expression. "Why dost thou wear such a silly costume, little one?"

Hew didn't reply but he gave me a sideways glance.

The spokes-fluff continued. "Remove it."

Hew wasn't in a big hurry, but he didn't hesitate either. He took off his boots, followed by the braces of bone and pauldron, then the heavy white shoulder pieces. Each part clattered on the other. The helmet was the last to go.

The revelation was shocking. So shocking I almost had to sit down.

Hew was adorable.

There was grime on his hands and he was definitely in need of a bath, but Hew was the most-cuddly fuzzbutt ever. He was twice as tall as the miongabhálaí, but undoubtedly a related species. His large eyes would melt the heart of the most hardened cynic. His horns grew in curls that were nearly complete circles. One teddy-bear ear had been mangled, but the notches only made Hew more endearing. The fluff of his coat was infested with even more fluff. He was a goose-down pillow, covered in lamb's wool, and wrapped in a cumulonimbus cloud.

Having stripped down to his original, factory-installed fuzzies, Hew gave a little bow in the direction of the swan. Then he squinted at me sideways again. The look told me to keep my trap shut.

Sure.

"Looks like a nasty wound you got there." I pointed at his butt. "Is it painful?"

Hew looked at his backside. He ran his hand over the spot, his fingers disappearing beneath the fuzz. "What wound?"

I paused, savoring the moment. "The wound you got when they tore off the sales tag at the toy store."

Hew turned away slowly, breathing nearly-visible fumes.

I grinned. Inwardly, of course. Outwardly, the goddess had me petrified.

The goddess's spokes-fluff locked her gaze on me. My chill, half-forgotten, returned full force. I swallowed. Or tried to.

"Prince Luck. Son of the Alder King." The swan's gaze locked on me, too.

*Caer Ibormeith, goddess.*

"Yes, goddess." My voice rang out in the silence.

The swan lifted her head, the blood-red drop on her beak centered between my eyes.

"Dream thou for me."

# CHAPTER 27
## The Dreamer Must Dream

I ran. I couldn't forget my purpose. Not even for a joke. Or a goddess.

I'd seen things in Béil's dream that had to be acted on. Now. No time to rescue Béil. No time for dreams. Children needed me. Abducted children. I knew how to find them. I needed to find them.

With my last reserves of energy, I sprinted for the forest of stones. No matter how clever or powerful the birds were, they'd have a hard time catching me in there. The stones were too tall and close together for flying, and with luck I'd lose them in the maze.

Hew had said it would be better for us both if I surrendered. I hoped the queen wouldn't be hard on him because I hadn't cooperated. I didn't want anyone to suffer for me.

But that included the kidnapped children.

There were a whole lot of those suffering already. If I had the ability to help them, I had to do it. Even at the expense of other people.

Innocence should never suffer. Would not suffer. Not on my watch.

So I ran.

I didn't dare look over my shoulder. If I was being followed, I didn't want to know. I prayed they wouldn't catch me, though. I prayed I'd find the way out.

I prayed for no dullahan.

Good prayer, that one.

I prayed for the children.

The green of the forest gave way to mist, a curtain of deep gray that slowed me down for the worthy cause of personal safety. I couldn't see more than a few feet in front of me, and there might be a chasm between me and the stones. I was fine with going slower. Too tired to run now, my breath going ragged.

The gray gave way to charcoal.

Where were those stupid stones?

A little farther.

That's all.

My feet were sore. My legs quivered, carrying my weight. I needed to sleep.

But if I slept I'd dream.

I couldn't dream.

The goddess would find me.

Oof. Maybe a little sleep would be all right.

A short nap. Just to recharge my batteries.

I couldn't though.

No, no, no. Not out here. They'd find me out here for certain.

I needed a place that was sheltered. Secluded. Hidden from fuzzbutt scouts and flying screechers. And dullahan that could smell the magic I carried.

My walk downgraded to a plod.

Would it be easier to find the stone forest in daytime?

I could nap until then.

I prayed for a cave or a crevice where I could lay down. At this point, I'd settle for a Hilton or a Marriott.

Heh heh.

A torch. Lighting a patch of pretty much nothing.

Out here. In the middle of nowhere.

Sure. Why not.

This was Tír na nÓg. Inspiration for Dante's Inferno.

I approached cautiously, perfectly aware that suspicion must follow when the one thing you're hoping for materializes out of nowhere. Things are only too good to be true because they are.

Stopping outside the circle of torchlight, I saw no leaves covering a pit or ropes waiting to snare my ankle. Anything more sophisticated than that wouldn't work. Only the most primitive technologies functioned in the Behindbeyond.

The fire of the torch bore no heat. I knelt and reached out. Touched the ground within the circle of light. In the distance, another torch flickered to life. The flame grew by degrees, as if it didn't want to spook me. Yup. That spooked me.

It didn't feel like a threat. If a dullahan were after me, it wouldn't light torches.

Walking to the next torch, I had to step around the bushes that grew here. They were stunted and black, but grew taller farther along whatever path I was being led down.

As I approached the next torch, a third torch sparked and sputtered, creating a new oasis of light another hundred yards away.

The bushes were waist high there. Like ebony coral, they fanned out in little branches. The path wandered by one of the taller ones. The branches looked like they had four little fingers and a shorter thumb on the ends, as if they were constructed of children's dismembered arms and hands. The thought made me queasy. Of course, it was just my imagination.

I took a closer look and realized bushes should not grow little fingernails on the ends.

I didn't look at the bushes anymore.

Torch number three marked the entrance to a small cave.

On the ground, a welcome mat.

The mat had a message written on it: "Mat Was Fired for Lying Down on the Job. I'm His Replacemat."

Well, that's just my kind of stupid.

Maybe this cave belonged to me.

I went in, hoping for a nap.

The cave meandered back into the rock with a narrow passageway that opened into a cavern. The ceiling was responsible for the faintly green glow that illuminated the space. Far overhead, pinpoints glowed like millions of stars. Rough-cut steps in the rock led down to the floor of the cave.

The floor was paved. Or tiled. Precisely-laid stones, cut and formed into patterns, made the floor feel like the floor of a cathedral.

**240**

I didn't notice the corpses until I'd stepped into the middle of them. How does that work?

Thousands of bodies had been arranged on the floor, wrapped in maroon death shrouds so dark they were nearly black. They all radiated outward from where I stood, feet pointing toward me. The chill that hadn't thawed at all in the heat of running surged in my core like the twist of a frozen dagger.

I took a step. The corpses near me tilted up, pivoting to my face. The corpses behind them tilted up as well, at lesser angle. Behind them, more corpses tilted slightly. I stood like the pistil of some mutated aster or demented dandelion and the dead were the petals.

Dry, rotted flesh. Decay. Air like the exhalations of ancient pharaohs. The smells mated with the images. This wasn't fun anymore. My instincts told me to go deeper into the cave. If I wanted answers, they'd be there. Nothing but capture awaited me outside.

I walked. All the corpses shuddered, fluttering, reorienting to align themselves with me again. I kept moving. The corpses didn't follow me. Didn't touch me. The bodies behind me gradually pivoted to the ground while the bodies closest to me rose, the dry, rustling sound of their shrouds scraping on the stone like secret whispers.

Ahead, the corpses began their tilt, waiting for their turn to rise and stare me down.

The shroud from one corpse's face slipped completely away, revealing his features. Emaciated and corrupted, I still remembered the structure of bone and tendon beneath the parchment skin.

I knew this man.

Memories rushed up from that quiet place where memories you wish you could forget go to live permanently. I remembered him because he'd been the first person to die while I'd watched.

Ten years old. Sluffing school with another one of the foster kids living with The Mama. It was the last week of May and the teachers were just as bored and ready for summer as the students. The two of us dug up some earthworms and headed to Lake Verret to fish. If we were lucky we'd be able to catch a crappie or a perch or a nice black buffalo before the truant officer tracked us down.

We hurried down the dirt path to the lake. When we heard an explosion, we hurried faster.

A rowboat was half-sunk in the shallows, with water almost over the gunwales. In the middle of the rowboat, a man fallen backwards over the center thwart. We dropped our fishing gear on the shore and jumped into the water. He had a creel and a net and a pair of sticks that I knew to be dynamite. The man had been "skipbait" fishing, which meant he was throwing dynamite to explode in the lake. The resulting shock stunned the fish and they floated to the surface where they could be scooped up with the net.

Completely illegal and, this time, the dynamite had gone off in the boat.

We waded in but stopped before we got close. The dynamite had done more than damage the boat. I was no stranger to innards. Hunting and fishing had inoculated me against that revulsion. Seeing the insides of a human being, however, was not the same. At all.

It took a conscious effort for me to look up from the wreck of his body to the man's face.

His eyes were wide. His mouth moved but he could only manage choking sounds. The man was shaking, staring at the sky. Long minutes passed before the light went out of his eyes and all I'd done was watch.

He had the same eyes now.

Over the years, I'd regretted not doing something helpful. I never could have saved his life. He was all but gone from the moment the dynamite went off. But I wished I could have given him some kind of comfort. A final moment of reassurance that he wasn't alone and didn't need to be afraid. A touch or a word. Anything but just stand there.

Now, I found myself in the same dilemma. Unable to think of anything to do or say and feeling only loss. I stepped away. The corpse of the man tilted back as I walked, but more rose up to greet me.

The collection of corpses stretched on into the misty light.

How many could there be?

The fluttering and scraping of the shrouds around their bodies wore on my nerves, and I longed to hear some other sound. The face of another corpse revealed itself. I averted my eyes, but the face belonged to Blake, who had been Erin's first husband, now dead.

I raised my hands to block the visage. The gesture felt like supplication—and surrender.

A thousand new corpses rose to meet me as I moved through their midst. The same thousand returned to their rest after my passing. Some revealed themselves. Some I knew. Some not. Their purpose eluded me, but I felt irresistibly drawn to the far side of the cavern, even if I had to swim through this ocean of the dead to find it.

Time passed, but I had no feel for it. Quicksilver and molasses. Both and neither.

An encouraging flicker of white beckoned, urging me on through the rotting tide.

The figure of a woman, clothed in white, stood mute. Head down. In her arms, two bundles rested. She cradled them as if they were fragile. Curled against her body, unmoving, they bore auras of living things nonetheless. Life clung to them, drifted from them, and the tangibility of that sensation was all the more apparent in its contrast with the surrounding decay and death.

The cloak she wore was spotless. The cowl obscured her face in a way that was almost coy. The fluttering and rustling dead fell silent as I finally approached the woman in white. I was tempted to lift the cowl to see her face, but it felt too intimate a gesture. One of the bundles moved. A foot with five perfect little toes stuck out from its swaddling blanket. A soft curl of dark hair poked from the crown of the other.

A rolling sound, imperceptible at first, rose beneath my feet. It grew like a machine manufacturing distant thunder. Behind the still statue of white, a portal opened in the middle of the air. No liagán stone. Just a crack in the middle of the air that widened in jagged pieces as if a mirror were breaking and the glass falling out in shards from the center.

On the other side, a throne room.

I stepped through the portal.

The floor of the throne room was covered with water. The stones created patterns, and I knew the design to be the same as the design in my father's castle. I sloshed through the flood. Minnows darted away, zigging and zagging to find refuge in the shadowed corners.

A figure on the throne.

My father.

I waded on, making tiny waves. Each step was a toy-sized explosion and the ripples bounced off and over each other, not diminishing but expanding into the distance. The Alder King never moved. Another statue. He reposed in an attitude of meditation. His elbow was positioned on the arm of the throne and his hand curled against his forehead. His eyes he held closed, and his compact frame slumped into the corner of the throne as if the meditation had failed to ease the weight of his many burdens. He had removed his crown and it dangled from the fingers of his other hand as if a moment away from falling to the floor.

The color in his face faded away. Flakes of skin fell down. Drifted up. Softly bounced and swirled. His clothing followed. In moments, the outer layers of the statue were orbiting motes of strangely-colored dust. What remained was dark. Burned long ago. Charcoal and ash.

I stood before the figure of the immolated king. It sat as if bonded to the stone seat of power, a blackened shell that somehow cast a reflection in the water that was unchanged. His reflection had nothing wrong.

Which was very wrong.

His reflection was unburned.

And moving.

And staring at me.

# CHAPTER 28
## Mansions and Miongabhálaí

The Alder King's image quavered beneath the unquiet surface of the water while his statue above remained eerily still. In his reflection, he wasn't slumped over. He wasn't lost in a reverie of thought. He leaned forward in an attitude of readiness, as if waiting for his cue to leap from the throne. His crown hovered majestically over his head, and his Stain shimmered with boldness.

This was the king I knew.

"Can you hear me?" I spoke to the reflection.

The reflection raised a hand like a piece of film set on slow replay. The focus of his eyes landed somewhere over my shoulder and the hand unfurled palm up in response to my question.

As I turned my head to look where he indicated, the walls flickered out of existence. The stones melted away as if I'd just imagined the walls in the first place. With the fading, a condensed version of my father's kingdom revealed itself. All of the places I was familiar with lay arranged before me. There was the lake behind my father's castle, Béil's castle home, the Palisade with its walls of living trees. The rivers and mountains where I'd taken Fáidh hiking. The hundreds of liagán circles with their standing stones. The three Scian bays to the south. The Fuilaseum and city of Áit Choinne that resided in the kingdom to the north were visible in clear detail.

All had turned to desolation.

The lake was black and turgid. The walls of Béil's castle crumbling. The Palisade's trees were overgrown and choking one another. The once lively rivers were befouled, and the mountains broken, emitting deadly vapors. The liagán circles all but destroyed, stones cracked and fallen. The bays that had shimmered with crystalline waters were flat and gray, filled with detritus. To the north, the Fuilaseum was empty and crumbling. Áit Choinne devoid of people and overgrown with trees and vines.

Stinging tears threatened to fill my eyes.

This is all wrong.

"What happened?"

I turned back to the throne with my father's ashen corpse and pled with the reflection for answers.

"Is this real?"

The reflection lowered his hand, almost mechanically. Eyes closed, he retreated into the depths of the throne until he rested against the back. His face descended into shadow.

A set of narrow steps offered the only exit. I took them. They curled around the walls of the tower that had materialized beneath my father's throne room. The air of my father's kingdom had become rank. Primordial. Heavy with unpleasant odors and wild, devolved sounds.

At the base of the tower, the ground felt too soft. Too loose.

I don't know this place anymore.

My knees felt wet.

Did I fall?

My chest and arms and face grew damp.

Did I fall?

Exhaustion swept over me like a predator.

I was fallen.

Aching.

Shoulders in pain as if dislocated and shoved back. Wrists burning as if tied with hard, heavy cords.

Breathing.

Lungs filling with clean air. That, at least, was an improvement.

Shining.

Light turning my eyelids orange. Compelling me to open them.

Sure. Why not.

From the ground, looking up, the clouds above me looked like mashed potatoes waiting for butter. Behind them, the sky offered an opulent shade of light blue normally reserved for artists and poets.

I would just have to lie here and appreciate that for a minute.

Then two.

One more.

With a sigh, I sat up.

The knees of my pants were dirty, along with the front of my shirt. I scrubbed my hands over my face and felt dirt there as well, along with bits of grass and leaves. Apparently, I had indeed collapsed after . . . I had to think. Then the memories landed on me like a dump truck full of bricks. The field of corpses. The white statue with two children. The throne room with my father's immolated figure but the reflected image unburned. Trying to tell me something.

Something . . .

I'd abandoned Béil. That memory tasted bitter too. But I needed to get away to save the children.

The children . . .

I needed to get out of here.

First, I needed to find out where here was.

"Highness, you're awake." The voice startled me, coming out of the foliage nearby. Hew stepped forward, amused because he'd made me jump.

"Knock that smile off your fuzzy face." I waved him off. "I yelped like that because it is the traditional greeting of my people."

Hew remained without his bone armor and without his weapon. He regarded me with his overlarge eyes, his little horns catching the sun in their curves, and I didn't know whether to kick him in the backside for spooking me or pick him up for a cuddle.

"So, Hew. Yipe." The second yelp sounded far less authentic than the first one. "Let's get out of here, shall we?"

Hew's face lost the smile. His head tipped forward and he wrung his hands as if he were preparing to make a confession. "Come, sire. I have much to show you."

Hew led the way. We didn't walk far.

A trim bungalow nestled beneath a rank of towering beech trees. The house had a broad front porch and plenty of large windows. Hew walked up to the front door and opened it.

"Welcome, sire."

I nodded and walked into a sitting room with comfortable furniture and a fireplace. "Is this your house? Not bad, Hew."

"No, sire. This is your house. Courtesy of Caer Ibormeith. Her name be ever praised."

I wanted to ask Hew what the ramifications of such a gracious offering might entail. On the other hand, if I didn't ask, I wouldn't get answers I didn't like. "Well. Extend my appreciation next time you see her. Maybe I'll come back for a vacation sometime. Now let's get out of here."

Hew continued to stare at the ground. "You have been"—he cleared his throat—"invited to stay. The goddess was most insistent."

"Invited to stay?" The chill I'd felt not long ago returned, cooling my tone.

"If you wish, you may petition the queen for release."

"Sure. Let's do that. Where do we sign up?"

"We must wait seven years."

I knelt, putting myself on Hew's level. The words I spoke were measured and icy. "I do not have seven years to waste. People need me."

"Those are the edicts of the realm."

"I didn't agree to any of this."

"You came into her realm voluntarily. If someone entered your home without permission, what agreements would you proffer them?"

He had me there.

I stood up and surveyed the house. It was well-built. Comfortable. Attractive. Far larger than I needed. With a sigh, I looked down at the little fluffnut who was, apparently, my new butler.

"Bye," I said.

I walked into the trees. There was something about beech trees that was kind of neat, but I couldn't recall what it was. I didn't really know where I was going, but I wanted to get a look around, so I walked uphill. The sooner I could figure out the layout of this place, the sooner I could find a way out.

Little fluffy footsteps followed me.

"Sire?"

I ignored him.

"Sire? Where are you going?"

A creek ran down along a gully near the house, trickling over rocks in a musical fashion that I would have found soothing under different circumstances. Following it upstream, I came upon a pristine lake surrounded by more beech trees. The shore was wide and sandy, which made me think of bringing Erin here to camp and roast meaty things and sugary things on sticks over a fire. That thought made me ticked even more because the edicts of the realm meant I'd have to wait seven years to get out of here before I could.

My frustration turned into action. I fed my stride with anger and disappointment.

Hew kept pace.

"You shouldn't stray, sire."

My boots crunched on the stones at the water's edge while Hew's hooves tapped quietly behind me.

"I'm not sitting around here for seven years."

Hew persisted. "There are dullahan in the forest. If you go into the woods, especially after dark, you'll be in danger."

With anger barely held in check, I stopped and pointed at the water. "Can dullahan swim?"

"Why do you ask?"

"If they can't swim, then they can't follow me if I go into the lake."

"I believe dullahan can swim, sire."

"Okay. Can you swim?"

Hew seemed mildly panicked by the question, wringing his hands again. "Me?"

"Yes, you. So you could protect me?"

Hew shrugged. "Not well, but—"

He didn't have a chance to finish his sentence. I grabbed him by the fur and with a backwards spin worthy of an Olympic track-and-field champion, I turned a half-circle to gain momentum and flung Hew out into the lake. A string of words in a language I didn't know erupted out of him as he arced into the water, hitting the surface with a satisfying plunk-and-sploosh. I didn't understand the words he said, but I got the message.

Pretty sure he got my message too.

Returning to my hike, which doubled as my physical venting program, I felt my muscles loosen. I settled into a moderate stride that would carry me a respectable distance without wearing me out. Yesterday had been a heavy dose of exhaustion, and I worried I'd need my strength today.

The lake narrowed to a small neck of water less than a hundred yards wide. Behind that there was a second lake. I had a moment to wonder about magic. I picked up a leaf and called to my power. The power was there but when I said "Tine," the spell fizzled. I got a wisp of smoke, but nothing you'd be able to call a flame.

Figures.

No magic in this place. Another reason to escape, although it would be more difficult.

Unless.

I did have a few tools. Tools given to me by powerful, non-mortal beings. If my magic didn't work here, maybe theirs would. I made a mental note to try the Heartpiece first. If there were Dubhcridhe here, I'd find out, and that would be worthwhile.

I felt eyes on me.

Dozens of the small miongabhálaí peered out from under the ferns and behind the tree trunks. They stared with those enormous eyes. I half-expected some of them to wave or come closer but they only gazed at me as I intruded on their territory. Dozens turned to hundreds. There had to be a nest nearby. They may have felt the magic I called up and if that was the case, any dullahan would smell it too.

Curses upon them all.

More miongabhálaí gathered to the point of becoming extraordinarily creepy.

"Go back to sleep," I chided. "You have dreams to catch."

They didn't move.

At the top of the lake, I found a little castle. The stones were rough-hewn, dark gray granite. At some point, there had been a stained-glass window in the wall facing the lake, but the glass was all broken out now. Only stubby teeth of color remained sticking out of the framing. Much of the outer walls had tumbled down, but the rooms in the center remained intact. I ventured through a split wooden door and saw a sitting room with a fireplace, and an archway with carved columns leading to a stairway going up to the second floor.

If I ever came back this way, I'd have to explore further.

Now and again, I came across more miongabhálaí. They nested beneath the broad, fan-shaped leaves of forest shrubs and in the crevices between the rocks. I also found people.

The goddess was really into real estate. The house that sat at the top of the hill was one of those goofy modern glass monstrosities that are usually set on the side of a hill in Snobbywood, California. There were rooms full of curving metal furniture and a painting that was thirty feet wide hanging on a stark white wall. The painting looked like it had been done by a dozen elephants sneezing paint through their trunks. Considering where I was, that was a likely possibility.

The figures moving in the kitchen were ghosts. The wife mixed something in a bowl on the counter while the husband squeezed juice out of oranges. The third person, a girl, was in her early twenties and had the same eyes as the husband. The scene of domesticity was so out of place here, I had to pause and watch. They carried on, oblivious to me even though I passed in front of their floor-to-ceiling window.

On the crest of the hill, I got a panoramic view of my prison.

Tír na nÓg wasn't circles of Hades. Here, it was a rolling valley, far longer than it was wide. If I had my directions right, I was located on the western side, six or seven miles from the border. The border

251

wasn't hard to define. It was a wall of purple stone several thousand feet high. Another wall lay across the valley, just as high; however, I wasn't able to see where the two walls met. The walls faded off into a misty distance both north and south. I looked west again. The wall wasn't precisely vertical, but leaned in to glower over the valley like a disapproving middle school teacher.

I needed to get there.

My departure had been hasty from the house the goddess had built. That tended to happen when I got ticked off. I had no food or water, but the stream at the top of the lake was refreshing and I drank. I did have my knife and I could make do if I got hungry. If I found a need for my other tools, I'd get them. The sun wasn't overhead yet, and I'd reach the wall in a couple of hours. Then there would be time to search for a way out and time to decide if I needed to find shelter or make my way back.

Going back to the house would be a last resort.

There weren't trails to speak of. My hike took me over meadows and through patches of low-lying grasses and shrubs. The view was pleasant. My mood was not.

By now, Nat would be calling out the National Guard. Erin would be worried sick. She'd already had one husband disappear for five years. I was slated to be gone for seven.

This could not stand.

As I hiked, I calculated and came to the conclusion Tír na nÓg was huge. Between the walls I could see, there were at least twenty-five miles, and the distance north and south I could see was more than thirty miles in either direction.

The result was more than 1,500 square miles.

And there was no telling how far north and south this realm went.

Fine.

I'd search the first five miles of wall today and take it from there.

For the children.

I passed more ghost-ridden houses with varying designs and more pockets of fuzzbutts, too. I ignored them all.

Around noon, I arrived at the wall. Or as close to it as I could get.

The wall was warded. A web of silver lines shimmered and pulsed at the edge of the forest where I stood, creating a barrier more than forty feet away from the purple stone of the wall. The power of the ward was palpable before I even got close to it, warning me to stay back. The power of a goddess, immense and irrevocable, stood as a force to never reckon with.

Wards were fashioned according to the desires of the caster. They could be simple barriers, like a magical chain link fence, or more complicated spells that targeted specific people or qualities. They could even stun or kill, although I doubted the queen wanted to zap to death the inhabitants she'd gone to so much trouble to contain.

There was no telling how high the ward had been constructed. Certainly higher than any of the trees I might climb to get over it. I'd used my magic to cut stone before, but with the ward in the way and with my magic stifled, I'd have to find a different solution. The only other way to disrupt a ward would be with iron. The chance of finding iron here was zero.

Another thought. With my knife, I dug a hole at the base of the ward. The silver attracted power from the ward in tiny little bolts of light, but the leather handle kept me from feeling any effects. The hole I made wasn't deep, but it was deep enough to see that the ward went into the ground.

Maybe there would be a tunnel going under the ward.

I had to look.

Onward.

Overhead, the sky grew dark as a voluminous cloud drifted in front of the sun.

Splendid.

The hike was cooler then. I continued for an hour, following the barrier and looking for any point of access or any flaw I could exploit. When I got hungry, I looked for a lake or a stream. I was fairly adept at fishing with my hands and a lake trout would be delightful for lunch.

The lake had no fish.

With a jolt, I realized I hadn't seen any birds. No mammals. Not even a fly.

Usually, in a forest, you can't move a millimeter without seeing something buzzing or flitting or floating somewhere.

The land here was devoid of wildlife.

What I did find was a small brick house. There were two women inside, faintly transparent. One sat on her bed reading a book while the other stared through a window with a drink in her hand. The back door opened for me and so did the refrigerator. While the people were phantoms, the houses were real. As it turned out, the food was real as well. There were sandwiches in the fridge and some fruit. I took one of each and walked out, shutting the door behind me.

If they noticed the missing food, they might wonder if a ghost had visited them.

Maybe they'd be right.

The first bite of the sandwich was delicious. Ham with Swiss cheese and tomato. I kept hiking, as a precaution, but all I felt after fifteen minutes was hungry. I finished the sandwich and then the pear, which was juicy and sweet.

My questions about food were solved.

On I went. The barrier and the wall of stone remained unchanged as I searched, but I persisted until the sun started to set. It felt early for twilight, but the giant wall cast a long shadow. The valley was dropping into darkness fast.

I needed shelter. Hew had warned me about the dark. Moving away from the wall, I looked for a place where I could bed down for the night and it occurred to me that I could slip into one of the houses. All I needed to do was find one and settle into a corner out of the way.

Ten or fifteen minutes went by. The light had faded faster than I could have guessed. No houses found. I heard the dullahan before I saw it. When the heavy gallop registered, I broke into a run. There were beech trees to climb and I took advantage, reasoning that a creature with hooves would be unable to climb. I pulled myself up to a branch ten feet above the ground as the creature thundered to a stop beneath me.

Instinct dictated higher would be even better so I climbed some more.

When I finally looked back down, I was well above the ground.

The dullahan circled the tree, and it appeared to be watching me except the phony eyes never blinked. The feelers around its head and neck tasted the air. The part of the dullahan that looked like a headless rider had those gleaming button eyes, and I knew that's what was watching me.

Creep-o-rama.

The thing tilted its fake horse head up at me and its long, sword-like tongue extended upward but it wasn't long enough to reach me.

"Ha, idiot!" I grinned down at the creature. "Neener. And also, while I'm thinking about it, another neener."

That's when the back of the dullahan rolled open and all the spindly legs came out and the idiot beast starting climbing the tree.

# CHAPTER 29
## Dance of the Dullahan

The spindly legs had no trouble wrapping themselves around the trunk of the beech and they were strong enough to haul the weighty bulk of the dullahan off the ground.

This was a nightmare.

With its tongue probing the air, the dullahan wasn't shy about making its intentions clear. I took a quick peek overhead. There was little refuge above. I readied my knife. The tongue lashed at me, cutting through the air with an audible snik. I dodged the strike and the point of the tongue took a divot out of the tree trunk. The dullahan hitched itself higher up the trunk. The tongue curled away and back again, like a snake preparing to strike.

I changed my grip on the knife and waited, my legs quivering as I held the branch, my stomach feeling tight.

One of the spindly legs curled gently around my ankle. I was lucky to feel it. Intuitively, I knew the dullahan was going to try to distract me. The spindly leg wasn't important. It wasn't going to kill me. For a moment, I admired its craftiness.

No matter what, I had to keep my eyes on the tip of the thing's sharp tongue.

The leg snapped taut around my ankle and pulled. It was counting on me looking down but I didn't. When the tongue drove toward me like a spear, I was ready. I turned sideways to dodge the strike and slashed with my knife. Behind the tip of the tongue there was soft muscle and tendon. My knife cut cleanly through the flesh.

With a screech, the dullahan recoiled. I let myself fall, slipping around the branch without letting go. I cut and stabbed at anything and everything, targeting the spindly legs. With all the efficiency and power I could muster, I sliced the legs and feelers.

Ichor made the bark slick, and the few legs I hadn't cut lost their grip. The dullahan slipped. Then fell. Time flowed at half speed. With almost balletic grace, the monster descended. Feelers and legs waved and the tongue spewed more gray-green blood. The beast hit the ground, sending tremors reverberating up through the tree. The thing lay still for a heartbeat. Then two. It twitched. Tried to get its legs underneath it.

A shriek split the air as a seabhacmór swooped out of the sky like a dark, feathered shadow. It paused long enough to clamp a talon around the dullahan's head before taking off again.

Holy whoa Betty.

Dust and leaves scattered as the giant bird lifted the dullahan into the sky. The monster struggled weakly in the bird's grasp, wanting to be free. Five hundred feet above the ground, the seabhacmór granted the dullahan's wish.

It fell again.

Like a stone.

I felt that impact as well.

The seabhacmór drifted over my tree and screeched.

"You're welcome," I shouted at the sky. "I mostly killed it, you know. Pretty much had it dying already."

Probably.

Hew had said that it's difficult to kill a dullahan except when it was eating. Breaking a lot of its bones seemed to work just fine.

So.

I avoided the trunk of the tree, wet with ichor, and used the branches to descend. The lowest branch was ten feet off the ground. I hung from that and dropped the rest of the way. None of my bones broke.

Hunters spend lots of money on things like camouflage and deer scent and duck blinds. They do so in order to mask themselves from wild animals and remain undetected by the better senses of the animals. If the dullahan could smell my magic, maybe there was a way of masking my scent.

There was a giant wall of magic rather handily placed. Unfortunately, there wasn't a good way to test my theory without another dullahan around and I'd had enough of those for one day. The opposite side of my problem was inherent in the houses scattered around the landscape. Even if the ghosts inhabiting those houses were lacking in magic, the dullahan weren't blind. They'd be able to see something resembling dinner from time to time. How would the queen prevent her guests from being eaten by the things in the dark?

A question worth pursuing.

I hiked away from the wall, the little hairs on the back of my neck on high alert. It shouldn't be too difficult to find a house in the dark. There should be lights, at least in the more recently built ones. The purpose was to let the people live here in the manner they'd been accustomed to before coming, or so it appeared.

Deeper into the forest I went, my breath quickening and my unease growing more urgent. How hard could it be to find a house?

After half an hour, I looked for a hill to climb. I finally found a craggy hunk of rock that would do the trick. From the top, I could see thirty miles in every direction that didn't have a wall.

No lights.

No man-made structures.

No people.

Only wilderness.

My eyes weren't failing. My sight was as sharp as a hawk's.

There were simply no shelters to be had.

An electric shiver coursed from my shoulders through the base of my spine.

I'm in trouble.

Shelter in place. The advice given in countless situations when danger may be looking for you was to hide where you were. Don't try to get away. Danger could find you more easily. I scoured the rock beneath me. Often, cracks developed when the climate was cold enough to freeze. Water that collected in crevices expands when it freezes and cracks the rock wider over time. This rock was relatively smooth across the top, and I wasn't sure it ever got cold enough to freeze here.

Clambering down, I circled the base of the rock. There were plenty of outcroppings and prominences. No crevices.

Come on, Nature. Help me out here.

On the other side of the rock, more rocks. Sooner or later, there'd be something I could use.

Please.

The feeling of dread pursued me as I crept from one boulder to the next. I felt like a clown fish, scuttling from one anemone to another, trying to avoid predators. Maybe I was just a clown.

There was a fallen log, but it held sleeping miongabhálaí. And it wasn't sturdy enough to protect me.

Eventually, I found a pair of stones huddled together like a couple of old drinking buddies, each leaning into the other for support. I scrambled between the two, finding a hollow underneath. It was damp and cramped but it would have to do for tonight. Any dullahan who smelled me here would have a hard time getting at me. My arms and legs and head were tucked in from the edges. Like a turtle who had borrowed a larger turtle's shell.

Although a sword-tipped tongue could stab at me.

Well. I'd gone a night without sleep before. I could do it again.

A stupid house. Right there. Thirty yards away from the pair of rocks where I'd spent the night with my own shivering panic keeping watch with me. At some point, as the sky had started to lighten, I'd dozed off for an hour to wake up again with sticky eyelids.

And the first thing I saw was a stupid house.

The architecture, Swiss Chalet. The ghosts inside, pale and oblivious. The food I scavenged, hearty and easy to snitch. I refused to feel any guilt whatsoever and dismissed the very thought as I stuffed a third oatmeal muffin into my mouth.

I deserved compensation for my misery.

A significant percentage of felons would understand that.

With a quick pace, I got back to the wall in fifteen minutes. I even found the tree where I'd fought the dullahan. The cut it had made in the trunk was there, but I didn't find the creature's body when I checked the spot where it had fallen.

Didn't matter.

I had a quest to finish.

The landscape flattened out significantly. Hundreds of those gigantic, rounded stones were strewn about but the hills were more even. The beech trees mingled with other adherents of the deciduous lifestyle, like maple and elm. On occasion, an errant pine claimed a piece of real estate as well.

Now there was another theory to test. If the dullahan only come out at night and the houses only appear during the day, problem solved. No mortals were harmed in the making of this insane asylum. Tonight, I'd try to see if it was true, primarily because I didn't like unanswered questions.

Tonight.

It made me sad to feel that I wouldn't be going home today. That I'd accepted being stuck here, at least for another day. That such a thing was becoming an accepted reality in my mind bothered me.

No.

People were looking for me. And I had people to look for.

Today, I'd find a way out. Today, I'd be leaving Tír na nÓg.

I sent my wish out to the universe and set off along the wall.

The universe sucks.

For most of the day, I zigzagged along the barrier looking for a tunnel below the rocks or a flaw in the ward. Overhead, the clouds languidly drifted along as if following me, but they never showed a shred of common courtesy by interposing themselves between me and the sun to provide a smidgen of shade. Jerk clouds. Thankfully, there were plenty of trees.

With an hour to go before sunset, I was forced to scout for shelter and a house to raid for food. There was a set of rocks with enough space for me to squeeze between them, but it was fifty yards away from the ward. I wasn't certain a dullahan would be able to follow me in or not. With the sun going down, it was the best option I could find. Nearby, a stately colonial-style home yielded baked chicken and something to do while the sun went down. I crept in to thieve and crept out to stand by the cluster of rocks and watch.

It occurred to me to stay in the house. It was probably safe to do so, but this was a particularly crazy corner of the Behindbeyond and the rules were often irrational. If the house disappeared at dusk, I might disappear with it and never return. Alternatively, my theory could be wrong, and some lucky monster would sniff me out in the house and eat everybody.

For the first time since tossing him into the lake, I wished Hew were with me.

Instead, I gnawed a drumstick down to the bone and observed the shadow of the wall crawl over the scenery.

I had never been certain when "twilight" occurred, but Tír na nÓg knew the moment precisely. With a shimmer of edges and corners, the house and the ghosts inside it vanished without a trace. Moments later, I felt the impact of hooves pounding the ground.

Another day, another dire circumstance.

I peeked around the stones and saw the dullahan heading straight for me.

Poodle noodles.

Ducking into the space between the stones, I waited, my heart thudding through my chest against the rock. The dullahan stopped at the gap, feelers waving. Smelling my magic. I scooted away from the thing. If it followed, I had an opening behind me and I could make my escape. The dullahan backed off and ran to the side.

Clever girl.

I slid back into the middle of the stones as the thing huffed to a stop at the back door. It smelled some more. Then it ran around again and I waited it out.

I can do this all night.

I may have to.

Finally, the monster decided to come after me. It crouched to fit between the rocks and I held my knife at the ready in case it tried to stab me with its tongue. By the time I'd made it to the opening, it was down in the middle of the crevice. Instead of running around, I scrambled up the stones to the top and lay down as flat as I could. It was possible for the dullahan to follow me there with a decent jump, and if it did, I'd drop down and run into the crevice.

We'll see how smart these things are. Hopefully without dying in the process.

I couldn't see the dullahan while pressed against the rock, which meant it couldn't see me either. I heard the thing pull itself from the gap with a snort. Its breathing remained heavy and it pawed the ground with a hoof. It shuffled around the opening and I heard it sniff in the gap. It plodded around the rock, looking for me. It went into the crevice from the other side and then backed out suddenly, running around once more.

Heh heh.

It could smell me but it didn't think to try going up.

The thing stopped, choosing a place where it could watch the crevice. If it was waiting for me to reappear somehow, it would have a long wait. I could lie on the stone all night and maybe give my heart a chance to calm down.

A soft crackling sound, which I associated with the opening of the dullahan's back, was followed by a shriek that almost knocked me off the rocks. Shrill and chittering, the sound was like the cry of a child and the warning of a hawk multiplied by all the things that sought to ruin everything beautiful in the world.

If that's a cry of frustration, I'm good with it.

It wasn't a cry of frustration.

It was a call for backup.

A second dullahan ambled out of the forest.

Of all the stinky butt nuggets. That's not right.

The second monster spotted me right away. It was far enough away to see me lying on top of the rocks like an advertisement for dullahan snacks and it galloped over, calling to the first one.

They squealed at each other. The first one turned and looked up at me.

Time to go.

I slid back off the rocks and made a run for the ward, hoping against hope my theory on the barrier would turn out to be right. I knew how to cut the tongue off a dullahan, which was a plus. And if one charged me, maybe I could dodge it and see what happened if a beast landed on the ward. Maybe it would leave an opening.

If I could pull it off.

Without dying.

Note to self: they will work together if necessary.

The pair of nightmares thundered after me. In life-or-death situations, it's comforting to think there won't be time for fear. Sadly, there's always time for fear, and the adrenaline in my system doubled to prove it.

When I reached the ward, I turned and sprinted parallel to it. On my left, the shimmering web of power gave a soft blue glow while on my right, two massive black dullahan vied for the first chance to taste something more meaty than my scent.

They could have fought each other for me. That would have been cool.

Instead, they kept pace easily and kept their distance.

Waiting for me to tire myself out.

Which would take as long as I could make it.

I ran for half a mile, feeling as if the creatures were toying with me and waiting for a sudden attack. A few trees grew near the ward but I ran around them. They were too small for cover and too short for climbing. I also spotted a nest of miongabhálaí but didn't have time to even think about how to use them for a distraction until I was well past them. With my stamina flagging, I spotted a pile of craggy rocks and made for it. A span of ten feet existed between the rocks and the barrier, which was too wide. No choice.

Panting and sweating, I pulled up in the sheltering space with my back to the ward. My knife fit into my hand as if I'd been born with it, and I faced the dullahan with what I hoped was an intimidating glower.

What's next dumb-uglies?

The nearest monster stayed put while the other one went around the rock. It took thirty seconds, so the rock was large. Or the dullahan dull. When the second dullahan found me again, he called out to the first one who called back. This time, the voices were guttural and throbbing, but I still never wanted to hear them again. Unless, of course, dying was the way for that to happen. In that case, I could listen to them talk forever.

The first beast edged closer while the second one barred my escape. The sword point of its tongue slipped out of its mouth, and I couldn't tell if it was being cautious or just tormenting me. Either way, the adrenaline in my system was processing off, leaving my arms and legs and gut jittery and aching.

Slowly, the hard point snaked closer. I kept my knife in front of me, checking over my shoulder to make sure the runner-up was staying put.

The tongue found the end of its reach, which was only a few inches away from my face. I nearly felt its edge cutting my skin and gripped my knife even tighter. When the dullahan struck, I'd strike back.

The dullahan took a step closer before lightning erupted from the ward, wrapping around me. My skin prickled, but there was no heat. Electricity coursed up the dullahan's tongue and coruscated around its head. Shrieking, the dullahan fell back. Its partner wheeled away, huffing in panic.

A seabhacmór descended, sentinel of the sky, a flipping minute late again. It grabbed the dullahan in front of me, crushing the middle of the "rider" from above in its talons. It half-carried, half-dragged the thing across the meadow in pursuit of the second one, which was beating a fast retreat toward the trees. The seabhacmór let go of the first dullahan and stroked the air with its massive wings. It caught the second dullahan before it could disappear between the heavy elms. Another stroke of wings, and the seabhacmór yanked the dullahan skyward. It flew higher, the creature in its grasp crying out. A thousand feet above the ground, the seabhacmór let the dullahan drop. It plummeted toward the earth. Halfway down, I realized what the seabhacmór was trying to do. The first dullahan was wounded, twitching but not dead. It was limping its way to find sanctuary. I had to admire the seabhacmór's creativity.

The second dullahan slammed into the first. Ichor and meat and bone erupted from them both, spattering the ground in a stomach-churning mass of red and gray-green and black.

Extra point for the seabhacmór.

And also, blech.

Beast bait. At least I'm good for something.

"Let me know if you ever want to do the whole job yourself for a change," I yelled, but the seabhacmór had already disappeared into the clouds.

The moon peered over the wall, casting silvery threads, and I settled in with granite slabs at my back. I'd learned another important fact. The ward would fry the dullahan if they got too close.

So, while I slept, I'd have a soft blue nightlight to go with the soothing coppery tang of blood in the air.

I could make that work.

# CHAPTER 30
## Mashed Potatoes

The twenty miles I'd covered helped sleep to come, but I managed to wake up before the sun rose, which is what I wanted. There was no sign of the dullahan corpses. Nothing decaying. Not a wildflower out of place.

Hmm.

I backtracked a mile, sticking close to the ward because The Mama don't raise no dummies. I recognized the set of rocks I wanted and resumed my spot on top of them. I was slightly less worried about dullahan attacking now. Panic was a decent teacher, and it was close to dawn in any case.

The moment arrived as the sun tinted the top edge of the western wall with a golden thread. The colonial faded into view, the ghosts already going about their business inside as if they'd been waiting for the new day.

There were sausages and fried eggs and toast, and I stole provisions while the ghosts were busy not seeing me. It wasn't as tasty as the breakfasts Dad made, but it was close. I was happy to see the house return. It confirmed another theory. I still didn't want to disappear at dusk in one. Maybe if I were in the one built for me.

First things first.

There were no clouds today, but the air was cool. I set out with a fresh day and I didn't want to waste a minute.

I missed Erin. And Nat. And Alyce too.

I hoped the abducted kids would be okay.

Okay until I could find them.

At the end of the day, I was another twenty miles more clueless. The trees changed somewhat. More pines and spruces. There were more rivers and streams too, and I took advantage of a quiet pool to wash out my clothes, which had gotten rank. While they dried, I napped. Socks, shirt, pants all turned stiff, but I didn't care. I also used my knife to trim my beard. It wasn't shaving by any means, but keeping the hair short kept my face from itching.

A log cabin waited for me to raid it and a cave beckoned nearby. I decided to stay the night in the area. I wouldn't sleep in the cave because it wasn't near enough to the warded barrier to be safe. I explored the entrance, which gradually descended into the ground. The cave didn't turn into a tunnel beneath the ward, however, and it went away from the wall instead of toward it. It also held the largest collection of miongabhálaí that I'd found so far. Hundreds of the little fuzzbutts piled on top of each other, each one dreaming away. Because I could, I picked one up and closed my eyes.

A housewife in a kitchen. She was making dinner and it felt very important. She stood in front of an appliance that was styled like a standard stove with an oven and four gas burners on top, but it was small, like a toy. There were four tiny, boiling pots with different side dishes. Peas, potatoes, corn, and green beans. She bent over and looked through the glass at a tiny roast, browning, almost done. She wrung her oven-mitted hands together.

I put the miongabhálaí down. Wherever the housewife was, and whatever her neuroses, she was on her own. I left the cave and stole food from the cabin. A small grove of maples stood within a few feet of the barrier and that's where I camped. As I drifted off to sleep, it occurred to me that I hadn't dreamed here. Maybe because Hew wasn't with me. Maybe because I didn't have any dreams in my mind, except to get out of this place. Caer Ibormeith wouldn't have any interest in that dream.

Good.

Maybe if I wasn't interesting, she'd let me go.

I drifted off. At some point, when the moon was high, I found myself half awake. Miongabhálaí emerged from their cave. They didn't walk so much as tumble and roll. And when they were clear of the cave, they floated off the ground. Like bits of dandelion fluff, they sailed skyward. Up. Up into a cloud above them. A cloud guarded by two flying seabhacmór.

In the morning, the cave was empty. I went back to make sure I hadn't dreamed the whole thing about the fuzzbutts floating up into the clouds and, apparently, I hadn't. There wasn't even a scrap of fuzz in the cave anymore.

I bet they shed like crazy in springtime.

At least they were safe. I was glad of that. Safe. Backed up in the cloud. Like data. Or vacation photos. Ha. And also ha. The cloud had drifted down the valley. The texture was a little more like a massive cauliflower rather than mashed potatoes, but the dawn still painted the edges golden like butter. The cloud was situated at the top of a pillar of rock, as if roosting. Maybe it had gotten snagged thanks to a mischievous breeze.

Time to raid the cabin again.

I trudged on.

At day's end, I hadn't learned anything helpful. Hadn't learned anything new.

I missed Erin. And Nat. And Alyce. And Max and Sandretta. I even missed my father. Maybe even Mads.

Maybe tomorrow, I'd find what I was looking for.

I slept beside the blue light of the ward.

The cloud today looked like mashed potatoes with butter again. Fluffier than yesterday's cauliflower.

The cloud today was dark. The potatoes getting old. Joined by a whole buffet table of gray potatoes making rain. Today the cloud sat in the branches of a tree, as if the tree were a massive multi-fingered hand playing catch.

Another day. Another scoop of potatoes. The stupid cloud may be following me.

Clouds everywhere. I'm thinking of giving up starch. I may be lost.

I hate potatoes.

    I hate potatoes.

        I hate potatoes.

            I hate potatoes.

                I hate potatoes.

                    I hate potatoes.

                        I hate potatoes.

                            I hate potatoes.

I hate potatoes.

                                                I hate potatoes.

               I hate potatoes.

                                        I hate potatoes.

       I hate potatoes.

                                                    I hate potatoes.

                   I hate potatoes.

                                    I hate potatoes.

       I hate potatoes.

                           I hate potatoes.

               I hate potatoes.

                                            I hate potatoes.

   I hate potatoes.

                       I hate potatoes.

                                        I hate potatoes.

       I hate potatoes.

                           I hate potatoes.

                               I hate potatoes.

                   I hate potatoes.

Alone.
    Dreamless.
    Lost.

# CHAPTER 31
## Troubled Fuzzbutts

A month gone. I was no closer to finding a way out. I'd started to think this whole quest had been a waste of time, but I'd needed to try. I must have traveled six hundred miles away from where I started, and the walls simply kept going. The trees had been pine and spruce for a few days, but I'd started to see maples again and other leafy shrubs. My boots were worn out. I'd had the same clothes for weeks. Undoubtedly, I was a scruffy-looking nerf herder, but I had to think Erin would be glad to see me anyway. If only I could find my way back.

The house nearby had a couple of thin-shouldered guys in it. They resembled one another in the way of father and son, which made me think about my own father. I stole a half-empty box of cereal and ate handfuls of it as I looked for a hill to climb. Close by stood one of the craggy pillars like those where the clouds sometimes rested. It didn't have a path, precisely, but there was a route I could see from the ground that was an easy ascent, and I decided to see how far I could go. With breaks for rest, I made the top after two hours, and wondered, not for the first time, if I had the skill to build a glider to fly over the wall. It wouldn't make a difference. No matter how high I got, the barrier warding the walls continued up as far as my eyes could see with no sign of ending above or to either side.

What place had walls that continued on with the same landscape forever?

This place.

I clambered down and stretched, finishing the cereal and leaving the trash in the house I'd taken it from. You're welcome, Caer Ibormeith, may your lands be ever free of non-recyclables.

I'd gotten used to hiking twenty miles each day, but the climb had used muscles differently, and I knew I'd feel it in the morning. I could still make some progress today though. The ground was friendly and my pace unforced. The afternoon was pleasant enough. The sun thoughtfully ducked behind the stupid mashed potatoes in the sky. Wonderful shade.

I found a cave. From the outside, the hole in the rock was like others I'd run across. Wall of stone. Dark opening. Probably full of sleeping miongabhálaí. Standard stuff.

The whimpering fuzzbutt was non-standard.

Swaying at the edge of the cave mouth, as if he wanted some fresh air but didn't have the energy to make it all the way out, the fuzzbutt bent over. A purplish goo dribbled onto the ground. The little guy shivered. A high-pitched sound escaped his throat in rhythmic bleats, a blend of whining and panting. I felt I should do something for him, although I was completely at a loss to know what was happening.

Thoroughly miserable, his eyes were closed against the bright day, the lids red. His fuzz was matted as if he'd been spattered with grease. I stepped closer for a better look. From inside the cave, more sounds drifted out, echoing against the walls.

Feeling like it was exactly the wrong thing to do, I went into the cave, steering clear of the wretched little guy panting outside. The cave went back into the rock several paces before opening into a cavern big enough to house a house. Dozens—hundreds—of fuzzbutts littered the stone floor.

They were all infected.

The rasping sounds were worse than the bleating sounds, but the whole cavern was a symphony of high-pitched squeals and lower-end barks of sickness. I kept away from the nearest nest. Whatever afflicted them could be contagious.

It could even be airborne. Wouldn't that be a full can of splendid?

I retreated from the fuzzbutts. My foot landed on a slick stone and I had a moment to consider changing where I stepped when there was a sharp cry from one of the miongabhálaí. It was loud and wrong and too close and it caught me by surprise. My foot slipped off the stone. I fell. My hands reached down automatically but landed on something fuzzy and wet and—

Sudden fear, like a knife in the gut.

The bad man was here.

This place was too confining already. Too many kids and not enough room.

Some of the kids would be going away today.

That was why the bad man was here.

He comes to take kids away.

He takes them to a factory where they chop them up and make soup out of them. The same soup they feed us here. That's why the soup is so salty.

That's what the big kids say. But they're lying. Just to scare us.

The thoughts were potent. The girl's mind dominated by fear. It took only a moment for her feelings to flood my system with the same urgent panic that stayed with me even after I pulled my hand away from the fuzzbutt.

What's going on here?

Another cluster of miongabhálaí hunkered down in a hollow close to the entrance. They were panting and shivering like the others, although none of these were throwing up. I touched one.

The only sound in the closed space was soft crying. The guards tolerated emotion as long as it couldn't be heard in the office. If it couldn't be heard in the office, it couldn't be heard outside. The warehouse was dark. The kids were all lying on cots but only the most exhausted could sleep. The only light came through the highest windows. Most were covered. The corner of the building across the street had a single blue light on it, which pulsed every five seconds. It offered a hint of comfort in the night, saying, "I am watching over you. The real world is close. Don't give up. There's a light in the darkness."

I let go of the miongabhálaí, realizing what I was seeing.

These are the nightmares of children. Children in the mortal realm.

274

GOT HOPE

The children on the other side of the door, glimpsed behind Aoife.

The children I needed to find.

I retreated from the cave.

More than ever, I had to get out of here. I had to find those kids.

There had to be some concern for the goddess's miongabhálaí, didn't there? The goddess wouldn't want to float this batch of fluffbutts up to a cloud. Would she?

Hew would know what to do. How to reach the goddess. If helping the kids would help her too, maybe she'd let me go. I put a finger on the miserable fuzzbutt by the door. Though the perceptions were dimmed and distorted by worry and exhaustion and pain, the child was living in the same warehouse, living the same horrendous existence as the others.

The fuzzbutts in this cave were linked to the same group of kids.

Change of plan. Time to turn around and work my way back to Hew and my little house.

Hiking back with the fuzzbutt would be a problem, but I needed to take him with me. He was my link to the kids in the warehouse and my evidence that something was wrong with the goddess's dream catchers.

Maybe he could be cured.

I couldn't hike while holding the miongabhálaí or I'd be caught in his dreaming, unable to see where I was going. Nearby, a number of those broadleaf plants waited. I pulled off a few leaves and quickly wove a basket. It wasn't pretty, but the fuzzbutt wouldn't care. I used a few additional fronds to make straps. The result was an ugly green backpack, perfectly serviceable, and the right size to carry the little guy.

I scooped him into the backpack.

Then I headed back the way I'd come.

As I hiked, I calculated. Coming up, I had paced myself for a long haul. Going back, I needed to pace myself for speed. Even if I pressed hard, I'd only be able to save myself a few days. There were limits to how far and how fast a Halfling could travel.

I hoped my boots would hold together.

The best of things. That's what I'd have to make.

So I would.

Almost, I forgot to eat. My flagging strength and generally contentious tummy reminded me as the sun was about to set. I found a bungalow with salty things on skewers that I barely had time to inspect before snatching them and trotting back outside. Taking care not to stab myself in the face, I pulled chunks of beef and chicken and shrimp and peppers and onions off with my teeth as I walked.

Delicious.

Someday, I'd work my way back here and steal from them again.

My path strayed toward the barrier. Whether by choice or accident, I wasn't sure, but the soft blue glow was reassuring to me.

Not so much to the fuzzbutt.

Over the course of the day, the little guy had slept. Once or twice, he squeaked and I found water, which he lapped up drowsily from my hand. It didn't seem to help. I worried he'd never survive long enough for me to get him back to Hew or the goddess if I didn't get him something to eat and drink. He refused everything I offered him.

Time to find a place for the night. It looked like it might rain, so I found shelter near the barrier that would also keep us covered. He started to cry as I searched near the barrier, and his cries turned to wails the closer I got.

Maybe the barrier affected the miongabhálaí too.

At a loss to know what to do, I left the little guy inside a log that had fallen over. He wouldn't be close enough to the barrier to be protected from marauding dullahan, but he wouldn't be easy to find either.

Feeling unsettled and without comfort as well, I shouldered my way under a shelf of rock where I could keep an eye on the log. My body was worn out, but I was wired enough that I couldn't find sleep. My eyes wouldn't close, wouldn't close, wouldn't close.

Fry me two baboons
And let me taste a monkey's heart.

Heh heh. Frank.

"Wake up."

Some idiot didn't know when to quit. I didn't wake up the first five times the voice had asked and I wasn't going to wake up this time either.

The magic flowed into me gently, insinuating itself like a whisper.

Snap.

I awoke. Not just drifting from sleep like a diver rising up from a tranquil sea. More like how a diver comes to a stop when eaten by a shark.

Senses instantly on full, I sat up.

"Good. You're awake."

Hew stood before me in full bone regalia, including the skull helmet and his jawbone-on-a-stick, which was still glowing blue.

"What are you doing here?" I asked the question before I had a chance to look around or even remember what I'd been doing before falling asleep. I pointed at his weapon. "Did you use that thing on me?"

Hew shrugged. "I'm where I've always been." He gestured to the space over my shoulder.

Behind me, my gifted house sat in the midst of its guardian beech trees.

Swell.

"I'm back where I started? How did that happen? Did the goddess bring me here?"

A sigh escaped Hew. "Not exactly."

"Not exactly?"

Hew shifted from foot to foot. "The land in Tír na nÓg isn't entirely . . ."

I waited. As long as I could. "Isn't entirely what?"

"Permanent?" Hew was trying to find the best word and failing. "Solid?"

"What are you saying?"

"The land can be changed, if the goddess wishes it."

She can change the land of Tír na nÓg. Oh, yippee. "I'm going to need more information about that."

Hew took a step back. "No."

I took a step forward. "Why not?"

With a jab of his pointy thing, he said, "You'll toss me in the lake again, which was insulting."

"You're right."

"And cold."

"Had to be."

"And my underfur took days to dry."

"I shouldn't have done that."

His eyes rolled at me from behind the helmet. "Jerk. With all due respect."

I nodded. "What I did was inexcusable. With all due respect, I give you my solemn oath it won't happen again."

Hew shook his head. "I do not trust you. Halfling."

"Hmm." I scratched the side of my chin, which was overdue for another knife scraping. "I think I only have two oaths available. A solemn oath and a comedic oath. Of the two, the comedic oath is far less trustworthy than the solemn oath."

With his head cocked sideways, Hew rolled his eyes at me some more.

"I don't know what else I can promise, Hew, but I have never broken a solemn oath. I hope you can sense the truth of that."

Hew shook his head with tiny motions.

What a touchy swimmer.

I finally knelt down and infused my voice with all the sincerity I possessed. "I give you my solemn oath. I will never again throw you into a lake, stream, pond, or puddle, regardless of what you tell me.

Ever. On the other hand, I'll toss you into the nearest volcano if you don't tell me what I want to know."

Hew flinched. Then, "There aren't any volcanoes in Tír na nÓg."

"It's okay. That was only a comedic oath."

I got another eye rolling moment. "Idiot."

"Technically, Prince Idiot." Maybe he was entitled to couple of insults, but it seemed like a good idea to remind him of his place. "I've been wandering here for a month, Hew. I need to understand."

The moment when Sir Fuzzbutt decided to let bygones be goners was plain in the way he dropped his shoulders.

Finally.

He gave a "follow me" gesture with his weapon.

I followed.

# CHAPTER 32
## Dream Harvest

Hew led me to a familiar log. "I have questions for you as well—the goddess's questions—but we have a bit of business to take care of first." A wheezing whine reminded me that I'd left the sick fuzzbutt inside the log last night.

I crouched down to get a look.

He'd gotten much worse.

The most shocking thing was how he could still be asleep. His eyes were closed and crusted with muck. His nose dripped with heavy mucus, forcing him to pant through his mouth. His tiny hands were twitching, and his fur was damp.

Hew regarded the fuzzbutt blankly.

"What can we do for him?" I asked.

"We can do one thing for him. Kill him."

"Kill him? Why?"

Hew shifted his weapon in his hands. He hesitated long enough that I wondered if he was worried my solemn oath would not remain solemn. Finally he said, "He is linked to a child having nightmares in the mortal realm."

"Yes, I know that. How do you know that?"

"I have been in your dreams for the past month."

"Ha. Joke's on you, Hew. I haven't had any dreams since I got here."

Hew's gaze drifted from the suffering fuzzbutt to me. "You have had dreams. Rather, you've had the same dream over and over again. Until last night."

What?

"What are you talking about? I don't remember any dreams."

"That's because . . . well, it's possible to have dreams and not remember them."

I let that statement swirl around in my mind. "Have you been in my head?"

Hew looked stricken.

"Is that why I have the mangled lyrics from 'Fly Me to the Moon' in here?" I pointed at my temple.

"'Fly Me to the Moon?'"

I nodded. "Except in my dream I heard the lyrics 'fry me two baboons.' Nobody else gets Frank Sinatra lyrics wrong except you.'"

Hew sidled away from me, taking tiny steps. "It was Mr. Sinatra's fear, expressed in his dreams. He worried he'd get the words wrong in concert."

"Hold on. You were in Frank Sinatra's dreams?"

Hew shrugged. "That's my job, under the goddess's mandate. To guard the dreamers. Follow their dreams. Harvest them if needed. Sinatra rubbed off on me. Dreamers often influence grand-gabhálaí and miongabhálaí."

I heard what he said but couldn't shake the word harvest. "You were a parasite in my head when I slept?" I wanted to be mad, but I'd given a solemn oath. I held my hand up in surrender. "It's okay, Hew." He seemed surprised at my calm. "What have I been dreaming about?"

"Until last night, you've dreamed about plants with fronds like children's arms. Hosts of the dead giving tribute, a woman in white carrying children, and your father, the Alder King. He sits on his throne, burned, but his reflection is alive. You have had that same dream every night. Until last night."

"I remember that. From a month ago. What was different last night?"

Hew chuckled. Coming from behind the skull helmet, the sound was hollow. "First things first," he said, pointing at the fuzzbutt. His panting and wheezing from the log sounded hollow as well.

A hand grenade of dread sat low in my stomach. "Tell me why we have to kill him."

Hew tilted his head so he could get a better look at the suffering ball of fur. "We have to kill him before he tries to kill us."

I didn't know how that was supposed to work, but I knew Hew believed it.

The fuzzbutt squealed. I recognized the sound. I'd heard it in the cave, visceral and shrill, and it had startled me. It startled me again now. Along with the squeal, the little guy shook violently. I felt bad. Then I felt nauseated when the miongabhálaí's horns started to unravel and become feelers.

The squeal of the fuzzbutt deepened to a growl. The feelers grew and lengthened like dozens of slender purple snakes pushing each other out of the way. The miongabhálaí's eyes flew open. They were clear and dark and I felt the weight of something prescient when he looked at me. His squeal turned to a scream as his belly split open and hooves thrust themselves from his abdomen, twitching and kicking. The log seemed to be shrinking for a moment, but I realized the miongabhálaí was getting bigger. Not only was it growing, it was coming after me.

Inside my gut, the grenade went off.

I called up my power, forgetting in the moment it was no use. The blue light sputtered and faded in my hand. I needed a different option. Hew watched me, unmoving, although he held his weapon in both hands, ready for business.

The idea of a mercy killing wasn't new to me, and it was the right thing to do.

I didn't have to like it.

There was a grapefruit-sized rock nearby. I picked it up and when the emerging dullahan's head ventured out of the log, I bashed it in. The former fuzzbutt made no sound, for which I was grateful.

Hew and I stood over the body.

"The goddess has a problem." Me. Stating the obvious.

"Yes. She wishes to see you."

"Really? Don't mess with me."

"Why do you think I've revealed myself to you?" Hew glanced up at me.

282

"I guess you'll tell me. But I don't trust you as far as I can throw you. Oh. Wait. I guess I trust you about twenty yards."

Heh heh.

"Jerk."

"Prince Jerk to you. Speaking of which, you're a jerk for invading my dreams and harvesting them. Even if the goddess asked you to."

Hew looked back at the corpse.

I didn't want to look at the thing the fuzzbutt had started to become. "You said this miongabhálaí was linked to a child's dreams?"

"Not dreams. Dreams are benign. Nightmares. Once a miongabhálaí is connected to a child's nightmares, it's ruined. It can't connect with other children. Nightmares are like viruses. They can infect other children. And every time that first child has a nightmare, the miongabhálaí is drawn in again. Eventually, if the nightmares are strong enough and never resolved, the miongabhálaí is trapped. Then it changes. There's nothing more powerful than a child's dreams. And nothing more damaging than the nightmares of the innocent."

Soberly, I said, "That's how dullahan are made." It was frightening and sickening and the revelation only made things worse. Such horrible creatures, born through the union of Tír na nÓg's meekest creatures, the miongabhálaí, and the burdened psyches of children who should dream of laughter and hope.

I gestured in the direction of the body on the ground. "He's got a whole cave full of friends. They're changing already, most of them."

"It's been happening for as long as there have been dreams, but the dullahan have always been manageable. Until recently. In the past few months the problem suddenly manifested far more frequently. Exponentially. That's why the goddess wants to talk to you."

Something about this didn't make sense. Caer Ibormeith had tasked Hew with following my dreams for more than a month and six hundred miles. What felt like six hundred miles. The queen had to know where the cave was with the transformer fuzzbutts. In fact, it was probably a short hike away, if the land was easily changed. So that left me with one big question.

What does she need me for?

283

One of my mental magnets found a mate and clicked.

I'm a little slow but I get there eventually.

She knows everything.

Assuming the queen has been given my dreams and Béil's dreams, she knows I can find the kids having the nightmares. And if the kids having nightmares are turning her lovable miongabhálaí into dullahan, then maybe we had a common goal but somehow, she needed me to put it all together.

"When does she want to meet?"

Hew nodded. "As soon as you can get cleaned up. You're rather . . . aromatic. And unkempt. And—"

"I get it. Shut up. It's her fault."

Finally, I took another look at the half-dullahan on the ground. He didn't seem so fearsome now. Just small and sad. "What do we do for him?"

"Nothing. Upon nightfall, his body will return to the essence of dreams and nightmares that created it."

I see.

"All right. Show me around this house then." Hew turned to lead me. "Are there good schools nearby? How's the crime rate by the way? I hear there are a lot of break-ins in this neighborhood. People having food stolen right out from under their noses."

Hew ignored me.

Probably for the best.

The house was nice. Fully stocked larder. Fresh fruit on the kitchen counter. Refrigerator with bottled water and cold cuts and cheeses. It was almost as if somebody could see into my head and find out what my dream lunch might be.

First, a shower.

Hot. Soapy. Water pressure perfect. I could've spent another month soaking.

But I didn't.

The razor at the sink was finely-honed. The shaving cream nothing less than shavy and creamy. The soother pleasantly manly. I could have gone slowly, making my strokes with precision.

Maybe next time.

Ten minutes later, freshly scrubbed and shaved without so much as a nick, I found clothes in the nearest closet. A minute thereafter, I was in a new pair of khakis and a pale-blue button-down shirt with a staggered pattern of tiny gold crowns on it. What good would the joke be if I didn't play along?

I paused when I noticed my bag had been unpacked. My tools were all laid out on a dresser. At one point, I'd considered trying them out to see if they worked here, like the Heartpiece, which Hope had told me I'd need. Well. If there were Dubhcridhe here, the goddess would know, right? I'd just ask her. Maybe she'd even know how to use it since I'd never tried.

In the fridge, I found bottled olives and Italian giardiniera and a dozen other bits of delicious that I used with the sliced meats to make an impromptu muffaletta sandwich. Eating took longer than showering, I confess, because nobody could stock a cupboard like Caer Ibormeith. May she always honor double coupon Tuesdays.

Finally, clean and well-fed, I felt prepared to deliver my case to the goddess with unassailable logic. Yup. Even if you strapped my logic to a boat, it could not be sailed.

Hew waited for me outside. He eyed me from basement to belfry and approved. Or, at least, said nothing. Holding his jawbone-on-a-stick like the leader of a marching band, he led the way. We turned up a path through the woods. The morning was turning to afternoon and I felt a soft energy sifting in my veins, as if the Earth had remembered me at last and decided to send me happy Nature vibes. I had no idea what was about to happen, but the mere possibility of getting away from this place lifted my soul.

Hew felt uplifted too. I heard him singing.

I'm a little spam who's boss in the 'hood,
The snow, it should always be good
To wear a watch over tea.

The lyrics didn't make a lick of sense, but the tune was recognizable and I found it funny in this situation that Hew was singing a messed-up-Sinatra version of "Someone to Watch Over Me."

We came up on the little broken-down castle I'd peeked in a few weeks ago and I nearly laughed out loud. "Hew." I looked at him sideways. "Why take this path? It's not nearly as scenic as the path by the lake."

"Oh?" He feigned surprise. "Guess I thought this way was more direct. The goddess is waiting."

Hew the Sly.

"You sure? Seems like this path was the long way."

He shrugged. "Perhaps I misjudged."

Was this the mighty warrior? Ah well. Mighty warriors could be afflicted with hydrophobia. Or my-underfur-is-still-wet-ophobia, and it was difficult to begrudge Hew his precautions.

Yet, as we walked into the castle, I found temptation. There was a fountain inside the foyer, a half-filled, stagnant kiddie pool made of granite.

"Look, Hew. Water."

Hew's head snapped around to look at me. "You gave your solemn oath."

"Solemn oath? What? Oh, come on, Hew. I was just pointing out the features of the foyer. Look. A tapestry."

I could feel the scowl through his skull helm.

"Although, as I recall, when I gave my solemn oath, I didn't include fountains."

Hew stepped to the side, putting himself out of reach until we were well past the fountain.

As inwardly as possible, I grinned.

We reached a flight of stairs leading up. A few of the stones from the wall and ceiling overhead had landed on the landing.

Good shot.

We picked our way around the rubble until we reached the top floor. Without hesitation, Hew turned down a balcony hallway and I followed him to another stair going up. We climbed again and emerged on top of the castle tower. The sky overhead was a crystalline blue with a few cirrus clouds and the one gigantic scoop of cumulonimbus. Hew stood by the stair and looked at the cloud.

"I hate potatoes," I said.

Hew didn't say anything, keeping the "non" in my non-sequitur, I suppose.

I extended an olive branch. "Wanna sing 'Stranglers in the Night' again?"

"No." Gruffly.

"How about instead of 'My Way' we sing 'Guy Way' since us two guys are here?"

Hew ignored me.

"We could put your name in the song. Maybe 'The Way Hew Look Tonight?'"

No response.

"'I've Got Hew Under My Skin?'"

Nothing. I turned to look back up at the cloud. "'Hew Make Me Feel So Yuck.'"

The cloud started moving toward us like the world's largest, fluffiest dirigible.

"The goddess is coming." Hew's announcement came out in formal tones. "Behave yourself this time."

# CHAPTER 33
## City of Dreams and Nightmares

Watching the cloud drift toward us, a whole lot of things began to make sense.

"The goddess lives in the cloud," I said.

"More precisely, her city resides within the cloud."

"Uh-huh. Uh-huh." Rocking on my heels, hands clasped behind my back. "Which means she's been watching me since I got here. That cloud has been following me."

Hew gave me his most patient voice. "Your Highness, as I mentioned, the land changes. The cloud watches over all of Tír na nÓg and goes whithersoever the goddess wishes, but she may also alter the land to keep you beneath her city."

"Yeah. Yeah."

"It's no surprise she's kept you under watch. Your dreams about your father, a king, have a touch of prophecy, and you kept having the same dream."

"Sure. Sure."

Hew shifted on his feet. "What does it mean when you get monosyllabic and repetitious?"

"Me? Me?" I paused to let him worry.

The cloud arrived. Its underbelly turned the air the color of wood ash, and the temperature dropped twenty degrees. The chill reawakened the pit of worry in my gut.

Please let this be my way out.

I miss my friends and my wife so much.

The mists grew denser until Hew was a solitary gray silhouette by my side. When the change happened, it was like waking from a dream, which was appropriate. A blink of my eyes, and the fuzziness cleared away and we were standing on a cobblestone street surrounded by towering spires edged in silver.

The place was beautiful, as you might expect from the city of dreams.

The style of the buildings whispered romance and old-world charm while remaining utterly otherworldly. At first, the street felt generously broad, as though made for carriages to go abreast with room to spare, and the buildings all extended over the street like those in a Tudor village. Then I realized that none of the buildings were anchored to the street at all.

They were floating.

The street was an endless rolling plaza that undulated and climbed toward the center of the city. Among the buildings, thousands of warm spheres set in baroque silver lanterns hovered overhead, illuminating the spaces between the spires. The buildings were constructed from shining glass that appeared to reflect the light but didn't reflect the neighboring towers, which gave the city a bright, calming existence that wasn't as frenetic as it might have been.

"This way."

I followed Hew toward steps lit from below. There were trees in the city, but I felt they didn't exist until I looked for them. Tall, crystalline poplars reached skyward, their bark the color of bone. Statues and monuments came into view as well, with sculpted figures and faces covered in lichen and moss, and they faded to translucent ghosts when my gaze moved away. At the first landing, I spotted a fountain with a basin at the bottom and dome above it made from enormous clamshells.

The water was flowing up.

Shazowie.

Hew continued up the steps and I tagged along. There was something off-putting about the city, and I finally realized what it was.

No people. No animals.

Where is everyone?

We climbed in silence. I started noticing differences between buildings. The architectures were like a history book organized by era. The farther up the hill we went, the more antiquated the styles became. The buildings were still constructed of the same glass-and-silver material, but the designs flowed from newer to older in a gradual march. At the top of the hill, there was a small stone-and-silver castle. Simple. Blocky. Barely more than a tower with heavy walls and slitted windows. Several hundred yards of open space surrounded the tower as if the other buildings were afraid to get close to it.

Maybe they knew something.

The cobblestone way ended. Hew strode across the grass toward the castle like we were out for a picnic. At the gate, Hew stopped and gave a little bow.

"Welcome to the castle of Caer Ibormeith, Goddess of Dreams. Long may she reign." He waited.

I realized I was supposed to go in first.

All right.

The entryway was simple. An open room. More glowing lanterns floating in the air. Stairs leading down. Down we went.

Cold dread settled over my shoulders like a cloak. I'd been down places like this before and almost lost everything. With a shrug, I forced the feeling of incipient panic off. This wasn't the same place. This visit was by invitation. This wasn't the time for nerves. Because nerves led to a bad attitude and me not knowing when to shut up. Plus, I'd already mouthed off to the goddess and found she had no sense of humor.

Great. A new dread formed. Possibly worse than the first one.

Down.

The castle was far larger than it first appeared. The tower at the top was just a hatch, essentially. From there, each level appeared to be more vast than the last. Through narrow stone archways, I caught glimpses of distant machineries, laundries, kitchens, and barracks filled with fuzzbutts.

Everything for a well-stocked goddessdom.

There were children. Children running errands. Children

polishing the fixtures. Children folding clothes. They had glowing thumbnails of silver light shining through their tunics. Lights like the one Alyce had. Alyce had said she'd worked at the border. Maybe there were kids there, too. Maybe she didn't remember correctly, or maybe she didn't know this castle wasn't at the border all the time.

Another shard of desperate worry wormed its way into my belly as Hew prodded me to keep moving.

The goddess used children herself. How sympathetic would she be to my cause? Would she respond to my appeal when she had this in common with Urlabhraí and Aoife and however many other kidnappers are in the business of child labor?

"We're here."

Hew put his jawbone-on-a-stick in front of me to slow me but we were expected. The silver doors in front of us opened, ponderous and silent. The opening in the floor was the first thing I noticed. The middle of the floor was missing, the gray-blue light of the air beneath the castle adding a thread of vertigo to my dread.

It's not just a throne room. It's an observatory.

That's why the stairs led down. This was the basement.

Or the dungeon.

On the other side of the room sat a small throne of simple stone with luxurious cushions. The throne was flanked by a pair of large wooden beams, and in front of the beams were a matched set of enclosures. Open at the top, but surrounded by bars like a pen at a petting zoo. As we walked in, a breeze curled around my face. To the left and right, archways opened into the cloud.

"You could store a whole lot of data up here. In the cloud."

Hew jabbed me with his pointy jawbone thing.

"Hey," I complained. "She's not here yet."

Hew pointed at the throne.

There she was.

A petite woman sat on the throne dressed in a satin gown. And an obese woman sat on the throne with boils on her face. And an old woman sat on the throne, knitting together skeins of imagination and time.

This was what my eyes and mind told me. Thoughts projected into my thoughts.

Another certainty jammed itself into my understanding: all of the women were the goddess. All at the same time, occupying the same space together, but somehow always apart.

She made me afraid.

This wasn't the swan I'd met before, even though it was. This was someone altogether different. A creature more strange than the swan. More capricious.

More lethal.

That certainty was projected into my thoughts as well. Unlike my father's influence, which inspired loyalty by virtue of his glamour, the goddess's influence was shoved down your throat. Not cool. More people filed in. With a conscious effort, I managed to take my attention off the ever-changing, ever-constant figure on the throne to see who they were.

Oh no.

Three men wearing insignia from the realm next to my father's. Sómasach. I recognized the man with the gray hair: Spreasán's father. He took a moment to glare at me.

Underjoyed to see you, too. Whatever he was doing here, it wasn't good.

In human form, Caer Ibormeith didn't need any fuzzbutt to speak for her. Her voice constantly changed, however, along with her image.

"Welcome all." She looked at the three men. "State your business."

Her sentences were brief. Perhaps when you are constantly receiving dreams, there isn't a lot of mindshare left for talking.

Spreasán's father gave a bow. "We have come to ask for the release of Prince Goethe Laoch, son of the Alder King, to stand trial for murder."

Uh-oh.

"No," the goddess replied.

Okay then.

Spreasán's father took a step closer to the throne, ignoring the opening in the floor. He wasn't giving up on a single word of denial, even from a goddess. "Your Supreme Majesty, the prince was alone in a room with my son. The prince is famously ill-tempered with a penchant for using fire wantonly." The sound of grief in the man's voice was genuine. "There was nothing left of my son. Nothing but ash. Nothing for us to carry home and bury with those honored dead who have given their lives in the service of our lands."

The goddess listened. An auburn-haired woman with a slave's brand on her chest and a broad-shouldered farmwife and a thin, haughty-looking spinster with an aquiline nose and wheat-shaded eyes.

"All we have left is our honor. The only thing that will give us solace is to bring this killer"—he pointed at me—"to justice. By right, the prince is ours. By principle, we demand thou release him."

The goddess tilted her head to the side and regarded me next. Her power lanced into my heart through her gaze. I nearly grunted from the impact. "Didst thou kill this man's son?" She used no name or title. Quicker that way.

"No. I—"

"Lord Lúbaire, thy request must be denied."

I didn't mind her interruption.

"But, Your Majesty—"

"The prince is innocent," the queen hissed. She stood up and walked towards the men. Her voice rose and fell with her changing faces. "I can see no guilt in him for this issue. On the other hand, thou art guilty of a great many things. If thou wouldst seek justice for the death of thy son, look to that mongrel who is thy master for it."

With a groan, knees buckling, Spreasán's father crumbled to the floor. He struggled to get up and found himself kneeling before the indomitable ire of the goddess.

She stepped over the edge of the hole in the floor but didn't fall. Whatever there was beneath her feet—a force, a barrier, sheer willpower—she remained supported and came over to Hew and me as if she were walking on glass.

"I have claimed the prince for myself. Seven years shall he serve me." Her glare fell upon me and my knees nearly buckled as well. My heart certainly did.

Seven years.

"His dreams unlock secrets." Her glare turned to a smile. The smile didn't make me feel at all better. "And those secrets will have import upon the entire Behindbeyond and all the known realms for centuries to come."

I replayed her words in my mind because they made no sense.

Import? Centuries?

Wait. There had been other words. "The survival of all the Fae depends on it." Hope's words to me on the edge of the cliff. Maybe this is supposed to happen. Standing in the middle of the eye, the goddess raised her hands. She looked to her right and I followed her gaze. The clouds outside the archway swirled, and one of her massive seabhacmór glided into the chamber. A last beat of his wings stirred the air briskly as he landed. I looked the other way as the second seabhacmór entered through the archway at her left. They walked on ungainly talons to perch on the beams next to their mistress's throne.

Creatures both handsome and terrifying.

With the birds settled, the goddess looked down. "Thanks to the prince, a nest of dullahan has been found. There will be a glorious hunt." She waved her hand and the land far below began to move as the castle flew over it. I didn't feel the castle lurch or even bump, but the sudden shift in the view made me queasy.

If I throw up, her floating mashed potatoes will have the world's worst gravy.

A minute passed. Everything came to a halt again. Thankfully. The perspective from here was far different, but it looked like we were floating over the cave where I'd found the sick fuzzbutts.

Oh boy.

The sun was still high in the sky, and the dullahan wouldn't come out until dark. Additionally, the seabhacmór would never be able to get inside the cave.

I leaned over and whispered to Hew, "There were dozens of sick

294

miongabhálaí in that cave. Hundreds."

"Be silent." The words of the goddess thundered in my ears though she didn't raise her voice. She moved her hands over the eye upon which she still stood. Below, the shadows of the trees and rocks lengthened. Realization swept over me like a cold bath.

She was moving the day forward. Accelerating time.

How is that possible?

That any being had such power was almost more than I could comprehend.

In minutes, hours passed. Dusk had barely a moment of glory and then it was gone, replaced by night. The goddess smiled. A child. A woman. A crone. Her seabhacmór eagerly left their perches and hopped through the archways. Below us, they soared down, down, down.

The hunt was on.

My instincts screamed at me.

This feels wrong.

My combat training urged caution. Maybe I saw things differently because I was looking at the landscape from overhead, but the view was similar to reconnaissance images, and my eyesight was sharp, so sharp, that I saw details. Details that—I wasn't sure what to make of the details yet, but I knew caution was needed. If there were multiple dullahan—

"Majesty," I blurted. "Don't let them attack."

"Silence!"

I blacked out. A moment. A minute. I wasn't sure. I opened my eyes and the view to the ground was beneath me.

Ungh.

I had fallen on the eye. I backed up until the solid stone edge of the eye was beneath me.

The dullahan . . .

The birds . . .

I saw everything in pristine detail.

The seabhacmór circled the opening of the cave, their outstretched wings in the moonlight painting deadly shadows on the ground. One of the birds screeched, the sound reverberating in my chest even though I was a mile away. From the mouth of the cave, a spooked dullahan galloped into the open. It streaked from beneath the overhang and headed for a clump of bushes. It was fast. Very fast.

The seabhacmór was faster.

I looked over the scene as cold lightning jammed my veins. My instincts had been telling me something. I knew what it was.

Ambush.

I bit back a warning. No! But I dared not make a sound. Not after the last psychic sucker punch.

The seabhacmór dropped. I couldn't see what was happening directly beneath the canopy of the bird's wings, but I could imagine. Talons coming down on the dullahan. Grasping. Piercing. The bird adjusting to the weight, pausing before taking off again.

Long enough.

The bushes flanking the seabhacmór erupted. Half a dozen dullahan burst from the undergrowth. Already turned over with riders open, they attacked the seabhacmór as a group. The bird threw back its head, beak gaping, eyes wide. A moment later, the bird's agonized cry tore open the castle's air.

The second seabhacmór tried to help. It flew to the first one's side. Beak slashing, it dragged one dullahan from beneath the first bird's wing, but the first bird was pounding the air, trying fruitlessly to escape. The birds were so big they got in each other's way, and the second bird had to back off. It shook its head, rattled, and lamely took to the air.

In stunned silence, we watched the seabhacmór fly, struggling to reach the aerie in the cloud. It beat its way upward, faltering. A dullahan dangled from its side, hooves uselessly pawing the air.

On the ground, the dullahan painted the grass with feathers and meat and blood. Tearing. Eating. Roaring victory. The goddess said nothing. Her several faces wept simultaneously and in succession. Despair. The flying seabhacmór disappeared from view for a moment, then crashed through the archway, trailing blood across the floor. Hew ran toward it, his weapon ready. Horrible moments passed. The seabhacmór cried out, pleading.

Hew shouted "Buail!" and a knife-edged flare of light cut the shadows beneath the bird.

Hew emerged, blood spattered over his bone armor.

The goddess ran to her pet, a fresh figure shifting into view with each footfall while Hew marched back to me. The coppery tang of blood came off him in a wave, stinging my nostrils.

"Stay here. I'll fetch a healer."

Cooing, the goddess gently rolled the seabhacmór onto its side. Hew had decapitated the dullahan, but the head was still half-buried in the bird's chest. It would have been excruciating to fly like that, using the thick pectoral muscles to fly while a beast bit into the flesh and hung from the bite. The seabhacmór was lucky to have made it back alive. Far below, there was little remaining of the other bird.

Movement caught my attention. A group of twenty dullahan or more were moving through the trees. Moving like a combat unit. The dullahan in the lead paused, sniffing the ground. Searching. Chittering at the others. Moving on.

I had a good idea what they were looking for. I prayed they'd be unable to find it.

Organized, the dullahan stayed in groups of two or three. One sniffed for scents while the others watched its back. They fanned out, covering several hundred yards, moving parallel to each other.

I checked over my shoulder. The goddess was calming the bird with quiet sounds. It lay unmoving, although its eyes were bright and its beak open, panting.

She might lash out at me again, especially since she wasn't in her normal frame of mind, and her normal frame of mind was frightening enough.

I had to try.

"Majesty?" I said with as much calm concern as I could muster.

She turned. All her faces were streaming with tears.

"The dullahan are hunting for a house."

She stood, wiping her wrist under her nose like a little girl. In her grief, she shuffled forward with little enthusiasm. Half-falling, half-kneeling, she dropped on the eye.

I pointed. The dullahan stood in ranks, surrounding a square space in a clearing among the beech trees. They faced inward on all four sides. Then they stretched their necks up and, as if one voice, began to shriek.

The sound pierced me to the soul. Harsh enough and loud enough to wake the dead.

Or the dreaming.

# CHAPTER 34
## Halfling Lives

The goddess moved the cloud—or the land beneath it. Her actions were hampered by her grief, but we floated to a point above the howling dullahan and there, we stopped.

I'd almost forgotten about the men from Sómasach, but as the cloud took its position, I looked up to see them standing around the eye. Two of the men gave their attention to the scene below with mixed expressions of horror and fascination. Spreasán's father stared at me instead.

Making certain to hold my gaze, he held his finger horizontally and drew it across his throat. Regardless of culture, that gesture would mean the same thing. Sooner or later, he planned to end me.

I held my finger horizontally in return. Then I touched my right cheek and my ear and drew the number nine on my forehead and tapped my nose three times as I glared at him with a deadly squint and a final nod. Regardless of culture, that gesture would mean the same thing. Sooner or later, he should try to steal third base.

When he finally realized I was messing with him, he set his jaw and clenched it.

I gave him the sign of the Dubhcridhe, bunny ears and chomping teeth included, and then I pointed at him. This time, I was as serious as a deamhan invasion.

I know what you are. I know who you work for.

These men wanted to kill me. They might be claiming justice, but I was the man who knew too much and if I got away from them, I'd cause them a world of trouble. They had no idea how massive that world would be, but it would be epic. That was a promise. And I would enjoy it.

The goddess gasped. Something was happening below.

A shimmer of a house was sketching its way out of the dream. The howling of the dullahan was bringing it out of the void and into the real world again.

"Can you do anything? Your Majesty? Can I do something?"

She didn't answer. The stream of tears threatened to become a flood but she stood taciturn and resigned.

The house was compelled from its hiding place, from whatever land it went to when the light faded to night. When the house was fully solid, the beast nearest the door reared up and kicked. The door held until it was opened. A man emerged, scowling, bare-chested, and yelling. The dullahan's tongue lanced from the creature's maw, piercing the man's neck. It lifted him up, pulling him out of the doorway, limbs flailing, as the next dullahan rushed through the door.

The goddess screamed. Her voice this time was unwavering: a clear, full-throated cry of anguish. Further sounds of violence drifted up to the castle, but I didn't need to see anymore. Whoever lived inside that once-sheltered place stood no chance against the beasts. I only hoped they wouldn't suffer long.

Momentarily forgotten, the seabhacmór remained on the cold floor. He watched, unblinking, as I approached. I went forward slowly. The bird could rip me in half with its beak if it wanted to, but I didn't think he would. I got close enough to touch his feathers and copied the cooing sounds I'd heard the goddess make. The bird turned his head away from me and raised his wing so I could see the head of the dullahan beneath.

Permission.

Cautiously, I probed between the feathers, finding where the dullahan's mouth was attached. The muscles of the mouth were slack, which told me the jaws weren't clamped down on the bird's chest anymore. Instead, the head was hanging there, teeth hooked into the muscle. That was some good news at least. The teeth would have to be extricated, but we wouldn't have to fight against it to do so.

Hoofsteps came up behind me. Hew and another grand-gabhálaí. The healer's eyes were frozen so wide, I feared her eyeballs would roll out of her head. She carried a large bag that clattered as she trotted over.

"What took so long?" I growled. "Doesn't anyone ever need healing up here?"

The healer shook her head. "No, sire. Almost never."

Oh.

"All right. I've field dressed wounds before. Would you like some help?"

The healer nodded vigorously. I swear her eyeballs rattled.

"First thing, we'll need something to dull the pain. Make it stop as completely as possible. Do you have anything like that?"

She checked her bag and found a stick with a hand of bones on the end, forming a clenched fist. With a hopeful expression, she held it out to me. "This one."

"You'll have to use that. Where I come from, magic comes from inside and we heal with medallions." The healer looked crestfallen. "I'll hold the feathers out of the way. Use that to deaden the pain. Then we'll get this thing's head out of the bird's chest. How about stitches? Or some magic to close the wounds and prevent infection?"

More bag checking. Another stick. The one had a small skull on it from some creature with more teeth than one would think necessary. Or desirable.

"Great."

It was tough going at first. The healer went instantly to woozy at the first sight of blood, and it took her a minute to remember the correct word to trigger the magic. After we got going, however, she hung in like a trooper. We used the fist all around the outside of the bite, the little healer sticking her tongue out as she concentrated. There wasn't a way to ask the bird how he felt, so I watched carefully as I started lifting the dullahan's jaw. The seabhacmór closed his eyes. Once or twice, his beak crept open and he snapped it shut with a click, which made me want to be nervous. Hew reached up and helped then. Once the upper jaw was free, the lower jaw slipped out and the head fell to the floor with a wet smack.

Taking additional care, I checked around the wounds. No broken bones. No spurting blood. Thankfully, there weren't any severed arteries. Trying to repair something like that would have done the healer in. I pinched the skin together while the healer brushed it with the skull stick. The blue glow felt warm between my fingers, mingling with the bird's blood. Hew did what he could to sop up with a cloth.

Finally, shaking and sweaty, my blue and gold-crowned shirt thoroughly ruined, I backed away. The seabhacmór lowered his head to the floor, eyes closed, and sighed.

Me too, brother. Me too.

I spared a glance around the room. Spreasán's father and his guard dogs were still there, standing in the corner, studiously unhelpful. I'd almost forgotten about them in all the tumult. A woman stood in the room, regarding me soulfully as only a goddess dealing with serious loss could do. There was power there, tangible power. She wore only one face now. I was seeing her true form—or the form she wanted me to see. She was lovely, although her softness was polished down to the foundation from the burdens she had taken upon herself, adding a hard line to her girlish expression.

I gave her a small bow. "How may I serve thee further?" Me. Captain of the U.S.S. Magnanimous.

"I will not forget thy help, Prince." Like her form, her voice remained on a steady timbre as well. She put a hand on my arm. Her touch was cool and soothing.

"The dullahan down there. Can you destroy them?"

She slipped her arm through mine and spoke as she guided me around her guardian bird. The intimacy of her touch surprised me. Her eyes studied his feathers, but her words were for me. "The dullahan are beyond my reach. They dream not. The neither think nor feel. They are the balance to my control of other things. Because I'm able to do so much, there has to be something over which I can do little. This is why I had my birds. Only they were strong enough. And now I've lost one and the other will need to heal. The dullahan will overrun the land now, I fear."

How about that? The goddess of dreams was an existentialist at heart.

"Perhaps you could alter the land to confine them? Keep them separate from the people in the homes."

Caer Ibormeith considered my words. "Residence in this part of Tír na nÓg is reserved only for my most-honored guests." She pursed her lips.

Most-honored? Really?

"Those who need to be apart from the waking world for a time. There is no guarantee of safety here." She and I stepped together, turning back. "If that were so, no one would die in their sleep. But your suggestion has merit." She focused on the knot of men from Sómasach. She spoke loudly enough for them to hear. "And now, five Halflings are dead in my realm. Those people were your kin, dogs. The Dubhcridhe are responsible. Their blood is on your hands."

Caer Ibormeith slipped free of my arm and went to the eye with a purposeful stride. Instead of following her, I sauntered to stand beside Spreasán's father. I said, "She knows you're here doing Urlabhraí's dirty work for him. That's his style. Sending his motherless puppies on errands he should be doing for himself."

I had the beginning of a plan in mind, and I needed to provoke him while the goddess was distracted. To his credit, he wasn't instantly provoked.

His tone like glass, he replied with narrowed eyes. "I don't know what you or the goddess are talking about. I have heard of a Lord Urlabhraí. From what I understand, he was injured by a coward and is rarely able to go anywhere. He guides the Máithrín's affairs from his bed, where he lies constantly bleeding from an iron-bred wound that will not heal. Fortunately, there is a line of loyal subjects all the way down the hall prepared to volunteer their blood to keep him from dying. He may be a mongrel, but some Halflings are as noble as any Eternal. Not that you would know, Prince." He all but spat the final word.

Nice.

I needed to escalate the discussion as quickly as possible. I felt bad about the words before I spoke them. "At least Urlabhraí had good role models, then. Not like your son. Eternals shouldn't cower before Halflings like me. You should have seen Spreasán before the curse burned him to ash. You should have seen your boy, in the corner, crying as I stood over him asking simple questions. Which Eternal did he learn to wet himself from, Lúbaire? You?"

Did the trick.

Lúbaire lunged for me. "I'll curse you too!"

Oops.

Realizing his slip, his rage deepened, and he reached for my throat. I let him come.

Most Eternals—especially those in power—learn some hand-to-hand fighting, but unless a knife or a sword is involved, it's really brawling. Useful in a tavern but useless in a street fight. I was a little taller and outweighed him by at least thirty pounds, but I let him get his hands around my neck. We turned and I made choking sounds for his benefit, my hands on his coat more than on him. The other men cheered him on.

I tugged on his coat, pulling him in a circle but I needed to end this in case the goddess decided to intervene. I let go and with a quick sweep of my arms, knocked his hands free. I slammed a fist hard into his belly and he whoofed as his breath escaped. He doubled over and I grabbed the coat at the shoulders, pulling it down and trapping his arms at the elbows. He practically toppled to the floor face first, gasping, but I kicked him for good measure. Not to hurt him. More to embarrass him. Then I went back to his coat and kept pulling until I'd yanked it off him entirely.

"You live in a proud realm, dog," I snapped. "But you are unfit to wear this. You are unfit to represent the good people of Somesuch."

I looked at the two men accompanying Spreasán's father. They regarded me, aghast. Probably because I had the name of the city wrong. "Somesuch?" I asked. "Is that right?"

In quavering tones, one man replied, "Sómasach, Your Highness."

"Right. Sómasach." I went back at Lúbaire. "You cursed your own son. You murdered and lied for Urlabhraí's favor. You are not fit to wear this fine coat and I shall keep it."

Turning my back, I stormed away, feeling as though they'd follow and retaliate.

They didn't.

Through the eye, the landscape below had changed dramatically. Where a cave had been there was now an open pit. Water cascaded down the side into a pool, and tons of trees remained for shade. In the distance north and south, steep cliffs hemmed the valley in.

That should work.

The goddess sat with her back against her seabhacmór. The rise and fall of the bird's breathing was steady as he slept.

The goddess looked like a sad little girl almost, her potent power having retreated somewhere deep and sheltered. She ran her fingertip along the edge of a feather, which was almost as long as she was tall. "They loved to hunt so. Especially together. But now there's only one."

There was nothing I could say. She had paid a price in losing one of her guardians, but I had a feeling she had known how events would play out. She had known her bird would die and she had known the dullahan would call a house out of shelter and eat the residents. She had let it happen anyway. Now she could further justify her obvious hatred of Urlabhraí and the Dubhcridhe, a sentiment we shared.

"Hew tells me thou hast had the same dream for a month." The goddess locked eyes on me and knew my thoughts were an open book to her. "I am most interested in the part about thy father on his throne, burned to ash and only his reflection reacting to thy presence."

I nodded.

She asked, "What doth such mean to thee?"

"To me?" I shrugged, surprised she would ask. "I would think you'd be the expert."

"I'm a gatherer," the goddess replied. "Occasionally I share what is harvested, but the centuries have taught me that a dreamer's subconscious is a better interpreter than I could ever be. So, again, what thinkest thou?"

"Does it need to mean something?"

"If thou hadst dreamed it but once, perhaps not. But over and over again?"

She had a point. "If I had time to think about it, maybe I'd come up with something. Anyway, Hew erased my dreams. The ones I've had here at least."

"That is true." She put her hand on my arm again. I didn't mind. "Hew said thou didst have a different dream last night."

"Really? I don't remember what it was."

The goddess stood and beckoned me. "That can be remedied."

We were in her chamber alone now. I had no idea where the men from Sómasach had gone. Or how long ago. The door to the chamber opened again on silent hinges. A figure came into the room. Not very tall but very familiar.

Laoch.

# CHAPTER 35
## That Golden Maze

Laoch was a contradiction. We were essentially parts of the same person, but I was fully-grown and could age while he had experienced decades more of life than I had but would always look like a nine-year-old kid. He had come into being when Béil had made a deal with a deamhan and the deal hadn't turned out as expected. These things happen in the realm of the Fae.

Laoch and I shared the same smoldering good looks though, and I was happy to see him healthy.

He gave me a nod. In his strikingly deep voice, he said, "Hey, Pops."

We also shared the same insouciant sense of humor.

I nodded back. "Juvenile. Noun and adjective."

The boy grinned. "How is Alyce?"

"She's okay." I noticed our friendly neighborhood goddess out of the corner of my eye, standing motionless. "Can we talk about Alyce here?"

"Caer Ibormeith, goddess of dreams, knows everything." Laoch gave her a sincere bow. "May her light never wane."

Never wane. Wow.

"Alyce was exhausted after she delivered her message. I'm not sure she'll ever wake up."

Laoch explained. "That is a safeguard. Children who leave Tír na nÓg without permission fall asleep in other realms to prevent them betraying this land."

"I see." I considered how much to reveal, but the goddess could easily know anyway. "I tried to find out more about her. Her father passed away and her mom isn't well. Alyce would like to be an adult and have a normal, mortal life but I'm told she must remain in the Behindbeyond. She served here for twenty-five years, in mortal reckoning. I'm hoping to help her. Helping people is what I do."

Caer Ibormeith lifted her chin. For most people, that was a sign she disagreed with what she was hearing.

"Time to review thy dream." Imperiously dictatorial, she changed the subject and waved her hand.

Hew came forward.

"Explain to the prince," the goddess commanded.

Hew nodded. "The miongabhálaí sift through dreams but are limited in how much they remember. They also are unable to erase dreams. I, as a grand-gabhálaí, have the ability to keep dreams entire and erase them. To share dreams, however, you'd have to be sleeping, unless"—he indicated Laoch—"there is an intermediary with a gift for telepathy. With Laoch joining us, we can share the dream together while you are awake."

This was why certain children ended up here and why the goddess wanted to keep them. And why Alyce was able to share things with me the way she had. And why Laoch had been taken and brought here. Alyce and Laoch and all the little telepaths permitted others to join in waking dreams. It meant the goddess had a unique need for these kids.

It also meant she had little interest in other children.

"Changes are in order." I pointed at Hew. "Your name is now VHS." I pointed at Laoch. "And you are VCR."

Hew looked at Laoch. "Do you know what he's talking about?"

Laoch shrugged with all the profundity of a two-hundred-year-old nine-year-old, which was substantial. Hew removed his skull helmet, possibly just so he could roll his eyes at me more obviously. He grasped Laoch by the fingers and pointed at me.

"Take Laoch's hand."

I did.

Myself. A small boat on an endless sea. The moon perfectly centered overhead like a spotlight in a stage play. Ripples on the water so precisely ordered as to create a soft lap-lap-lap of rhythm. A soundtrack to break the silence.

The version of me in the boat looked over the gunwales. Port. Starboard, Port. I had no sense of my body as an observer. I looked down, but I was a camera without a housing. An invisible witness, alone. No Laoch at my side. No Hew.

The waters rippled, burbled, boiled. Minnows below the surface. Agitated. Small fry trying to leap from the depths but barely able to launch into open air before bumping into the side of the boat and dropping back into the ink. Thousands of minnows, stirring, splashing.

Below them, the predator.

Its movement was a great swell that lifted the water, carrying the boat up, six feet up. The same distance up that a body is buried down. The wave leant panic to the kinetic, frenetic frenzy of the fry.

My dream self should find a shore. Escape the leviathan.

This was not our world. Not the world of the fin-less, gill-less, guileless.

It was his.

The sleek monster of the unfathomable fathoms.

My dream-self seemed unconcerned.

Or—even worse—unaware.

What an idiot.

He smiled. I wanted to warn him off. Get away! But I had no voice.

He leaned over the side. He had no oars with which to escape, but he had hands.

Don't let them get bitten off. Who knew how many rows of teeth the predator had?

He called up his power. With a fingertip, he touched the water.

The waves becalmed as light suffused the deep with a cerulean glow. The glow spread outward, encircling the boat, filtering down inch by inch like slow-moving sunshine.

The minnows responded. Rising to the surface, bathing in the glow of magic. Then leaping into the air with starlight flashes and transforming into birds. Up from the water. Up to safety on the wing. Flying moonward, making room for the fish below to gain purchase over the water, changing, flying, soaring to sanctuary.

Until the water was devoid of minnows and the sky full of sparrows.

Now only the monster of the water remained.

And only one thing left to eat.

The leviathan flicked his tail and turned toward the boat.

The water surged upward again, filled with rows, rows, rows of teeth.

Wake.

The dream ended as quickly as it had begun.

The thudding in my chest was slower to stop.

So was the blue glow shining through Laoch's shirt. There would be silver embedded there.

I wanted to ask Laoch if he was all right with the implant. If he even knew about it. Did it ever hurt? Did Béil know what happened?

There wasn't time.

"What thinkest thou?" the goddess asked.

"I'm no stranger to symbolism." I scratched my jaw. "I got a C+ on my Emily Dickinson essay in high school."

"What thinkest thou?" More insistent.

Right.

"The little fuzzbutt I tried to bring here would have had an answer to that question, I think. But he grew feelers and a set of hooves and I bashed in his head."

The goddess look annoyed.

"Hew knows."

Hew cleared his throat. "A miongabhálaí from the cave. Prince Luck carried him here. It transformed this morning."

"He was linked to a child having nightmares in the mortal realm. And he wasn't the only one." I told the goddess about all the children I had seen in all the miongabhálaí and the fears the children were poisoning them with. I told her about the view out the window. I told her what Béil had dreamed. As I talked, I went to the eye. With as much grace and gravitas as I could muster, which wasn't a lot, I

310

swept a hand toward the dullahan on the ground.

"Goddess. You know these are the nightmare children of children with nightmares. There will be many more because the nightmares of the children aren't going to stop. And I'm afraid it will simply grow. Because the people giving the children nightmares are getting more bold. Taking more children, both mortal and Halfling. The dullahan will increase."

Pausing to breathe, I let that sink in.

"It's like the measles. If enough children are vaccinated, the few cases that come up are manageable. But when there are too many vulnerable, exposed people, the chance of an outbreak increases exponentially. Maybe you know this already. Maybe that's why I'm here now, when the outbreaks of dullahan have grown."

The goddess gave me a perfectly expressionless expression.

Okay.

"I can find them. That's what my dream is about. I know it. The minnows are the children, unable to get away. But I can find them. I can find them and give them wings. I can set them free. Do you see it?"

The goddess tilted her head. She looked past my shoulder, her eyes unfocused.

"You said you cannot stop the dullahan here. You said the land could be overrun and you only have one seabhacmór remaining to fight with. I can help you on the other side. In the mortal realm. Let me go back. Let me finish the job I was doing when I came to Tír na nÓg. Let me set the children free and stop the people who are giving them nightmares. You'll have fewer outbreaks. Fewer dullahan to deal with. You won't lose control."

Her gaze landed on me with a full weight, but I couldn't read the goddess at all. Her expression was so neutral I wondered if she had heard anything I'd said. She wanted something more. I took a guess. "I'll come back here when I've completed my task and serve thee for seven years."

The goddess blinked. "All thou wouldst need to complete this task is permission to leave?"

The coat I'd taken from Spreasán's father lay on the floor where I'd dropped it. I picked it up. "And this."

The goddess said, "Hew. Take him to the gate room."

She vanished, and Laoch vanished with her.

Blink.

Hew paused for only a moment before trotting out through the door to the stairs. I kept up, but it was not a saunter. A look of disbelief was plastered on his face.

I wanted to be happy.

She's letting me go.

I wanted to jump and yell and get excited, but Hew's stupid expression of concern wasn't good. "You're worried, Hew. Why?"

"You don't know the way. There hasn't been time."

"What do you mean?"

"You don't know the way to get out of Tír na nÓg without dying."

"Sheesh, Hew. Ominous much? What's there to know?"

Hew started to ramble. "She's supposed to tell me. Then, as you do her bidding, I teach you how to get out. None of that has happened."

If the goddess didn't want to let me go, then what would she want? Suddenly, I was a lot more concerned about the goddess's many faces. Was it safe to trust the face she had shown me?

"It takes seven years to earn release," Hew mumbled. "A starting place and six paths through, one part for each year."

We ascended. There were more children than before, leaning out of windows, peeking around doors. Perhaps they knew what I wanted to do.

Find their friends in the mortal realm and set them free. If I can find my way out.

My month of conditioning meant that I could keep up with Hew and not change my breathing. My ability to count was in good shape as well.

"Haven't we climbed a lot more stairs than we came down?"

"Oh, yes," Hew panted. "The entryway would have been several flights back."

"Why didn't we see it?"

Hew waved his weapon in a circle. "Goddess of dreams. Ability to change stuff."

Yup. That explained it.

Going down from the entry, the levels had felt larger, like descending through a pyramid from the pinnacle. Now, as we climbed, the levels felt larger the higher we went until we reached the top. The pyramid upside-down.

A room opened at the top of the stairs, a grand ballroom with vaulted glass ceilings. Ancient trees grew along the walls and balconies with their branches clambering up past the roof. Many of the roots trailed into the room and over the sides. The view from the windows was unobstructed and breathtaking. We were above the cloud that masked the existence of the castle, and the sky outside was a pale, pre-dawn pink. To the west stood the Eternals Tower. Lights sparkled from some of the structures. Other dwellings were dark and shifting. It had been behind the wall on the ground where my house had been and not visible from there. Here, it stood out like a monolithic tribute to dreams and dreamers.

Béil was still there. I hadn't forgotten about her. I needed to help her.

The goddess had a simpler throne here, but her presence still captured my attention. She sat with Laoch by her side and assorted children and grand-gabhálaí around her.

A sour voice spoke. "Oh, good. The prince is here. We're all saved." Lúbaire stood with his puppy pack of sarcasm.

Fantastic.

The goddess set a reminder. "He is here at my request. As are ye." Her words included a threat: do not forget you exist in this place at my will and pleasure.

Lúbaire had to rant anyway. "Our agreement was to deliver our petition and return immediately to our realm. We have been made to wait far too long."

"Yes," the goddess said. "Please let The Máithrín know there were unfortunate delays."

At that, I had to jump in. "You made arrangements with the queen of Tír Dúchais?"

"The Máithrín knows when a wrong must be righted," Lúbaire barked. Defensive. "Much more than anyone, including thy father."

"She also lets Urlabhraí do whatever he wants."

"Lord Urlabhraí has an interest in justice."

"I think you said that perfectly. Urlabhraí has an interest: injustice."

Lúbaire looked at me blankly.

He didn't get it.

Caer Ibormeith ended the repartee. "Which of you would like to leave first?"

Lúbaire knew to get while the getting was good. "I would."

"Very well. Please find the wolverine." The goddess indicated the tiles on the floor with an outstretched hand. We all looked down. Most of the tiles were simple, unadorned marble. A number of them, however, had animals carved into them. There were dozens of those, arranged to form the perimeter of a rectangle. Inside that rectangle, the tiles were accented by precious metals.

"The wolverine?" Lúbaire asked.

"Yes," I said. "The largest member of the weasel family. Like you."

Lúbaire glared in my general direction but refused to make eye contact. He focused on the floor. There were all sorts of different animals on the tiles. Birds, mammals, reptiles, fish. Finally, he found the right tile.

"There you are," I said. "Pointy nose, beady eyes, cranky demeanor."

Lúbaire sighed. "What's next, I pray, that I may be rid of the prince's insults?"

The goddess gave the answer. "To exit the maze, walk to the matching symbol. It lies somewhere on the floor."

Lúbaire looked around. He sensed this was some kind of challenge. Maybe he wasn't entirely stupid.

314

Finally, he spied the starting tile's twin on the other side. He stepped toward it.

He covered six feet of floor when a gash appeared on his thigh. With a shriek, he sank to his knees. His hand went to the wound. A crimson stain seeped between his fingers. His wild eyes searched the room for his assailant. There was no one.

Curious.

"I would suggest a different path." The goddess smiled a half-smile.

Lúbaire stood up and looked like he was going to ignore her advice, the second wolverine tile sitting ten steps away.

"I pray thee. The path is not direct." The voice of the goddess was full of power again. Her face started shifting to other faces.

Lúbaire stopped.

Mental magnets slammed together.

Moly with all its holies.

I know what this is.

I glanced at Laoch. He was looking straight at me as if he'd been waiting for me. He gave a tiny nod. Almost imperceptible.

Lúbaire changed direction. He walked perpendicular to his original course. Three steps later, he screamed again. A second gash bloomed on his shoulder.

"I would suggest a different path," the goddess repeated.

Lúbaire yelled again. Anger and pain in equal measure. "What is this deception?"

The goddess quoted:

I strongly wish for what I faintly hope;
Like the daydreams of melancholy men,
I think and think in things impossible,
Yet love to wander in that golden maze.

I recognized the quote. We'd studied John Dryden in high school too, along with Emily Dickinson. He must have lived here for a time.

"What does that mean?" Lúbaire spat.

"There have been many who have visited my realm. Poets and playwrights, deviant and devious. I take inspiration from the dreamers and make rules to govern who should leave my realm."

"You're insane."

The goddess's face changed at that. Dark eyes, black hair, skin like crepe paper. The visage remained. "Lord Lúbaire, if thou canst not interpret the maze, thou shalt serve me for seven years. Over time, thou mayest learn the path to freedom."

"Seven years?" Lúbaire spat. "I cannot afford to waste time here. Release me."

"Ask them to show you this thing with leaves in a whirlpool," I offered. "That'll help a lot."

Cornered animals know when they're cornered. Lúbaire was no different. And cornered animals turn dangerous. He looked again to his exit.

"Commit to seven years of service and thou shalt be released."

Lúbaire had one hand on his thigh, covering the wound. His other hand pressed the wound on his shoulder. His eyes were feral.

A low growl tumbled up from the center of Lúbaire's being, growing in volume and ferocity.

Oh no.

Don't do it.

I guessed his intention before—blink.

Lúbaire shifted to the exit tile instantly.

Wait.

He used magic.

How did he use magic?

Lúbaire was an Air Mage, like so many of the Dubhcridhe. That meant he could teleport to any spot he could see. But magic wasn't supposed to work. Not personal magic. Not in the heart of Tír na nÓg.

Lúbaire stood straight on the wolverine tile. Unbowed. Victorious. He took a step, tried to take another, then slumped to the floor like a bag of wet oatmeal. Strangled sounds threatened to make sense, but all I could hear was "K-k-k." He bled from a dozen wounds.

Lúbaire's friends huddled together, staring. Maybe they were afraid to move and offend the goddess. Maybe they were just crappy friends.

The man was conscious. Fear infested his eyes. I remembered the man in the boat when I was a kid. The first person I'd ever seen pass from this life into the next. He had worn the same expression. I hadn't known what to do or what to say back then. I didn't really know now either, but I understood this moment was a testament to tragedy. Even if he was getting what he deserved, this was not a time to hold onto anger or spite. No man with a soul would indulge in gloating over a dying man this way. And no man should die alone.

I knelt by Lúbaire. Touched his shoulder. He struggled to look at me and tried to speak but blood welled up instead of words.

"Listen," I said gently. "You have to know that I'm going to fight them. The Dubhcridhe. But I don't have to agree with you to respect you. I'm here. I'll stay with you. As long as you need."

Lúbaire was very pale, shivering on the floor. I couldn't be certain what he said. Tried to say. There was too much blood in his mouth and he didn't have enough strength to cough it out of the way. There was fear there, in his eyes, but his gaze locked onto mine and there was a second where our souls met and he relaxed, knowing I was there with him. He nodded, just once. Then he was gone. His gaze lost focus and I looked away.

It was impossible, but the face of the goddess changed to women I knew. My mother. Erin. Hope. Béil.

Mother.

Erin.

Hope.

Béil.

Mother.

Erin.

Hope.

Béil.

"Who will try next?" She looked at me. "Who is ready to leave

Tír na nOg?" Her voices were familiar as well.

"Him." One of the puppy pack pointed a quivering finger at me. "Let Prince Luck try."

Try his luck. Ha ha.

I had to remember what Alyce had done to me. It seemed like a year had passed since the rehearsal of the wedding when Alyce had appeared and she'd forced me to walk up and down, back and forth, over chairs and across them. Even through a wall. A starting point and six parts of the path. She'd done so under Laoch's direction.

She'd done so for this moment.

# CHAPTER 36
## Path of the Raven

With a graceful gesture, the goddess indicated the floor. "Please find the raven."

The raven. Good choice. My raven, Midnight Dreary, had never failed to guide me.

The goddess knows everything.

I searched the floor. The raven was not among the tiles on the bottom of the maze. I found it along the edge of the rectangle to my left. My starting point.

Here goes nothing.

And everything.

Something waited in the maze. An invisible mechanism. An arsenal of phantom weapons. I couldn't see a thing. Maybe I could pull up a flame. The light could be useful.

"Tine," I whispered. The power lay drowsy in my hand and refused to ignite. Was worth a try.

And also, how is that fair?

I took a deep breath, my heart pounding. If I remembered what Alyce had done, I was supposed to move east first. Was it three steps? I stepped once, twice, thrice. The sun still huddled behind the horizon, but a glimmer of light drew a thin line in the air in front of me. The edge of a sword. A sword preparing to strike.

Whoa.

Three steps it must be. One more and I'd get slashed.

My eyes, with their enhanced sight, picked up tiny motes in the air. Minute bits of stuff scattered, floating, in the spaces over the tiles. I leaned to the side, observing how the bits shifted in relation to each other. All those floating bits were edges of larger bits. Bits of patterns that were familiar.

Bits of Stain.

It's not a something there. It's a someone. A knot formed in my throat and I tried to swallow it away. The sun thrust a bright edge over the horizon, catching more of the motes. More Stains. Everywhere in the maze. There had to be at least two dozen of them. Two dozen collections of motes in the air, turning in languid rings. Two dozen phantoms with weapons waiting to cut me and kill me if I made a wrong move. Made it so much easier to concentrate. Be grateful. I was able to see their Stains.

Time to rack the brain again.

Alyce had turned me north. I pivoted to the left, using the tiles to make sure I was lining up straight. How many steps had I taken next? The actual number escaped me. I'd been focused on what was happening to me and then getting Bromach awake instead of counting steps, even though Alyce had told me not to forget.

Deep breath. A step. Another. Another. An—there! On my right, the outlines of a broad-shouldered warrior flared to life in shimmering bits of light, like crystals in sunshine. As he turned to look at me, the ghost acquired features and details although he was still translucent. He wore ancient armor and held a longsword ceremonially, pointing up.

He opened his eyes and tilted his head down to look at me.

Gulp.

In life, he had been a magnificent specimen. In death, he was terrifying.

If I took a step in his direction, he'd use that longsword.

With extreme care, I took another step. I passed the warrior and he flickered out of view.

Another step. A third ghost waited for me. I knew from the circling Stain. A feeling of bugs crawling on my back tracked up my spine, over my shoulders, and up my neck to the top of my head. Walking down the path was like walking a tightrope. Straying from the proper line wouldn't cause a fall but would be deadly.

I passed that specter, then passed another. Step number ten—a fiery pain raked along my arm. In front of me, a tall, gaunt woman shimmered. She wore an over-sized tunic and held a halberd. She regarded me with blank eyes. Instinctively, I stepped back. She faded into invisibility, leaving only a few motes of Stain turning in the air.

Nine steps. Not ten. I'd been distracted by the ghosts to the side and had forgotten to check ahead.

To my right the path was open, leading deeper into the maze.

I pressed my hand over my wound. My shoulders and chest and neck ached already. I was far from becoming panicked. Lúbaire made for a good reminder.

Alyce had turned me east again. Yes. This was where I'd been forced over the benches, staggering and stepping on the seats like an idiot. There had been a lot of steps. At least ten.

Blowing air through my cheeks, puffing them out to release tension, I walked.

Phantoms manifested on both sides this time, staggered along the path, all of them dangerous. The faces of the ghosts remained grim, each one armed, awakening and flickering into view as I passed, then returning to sleep. Part of me wanted to study them. Examine the armor and weapons they'd had in life. Examine their Stains.

Now was not the time.

At step number ten, I stopped. There was a specter to my left, but I was sure I needed to turn that way. Alyce had directed me east, then north, then east, then north again. Right? If I went up the next row of tiles, however, I'd be next to a sinewy specter with a sickle. No. A silver sickle. A sinister silver sickle.

Alliteration did not lead to safety.

Checking all around, I went one more tile. Eleven steps. That had to be correct.

The path north was open. This was where I'd almost run into the chapel wall. My face had come right up to it after only a few steps.

I shook my hands, getting out the nerves.

I'd better be right. I didn't want to bleed any worse.

A brace of barely-seen barbarians—alliteration stop!—waited to my left. Seven steps. Where was my exit? Too soon. I had more maze.

I'd only gone halfway through the steps Alyce had given me. Forced on me. I spotted the other raven tile ahead and to the left of where I stood. A forest of floating Stain stood between me and the tile I needed. From here, it looked like I'd pass next to a specter on one side or the other. All the paths had a Stain floating near. Except to my left.

Yes. I had walked parallel to the chapel wall here. That path had an extra row of tiles between the Stain. Therefore, I could walk between the sentries without injuries. Inquiries. Or soliloquies.

How was I getting loopy? I hadn't lost that much blood.

Focus.

Four steps to the west. I ran out of blade-free real estate. To the south, the only open path. Three steps to remain safe. I took them.

Right. There had been a pillar not too far ahead of me at this part in the chapel. I stepped west. The specters gave passing interest as I passed.

Seven steps. There. To my right, the raven. A straight shot past the specters.

A leisurely pace despite the pounding of my pulse in my ears. Then out. Points for keeping my head. Literally. And keeping my cool. Maybe I was part cucumber.

"Thou hast earned the right to depart Tír na nÓg." The goddess stood from her throne.

From the other side of the room, the mongrel dogs glowered.

What? No applause?

"Heal him," the goddess commanded. The little grand-gabhálaí appeared almost instantly with her bag of rattling sticks and bones. She nodded in greeting, her eyes wide as always.

The goddess came to my side. She spoke softly. "It will be quiet in Tír na nÓg without thee."

I smiled. "I'll make Tír na nÓg quieter still by finding the children and ending their nightmares. There will be so few dullahan, your seabhacmór will need a hobby." I took a deep breath, thinking about Erin and Nat. How to explain I'd need to return here for seven years. "Then I'll come back."

Laoch materialized beside the goddess. In his odd man-voice, he said. "I'll serve the seven years."

The goddess did not find this a surprise. "You're both parts of the same soul."

Shaking my head, I said, "I can't let him do that."

Caer Ibormeith replied, "I accept his offer."

"I had a great time."

A girl appeared next to Laoch. She had a silver piece in her chest. She also had dark hair, rich amber skin, and a dimple at one corner of her mouth that deepened when she smiled. She slipped her hand into Laoch's, and all the world made sense.

Béil was going to have a fit. A bigger fit.

The goddess rested her hand on my arm again. "Ask thou of thy father what it means for him to become ash upon his throne. If he will tell thee, I would also like to know."

I promised I would ask.

The goddess headed back to her throne. I remembered Béil and turned to propose a deal but Caer Ibormeith had evaporated.

Aw, crap.

I'm a dead man.

Well, Laoch was having a good day. He wasn't letting go of the girl's hand. Good. I asked, "How did you know the safe path through the maze?"

"The goddess gives the raven path to those who earn it."

I thought about that. "Did I earn it? Or did you?"

Laoch shrugged.

"Does she know you used Alyce to get the directions to me?"

"The goddess knows everything."

"Laoch?"

The new voice came from behind us. Béil.

Laoch tolerated her throwing her arms around him. Checking him every inch. She acted like she hadn't seen him for years. It probably felt like it.

I hoped Erin would do the same for me.

We men are willing to put up with a lot.

Béil eventually noticed me. I said, "I was going to come back for you."

She stared me down. I expected a slap but when her hand moved, she held something for me. "Luckily. For you. The goddess. Explained everything." She dropped a glass vial into my hand. Inside was a teaspoon of dirt.

I took it. "What is this?"

"The goddess. Didn't say."

There was a label tied to the bottle with a ribbon. The label read, "Me."

"Okay." I put it in my pocket. Béil had something else in her hand.

Béil nodded. "This. She did. Explain." She kept her hand closed. "I will. Only give it. To you. If you. Promise. To bring me. Back here."

She put her free hand around Laoch while his girlfriend looked a little less dimply about it all. "Okay." With a nod, Béil gave the object to me. "It's a ring." King of the detectives.

Laoch explained. "It's like a barrow key, except you can use it to enter Tír na nÓg whenever you want. You can also use it to leave."

I turned the ring in my fingers.

"This is an extraordinarily bad idea."

"Why?"

"First, men cannot be trusted with magical rings. Ask J. R. R. Tolkien."

"Don't be. Stupid."

"But I did promise to bring you back here, Béil. It's the least I can do."

"The goddess said to give you this as well." She handed a small square of parchment to me. I opened it up. There was a drawing of a dog in quill and ink. Below the drawing, the words:

One dreamer must not dream.

An idea began to form in my mind. An idea that would make

rescuing children even more useful. To them. To my father. And to the Caer Ibormeith, goddess of dreams, long may she know everything.

Mads had taken Agent Scarsdale's essence again so she'd be able to speak. She was delighted to see me with Béil but surprised I didn't have Laoch. I told her Laoch had chosen to take my seven years of service and he had also found a girlfriend. Besides, when a child is over two hundred years old, he should move out of the house and get a job.

Béil was less accepting. Her motherly instincts had been honed for centuries, and I felt like her worries were less about Laoch and more about being afraid to be alone.

"I will bring you back to visit. I promise."

"Your promises. Leave much. To be desired."

She wasn't wrong.

I vowed to repair my reputation on that score. I stared at my boots.

"Is something wrong, sire?"

"I need to help those kids, but I've been gone for so long. Nobody seemed willing to help me get a message out. Erin will be worried out of her mind. And Nat—"

"Are you sure?" Mads-Mully wore a wry smile.

"What?" Me, indignant. "Are you saying Erin doesn't love me? She hasn't missed me while I've been gone for over a month?"

"I'm sure she loves you. I'm not sure she misses you." If she thought she was being helpful, she was wrong. "You haven't figured out the leaves," Mads-Mully said.

On that, she was correct.

"Tír na nÓg is a land of symbols and hidden meanings."

"And obstinate Púcas."

Mads-Mully crossed her arms, disgusted. "What do you remember from the pool?"

"Come on."

She was serious. "Tell me."

Fine. "Water and leaves."

"What about them?" The expression on Mully's face went beyond challenging. "Dee-tek-tive."

"All right. There was a small red leaf that turned into seven big green leaves."

"Good. What else? What about the water?"

The pool of water had been part of a stream. The water had carried the leaf around an eddy. I squeezed my eyes shut to picture again what had happened. "The water went full circle. Clockwise."

"Yes."

"Don't sound so shocked, Mads."

"Put it together then."

I sighed. "The small red leaf went around clockwise. Then went pop, becoming seven bigger, fresher leaves." It had to mean something. Nobody makes such a big deal about a magic trick unless they're in a castle in Hollywood, which I'd always wanted to try. "Like a clock." I processed the sequence again. It didn't make sense with little hand and big hand. It made sense with units of time. "Once around is a minute, which is a small unit. The next largest unit is an hour."

Mads-Mully nodded.

"The only way it makes sense is if one minute equals seven hours."

"Finally."

I gave my brain a chance to calculate. Numbers and clocks. "Are you telling me that only three minutes pass in the mortal realm for every twenty-one hours here?"

"I'm not allowed to tell you that." Mads-Mully, self-satisfied. "But the leaves are."

I felt like sitting down.

Extrapolating further, I reasoned that a month spent in Tír na nÓg was something like a hundred minutes in the mortal realm. Setting aside why it worked, I realized I could spend a few more days here and I'd still only be gone two hours in the mortal realm.

Well dang.

# CHAPTER 37
## Contingencies

For a heart-stopping moment, I envisioned myself coming out of the portal and finding out the whole thing had been a dream. I was wrong. It had all happened. My feelings were mixed.

Nat's stony expression didn't twitch an iota when Mads-Mully and I co-sauntered out of the bayou. He didn't say a word either as we marched down to Eustace's cabin. We waved at Eustace from the dock where Nat had tied up kayaks and Eustace looked at me from the porch with a knowing stare. His eyes seemed to say, "Y'all come back and share your story when you have the chance."

Will do.

The morning sun painted dapples on the water, easing between the trunks of the cypress trees slow and thick somehow, like syrup. The lightning bugs had gone to bed, but tiny morning bugs danced over the shoreline, adding bits of light and motion. I'd grown accustomed to having high walls hemming me in, and the wide-open skies liberated more than my view. They liberated my spirit. I found myself humming.

At Gatorbait Excursions, Mads-Mully and I hung out in the parking lot while Nat went inside.

"You're not going to talk to your father?" she asked.

"He doesn't know about the dreams. I'll go talk to him after we make this better."

Mads-Mully gave with the narrow eyes. "What do you mean 'we?'"

"I need your help, Mads." I rummaged in my bag and pulled out a bundle for her.

"What's this?"

I opened the bundle, which held Lúbaire's jacket. "First things first. Have Petit-Palais make some calls."

"He's in the hospital."

"Yes. You put him there. Let him know I'm going to Boston and I want to meet with the FBI there."

She looked at the jacket while she spoke. "I'm not sure how cooperative he'll be."

"Tell him he deserves the credit. This information came down due to his excellent field work and there's a promotion in it for him."

"So I should lie to him."

"Make this all about him. He'll follow through. Then you can bow out before there's trouble with the real Scarsdale and the spotlight will be on him. And for heaven's sake, make sure you get Scarsdale out of that tomb and home again. As soon as possible."

Mads-Mully looked at me sideways while I gave her a quick run-down regarding Lúbaire's jacket.

Nat came out of the office, making me wish my saunter was half as cool as his. I looked at Mads-Mully until she got the hint, got into the Cadillac, and drove away.

Nat and I clambered into the SUV. Finally, Nat asked, "Long night?"

When I laughed, I tried not to sound like a maniac. It wasn't easy.

"Worth it though." I wiped a mirthful tear from the corner of my eye. "I found out more than I'd hoped about Alyce."

The bounce that woke me up wasn't Carlene's fault. The weather in Miami was unseasonably cold and wet, and the jet was subjected to a swirling wind that slipped out from under the wings. Carlene rocketed out of the cockpit as soon as we stopped at the gate, squealing. I was busy retrieving my bag from the overhead compartment when she threw her arms around my neck and planted a kiss on my mouth, which wasn't the post-flight "Buh-bye" I usually got from airline pilots.

"Oh gosh! Sorry! Sorry! Sorry!" She was medium-horrified when she realized what she'd done. "I just got so excited."

I laughed. "I understand. Congratulations."

"Um. Thanks." She backed away, grinning, and managed to make it out of the plane before losing control again.

Cute gal. Glad her dreams are coming true.

Now for mine.

Erin's embrace felt like heaven. Her arms held me tightly while her hair tickled my neck. She smelled like cinnamon and butter and blissfulness, and she didn't question or resist when I squeezed instead of letting her go. For minutes. Many minutes. We started swaying, eyes closed. She sighed and said, "Mm," and just let me hold her.

She got me.

Got Got.

Not the easiest thing, but she rolled with it.

Reluctantly, I relaxed my arms so she could move back but I didn't let her go. I looked at her. Her toffee-colored eyes and flowing hair and perfect, smiling lips that I hadn't even kissed yet. She ran her hand down the side of my face.

She asked zero questions. Didn't second guess. She was simply there.

Her open expression let me know she wouldn't turn down an explanation though.

"I just spent over a month in the land of dreams and nightmares. Tír na nÓg."

"Oh."

"I had a house. Never stayed in it. But it came with an adorably furry assault butler who stole my dreams and sold them on the black market. Or something."

"The fiend."

"And I didn't stay in the house because I was afraid I'd be stuck there for seven years and that's far too long to be away from you. So, I tried to find a way out."

"Mm. You did find a way out."

"I did."

That was it. Accepting what I gave. She drew me in again, and we held each other and danced to the rhythm of our own breathing.

Time passed. I finally said, "I'm going to kiss you now, but if you do your psychometroid thing, you'll find the history of my lips includes a recent encounter with Nat's girlfriend's roommate who got a little overenthusiastic because she's going to get her pilot's license."

"Uh-huh. I think I actually followed that sentence. Is she a good kisser?"

"No. The sample size was admittedly small. Over with before I knew it."

"That's too bad. Let me show you how it's done." Erin kissed me then, making it clear why she was team captain of the Lambda Iota Pi sorority smooching team in college.

"I can't stay." When I was given use of my facial features again, those were the first words out. "All these kids have been abducted. Like the ones at the wedding. I have to help them. Their nightmares are spawning evil in both realms, and every minute here creates more disasters for the goddess. There's a chance I can take out Urlabhraí as well. I can't stay."

"I know." Urlabhraí wasn't one of Erin's favorite tyrants either. "Don't go alone, Got. Take people with you. People who can help."

Already on it.

Sir Siorradh tilted through the portal with me. It felt good to be in the Behindbeyond again, because time flowed differently here too, giving us an advantage. There were no Dubhcridhe guarding the access point, which was precisely as Madrasceartán had reported. We set off at a brisk pace, following a narrow road that bordered a forest of ash trees. The ash were tall and narrow and dense, crowding out most other trees, but there was an occasional birch or oak braving the status quo.

"Dude." Siorradh paused. "You sure this will work?"

"I have every assurance."

"I'm here as the muscle?" Siorradh flexed an arm.

"With the added benefit of never going to sleep. Unlike me."

The moon overhead was red-hued and waning. There were some billowy clouds threatening beauty and captivation. I tried to remain unprejudiced since the clouds were letting the moon play hide-and-seek. We hiked for a quarter of a mile before the encampment came into view, more than five miles away. Big deal for hikers, but no big deal for those mages who could blink.

"The guards should be able to spot us, but we'll stick close to the trees."

Mads had told me how the Dubhcridhe set their portals a few miles outside of their camps because so many of them were Air Mages. They could blink as far as they could see and carry any non-blinkers with them, but anyone trying to attack the encampment would be spotted and dealt with long before they got close.

Sir Siorradh asked, "What happens if we make it all the way to the gates?"

"Good question." I scratched the back of my head. "Can you tap dance?"

"Do I look like I'm Fred Astaire?"

"I don't know. Are you afraid of escalators?"

Siorradh stood frozen for a couple of seconds. "Heh heh. I should have said Gene Kelly."

"Too late. No backsies."

Siorradh didn't need help with mortal realm pop culture.

With my hawk-like vision, I picked out the sentries where they patrolled the perimeter of their camp, moving from one torch-lit patch of warmth to the next. Under the gray-deepened cover of twilight, we were less visible than we could have been, but being here in daylight would have been too obvious. I did want to be caught. Heh heh. All part of the plan. But I didn't want the bad guys to know that and become suspicious.

Madrasceartán and her Púca pals had assumed the essences of Lúbaire and his cronies. The Dubhcridhe didn't know Spreasán's father was dead yet, and they thought the others had returned with him. It had taken twelve hours for her to reappear and tell us what was happening, which killed me. Months had passed in Tír na nÓg over that time. Mads tried to calm me down, telling me the goddess had cut the number of miongabhálaí on the ground so fewer dullahan would be created, and confined the infected to a very long, very deep pit. I imagined the pure fluffbutts floating up to the cloud while a roiling mass of equine beasts snapped and shrieked.

These nightmares must end.

Two shadows detached themselves from the midnight pillars between the ash trees and stepped out into the road where we could see them. Someone had been watching the access point after all. Siorradh took one more step after I stopped and half-shielded me.

I cleared my throat. "It's about time. Did you bring the pastries?"

One of the two shadows hesitated, stopping to look at the other one.

"Well? Come on already. We've been waiting out here for hours. You know how much he likes his pastries. Hand them over."

The shadow who had been the recipient of the look from the first one said, "We don't have pastries, moron."

"What? You're kidding. We came all the way to get pastries for nothing? I'm afraid you'll both have to come with us then. If you explain nicely, maybe he won't kill you."

The first shadow finally spoke, addressing the second one. "What's he talking about?"

"Who exactly wants pastries?" the second one asked in the same moment.

"Wait a second." I pointed over their shoulders. "Isn't that the fabled city of Stratford-Upon-Dunkin'-Donuts?"

Both shadows turned to look where I was pointing. Sir Siorradh and I rushed them. Siorradh's gauntlet made a satisfying clank as he struck. My punch was far less melodious, but the other shadow crumpled to the ground with a groan just the same.

We stood over the lumps, melted shadows on the ground under their black cloaks.

"Nice outfits for running around in the dark," I said.

"These are not the droids you're looking for?"

"Not even close."

No footsteps approached. No voice reached my ears. With a brief shoosh, strong arms came out of nowhere and clamped down on my shoulders. Then a gut-wrenching lurch covered the distance from the spot on the road and I came to a stop outside the encampment. An additional shoosh brought Siorradh as well.

Dizzy and nauseated, I managed, "Looks like the droids found us."

Good. Someone had taken the bait. Then silver manacles encircled my wrists and I no longer had any thought of resistance. On some level, I knew what was happening, but at the same time couldn't turn that awareness into action to struggle. Sir Siorradh kept still as well, but my sheltered inner self didn't know if the magic was working on him too or if he was just playing along.

"Inform Lord Urlabhraí we have Prince Luck." I finally got a look at the men who had captured us. The surly, sneering one who had spoken was another of Spreasán's clan. Bright blue collar. Insignia of Sómasach on his jacket. He said, "Now we'll have justice for my nephew."

"Justice? The only way to get any more justice for his crimes would be to kill him again."

This one was easy to provoke. The fist in my belly knocked the wind out of me and dropped me to my knees. I tried to cough. It took a minute to get there and then the pain of coughing was decidedly not worth it.

"Do you have any other last words?"

"Flibbertigibbet. Bamboozle. Perspicacious. Buttwad. I can't decide. Although that last one reminds me most of you."

The next punch caught me in the face, sending me to the floor. Sir Siorradh had enough and knocked my adversary into the wall, then sent a knee into the man's side. We all heard ribs crack.

"Stop." It hurt to speak loudly. "Sir Siorradh. Stop."

"It will be the furnace for you." I didn't see who issued the threat to Siorradh, but it was very real. Intense heat would do my friend in.

"Leave him alone. He's only here because I asked him to come."

I sensed people moving back. The space around me opened up with a shuffling of feet and the air felt less dense. Easier to breathe. I heard a familiar voice. "Weep not for the minnow who swims into the shadows only to be eaten by the trout. Of such are life and death."

The voice sent a shiver through my veins. Urlabhraí. Yes.

From the floor, I said, "Hey, Urp."

"Please call me by my full name. Only a commoner would call me 'Ur.'"

"Oh, I didn't call you 'Ur.' I said 'Urp.' It's when gas bubbles up from your stomach and escapes. In the mortal realm we call it a 'burp,' which is funny because nobody actually 'burps.' They just 'urp.' Anyway, I can see how you might have gotten confused. Urp."

"As ever, little prince, your scintillating wit dazzles."

"And your wit bedazzles."

Pause. Then, "I'm certain that's an insult to someone, somewhere."

There was something in Urlabhraí's voice. A wheeze. A weakness. I looked up to behold Ur in all his martyr's glory. He had an elaborate apparatus covering his left shoulder, made of silver, with the top half hidden beneath an embroidered cloak or cape. Based on what Lúbaire had said the last time he'd been annoying, the apparatus kept Urlabhraí from bleeding to death.

"I knew you would come searching for us sooner or later. You're quite predictable. That saves us the trouble." Ur's gaze drifted from me to Sir Siorradh. "I did think you'd bring more reinforcements."

"Sir Siorradh is all I need. For the moment."

A portly young man in a white robe stood behind Ur. Nervous.

Ur pressed his hand against the center of his chest. "My poor health. The wound from the iron-tipped arrow." A momentary grimace surfaced on Ur's face as he lifted his arm to raise the cape from the apparatus. Under the silver cage of the device, Ur's tunic was splashed with red. "The constant bleeding is so difficult. If only the injury could be healed."

"It's all my fault, Urp." I coughed after all. "This wouldn't have happened if I'd managed to kill you."

Ur chewed back a retort. "As it happens, I am feeling too weak to argue. While it is a vulgar process, I must care for myself."

The guy in the robe was reluctant to move. Two men clapped their hands on his shoulders and helped him with his volunteering, shoving him to his knees in front of Urlabhraí.

Ur made soothing, shushing sounds as he placed his hands on his shoulders. A pair of silver rods snapped against the guy's neck without warning. He flinched and grunted. The silver turned red and the color followed the rods to Urlabhraí's chest. He closed his eyes as the blood from the young man flowed in. I hadn't realized just how pale Ur had been until I saw his face turn more pink and then run to florid.

Quite the sideshow.

No one moved as the bizarre process continued. The silence was stunned and sad, at least for me. Ur's men all but yawned while the boy moaned softly.

What a waste.

At last, the rods snapped back. The reluctant donor slumped forward, hands on the floor, then leaned back, relief adorning his face. He was alive and that was a happier outcome than it might have been. I hoped he was going to be rewarded at some point for enduring this charade, but most likely he was from a family with no status.

Ur shrugged the cloak back over the silver cage. I saw the purpose of the silver apparatus now. It held the rods precisely where they needed to be to feed blood to Ur's system. When he was reassembled, he looked around sheepishly as if he'd just been caught picking his nose or scratching his backside.

He swallowed with a dry click. "Now you will tell me why you have come to the Dubhcridhe training camp."

"Good work, Urp. You admitted this is a Dubhcridhe camp."

Ur shook his head. "Any words between us will not matter. You will soon cease to cause problems for anyone. Your father included."

Okay. That hurt.

Ur started to bend down so he could stare me in the eyes, then pressed his hand to his chest and thought better of it. He straightened. I stared at the bloodstain on his tunic.

"Your father is looking for a place to shift the Eternals."

What?

Ur smiled at my obvious surprise. "You didn't know? He is abandoning the Behindbeyond because we have stepped up the Dubhcridhe's plans."

My father on his throne. Turning to ash.

"We stepped up our plans due to your meddling."

The Alder King, in a place where I couldn't talk to him.

Moving the Eternals?

I said, "Good." Doesn't feel good. "If you're changing your plans, then I scare you. I'll take that as a compliment."

"Take it," Ur sneered. "Take it to your grave."

Dang. He out-smugged me.

I looked past Ur and his hench-weenies. My surprise should be here by now. "Aren't you going to try talking me into joining your merry band of Halflings again?"

Where is Hew?

"No, Highness. The Dubhcridhe don't need you. Neither do we want you."

"Are you sure? C'mon. Try. I might agree this time."

"No."

"Pretty please? Once more? For old time's sake. It would mean so much."

Ur took a step back, eyeballing me. Thinking.

He's on to me.

Now is good, Hew. Where are you?

"Are you stalling, Prince Luck?"

"Stalling? Is that where you put horses in a barn? I mean not the barn. When you put a horse in a stall in a barn? Stalling? Is that stalling? I guess I have. Not now. I'm not stalling now. I'm busy being interrogated. But I've put horses in stalls before. I've definitely been stalling. Nothing better than a session of stalling."

Ur pointed to his men. "Bring Prince Luck and his metal friend."

"Wait. You haven't seen Sir Siorradh lap dance yet. Oops. Not lap dance. Tap dance." I laughed. "Boy, I almost messed that up."

Hew stood in the doorway.

About time. That meant the goddess had done her part as well.

Nobody moved. Hew wore his armor and held his jawbone halberd. He was intimidating to look at, despite his short stature.

"Uh-oh." I was determined to get my title of smuggest back. "Now you're in for it, Urp."

"I think not." Ur blinked away.

Once again, hands grabbed me. A disorienting lurch. We shifted to a spot that had been visible from the camp, quite close to the spot where Siorradh and I had been snatched before. We shifted again to another open spot and finally shifted one more time to the spot where the portal stood.

Or had. It was gone now.

"Uh-oh." It was hard to sound smug when you're trying at the same time not to throw up. "Now you're in for it, Urp. Did I say that already?"

"What's going on?" The edge was coming off Ur's smugitude.

Good. Thank you Caer Ibormeith.

"Where is the portal?"

"You're predictable too, Urp." I stood face-to-face with him. Hew had followed us easily and waited behind Ur and Siorradh and Ur's men.

"I'm going to drain your magical powers away now. When I count to three, you'll no longer be able to shift. Instead, you'll remain right. Where. You. Are. Ready? One. Two. Three."

Ur must not have believed me. He tried to shift away and expected it to work because he leaned into it. His eyes flared wide and he had to step forward to keep from falling over.

Hew made a sound. It was probably a chuckle or it might have been a snicker.

"No magic, Urp. If you ever hope to use magic again, you'll tell me where the rest of the humans are."

I chest-bumped his silver apparatus. He flinched.

"Step back from His Lordship."

One of Ur's hench-boogers wanted a rumble. "Hew, if you please."

Hew dashed forward. His weapon carved an arc through the air. The manacles on my wrists rang like a bell as the jawbone's magic severed the silver.

I rubbed my wrists and jutted my chin at the lackey. "You forgot, Mister Blinky. A prince outranks a lord."

He was quick. I was quicker.

His fist really wanted to find my face, which was a worthy goal. The fist maybe lacked self-esteem. The other fists probably made fun of him when nobody else was looking. It's good for a fist to have a purpose in life. Sadly, this fist would have to realize its self-actualization some other time.

I ducked under his roundhouse and jabbed hard into his midsection twice, causing him to bend over. Then I unleashed an uppercut into his upper-crust upper lip.

My fist complained. It hadn't collided with a tooth or mandible or stubble-covered face for far too long.

The pain felt good.

Another bell rang and Sir Siorradh was free as well. He wasn't really a fisticuffs kind of guy, more at home with a sword or mace in his hand, but he held his gauntlets up and assumed a defensive stance.

Three seconds. That's all I'd needed to take out the first snot-shot.

A second lackey came at me. Running with his hands out, all grabby-like. I stepped to the side, slapping his nearest hand away. I pushed down on his shoulder as I brought my knee up to his face. He crumpled to the ground. My knee hurt so good.

"Magic is great." I shook out my hands. "As long as you have at least one other sleeve to pull a trick from."

One guard remained. I gave him a jut of my chin. "So, nostril-fruit, what's your preference? I'll even let you pick. Fight me. Fight

Sir Siorradh. Or fight my buddy over there with the Napoleon complex."

Hew twirled his weapon for emphasis.

The guard took off running and headed for the trees.

"Just you and your strolling blood bank over there, Urp." I got back in Ur's face. "Tell me what I want to know."

"Whatever you're doing, Highness, you'll never succeed. I don't know yet how you've pulled this off but you're not the only one who can foresee the need for contingencies."

The guard that had run into the trees came back. With thirty friends. They surrounded me, swords drawn, except the returning guard who gave Urlabhraí the carnivorous bunny salute.

Ur inhaled like he was sad about something. "Alyce. Do what you've been told."

My consciousness slipped away as the ground rushed up to meet me.

# CHAPTER 38
## What Once Was Gained

Reflex shut my eyes as I fell. When I opened them again, a moment later, I was with Alyce. The sky was deep and dark above us, but a pool of light fell on a tree with golden boughs, and a rock served as a throne for the princess of dreams.

"Alyce? What are you doing? Send me back."

Alyce sat with her hands in her lap, palms up, fingertips overlapping as if she were reading an invisible book. "I had to. The Dubhcridhe recruit Eternals as well as Halflings. They also recruit mortals. Like me."

"What are you saying?"

"I've been helping the Dubhcridhe for a while. Years."

"Alyce? Why?"

"I've seen a lot of dreams. A lot of unfairness. So many of the Eternals dream about ruling all the realms. Taking all the power."

I ground the heels of my hands against my closed eyes.

Everything we've done, coming undone.

"Some Eternals feel that way. I also know for a fact that many don't."

Alyce didn't respond.

I pressed my point. "A lot of Eternals favor a balance. You can't condemn an entire group because a few people in that group behave badly."

"You're opposed to the Dubhcridhe."

"A group whose stated purpose is to oppose all Eternals. Alyce, just look at what I've done. My actions, okay? I'm trying to get rid of a murderer and return the people he's abducted and enslaved. Many of them mortals. And get them back to their families. If that results in the collapse of the Dubhcridhe, they weren't a strong group to begin with."

Alyce shook her head. "Lord Urlabhraí will set the captives free soon. He needs them for now, but once there's equality between the two groups, he'll set them free."

"I know you want to believe that and I can't discount all you've seen. Living outside dreams, though, I see what happens in the real world, and I can tell you men like Urlabhraí do not back away from power. They take what they can get and use it to get more. He won't free any children unless we make it too costly to keep them."

"I already promised."

She's changing the subject. She's not sure.

Urp knows what she wants.

"Let me guess. He'll make sure you get back to the mortal realm. Find your mom. Make you older so you can step into your old life. But Alyce, that's a life you've never known."

"Hey. It doesn't mean I don't want to."

A slip.

"You're right. I know I'd do the same thing." I can't make her mad. She's only human. "You should know I've started on those things for you. It's what I do for a living."

"Lord Urlabhraí already found my mom."

Really? How am I losing ground here? Again?

"That's great, Alyce. I asked a sheriff to help with that, too. Sheriff Holden in Donaldsonville."

Alyce looked surprised.

"I did that before I went to Tír na nÓg. Did Urlabhraí mention the same sheriff?"

Still no reply. Then, "His Lordship said you'd try to take the credit."

Uh huh. "Because that's what he's doing. Between the two of us, who is more likely to have had a conversation with law enforcement in the mortal realm?"

"Mortals, of course. His Lordship has mortals working with the police. The FBI. Everyone."

Uh-huh.

Alyce went back to her hands. Fiddling with non-existent dirt under her fingernails. "You say you want to help the mortal children first?"

"Yes. Mortals first and always."

Looking into my eyes, she knew her next words were going to hurt. "What about Hope?"

Oh boy.

There was room enough on the rock for me to sit next to Alyce, so I did. I wasn't sure what I needed to say since Urlabhraí was a step ahead of me on everything. Again. "It's been difficult to come to terms with that."

"Did she die?"

I had to be honest. "Yes."

"Weren't you supposed to protect her?"

"Yes."

"You can't blame Lord Urlabhraí completely."

My tongue felt thick and awkward and dry. She wasn't wrong.

Driving the point home, she said, "You let a mortal die while Eternals and Halflings were allowed to live, so why should I trust you?"

In Urp's version of the story, I was the bad guy.

There isn't time for this.

The rock felt hard and cold. I stood again and walked to the tree. The wood was textured in exquisite detail that felt like the real thing. And made zero difference to my day.

"Does Urlabhraí know how to age you?"

"Yes."

Of course.

"Did he tell you how?"

Alyce fidgeted again. "No. He said it's a bargaining chip to make sure I'll do what he needs me to do."

He doesn't know.

"How long are you supposed to keep me here?"

Alyce didn't answer.

A swan descended from somewhere north of nowhere. Its white wings were stark contrast against the background of the dark, empty bruise of the sky.

"He promised he'd let me wake you. As soon as he can."

"I see."

So, never.

My spirits sank. I'd gotten so close to finding out what I needed from Ur. I could have brought dozens of knights. Overwhelmed their forces. How many would have been killed? I'd felt certain this was a better way. And Ur never would have shown up if I'd brought an army. For him to take the bait, he'd had to think I was just here looking. And acting as stupid as he thought I was.

I'd proven him right.

He was in a place where he couldn't blink away, but he was still getting away.

A permanent nap was likely for me. Ur had my body. Siorradh and Hew might attempt to protect me, but they'd likely be killed if they tried. Ur might use me to bargain with, but he would destroy me as soon as he figured a way out of his predicament. I didn't think Alyce was prepared to let me die, but I wasn't sure she was ready to believe that's what was going to happen.

The swan in the sky was almost here. Black neck. Red spot on the beak. Perhaps she'd come to make me a permanent resident of Tír na nÓg.

Erin hadn't known how close she'd come to losing me before. If I died here . . .

Alyce looked at me, her expression fixed and determined. I couldn't be angry about her wanting to get back everything that had been taken from her.

The swan landed. She rolled her wings to settle them against herself and began preening errant feathers with her beak. I sauntered as best I could in her direction. If Alyce was aware of the swan, she didn't care.

I whispered, "Goddess?" Standing before her, in this place, made me feel stupid and frustrated. When she turned her gaze to me, it

343

held the wisdom of ancient beings. Her beak lashed out—the beak she'd killed her father with—but she just nipped at my pocket.

"Hey." Confused. My brain dusted off a few thoughts. I laughed out loud. A swan ducked out to come goose me.

"What's funny? Why are you laughing?"

"Uh. Me?" I looked around. Alyce doesn't see the goddess. I replied, "It's funny what you remember when your life flashes before your eyes."

Alyce looked away. Sad, serious eyes. The swan stabbed at my pocket again. Stop it. The swan shook her head from side-to-side, the long curve of her neck swinging in counterbalance. She hit me again in the pants, three times, rapid-fire.

Stupid goddess.

My hand covered the spot to shield it from further attack. There was a bump underneath. Something in my pocket. What . . . ? I reached in and found . . .

Maybe she's not a stupid goddess.

The little bottle of dirt with the label that still dangled from the piece of twine. It said, "Me" on it as before. C'mon detective. I turned the label over. The other side said, "Sprinkle."

Sprinkle Me.

Helps to stop taking things for granted.

"Alyce? I just realized something."

Alyce tilted her head sideways as she turned to look, steeling herself against a plea from me. Or a lie. "What?"

The swan curved her neck back, raising her head, then tilted her beak down. A nod. Then she launched herself into the air and vanished.

"What's that?"

"A gift. I thought it was for me because—" I raised my hand, stopping myself. "Doesn't matter. The important thing is I finally figured it out." I showed the phial to her. "It says 'Sprinkle Me' on it. It has to be for you, Alyce."

"Where did you get it?"

"The goddess. I helped her. Now she's helping me. Helping us."

344

We need to be on the same team.

"It takes years to please her. Decades. I should know."

"Well, I'm charming and quick." Usually. "I'm standing here instead of Tír na nÓg. Right?"

Alyce squinted. She wanted to believe me. The hunger was clear in her eyes now. The desire for the thing she wanted most and the possibility that I held the key for it in my hands.

"What's in it?" Her gaze was locked on the phial.

One step closer.

"Don't be disappointed." I held the phial by the cap. An inch-deep collection of gray-brown earth sat unassumingly in its cylindrical prison. "Dirt."

A spark of recognition lit up Alyce's face. "I've heard about mortals who tried going home. When they touched the ground, they aged." Her voice was warmer.

"Is that right?"

"And they died."

"That would be a drawback."

Her eyes refused to stray from the glass. "But that's only a little dirt. It's from the mortal realm?"

"I don't know." Truth.

"The goddess knows all things."

I would have said it. She beat me to it. Her pupils dilated, and the thrum of her pulse ran notably fast under the skin of her neck. She's excited. Maybe . . .

"I have this bottle in the real world. I just didn't know what to do with it until now."

She finally admitted, "I want to believe you."

There had to be a way. Had to. I needed to make her see what Ur was really like. "I've always been honest with you, Alyce. I've never withheld anything. Now I'm going to trust you with something very important. You can use your abilities to follow everything that happens."

"What did you have in mind?"

I wasn't sure how to explain, but I had to try. "One of the people working for Urlabhraí made some mistakes. It cost him his life. I sat with him as he died. I could have rubbed it in. I could have shoved it all in his face. I mean, I'd won and there was nothing he could do but listen to me. But I didn't mock him. I just told him I'd stay with him. I tried to comfort him until the bitter end." My dry throat didn't want to be bothered by a swallow. I sounded parched. "I want you to see Ur's true colors. A man is never more real than when he thinks he has nothing to lose. Watch me. Watch him. See who you can really trust when he thinks he's won. If it's not me, you can make me sleep again and let Urlabhraí have his way."

# CHAPTER 39
## A Promise is a Promise

"Alyce? I said do what you've been told."

Ur's eyes rolled aimlessly as he addressed an Alyce he wasn't able to see. His expression was perturbed. I was ready to perturb it more.

"Didn't you notice, Urp?" I got to my feet. "I went away, but Alyce sent me back."

Ur scowled. "You're lying."

The circle of Ur's soldiers tightened around me, a noose of bristling swords and spears. More than fifty soldiers created a wall of danger. "Better think twice, Urp. Without me, you don't get out of here."

"Perhaps."

"You don't know where you are. You think you do, but you don't." It was time to take Urp to school. "Your camp over there? Watch." I wiggled my fingers. "Na na na na."

Ur looked. A few of his less-disciplined soldiers looked. The camp was still there.

"Very impressive," Ur said dryly.

"Hang on. Gotta finish the incantation." I wiggled my fingers some more.

Now, goddess.

"Na na na na na."

The camp winked out of existence. The walls. The makeshift buildings. The torches. All of it gone except for a few dozen people.

Ur's eyes narrowed.

"Would any of your swordsmen like to take a swing at me?"

A soldier stepped forward. He was either eager or the point man. He raised his sword.

Pointing at him, I said, "Na na na."

He evaporated. There and gone with no trace. All except for his sword, which hung in the air for a split second and then fell with a ringing, awkward bounce on the ground.

Ur squinted at me. "Thou hast no real spell."

"Better than any of yours. Go ahead and try. Pull it off and I'll let you have the King of Smug title back."

Ur ignored me. "Hast thou become an Air Mage after all? Didst thou shift him? And the camp?" He looked all around, trying to locate his missing hench-weenie.

"Maybe he simply ceased to exist."

"Impossible. Matter cannot be destroyed. Not even by magic."

"It's mortal magic. Based on songs with 'na na na' in the lyrics. Maybe that was The Beatles. Maybe it was Roxette. You don't know." I picked up the orphaned sword. Hefted it. "How about this? All your soldiers. All your servants. All at once. This spell might have been written by Gary DeCarlo. Maybe Michael Jackson." I waved my hand over my head. "Na na."

The soldiers winked away.

"It's just you and me now, Urp." I hefted the sword again. The balance was a little off, but I could swing it.

I swung it.

The blade sang through the air, slicing toward Ur's neck. He twitched.

I ended my swing prematurely, bringing the blade to a stop an inch away from his neck. "Did you just try to get away? Blink to safety? Not going to happen. Not this time." I lowered the sword. "I'm trying to make a point. Your magic will not work to save you. There is no magic here for you."

Sir Siorradh and Hew moved around Urlabhraí, taking up positions behind him.

"You made a mistake last time, Urp. You left me and my friends to die instead of finishing the job. I won't make that same mistake."

Urlabhraí raised his chin, calculations rolling behind his eyes.

"You have children hidden away. Mortals and Halflings.

348

Different places. Not just at the camp. In warehouses and abandoned buildings. In the mortal realm and in the Behindbeyond. You're going to tell me where they are. All of them." I raised the sword again, preparing to strike. "Now."

"I'm curious." Ur held up his hand. The tone of his voice was condescending, but beads of sweat collected on his brow and ran down the side of his superiority complex. "How could you bring me to a place that's different from where I intended when I used my own portal to get here?"

"Great question, Urp. Very perceptive. I'd love to share, but you might cooperate with me and tell me what I want to know and then I'll have to be a noble Halfling and let you live. If I do that, you could use my strategy against me someday." As I spoke, I moved closer to Ur. He slowly backed away until he bumped into the wall of metal named Sir Siorradh. "Answer me. Or die."

Ur looked at the ground. Resigned. "Thou shan't kill me, Prince Luck. It's not in thy nature. Hurt me, thou might. Torture me. But I've learned to live with constant pain." His hand strayed to the bright red spot on his chest. "Thou mayest go to hell."

Shaking my head, I turned the sword down and let it rest on the dirt. I grasped him by the shoulder. The one without the contraption of silver. "It just so happens I know the way to that place. I'll take you there."

Hew stepped between me and Ur. He said, "Thou shalt leave Lord Urlabhraí here, Highness. By command of Caer Ibormeith, goddess of the night places. May she always deal fairly with traitors."

Ur grew heavy as his knees gave way. I tried to keep him from tumbling to the ground and hurting himself but only slowed his fall. His face paled like the moonlight upon it.

He said, "The cursed stars, not Tír na nÓg."

"You've been here?"

"I served the goddess." Ur's voice cracked. "For a time."

"He was cast out and warned never to return." Hew's voice rumbled hollowly from behind his bone mask. Footsteps padded over the grass. A lot of footsteps. Ur inhaled, sharp and quick. Rank after rank of grand-gabhálaí marched into view from the trees. They came from over the hills, from the road. Hundreds of them. Thousands. Many of them wore bone armor like Hew and carried pieces of bone on sticks. Weapons and shields. Others bore cages made of wood, carried with poles on their shoulders. "Now Urlabhraí has returned to her realm and she will exact her retribution." The hoard of grand-gabhálaí shouted, rattling their implements. For a mob of cuddly bear-sheep, they could make noise that sounded alarmingly vicious.

"Hang on." I waited for the roar to die down, shouting to be heard. "Wait."

Hew raised a hand and the roar abated to a murmur.

"I need him." And I need him to feel threatened. "He has to tell me where the children are."

Ur rasped at me, "Get me out of here and I'll tell you what I know."

I whispered back. "Can you run?"

Ur got to his feet. "Yes."

This was news. Good news.

"You won't bleed out?"

"I confess," Ur whispered, "it's not as bad as it looks." He still looked pale, maybe from fear instead of blood loss.

Faker. I whispered fast, "It can't look like I'm helping you or the goddess will have my head. The portal is in the same place. The goddess simply moved the land and us with it. If you run for the portal, I'll run behind. It will look like I'm trying to catch you, but I'll make certain you get there. Once we're through the portal, tell me where the children are."

Ur slipped his hand underneath the cloak and the silver contraption. "Agreed."

Alyce? I hope you're watching.

"Enough talk." Hew pointed his weapon at us.

Ur threw off the cloak and ran. He hurdled over the grand-gabhálaí and dodged the few with weapons, exhibiting more agility than I would have thought possible.

"Stop!" I hollered before I started running. "Come back!" I took care not to step on any fuzzbutts. My hesitation also helped Ur get farther ahead, which was part of our deal after all.

Ur turned the curve in the road as I trotted behind. "Stop!" From the curve, the portal shimmered a few hundred yards away. Overhead, there was a flash of lightning and a rumble of thunder.

The goddess's cloud.

Mashed potatoes in pursuit.

My feet lost ground. I was running at the same pace but barely moving. Ur ran in front of me with the exit close, but I wasn't going forward as fast.

Nightmare.

We've all had that horrible dream. Running but moving too slow and it feels like the ground beneath our feet is sliding backwards, carrying us away from our escape.

Like that. Only real.

The goddess controls the land.

The chase went on. I pushed harder to get farther. My breathing accelerated. The goddess was certainly making it hard for us to run. Good. Ur's wheezing was audible and arrhythmic, like a steam engine with a broken piston. Coughing, spitting, he was getting closer to the portal despite the uncooperative earth beneath his feet. I put my head down, shifting up to a sprint.

Ur made it to the portal well ahead of me and vanished.

The ground returned to its former non-reversing state and I rocketed toward the portal, entering a few scant seconds after Ur.

The room beyond was lit with torches, revealing a door on the other side and a fountain along the wall. I skidded to a stop on the stone floor with my heartbeat pounding in my ears. The portal closed behind me. No one would be following us in. For a long minute, we tried to catch our breath. Urp's deeper breathing had caused more blood to stain the front of his tunic, but the color stayed high in his cheeks. He coughed and spat on the floor, then resumed his labored breathing.

"You want the shirt that goes with those pants?" I asked.

"What is that"—he inhaled—"supposed to mean?"

I waved him off. "Just a joke."

"I should have known." Urp straightened to a standing position, his hand pressed against the wound in his chest. "Thou art very predictable. Always joking at the wrong moment."

I shrugged. There was a crate against the wall, which turned into a good place to sit. "Now that we're such good friends, I thought I could afford a joke." I leaned back against the wall. "Now you're safe, as promised. Tell me where I can find the children. Mortals first."

Urp's breathing had calmed. He went to the fountain and cupped water with his hand, which he drank politely.

"A promise is a promise." He gestured with an open hand. "One thing first. A test."

He blinked.

There was a door at the far end of the room. An Air Mage needs to see the place where he wants to teleport to. That spot was as far away from me as he could get. He arrived there instantly.

I met Urp's gaze. "Tell me what I need to know."

"So predictable," Urp replied. "Joking instead of pressing the advantage when thou hast it. Thou shouldst have interrogated me in Tír na nÓg. Right where thou didst want me. Thy tendency to be helpful has failed thee. I can shift here. And I have no reason to help thee anymore."

I stood up cautiously and lifted the lid of the crate I'd been sitting on.

"If I had the time, I'd kill thee, pathetic prince." Urp, threatening to out-smug me again. "I'm afraid I must go."

From the crate, I lifted out the Heartpiece. "Don't be afraid, Urp. It's going to be all right. I don't really need you. This device will lead me to every one of the Dubhcridhe."

Urp hesitated. "We'll move the children."

"How will they know to do that, Urp? You're never going to have the chance to tell them."

"Try thou to stop me." Urp turned toward the door. There was no handle.

I closed my eyes. My words sounded like a prayer. "Alyce? If you're watching, I think you've seen enough."

"Alyce?" Urp's words were not a prayer but a command. "Take him as thou didst promise."

Nothing happened. I felt sad looking at Urp. I prayed again. "You were right, goddess. There is no honor in him. I'll have to find the children the hard way, and it will take some time. But I will not rest until the job is done. Thou hast my word."

Urp stared me down. I said, "We're still in Tír na nÓg." I put the Heartpiece back in the crate. "I did tell you the goddess moves us by controlling the land. That's what happened just now when you apparently shifted. It was important to see what you'd do if you thought you had your powers back. If you thought you'd won. I was rooting for you to show some integrity. You didn't."

I sauntered to Urp by conventional means. The door evaporated. Outside, the hoard of grand-gabhálaí waited with Hew at the front and Sir Siorradh beside him. "I told you I would bring you here. And a promise is a promise. Welcome to hell." I shoved Urp through the door. He stumbled and fell onto the grass. Maybe it was an act. Maybe not. Maybe I was beyond caring.

The grand-gabhálaí bearing the three cages carried their burdens forward. Sounds of misery issued from each one. Wheezing and coughing and snorting and sneezing. Each one carried a miongabhálaí. They were all infected.

With great care, the cages were placed on the ground, the poles withdrawn from the rings of silver. There didn't appear to be doors on any of the cages, but I realized when the changes began, the newborn dullahan wouldn't need doors to get out.

Urp kept his chin up. Or nose. This was all beneath him.

The pole-bearers retreated behind their weapon-wielding cohorts. Columns of stone rose from the ground, reminiscent of the forest of pillars Hew had guided me through when I'd first arrived. These pillars were close together, too close to move between them.

Like a drumbeat, bone-on-bone, the grand-gabhálaí clapped their weapons against their armor and shields. A soft chant rose from their throats. It felt like a ceremony.

There was work I needed to do. Work in the mortal realm. Part of me wanted to leave, but a larger part bade me stay. The wait was short. With a cry, the back of the first miongabhálaí split open. Feelers waved in the air.

Urp took a step back, finally allowing his nose to angle downward in order to see the thing changing behind the slats of the cage. His voice trembling, Urp tried to put a sentence together. "I will tell thee anything. Anything thou needest."

Hew spoke in a clear voice. "Behold, Lord Urlabhraí, the children thou hast spawned."

The newborn dullahan whipped its sharp-edged tongue against the wood of its prison. With a snapping sound, the slat gave way. Feelers and abnormally-lengthening legs and a whipping tongue demolished the cage in moments. Urp retreated as far as he could, pressing his back against cold, unyielding rock.

The creature was only half-formed as it growled at Urp, stalking the perimeter of the stone circle, snarling, seething. The second miongabhálaí shuddered in its cage, croaking a birth cry. The first inserted its legs between the slats and pulled a piece of wood away, cracking, splintering. Then another. Shrieks split the air as the first dullahan began eating its neighbor, swelling, sprouting, squealing.

Urlabhraí's mindless scream cut the shadows.

# CHAPTER 40
## Inventory

The Heartpiece pointed up the dark hallway. Someone was there. An eater of the deamhan heart. Dubhcridhe.

Sir Siorradh would have been a good partner if we'd been hunting for Halflings in a different realm. A fast-moving knight in armor was a familiar sight to children who had been born in the Behindbeyond. At least they wouldn't have new nightmares. We were hunting for mortal children, however, and bringing Sir Siorradh and the king's guard to Boston would have created more problems than it might solve.

Instead, I had different help.

Béil wore tight-fitting, charcoal-colored pants and a jacket and looked like she had stepped out of an Avengers movie. When I'd reminded her that most of the children would never have seen an Avengers movie, she smiled and said when they did, they'd remember her.

So there was that.

We were alone here, as it turned out. My request to Petit-Palais for some FBI presence had gone unfulfilled. I was starting to wonder how committed he was to resolving the case. I'd make it a point to have a conversation with him when we were done.

"Ready?"

Béil leaned against the wall beside the door. She wasn't snapping her gum and filing her nails, exactly, but she looked bored. Rescue missions weren't quite up to her usual level of excitement, apparently.

"Ready?" I repeated.

She finally stuck her hands out at me, palms up, and rolled her eyes.

Great.

I called up my power. It was more than willing to awaken. The building here was the very one we'd explored in Béil's prophetic dreams. The roll-up door was intact in the real world. So was the locked door next to it. For the moment.

"Tine." The lock melted under my ministrations and the door swung open. "That felt good."

I was customarily a sidle-and-sneak kind of guy. Béil walked through the door like her name was on the building.

"Psst!"

She ignored me. Instead of slowing, she pulled the zipper partway down on the front of her jacket, her eyes fixed on a point across the room. I tracked her line of sight. There was a guard standing at a bench against the far wall.

Oh, boy. Here we go.

He heard her footsteps and turned, fumbling for his gun. Even in heels, Béil was barely tall enough to look the guy in the solar plexus. He hesitated as the short, smiling blonde approached. She put her finger up to her face. I could only see her now from a rear angle, but she'd probably stuck her finger in the corner of her mouth. Flirty.

"Hi," she said. Her finger moved to the man's chest. "Básaigh."

It almost sounded like she'd said, "Hi. Bye."

The man convulsed so hard, his feet left the ground as his legs spasmed up to his chest and his head snapped down. He went from standing to fetal instantly, then dropped and hit the floor with a resounding thud I felt through the ground.

I hurried over. The guard might as well have been fake. Bodies might twitch or quiver after trauma, but the poor guard was completely inert. His lack of autonomic response was frightening. I pressed my fingers against his neck, checking for a pulse. Nothing.

"Did you have to do that?"

"He was. A traitor. Yes?"

"Yes."

"Now. He is not."

She had a point.

"We agreed you'd put them to sleep so the miongabhálaí can collect information for the goddess."

She put her hand back to her face, feigning embarrassment. "Naughty me."

I sounded irritated because I was. "Make them sleep."

The next room led to the narrow hallway with the security slits. I opened the door and peered through.

No one visible. The Heartpiece was a risk, but I got it out of my bag anyway. A golden column of light shimmered up to the ceiling as I fed power to it. Little pointers and dials came to life. I knew precisely zero about them. I turned the device like a compass seeking true north, except I was seeking pieces of deamhan heart. Small black singularities, like black holes in space with purple and gold coronas, floated in the light of the device. The coast was clear, but there were enemies close by. I tucked the Heartpiece away.

"I'll take. That bauble. When we're done. My bedroom. Needs a. Night light."

Funny.

Béil and I slunk through the semi-darkness and down the narrow hall like ferrets hunting rats. Carnivores, lean and mean, on the scent of lesser meat. The next room was where I'd found the inventory sheets. French Vanilla and Toasted Almond with various symbols and numbers. I'd finally realized they weren't for coffee blends, they were inventories of children. Codes for their race, the color of their skin, their age, male or female, and whether they were mortal or Halfling. The back of my neck got hot as I spied a stack of similar sheets on the desk.

No time for anger.

In the dream, Aoife had come into this room with her associates while Béil and I had retreated, but not before I'd seen through the next door into the adjoining room. That's the room I wanted. The wall between the rooms had windows, grimy and streak-stained with whatever oils and vapors that had once been dispersed into the air had condensed in rivulets running down the glass. Near the door, someone had cleaned a circle at face height so the rooms could be checked.

And I thank you. I peeked. Cots filled with children. Sleeping. The light halfway between bright and dim.

Yes! This is it. Everything depended on the next few minutes. Can my heart hammer any harder?

Four guards stood against the walls, alert, scanning the perimeter. No. Five guards. The fifth was standing in a deeper shadow by the door at the other end of the room.

They had rifles. Spell time. A thread of power willingly trailed from my hand to the floor.

"Tine," I said.

The thread ignited with a soft phumpf. Chanting softly, my heart beyond racing, I guided the thread under the door with my voice. The cool orange glow blended with the light struggling into the room from outside, seeping in through the brown-papered windows high above. The thread traced its quiet fire around the room. I worked quickly to complete my trap before the light of the flame got noticed. I had taken a page from my father's book and stapled it to a page from the book of Caer Ibormeith. I wasn't able to use the same magic, but I could use the same strategies.

When my trap was set, I nodded to Béil.

She opened the door quietly, stepping into the room. In a clear voice that rang perfectly against the walls, she cried, "If you move. You die!"

No one moved, for a moment.

The moment passed.

One of the guards turned, pulling back the charging handle on his assault rifle. I changed my voice, tightening the thread of fire that I'd woven around his ankles. He screamed, falling to the floor, the rifle clattering against the cement without firing.

The guard nearest Béil tried to shift away. He vanished from his spot but reappeared a fraction of a moment later, tumbling to the floor and shrieking like a stuck pig. The slow learner next to him tried the same thing and also found his legs lacerated by fire as he moved through the white-hot threads I'd woven.

Béil was already moving. She reached the first guard whose hands were clamped around his bleeding legs. He was writhing, still shrieking. She slapped him across the face and said, "Codail."

Blue light flared. The man fell silent.

"She's putting them to sleep." I shouted the words for the benefit of the two guards that remained unburned. "Stay where you are. Don't fight. You won't be harmed."

The guards raised their hands, leaving their rifles hanging from their straps, surrendering. Their eyes watched Béil apprehensively and then looked at the ground to find the thread of fire. Béil sent another guard to the land of dreams, his whines falling silent.

One of the guards still standing glared at me.

"Are you an Air Mage?" I asked.

Air Mages could disrupt my fire.

He shook his head. "My father was an Earth Mage." This explained both his power as well as his lineage. A Halfling.

I spared a glance for the fifth guard. She was short, with dark, wiry hair and a flat face with a nose like a pug. She returned my stare and didn't move.

The kids. Finally, I looked. Dirty little faces peered out from under thin blankets. They'd learned to be quiet, it seemed, in the presence of weirdness. I counted noses. It didn't take long.

Only a dozen.

Where . . . ?

Keeping my thread of fire alive, I walked past small solemn expressions to a cot with a lump under its blanket. With my free hand, I lifted the blanket.

There were only more blankets.

"We knew you were coming." The tone of the guard felt like an inheritance of smugness from Urlabhraí.

"Really? Huh."

"We moved most of the brats already."

For the moment, I concentrated on the girl nearest me. Kneeling by her side, I looked up. Through one of the windows, a blue light blinked on the corner of the building across the street. "You look at that light a lot. Don't you?" I asked. The girl nodded her answer. I smiled. "You'll be safe now. Do you believe me?" She nodded again but I wasn't sure she meant it until tears welled up and spilled over onto her cheeks.

"Good girl."

Béil finished with the third guard who was now prostrate on the floor, asleep, ankles dripping crimson. She moved to the kids who were sitting up in their cots. Sniffs and soft cries. Béil cooed and put her arms around a little boy who could only have been five years old at best.

Amazing how quickly she could go to motherly from murderly and back again.

Taking the rifle from the guard, I retrieved a plastic tie from a small bag on my belt and zipped his hands together behind his back. "I'd like to say you're under arrest, but I think it's more honest to tell you you're going to the Alder King's dungeon."

"My death will inspire the Dubhcridhe."

"Will it? It'll probably be centuries from now. How's the longevity in your family?"

The man blinked. "You aren't going to kill me? The Alder King isn't going to kill me?"

"Nope."

He went from smug to sulk. "What about her?" He tilted his head in the direction of the female guard. Nothing like throwing your friends under the bus. I looked at the woman. "Do you want a plastic tie too?"

"Not really." She shrugged.

I let my magic go. The threads of fire evaporated. I said, "Guess she doesn't want one."

"What?" The plastic-tied guy was enraged. Good.

Checking the kids was my next priority. Béil joined in. The children's lack of reaction as we made contact with them was extraordinarily sad. They had become immune to fear. Maybe they saw me as another master and overlord. Another figure of power and abuse. They had to act apathetic because the alternative was to be afraid all the time. They would feel different emotions from now on. I had to make sure of that.

Squatting down by the nearest child, I asked, "What's your name?" The child stared at me with dry eyes and didn't respond. I tried, "¿Cómo te llamas?"

"Me llamo Camila, señor."

There was a Hispanic girl under all the dirt and tangled hair. She was one of the lucky ones. Many of the girls weren't here for sweatshop work. They'd been taken elsewhere to do other jobs. She slipped out from under her blanket. Her arms went around my neck as she looked into my eyes. Her hug was infused with the scent of unwashed clothes, but it was worth it. When I noticed her clubfoot, the heat in my neck doubled. I held my anger in check. The last thing this girl needed was another adult to fear.

This girl's family had probably sold her. Look at those beautiful brown eyes. How could a parent send away those beautiful eyes?

I carried my señorita. Some kids were coughing. Some were missing appendages. Walking among them felt like being in a hospital ward.

They'd taken the healthy kids. Left the damaged ones.

"Hey." The Earth Mage was losing patience.

Ignoring him was my pleasure.

"Hey!"

Fine. "Holler all you want, buddy. You're my least important concern."

"What about her?" He tilted his head at the fifth guard, standing quietly. Hands at her sides.

"You're still upset about your comrade there? She's being very cooperative."

A boy wearing filthy red pajama bottoms had an infection of some kind. He could barely lift his head and his breathing was ragged. He had red spots on his skin, and his stomach was misshapen even though he looked thin and malnourished. He was the one who pushed me over the edge. I put a reassuring hand on his shoulder and mustered a smile, trying to keep calm while my blood ran hotter by the moment.

Moving away from the boy, my power wanted to speak for me. I delivered the señorita to Béil, whispering, "Ve a ella," to the little girl. The little one let Béil take her. Béil stroked the girl's hair, but she smirked at me over her shoulder. She didn't need to be a seeress to know what I was going to do.

The blue glow flared orange-red the moment it touched the air. My fist was wreathed in flame as I hit the guard in the face. His head snapped back, rebounding on the wall, and the fire splashed off the concrete. The fire was weak, mostly for show, but I wouldn't have minded if the guard had gotten singed. My vision blurred. The guard kept his feet, which was perfect. I wouldn't have to bend down to hit him again. I pulled my hand back.

"Prince Luck," the female guard called out, suddenly standing beside me.

"Leave me alone." The fire around my hand went hotter.

Her hand rested on my arm. "Remember Spreasán? We're trying to clear your name, not prove them right."

I listened. Heard her words. She made sense. Of course.

"The boy is very sick."

"We'll do what we can, sire."

The guard in front of me looked up, nose bloodied, expression suspended somewhere between relief and mockery. "Who is she?" He's not too stupid. Maybe I knocked some sense into him.

"She has a tail, if that helps." I grinned and probably looked like my father. "We couldn't march an army through Boston." I shook the tension—and residual heat—from my hands. "But we needed to rescue these kids. We needed an insider to find out where you'd take them if you were spooked." I took a deep breath, my anger fading although it was hard to let it go. "Loser, meet Madrasceartán. Madrasceartán, this sack of stupid is Loser."

"Knowing the destination isn't going to help you," Loser spat. "We had an army waiting, and now the children are all where you'll never find them."

I let my fire jump up again. Just long enough for the mockery part to vanish off his face. "There was an army waiting, all right." I smiled. "About a thousand of the Alder King's best knights."

"That's impossible."

"Yep. Probably what His Lordship thought."

That made Loser pause. "Lord Urlabhraí is in hiding."

"Sure. I'm torn up knowing I will never see him again." Probably wrong of me to savor the moment. "We want you scared and running. Every time you move a group of children, you move them into our hands." I nodded to Mads, maintaining the essence of the female guard. "Get him out of here."

Béil waited for me, hands folded in front of her. "One of. These fools. Needs healing."

The temptation to ignore the needs of a traitor weighed heavily. All of these kids should get healing first. "Where?" I sighed.

Béil pointed to one of the guards on the floor. He'd been the first to try and teleport. He had a deep gash across one ankle, and my fire had almost detached his other foot before the fire had weakened and failed. The heat had cauterized the wounds, but not wholly. A pool of blood lay under the man's legs.

I pulled out my healing medallion. "Leigheas," I said as I pressed the coin to the edge of the worst wound.

Cool blue light trickled through me, through the coin, and flowed into the wound. I sensed the muscles and tendons knitting together, making soft crackling sounds. The nerves and blood vessels reunited with sounds like static.

The dumbbell slept through the whole thing.

A side effect of healing another person was the sense of fulfillment received by the healer. I needed that badly. The sensation of peace that flowed into me was like bathing in a pool of endorphins. I inhaled deeply.

There was a silver pattern in the floor at the back of the warehouse. My euphoria lingered as we escorted the kids through the Dubhcridhe portal, which actually opened into Tír na nÓg. With a measure of desperation, I clung to the feeling of peace and well-being as I carried out the little guy in the red pajamas and then the Hispanic girl. Their bodies were so small and frail, and I feared my healer's high would give out, plunging me into a bout of melancholy, weeping, and the burning anger of the righteous. If that happened, I'd just have to heal one of the other idiots. Heal until my power ran dry.

My señorita hugged me tight as we went through the portal. On the other side, her tiny voice said, "Gracias, señor."

I felt even more fulfilled.

# CHAPTER 41
## Foxes

Alyce pulled the cork, took a deep breath, and hesitated. She had only been awake for a day. It was as if she'd been waiting for me. As soon as I walked into her bedchamber, she'd popped up and asked for pizza. She'd spent twenty-four hours being fawned over by nurses and, as often as time would permit, Fáidh.

After a day, she said she was ready and I'd given her the phial. She took another deep breath and followed the prescription on the label. The dirt spilled down, sprinkling her hair, her shoulders, the tip of her nose.

Nothing happened.

Then something did.

Magical transformations in movies are always sweetly sparkling moments with music at a crescendo, golden shafts of light, and a wide-eyed character having the most beatific experience of a lifetime.

All a lie.

The bits of earth made holes in the air, floating down like shiny peppercorns. Dark ribbons of magic swirled jaggedly away from her and then back, seizing Alyce's Stain with a depthless black as if its edges had opened strings into parallel dimensions. The curves remained fixed, but inverted all the same. Warped.

Bending space. That's how time is altered. Realities reworked.

Alyce screamed. Something inside her popped and she cursed. More curses erupted as her skin stretched. Bones lengthened. She shuddered, exhibiting the mastery of a forty-year-old's vocabulary. Who was a sailor. In a locker room. With filtering issues. Forget potty mouth. She owned the entire sewage treatment plant.

No one could blame her.

It was over quickly. A person can tolerate almost anything for five seconds, and mercifully that was all Alyce had to endure. Less time than winning a bucking bull ride. Less time than a birth contraction.

She'd refused to tumble, staying on her feet in an admirable show of strength, but she was drenched in sweat and panting, bent over, a final slow moan punctuating the last moment of the change. Her arms hung down and her hair sat limply over her face.

Gradually, she straightened, finding her new center of gravity. She was two feet taller. Her waist had remained girlish while her surrounding real estate had gotten curvier.

"Um."

I pointed as artfully as I could at the seams of her clothing, which had split in several places. She wasn't showing anything revealing other than a camisole, but she was prepossessed sufficiently to understand there was a man in the vicinity and her level of modesty might not be where she'd prefer it. Erin was the smart one and found a robe Alyce could wear.

Her face was still damply draped. She raised her hands and parted the hair in front of her face like drawing the curtains open at the front of a stage.

Her eyes met mine and asked the question she didn't want to voice.

"You're beautiful." Truth.

She laughed. Short and deep. "Really?"

I upped my thumb. "Speaking as a man who is no stranger to staring at pretty girls. Yup."

Erin smacked my shoulder. Alyce's smile held up for a moment or two, then collapsed.

What did I do?

Covering her face with her hands, she didn't breathe at first. Then a sob got out. And another.

Oh man.

Alyce curled into my embrace. Erin put her arms around us both. Alyce wept against my chest for a minute before she was able to put words together. "I never . . . never really thought . . ."

"I know. But it did."

Sir Siorradh stopped at the massive doors. The wood had been burnished to a deep brown-red by thousands of polishing hands over centuries of time. The panels of wood were carved with scenes of hunting parties and forests and packs of wolves. Clad in silver, the hinges were thick and heavy with the remaining fixtures reflecting our images like mirrors.

The doors swung open silently. The room featured a solid line of my father's personal guard lining the walls. If anyone so much as sneezed suspiciously, he'd get a lance through the larynx. Bromach waited for us next to an empty throne along with a number of leaders whom I recognized as military officers from the insignias on their cuirasses and shoulders.

The throne was empty. The Alder King was pacing the floor. Clover sprouted beneath him at every footfall and then the tender fronds turned brown and dry as he moved on. The floor was littered with dead clover, raised and then abandoned under his boots.

"Has he been pacing long?" I asked.

"Far too long." Bromach frowned. "He is not eating either."

One of the dukes grumbled, "He makes us march with him all around the castle as if we were new recruits. We'll none of us sleep through the pains in our legs tonight."

"Thou couldst stand to work off that wagon wheel around thy middle, Báicéirfíle."

The other men laughed. Father stopped pacing.

"Knowest thou the total?" His eyes landed on me. The weight of his gaze brought with it a heightened sense of loyalty. I wanted to answer but felt confused.

"Sire?"

"We are dealing with more than 81,000 Halflings now, thanks to you."

Confusion permeated my thoughts. His expression was hard to read.

81,000 Halflings?

That would require a lot of resources. Was my father concerned about the costs?

The dukes and barons took me off the hook.

"We have our people back."

"Whole families are being restored."

"Good work."

Finally, Dad threw his stout arms around me. He pinned my own arms against me and lifted me off the ground. It felt like being hauled up by a python. My eyes threatened to bulge out of my head. Dad was laughing.

"Well done, lad."

My heart had been warmed many times over the past month, but it never tired of the feeling. 81,000 Halflings. Thousands of children and young men and women who had been reunited with their loved ones. Thankfully, my father had nearly squeezed me in half. That explained my watering eyes.

He leaned in to share something in confidence. At least as much as possible surrounded by people. "I had been considering a drastic exodus of our people."

The king of ashes. "I'd heard that."

He clapped my shoulder. "I think it's safe to set such plans aside."

"I'm relieved." Very, very relieved.

Bromach offered his congratulations as well. He was quick with a handshake and a question. "May I ask, Your Highness, how it was done? I've yet to get a good answer."

"I entrusted Madrasceartán and her pack with the secret. We have Caer Ibormeith to remember as well. Long may her lands be changeable."

Bromach nodded, not talking, but encouraging me to go on.

"The Dubhcridhe operate in hidden places, but their isolation makes communicating difficult. Using the gift of the Heartpiece, however, I'm able to find Dubhcridhe leaders. The Púca take on the essences of the leaders, allowing Mads and her pack to infiltrate their strongholds. Once inside, they discover the destinations of their portals, then the goddess creates a place in Tír na nÓg that looks exactly the same."

The queen of dreams knows everything.

Which helped a lot.

"When the Dubhcridhe open their portals, everything looks normal. When we're ready, we convince them they are about to be raided. They use their portals to escape; however, instead of finding Dubhcridhe on the other side, they find the armies of the Alder King waiting for them."

Bromach still looked perplexed. "But . . . how do you change destinations? The patterns of the gates would be familiar to them, but the patterns would have to look different if their destinations were different. If the destination is in Tír na nÓg, someone would have noticed a different pattern. Wouldn't they?"

"Oh, yes. We didn't change their portals at all. They worked precisely as they were designed."

"Then, how . . . ?"

The silver ring on my hand almost glowed as I showed it to Bromach. I grinned like a magician savoring his favorite illusion. "With this ring, I can access Tír na nÓg. A gift from the goddess that has proved itself many times over."

Bromach shook his head, thinking.

"Two portals."

Bromach squinted.

"Back-to-back portals. Portals are two-way passages, correct?"

Bromach nodded. Common knowledge.

"The first portal simply has a second portal exactly in front of it."

"So . . . "

"When the Dubhcridhe used their portal, they exited, encountered my portal, and went through that to Tír na nÓg. It seemed like they were going through one portal to their customary destination they wanted. In reality, they went through a second portal that exited to a place that only looked like the destination they wanted."

Bromach smiled. Then chuckled. Then laughed.

He stopped. "Does not one magic interfere with the other?"

Ah. "You'd think so. But their portal is opened in the mortal realm or the Behindbeyond. I create mine in Tír na nÓg. The goddess helps to line them up."

Bromach gave a sage nod. "The magic originates in different realms. No interference." He laughed again. "I'll be more careful about taking portals, I think."

"You'll be all right." I held up the silver ring. "I hear the goddess rarely gives these away." I thought of the goddess. Last I'd heard, the dullahan were appearing far less often now.

Far fewer children were having bad dreams.

Bromach didn't touch the ring, but he raised his hand near to it as if he could feel its power. "The king's generals have a nickname for you."

"Uh-oh. What is it?"

"Sionnach na Ádh."

The words weren't familiar. "What does it mean?"

"The Fox of Luck."

Well. That's twenty kinds of awesome.

"I'll take it."

Bromach gave a half bow and abandoned me to my own devices. I sought Sir Siorradh.

"You've done well, dude."

His helmet swiveled smoothly to look at me. "Many soldiers have been tireless in their service. You gave them a cause and they have united to fulfill it."

"I heard there were some casualties."

"Yes." His voice sounded hollow. "The Dubhcridhe became desperate after so many successful raids. We lost some men—but they lost far more. Now we have run out of places to raid, it seems. Any of them who remain have run to sanctuaries where we cannot find them."

"The Heartpiece isn't catching new leads either. But we're still a long way from snuffing them out."

"Agreed. The 81,000 we rescued were the ones who wanted to

come back. You'll be glad to know we've found and returned all the people taken from the wedding."

"That's wonderful."

"We have also arrested the leaders. In addition, we found more than 40,000 Halflings who have built a life over the course of the past few years. They were required to support the Dubhcridhe but are now content in their work, and we could not force them to leave their farms, their businesses, their opportunities. Even if they are sympathetic to the Dubhcridhe cause, they are spread out now. And virtually leaderless. Geographers will be adding new towns and villages and revising their maps to show the villages that are no longer abandoned."

They're rescued regardless. In a different way.

"You should be proud, Highness."

I couldn't speak.

Proud. Yes. Happy. Yes.

"And what of the mortals?"

If anything, I felt more happy and proud about them. "We found a lot of children. More than 2,500 kids. Those who had been taken by the Boston mob." After that, I couldn't speak again for a minute.

They were a drop in a very large bucket. A lot of different bad guys took kids for a lot of different reasons, and there were hundreds of thousands of missing children around the world. The ones we had found were precious. More so because they'd been so hard to find. Kids who had been swept up with the Halflings and not wanted by the Dubhcridhe. They'd been turned over to their partners in Boston and sold through the company that fronted the mob as a coffee distributor.

Finally, I found my voice. "Erin is helping coordinate their return. We're sending them to police agencies and child and family services as close to their homes as we can. A few might be adopted in the Behindbeyond."

The ones who can't go back.

The broken.

The abandoned.

The abused.

We'd find homes for them eventually. And we'd find more kids. I wanted to look into the Boston mob more deeply to find out why they were connected to the forces of evil among the Fae.

Happily, we'd been able to help the little guy in the red pajamas. He had leukemia, but the Alder King's healers were highly skilled at curing mortal diseases. They were also skilled at fuzzifying memories. The boy's family would be mystified about his improved health and equally mystified about his whereabouts.

All to the good.

I'd been wrong about the little girl, too. Her family had been looking for her desperately. I'd checked. Private eye. Good for something once in a while.

Then there was Alyce.

"Hey, honey."

Erin's arms—Fáidh's arms—wrapped around me. I turned and embraced her in return. "What a great surprise. What brings you here?"

"I heard your father had called for a gathering and I thought I'd join in. Good job, Got."

Her kiss was the best reward.

She took me by the hand and led me to the king. He'd stopped pacing long enough for a clover carpet to amass beneath his boots. It sounded like he was getting more details from Sir Siorradh about the redistribution of the rescued Halflings according to what they could do and where they were needed most.

Fáidh interrupted anyway.

"Your Majesty. Sir Siorradh." The king was always happy to see her. His broad grin lit up his face and she leaned over so he could give her a hug. She returned his smile when he let her go. "I have an announcement." She clasped her hands and, bouncing on her toes, stood up straight, which was a small breach of protocol as she was addressing the king with her head higher.

Turned out, he didn't notice.

Not after she said, "We're having a baby!"

# CHAPTER 42
## Seven Minutes Between Worlds

"How are you feeling?"

"Still hung over. All your fault."

"I didn't know your father would want to celebrate instantly."

"Neither did I, but you've known him for at least a century longer than me."

Erin laughed. Soft and husky.

"At least you had a reason not to join in on every single, solitary, stinkin' toast. You're expecting."

"You looked like you were having fun."

"When they said ginger ale, I thought they meant mortal ginger ale."

A quieter voice tumbled over from the back seat. "Oh. I think we're there." Then, even more quietly, "Thank goodness."

"Sorry, Alyce." She was mortal, which allowed me to apologize. I tried to turn and give her a suitable expression of regret but all I accomplished was a wince.

Erin braked and turned into a parking space. My head kept pounding. Through my sunglasses, I checked the sign on the building. Donaldsonville Parish Sheriff's Office. Yup. We were there. The wait was over.

According to Sheriff Holden, today almost never happened. Alyce's mom, Lorna, had quietly moved back to Ascension Parish, living in nearby Dutch Town. She attended AA meetings and worked as a stylist in a beauty salon to pad her social security until she could retire. She'd been happy to hear that Alyce had been found, but refused to accept a meeting. With a little gentle questioning, we'd found out her teeth were in bad shape, and an appointment resulting in a new smile sealed the deal.

We stepped out of the rental car. The change from the air-conditioned interior of the car to the humid interior of the state of Louisiana was like going from a soothing vacation in the snowbound castle of the Púca to being mauled by a Púca. Being mauled by a Púca wearing a wool suit. Being mauled by a feverish Púca wearing a wool suit. While breathing on you.

Wow. My head hurt.

I held up the handle of the door on the car so I could press it into place and then latch it closed without making a sound. The ladies slammed their doors, but my joy at finding out I would be a father meant I could choose not to take such thoughtless actions personally.

The ladies preceded me into the building. I watched their feet carefully because the sun was in the opposite direction and the ladies appeared to be amazingly adept at not stumbling over the curb or the steps. In heels, no less.

Four o'clock and the lobby was empty. I surmised this to be true because my keen observation skills were supplemented by some lady yelling, "Anybody here?" The door of Sheriff Monarch Holden's office was closed. There was a momentary pause, and then I heard two heavy feet land on the floor and start walking.

"Um."

Twenty-five years of worry and loss were embodied in that single syllable. I put my arm around Alyce's shoulder and pulled her in, exuding comfort while trying not to lean on her. Too much. Erin hugged her too from the other side. Erin had been so affected by Alyce's plight from the start. Today's meeting meant as much to her as anyone.

The door swung open and we were greeted by the beaming face of the good sheriff. He threw his arms wide. "Got!" His voice slammed down on my head like a hailstorm of hatchets. "Welcome back, son!"

I managed, "Good to see you, Sheriff."

He was a good enough sheriff to notice my hangover. He was a good enough person that he dialed down the volume. "I was delighted to get your call."

I nodded. Half an inch for a nod was noticeable enough, right?

Mon turned to look at Alyce. "You are the very one. Welcome home."

On the phone, I'd let Mon know that my story hadn't been filled out with perfect truths. In our first meeting, I'd told him that I was working on behalf of a little girl who looked like Alyce. That had been before there was even a possibility Alyce could be returned to her natural age. Now, for today's meeting, I'd brought the actual Alyce so I'd admitted to a fudging of the facts.

If he wanted more details, he'd ask.

Alyce drifted behind the sheriff as if in a dream. I knew that walk. She'd used that same walk in her actual dream.

There was a woman in Mon's office. All I saw from the back was a thatch of straw-like hair, reddish-brown, except for the roots that were silver-gray and long past due for a color. Hearing our entry, the woman stood and turned. Her face was lined, on the wrong side of sallow, and emblazoned with equal parts addiction and remorse. Still, I could see she'd been pretty once. Pretty in the same ways Alyce was pretty now.

"Oh."

She tilted to the side a bit but caught herself on the arm of the chair she'd been sitting in. Her eyes traveled the contours of Alyce's face, down to her feet, then back up. Her eyes shimmered. She trembled; her arms went out but hesitated as if she was worried about touching Alyce in case she wasn't real.

"Baby girl?"

Alyce was shaking.

Her mouth moved.

Moved again.

"Momma?"

The ladies slipped into each other's arms. Hugged each other like they might be fragile. Then hugged each other like they knew they were strong.

"I'm so sorry, baby girl."

"It's all right, Momma. I'm all right."

There were a whole lot of tears after that. Turns out Sheriff Monarch Holden is a huge, sun-tanned, trout-fishin', weepin' baby. Maybe it was all right to keep him company.

Erin found her way into my arms and we watched mother and daughter get reacquainted. Soft sounds. Soft words. Soft eyes full of love rekindled.

This is why I do what I do.

I'd have a child of my own soon. Erin would be a mom. The world—scratch that: worlds—we were bringing life into were all of them frightening and often unfair. But Erin was better qualified than anyone I knew to make that child happy regardless. And I was above average, at least, when it came to protecting the ones I loved.

We'd be all right. We'd make it all right.

I noticed the back wall of the sheriff's office. Alyce's photo was still on the wall, but a note had been added. "Found," it read. Lost. And now found.

Mon wiped his eyes with a white linen hankie as he slow-sauntered us toward the lobby. "Y'all are welcome to stay here in town. There's rooms already set at the hotel across the street. Gal named Crystal runs the place, and she'll get you some supper whenever you want."

Alyce and her mom followed the sheriff through the door with Erin just behind. "Thank you, Sheriff." Lorna didn't take her eyes off her daughter. "I'm fearin' if I look away, Alyce'll disappear again."

"No worry there."

Mon turned around to face us, his back to the front door. There was a certain joy in his eyes as he regarded Alyce and her mother.

The front door slammed open, and the gunshots came moments apart. Two shots, low and right, followed by two shots high and left.

Pop-pop. Pop-pop.

Mon's smile melted to shock. He shuddered first, then began to fall toward us. As a big man, he was slow to topple. Over his shoulder, the light bloomed as the shooters shifted position.

I opened a portal to Tír na nÓg behind me. The silver ring on my finger almost acted on its own and I felt a sudden pressure in my chest.

Get everyone out.

Everyone. Out.

I could step forward. Put myself in front. My shield coin would protect me from bullets, but there were two shooters. Only one bullet needed to get past me to cause more tragedy.

I stepped back.

There was a long moment where more information filed into my brain than I would have thought possible. Sheriff Holden, going to his knees and still tipping toward me, pain drawn in heavy strokes down his face. Alyce clinging to her mother, instinct just beginning to move them sideways out of the line of fire. Erin turning toward me, her eyes wide orbs with emeralds at the center, running into the frame of the door, her shoulder impacting the wood and throwing her off balance.

Behind them, the two shooters, adjusting their aim and lining up their shots. The one coming in high was a man, targeting Erin's head. Petit-Palais. Professional. Impassive. The other shooter, coming in low and preparing to shoot Alyce. Grim determination pasted on her face. Deputy Macy. Once friendly. Now enraged.

Alyce's words, spoken in a different context but more meaningful now: The Dubhcridhe recruit Eternals as well as Halflings. They also recruit mortals. She'd also said: His Lordship has mortals working with the police. The FBI. Everyone. The words were there but none of us could have known. Just facts. Not predictors of the future. Not clues for now. Just words that stung.

A bullet emerged from the end of Petit-Palais's revolver, wisps of smoke and expanding gas urging the projectile through the air. No sound. It would come. The bullet was intended for Erin. Intended to take away a life and the life she carried inside. The life we'd just conceived.

A moment later, a bullet exited Deputy Macy's gun. The bright fire of the load illuminated the throat of the barrel. The pop would reach my ears before the bullet would reach its target. Intended for Alyce. Intended to take away the life she'd only just resumed. The life renewed with her mother.

This cannot stand.

A bullet fired from a pistol travels at more than 500 miles per hour. My fire had to be faster.

"Tine!" My power hit my hands like electricity hits a resistor in a circuit. More power than I needed, and the excess bounded through my system and threatened to take the top of my head off.

Ow.

My head could pound later. Fire lanced out of my hands. The gout of flame from my left I directed between Erin and the sheriff. The gout from my right I curved under Alyce's legs. The molten fire streams bent themselves to my will, following the paths I desired. Bending like hot orange taffy. Looping, curling. Shifting as I moved my hands and chanted my commands.

If firecasters were orchestra conductors, I was Leonard Bernstein, Herbert von Karajan, and Sir Simon Rattle all rolled into one. I was master of my craft. Passionate. Inspired.

Desperate.

The fire flowed. I fed more into the stream, like forcing water along a hose. My voice brought the gouts of burning panic up and arcing in line with the bullets. The first bullet was ten feet away from Erin now and her colliding with the frame of the door had only kept her in the bullet's deadly path.

Pop.

The sound reached my ears at last, slow and drawn out, but there.

I sang to my fire to blossom, grow hotter, and bite. The tip of the stream flared white as it met the bullet. The metal resisted, relented, warped, withered. Like a meteorite, it flashed bright-hot and disappeared. Petit-Palais had fired again, the second bullet following the same trajectory as the first.

Butthead.

I drove the fire forward, accelerated it, guided it to ram down the barrel of the gun, taking the second bullet along the way. It just needed time.

The deputy's bullet was next to be swallowed by my swirling

serpent.

Bite.

Burn.

Bam.

This might work.

Please let it work.

The right-side lance thrust toward the deputy's gun. I fed it. Nurtured it.

Alyce and her mother continued their fall, forcing the deputy to anticipate and redirect her aim before firing again. My flame would get there first.

"TINE!" The extra power sought release down the pipelines of fury I'd created. The streams crossed the spaces with renewed speed and strength.

The second bullet from Petit-Palais fed the flame. Flared out of existence.

Gritting my teeth, I conducted my duet of fire.

Surging, singing, the left-side lance leapt into the gun. The expression on the Petit-Palais's face was halfway to stunned.

Good.

With red-orange-white brilliance, the muzzle melted and blew apart. A long forever later, the fire reached the guts of the gun. The loads erupted, setting each other off. The gun exploded. The powder chewing through metal. The metal chewing through flesh and bone.

Petit-Palais's hand shredded. The faults and fractures continued past his wrist, up his arm, separating meat and blood halfway to his elbow.

Crescendo.

The music of mayhem played on in stereo. Deputy Macy's younger reflexes had triggered her self-preservation instincts, and she had pulled her gun hand off her target, bringing her arm in to cover her body in the beginnings of a defensive reaction.

No defense for you.

The gout covered the gap, enveloping her pistol from the side. Her hand, her arm.

An inkling of a scream. She managed that before the gun surrendered to my fire. It tore through her hand and arm and into her body, lighting up her torso.

I fed the fire still.

They had come to steal all happiness.

They had to be stopped.

I bore witness to their fall.

And kept vigilant watch.

Sheriff Holden's knees hit the floor at last. I felt the tremble and it shook me out of my reverie. Erin was clinging to the doorframe, beginning to turn her head to look over her shoulder, not realizing yet that the danger had passed. Alyce and her mother were nearly on the floor as well. Petit-Palais was going down. Deputy Macy would be last.

I could let my power go.

Couldn't I?

It took effort.

I did.

The pounding in my head had not subsided. Without the distraction of the fight, the pain reasserted itself at the forefront of my consciousness. I groaned. Lights shimmered at the edge of my vision. It wasn't all from the headache. I stood in another realm. The daylight was much brighter in Tír na nÓg.

In dire circumstances, people often report that time seems to slow down. Perhaps that had been in the back of my head when I'd created the portal to Tír na nÓg and then stepped over the line. Instinct. Invention. The fox of luck. Maybe a little help from the goddess of dreams. Something had motivated me to take the step.

In the mortal realm, Petit-Palais and Deputy Macy had fired on Sheriff Holden. I'd used the silver ring to make sanctuary but only had time for me to cross. In the mortal realm, only a second of time had passed after that. A second of time for my enemies to fire. A second of time for me to react. But in the realm of the goddess, it had been seven minutes.

That was the ratio.

For seven breathtaking minutes, I'd conducted the music of destruction. Woven my spells. Chanted my songs. Done what I had to do. My enemies continued to fall, languidly suffering while I watched.

Forward then. Back to the realm of mortal time. I took a step and the portal of dreams winked out behind me. The cacophony of sound assaulted my ears instantly, sending jagged, slashing pain through my head. The last echoes of explosions and screams and bodies colliding with hard things.

No time to feel.

I checked on Erin first. She slid the rest of the way down the doorframe, shocked and confused, but she was okay. Alyce and her mother were on the floor together, panicked, but essentially unharmed. I ignored the figures of the shooters in front of me. One shrieking and rocking on the floor, the other disturbingly silent.

Sheriff Holden lay face down in his own lobby. Unmoving. Soundless. The four shots fired at him had hit him in the shoulder and lower back. I ran to the desk phone and called 9-1-1.

# CHAPTER 43
## Dream's End

True to Sheriff Holden's word, Crystal had supper for us across the street. The four of us sat together, shell-shocked, stealing glances through the window toward the sheriff's office. The waitress had offered to let us sit in the back, away from all the "trouble," but we'd needed to see.

The ambulance had taken Mon first. They'd been gentle enough when they'd moved Petit-Palais and Deputy Macy off the threshold of the building, but it was clear to whom they had given priority. The paramedics had rolled Mon out on a gurney, an I.V. already in his arm, and I'd seen Mon flex his hand like his circulation felt tingly. He was in serious condition, but he was alive, and the ambulance had fired up all the lights and sirens as it had sped away. I hadn't minded the sound.

Macy had been unconscious. Three paramedics had started working on her. Petit-Palais had refused to look at me or answer my questions, so I didn't know if he really was a Dubhcridhe sympathizer or just losing his mind.

The ladies had all been banged up. Alyce had a bandage on her chin and her mom had scraped knees and an elbow patched, but they were fine otherwise. Erin's knee had gotten bloodied on the baseboard, but she was fine too. I hadn't gotten a mark on me, which was a nice change from the usual. Just my head continued to throb.

I'd answered a few questions for the state police while the ladies had been attended. The cops would want to ask more questions later, and I'd said that would be fine. They'd gotten some information from each of us. After that, we'd decided to walk to the hotel even though we were too wired to eat or sleep.

We'd sat, not quite comfortable, looking through the window. They'd kept working on Macy while Petit-Palais complained. His exact words had been muffled, but he'd continued pestering and gesturing and it was clear from his actions that he wasn't happy about being ignored. They'd called in some backup from the hospital and someone had finally checked his arm. She installed an I.V. on the other side then and injected something in the tube. Within seconds, Petit-Palais relaxed against his gurney and shut up.

It was hardest on us all to watch Deputy Macy. All we'd been able to see from the cafe had been the top of her close-cropped hair. The paramedics had battled mightily to save her, unwrapping package after package of implements and materials. In the end, they had pulled her I.V. and slipped her into a bag with a zipper that went all the way up.

Alyce and her mother had cried.

Later, after the police tape had been strung and all the emergency vehicles had gone, the waitress was able to tease some food orders out of us. I got meatloaf and asked the waitress to please, for the love, substitute rice for the mashed potatoes. She did. We started eating with good intentions, but mostly picked at our food when it came.

"I still cain't understan' what happened." Alyce's mom shook her head minimally, carefully. "I heard gunshots and then Alyce was pushin' into me and there was a flash of light and things burnin'." She turned her hands palms up on the table. "An' then it was over."

She looked to me with questions scorching the edges of her eyes. I shrugged. "Sometimes guns jam. Sometimes they actually blow themselves apart."

That's the same thing I'd told the state police.

"Both of them guns? At the same time?" Lorna was no dummy.

"We're just lucky." I looked into Alyce's eyes and then Erin's. They understood.

"Lucky we are," Alyce said. "Lucky indeed."

Alyce and her mom had coffee and I shared some pie with Erin. We were reluctant to leave. Food and beverages were the mortar holding our little group together at the moment, even though we'd hardly touched any of it. But we needed the comfort of that routine after all we'd been through. Finally, Crystal came to find us and tell us our rooms were ready, hinting that six hours in the cafe was enough. We took the stairs at a slow pace. Alyce and her mom had the room across from us. I continued to feel their presence after the doors came between us.

Erin and I cleaned up quietly and got undressed. I hadn't even noticed someone bringing up our bags. I owed someone a tip. At last, lying quietly with Erin in my arms, I let myself drift toward the night places.

"They're going to be all right." Erin shifted in my shoulder. I liked the solid conviction in her tone.

"They will be. That's what families are for. To make each other all right."

"Mm." I listened to her breathe. Then, "I have to get back to Miami."

"Yes."

"Get to the office and figure out when to take maternity leave."

"Love that idea."

"Mm." She breathed for a while again. Her voice became dreamier. "More of the kids you found will be ready to go back to their homes soon."

"That's where I'll be." Helping more kids would soothe my aches and pains better than any medicine.

Erin's lips against my neck. Then, "Love you, my lucky fox."

I chuckled my softest chuckle. "I'm only lucky because I have you. Love you."

The goddess claimed me, and the dreamer dreamed. I walked through empty rooms of a castle. The stones beneath my feet were dry, and my father, the Alder king, sat on his throne in all his glory.

# Author's Note

As of this writing, more than 750,000 children every year are classified as missing—and that's just in the United States. This includes abductions, runaways, and "throwaways." The FBI's National Crime Information Center (NCIC) shows approximately 30,000 active cases for missing persons under the age of 18. The National Missing and Unidentified Persons System (NamUs) provides services to not only help locate missing persons but also to help resolve cases where a person has been found deceased but cannot be readily identified. This database can be used by law enforcement, but can also be used by anyone with missing family members.

Thankfully, miraculously, many missing and exploited children are recovered every year as well. The National AMBER Alert program and other similar efforts are a good start but we can do more. In the face of such sobering statistics, it's important to remember we live in a time when technologies and tools make it easier than ever to be aware and follow through on the edict "if you see something, say something."

# Never Miss a Future House Release!

Sign up for the Future House Publishing email list.

www.futurehousepublishing.com/beta-readers-club/

## Connect with Future House Publishing

Facebook.com/FutureHousePublishing

Twitter.com/FutureHousePub

YouTube.com/FutureHousePublishing

Instagram.com/FutureHousePublishing

# Acknowledgments

The vacuum. Nature may abhor it but not more than a story waiting to be filled.

I officially started work on *Got Lost* on March 15, 2017, within hours of *Got Hope*, the second novel in the series, being published. I don't count research and notetaking, which authors call "pre-writing," because I've been "pre-writing," in a way, since grade school. If you're enjoying the Behindbeyond series, you'll be pleased to hear that I have notes for more novels in the future. Can't get in all the good Got stuff at once.

This installment is the most lengthy of the series so far. It had to be. There's a whole new kingdom to explore, guarded by púca and ruled by the Goddess of Dreams, Caer Ibormeith, may she bless the night places forever. It has also been the most rewarding to write and so many people have been instrumental in the care and feeding of this story. First, my good friend Paul Genesse, who taught the fiction writing class that finally motivated me to take the "pre-" off "pre-writing." In 2015 I was hoping I could get him to put together a few nice words for the cover of the first novel and not only did he do that, so graciously, he has become a mentor and chief cheerleader for me and the entire series. Next, Mike Glassford, who is not only the world's best-dressed pirate attorney, but also number one fan, advisor, and friend in so many ways.

My editors. Emma Hoggan deserves a week-long standing ovation as an editor who delivers dedication and direction as constant as the North Star. She is always where she needs to be and always doing her job with a celestial brightness that lets me know there is a navigator at the tiller who will always safely steer the ship across the deeps and shallows alike with confidence. Emma Snow, Abbie Robinson, Stephanie Cullen, and Sarah Jensen have gone round after round with aplomb and professionalism and made the whole process thoroughly breezy. It's long past time for them to turn in their "Mean Editor" cards because they are doing "mean" all wrong—but doing editing all right. To Mackenzie Seidel, you've made Got and his world look better than I imagined and I'm supremely grateful. Well done to all y'all. There's a seat at The Behindbeyond table for you, forever and always.

My advance readers are invaluable, alpha and beta and as many Greek letters as they might need. You love a good story and your honesty with mine is appreciated so very much. Kayla Echols, Dalice Peterson, Vince Campanile, Nicholas Adams, Andrea and Dave Van Wagoner, and Josh Larsen; you are the sentinels of dangerous lands. May your vigilance never wane.

As always, the deepest, sweetest, most heartfelt thanks to Shauna for all your love and support.

# About the Author

Digital bestseller Michael Darling has worked as a butcher, a librarian, and a magician. Not all at the same time. He nests in the exquisitely beautiful Rocky Mountains with his equally breathtaking wife, their normal-if-you-don't-look-too-close children, and a disturbingly large St. Bernese dog named Appa. Michael's award-winning fantasy and science-fiction stories are frequently featured in anthologies. His first novel, Got Luck, was published in 2016 and the sequel, Got Hope followed in 2017. He continues work on that series as well as other projects.

Connect with Michael Darling:

www.michaelcdarling.com

twitter.com/michaelcdarling

www.facebook.com/michaeldarlingwrites